LAST-DITCH

Other Anthologies Edited by:

Patricia Bray & Joshua Palmatier

After Hours: Tales from the Ur-bar
The Modern Fae's Guide to Surviving Humanity
Temporally Out of Order * Alien Artifacts * Were-
All Hail Our Robot Conquerors!
Second Round: A Return to the Ur-bar
The Modern Deity's Guide to Surviving Humanity
Solar Flare * Familiars

S.C. Butler & Joshua Palmatier

Submerged * Guilds & Glaives * Apocalyptic
When Worlds Collide * Brave New Worlds * Dragonesque

Laura Anne Gilman & Kat Richardson

The Death of All Things

Troy Carrol Bucher & Joshua Palmatier

The Razor's Edge

Patricia Bray & S.C. Butler

Portals

David B. Coe & Joshua Palmatier

Temporally Deactivated * Galactic Stew
Derelict

Steven H Silver & Joshua Palmatier

Alternate Peace

Crystal Sarakas & Joshua Palmatier

My Battery Is Low and It Is Getting Dark

David B. Coe & John Zakour

Noir

Crystal Sarakas & Rhondi Salsitz

Shattering the Glass Slipper

David B. Coe & Edmund R. Schubert

Artifice & Craft

Stephen Kotowych & Tony Pi

Game On!

Troy Carrol Bucher & Gerald Brandt

Last-Ditch

LAST-DITCH

Edited by

Troy Carrol Bucher
&
Gerald Brandt

Zombies Need Brains LLC
www.zombiesneedbrains.com

COPYRIGHTS

Table of Contents

SIGNATURE PAGE

Troy Carrol Bucher, editor:

_____

Gerald Brandt, editor:

_____

Jason M. Hough:

_____

Tanya Huff:

_____

L.E. Modesitt, Jr.:

_____

D. Thomas Minton:

_____

Nemma Wollenfang:

_____

Hayden Trenholm:

_____

Edward Willett:

_____

Blake Jessop:

_____

Steve Perry:

_____

Ember Randall:

_____

Derryl Murphy:

_____

Chadwick Ginther:

_____

Russell Hugh McConnell:

_____

Gary Kloster:

_____

E.C. Ambrose:

_____

Donald McCarthy:

_____

Justin Adams, artist:

_____

Alavus

Jason M. Hough

And so came the moment of doubt. Where would they send him this time? To do what, exactly? The questions always bubbled up in the moments before the signal arrived, despite Peter Caswell knowing they would never be answered.

Laying back on the bed, he shut his eyes and pushed the concerns away.

"Close the blinds," he instructed the room. Off to his left came a slight whirring sound as the vertical slats rotated. The sunlight dancing on his eyelids diminished until only darkness remained.

'I'm ready, Monique,' he sent to his handler.

Her reply in his head came almost instantly. He wondered if she was here, in the same block of corporate-owned flats, or somewhere else entirely.

'Off we go, then,' she replied. *'See you on the other side.'*

He nestled into the bed, waiting.

'In five. Four. Three…'

Caswell, thinking only to himself, recited the first half of his memory bridge:

Speak the word.

Then the signal arrived, and the implant in his neck flooded every cell in his brain with the memory marker.

* * *

Two days later he lay suspended beneath a bridge in Mumbai, acting as a proxy assassin. The answers to his questions, he mused, fleeting though they might be.

He was on his back in a climbing harness, hanging mere inches below the span's grimy underside. Somewhere above, an endless stream of gently sighing electric cars and lorries slid across the concrete monster in computer-choreographed perfection.

Twelve minutes earlier he'd stepped out of a cab into the heat and energy of the midnight crowds moving like busy ants along the streets and alleys. In a restaurant perched on stilts above the riverbank, he'd ordered a curry and beer before asking for the restroom. A few minutes later he'd exited the structure via the back door, dressed in workman's overalls and a painter's mask he'd taken from his backpack. Listening to Monique's instructions, he'd descended a narrow stairway to a locked gate. The lock took only seconds to pick, and then all that remained was to attach the harness he'd brought to a pipe and start pulling. For ten minutes he'd heaved himself out toward the center of the span.

Caswell paused his efforts. Steadied his breathing. Cleared his mind. Wiped some foul oily grime onto his pant legs.

His curry would be ready soon. The tantalizing beer was no doubt already sweating beads of condensation onto the table he was supposed to be sitting at. He wanted to be back there, sipping that pint, before the waiter began to wonder if he'd be coming back for it. Before an impression might start to form, if questions were asked later.

Caswell glanced right, following the path of the river to where it bent sharply. His gaze drifted upwards, past a bustling promenade towards the dazzling lights of downtown skyscrapers. There was a gap here, between two hotels where, another hundred meters farther along, he could just make out the white pillars of a corporate office.

The view matched the image Monique had shown him. He was in the right place.

Caswell pulled the drone rifle from his overalls. A gray metal tube half a meter in length, attached to a flat platform barely a centimeter thick and equally as long.

He twisted it around to face those white pillars over a kilometer away, needing only an approximate angle. It looked good enough, but the concrete above was too narrow for an attachment. He slid himself backwards a few meters, found a better position, then confirmed he could still see the white pillars in the distance.

Holding the tube pointed in that direction, with the flat "base" turned upwards, he pushed a hidden button on one side and heard the quiet hiss as foam adhesive bloomed from an array of nozzles along the surface. He counted to five, then pressed hard, holding the rifle against the underside of the bridge for another count of five.

Gingerly he removed his hands. The drone rifle stayed put. His job was done, save turning it on. As for the rifle's job, that might be a month from now. A year. Maybe several years.

To anyone who might glance up here from a riverboat below, they would see a fifty-centimeter-long gray tube nestled amongst a dizzying array of pipes, wires, and conduits that spanned the underside of the bridge. In other words, they would see nothing at all. The weapon did not look like a weapon. It had no need for all the support protrusions or sighting aids a human-operated rifle required. No grip, no stock, no trigger. It was simply a barrel packaged inside a larger tube stuffed with enough computing power to run a fairly large corporation, and a few telephoto lenses at the business end.

Enough time had passed for the adhesive to set. Caswell reached up and yanked on the object. It did not budge. He twisted hard. Still nothing. It was solidly in place. He tapped another recessed button, then waited. Six seconds passed before a pinpoint LED winked green at him. The rifle's sighting camera recognized its view as the one it had been assigned. The motorized aiming system within came to life. Servos whirred as minute calibrations dialed everything in, down to microscopic tolerances. It had acquired its frame of reference and could aim within it.

The rifle peered between sagging old electrical wires, through the gaps of a billboard's support truss, and just beneath the fringed canopy of a café umbrella almost a kilometer away. Through all that it saw the rear exit of a building owned by the Runshaw Group, a mining conglomerate.

Once primed the weapon would wait, ever vigilant, never blinking. Pattern-recognition algorithms would analyze each face appearing in that doorway until the preprogrammed match was found. Then it would fire the only bullet it carried. A single round right through the center of the forehead. The target would die. Heaters would activate within the rifle, causing it to drip as slag into the river below. By then Caswell would be… well, very far away. Who the actual target was, he had no idea. After leaving this place and returning to the flat in London, he wouldn't even remember this rifle, this bridge, or the curry waiting for him back on the riverbank. All would be forgotten.

A voice in his head broke through the monotony. *'Status, Agent Caswell?'*

'Hello, Monique,' he sent. *'Just tidying up here.'*

'Good. Keep me informed.' Monique's presence in his head vanished.

Careful not to jostle the drone rifle, he turned the switch into the active position.

"We're not so unlike, you and I," Caswell muttered to the weapon. Sometimes his job was to kill, too, and neither he nor this weapon would remember their deeds. If not for a little trick he'd devised to keep track of his body count,

Caswell retained no memory of any such missions. What he had instead was memories of his handler, Monique, triggering the implant in his brain in order to preserve his memory state. Then, from his perspective, a millisecond later would be the memory of coming out the other side of the mission and being told, hopefully, that he'd succeeded admirably. Everything in between, gone, like a file deleted from a computer.

All in the name of operational deniability.

"Only difference is," he added to his conversation with the object, "they don't melt me down when it's over."

He expected no response from the inanimate object.

But he got one.

A thunderous *hum-THWAP* as the electromagnetic weapon fired.

Peter Caswell was so startled he simply lay there in his harness for a full two seconds, blinking. In his mind he ran through all the things that sound could have been. One of the ropes holding him in place had snapped? Two cars colliding on the bridge above? Denial, all. He might have had the memories of all his assassinations deleted, but he trained for such missions constantly. He had to, otherwise he'd be a rookie every time he received an assignment.

Still, he didn't move, his mind refusing to come to grips with the fact that the weapon he'd just installed had already spotted its target and fired. Someone, a kilometer away, would be having their brains sprayed out the back of their skull right about now.

'*Holy fuck. Monique!*'

'*Go ahead, Caswell?*'

'*The fucking thing fired!*' he growled. '*Not ten seconds after I turned it on it fucking fired!*'

'*Calm down,*' she sent, in her usual business-like voice. '*Have you moved away from the device?*'

'*I just turned it on! I'm right beneath it.*'

'*MOVE. NOW. It's going to–*'

The sound of her voice in his head was temporarily drowned out by his own internal cry of panic.

Above him, the rifle was turning red. *Glowing* red.

He tried to push the harness back towards the riverbank, but while he'd been holding his position here the straps had become ensnared by the thick grime on the pipes to which they were attached. Getting them unstuck and moving again would take seconds he didn't have.

A heavy droplet of molten metal dripped off the underside of the weapon and fell onto his knee. The cloth of his pant leg began to smoke, and a split second later the burning pain hit him. Blocking the intense agony and the smell of burning hair and skin from his mind, Caswell willed his implant to push him into a state of overclock. Chemicals flooded into his brain and forced his neurons to fire faster. He had twenty seconds now–twenty seconds of real time, which would feel like two hundred seconds to him.

With his left hand he undid the long zipper on his overalls and let the two halves flap open. His right hand came up at the same time, reaching under the fabric to pull a folded knife from a holster below his left armpit. Above him, another droplet of molten horror began to extend toward him. Several more were forming farther down the length of the drone rifle. In the languid world of his overclocked perception, Caswell diverted the blade in his hand. He'd been about to start cutting through the straps holding him to the underside of the bridge. Instead, he flicked it upwards and across, impacting the big glob of yellow-orange liquid metal, slapping it with the flat of the blade to propel it into the cluster of straps at the apex of the harness. He watched the molten metal fly towards the bundle of straps, kept his blade swinging in that direction. The metal hit first, the straps fraying and smoking almost instantly. His blade, now edge on, crashed in a split-second later. Caswell put everything he could into the swing. Watched it all in slow motion. The sizzling and flames of the molten metal, the blade cutting in just after, slicing into the woven straps and pushing the fiery glob in farther.

He could do nothing to avoid the next drip that fell toward him. This glob landed just to the right of his abdomen, searing along the side of his waist before falling down into the folds of his unzipped overalls. Nothing to be done about it except register the growing pain, knowing it would only grow for the next ten seconds. Knowing the same would happen a hundred times over if he didn't get out from under this melting weapon soon.

He reared back with the knife and swung it in again.

The harness came apart at once. All in the blink of an eye to anyone watching, though for Caswell it lasted seconds.

He fell. Arms wheeling, legs kicking. Above him a molten rain of red-hot droplets chased his descent. Wind rushed by his ears.

The river rose to meet him.

* * *

The word is all of us…

Peter Caswell winced as the second half of his memory bridge echoed through his head. A second ago he had closed his eyes and recited the first half, *speak the word.* Now the bit of old song lyric was complete, and so was whatever mission he'd been sent on.

His head pounded. A shockwave that ran up the back of his skull and around to his temples, then back again. This was not normal, and felt more like how a mission started rather than how it ended. He lay still and let the wave of pain dissipate. Only then could he take stock of the rest of his body.

Deep persistent ache in both legs. A stabbing pain in his lower back when he started to move. He could live with both, but hoped he wouldn't have to.

Then there was the headache, which was severe. Still, nothing a few painkillers couldn't sort out.

Aches and pains cataloged, Caswell turned his attention to everything else.

The room was dark, still at the perfect temperature. The bed felt the same. This was good. He'd returned to the same place and position as he'd been in when the mission began, which was always preferred as he found it the least disorienting.

"Open the blinds," he said.

The apartment complied. They whirred and rotated, but no light came in. Or, at least, not as much as before the memory gap. A soft shimmering glow danced lazily on the walls, the ceiling. Nighttime in London. The low distant hum of traffic down below. Headlights throwing shadows in hypnotic patterns across the room.

He opened his eyes fully.

'*How do you feel, Peter?*' Monique asked in his head.

Caswell held back his initial reply. Sometimes a new ache, or the itch of a freshly earned scar, would take a few minutes to register. But other than his legs and his back, nothing emerged. Something *was* different, though. He felt quite sure of this, couldn't put his finger on what the difference was.

'*I feel strange,*' he replied, moving to sit up. His stomach was empty, that was part of it. Just before the memory marker he'd eaten a light meal, as he always did, but clearly he hadn't replicated that step of his process before his memory of the latest mission was deleted. He wondered why, but knew answers were unlikely.

'*Before you stand up, Peter, I need to explain a few things. It is now February the eleventh.*'

Caswell blinked. 'Two weeks?!' A typical mission saw two days, maybe three, wiped from his brain.

'*You've been in hospital, and asked me to spare you the… recovery process.*'

He sat on the edge of the bed and digested that news. The peculiar feeling in his body made sense, now. Instead of a few new bruises and scars to process, his body had been through something major, and yet had already healed.

'*What happened to me?*' he asked.

'*You know I can't tell you the details. But the result… a broken leg, major bruising on your back and left shoulder. Some burns. A severe concussion. According to my post-op brief, were it not for the kindness of a stranger we would have lost you.*'

'*A kind stranger? Thought that species had gone extinct.*'

'*Well, lucky for you they haven't.*'

An awful thought flicked through his head. The kind stranger, lying dead for their troubles. A loose end tidied up. He hoped that wasn't the case, hoped he wasn't the type of person that could do something like that, but he'd never know.

Caswell stood slowly, testing his legs. He'd healed well, at least, as he could not tell which one had been broken. They both ached. He felt sluggish. Out of shape. He crossed to the kitchenette and opened the refrigerator. As always it was empty, save for a row of Sapporo beer bottles arranged perfectly across the top shelf. This was a secret part of his memory-bridge process, something he didn't share with Monique as it went against the protocols their employer, Archon, insisted on. The number of bottles facing backwards would tell him how many people he'd killed on the mission his employer had just deleted from his memory. He wasn't supposed to leave himself any information, especially details, but this one thing he felt he deserved to know. A tally of how successful, and perhaps how evil, his forgotten self was.

But this time, for the first time since he'd begun killing for Archon, all of the bottles faced forward. He hadn't killed anyone?

'*My injuries,*' he thought carefully to Monique, '*do they mean we were unsuccessful?*'

'*On the contrary. I'm told we performed admirably, but that the, uh, complications… they occurred during the extraction process.*'

He closed the fridge, took a shower, and dressed.

'*Our betters have awarded you an additional two weeks vacation, Peter. Plus a sizable bonus for the injuries and lost time. Two point seven million. Enjoy it.*'

Four weeks off. He nodded, pleased. A break sounded good. The money was nice, but he had more than he could ever spend already.

'*Can I make a donation to this kind stranger?*'

'*They remained anonymous. But even if they hadn't, it's best if they never hear from you again, Peter. Still, that's a lovely thought.*'

He took a company limo to Heathrow. Walking through the concourse he realized he was limping slightly. The left leg had broken, then. He'd have to work on that. A noticeable limp would be, well, noticed.

Caswell moved through the bustling crowd and made his way to the bookstore just past the sensory parlor. The place was nearly empty, physical books no longer the hot seller they'd once been, but that suited him. He found the travel section, knelt to the bottom shelf, and reached behind the row of books there for the one he personally had tucked out of sight. It was still there. Always was. He felt sure he was the only person who ever touched that shelf, not to mention that specific book.

It was a catalog of places the would-be adventurer traveler 'must visit', one location per page. Caswell, pretending to select a page at random, would instead turn to the page that matched his professional body count. Whatever place that was, he would go there. Today, though, he already knew the destination. He'd go to the same place he'd been last time. No beer bottles turned around meant no kills, which meant the same page. Mexico. Tacos on the beach. He could live with that. Still, he went through the motions. Cameras were no doubt watching. A deviation from his routine would be noticed.

He thumbed through the pages until reaching Fifty-Nine. And there he froze.

Inside the book, over the title at the top of the page, there was a sticky note. Two words, hastily scrawled:

Alavus, Finland.

Caswell snapped the book closed. Then opened it again, removed the note, and waddled it into a tiny ball. All the while his mind raced.

It wasn't his handwriting, but clearly it was meant for him. Someone had known what page to put the note on. Moreover, they'd known what to write as well.

Alavus. All of us. Speak the word, the word is all of us.

Whoever it was, they knew his mnemonic. Caswell never told anyone the bit of old song lyric he used to ease the transition across his memory gaps. And yet clearly he had. On the last mission? Likely. The question became: why?

Caswell returned the book to its hiding place and walked out of the store. The answers to his questions, it seemed obvious, were waiting in Finland.

* * *

Having only a destination and no timetable, Caswell decided to drive. Give himself time to process, and a few days for his leg to fully heal up.

'*A road trip?*' Monique asked.

'*Been a while since I sharpened my driving skills,*' he sent back, in a tone he hoped reminded her he didn't like her in his head while on vacation. It seemed to work, as no more questions or comments interrupted him as he made his way through the car hire pavilion. Caswell decided to splurge, opting for an early century Porsche Dakar, electric-converted sometime in the last few years and fully kitted out for winter driving.

As he cruised east he booked a sleeping cabin on a ferry that would take him across to Esbjerg, driving onto the ship mere minutes before its midnight departure. He woke at dawn just as the ferry was docking. They'd charged his car during the crossing, and by noon Caswell was pushing the classic Porsche past Malmö and into the center of Sweden toward Stockholm. Save for some automated cargo vehicles, the highway was nearly empty today and derestricted. Caswell pressed the car to its limit, smiling as he went. He couldn't remember the last time he'd physically driven an automobile, never mind one as enjoyable as this, either because it had been too far in his past or part of some mission now wiped from his mind. Either way, he found his excuse to Monique not such an excuse after all - this could be valuable training. Even if it wasn't, it was fun.

Another overnight Ferry took him to Finland, and by noon that day Caswell saw the first sign for the small village of Alavus, four kilometers distant. He stopped beside the road and pulled up a satellite map of the place, partly to figure out what his final destination might be, and partly to be sure he understood his exit options. Only two main roads in and out, roughly in the four directions of the compass.

He had no idea who he was supposed to meet here, or even *if* he was supposed to meet someone, but the location seemed obvious enough: There was only one hotel in the town, which housed the only proper restaurant and bar. Still, he studied the names of the other businesses and landmarks, looking for anything that might mean something. A dead-drop perhaps? Nothing leapt out at him. It was a small village in the middle of nowhere. The only reason for him to come here was the town's name, it seemed. Someone knew it would have meaning for him. Perhaps he'd receive a second note at the hotel's check-in desk.

Caswell set his implant to privacy mode, hoping if he only left it in that state for a few hours that Monique might not even notice. It wasn't against policy or anything, just something that she frowned upon. She could still request presence if she needed to contact him, but couldn't enter his mind uninvited.

He called the hotel's automated system and booked a room under a false name, then drove on toward the town.

Entering Alavus, Caswell turned down a side road. The map had shown a small alley across the street from the lone hotel. It took some time to find his way through the maze of narrow lanes, but eventually he found himself nosing the car towards the mouth of the alley. Caswell killed the running lights and waited a few minutes, watching the windows along the front of the building opposite him.

To the right he could see a check-in desk, two flat-screen kiosks providing guests with the ability to print keys or authorize their own smart devices to act as such. No actual person was at the desk, but that was the norm these days. Caswell scanned left. The restaurant had been designed to look like a classic American diner, for what reason he could not imagine. Red leather booths along the windows, and a counter lined with chrome stools on the interior side. Behind the counter was a wall with slots that provided access to the kitchen.

An older woman fussed with a coffee machine behind the counter. Someone moved around in the kitchen. As for patrons, there was only one he could see. A nondescript person wearing a hooded sweater, seated in the farthest booth from the door.

After one last look up and down the street, Caswell decided it was time to rely on his instincts and reflexes, and find out who'd summoned him here. He locked the car and crossed the street. Despite being just shy of 1 PM, it felt like dusk outside. Cold and dark, the sky a uniform gray blanket of clouds.

Using the kiosk he checked into his room, and waited as a keycard printed.

"Luggage?" the machine asked.

"No." He'd left it in the car, unsure yet if he'd actually stay here.

Caswell walked into the restaurant.

The lone patron was a young woman, he now saw. Indian perhaps, or Bangladeshi. She glanced up at his entrance.

When their eyes met she stood, tentatively, swallowed back some nerves, and gestured to the seat across from her. There'd been instant recognition in her features. Caswell had never seen her before, at least not that he could remember. The 'kind stranger' Monique had spoken of? Perhaps. He walked toward her along the row of booths, nodding towards the waitress behind the counter as he passed. In the same instant he brushed his left hand over the table beside him, swiping a steak knife from its surface and dropping it into his jacket pocket.

The young woman had a laptop computer to one side of her, by the window. It was open and turned on, but when she realized he was glancing that way she quickly pushed the lid down and then set the machine on the bench seat beside her. In front of her was a cup of coffee that looked cold, and a half-eaten plate of chips with a drying smear of ketchup along one edge. She'd been here a while.

"Speak the word," Caswell said.

"The word is all of us," she replied. Then she let out a breath through pursed lips. "I've been here a week," she said. "What took you so long?"

"No. We're not starting this conversation there," Caswell said. Her mouth snapped shut. He leaned forward on his elbows. "Who are you, and how do you know that phrase? How did you know about the book at Heathrow?"

"You said this might happen," she replied, but it seemed more for herself than for him. The woman leaned forward as well and held his gaze. "I'm Firecracker," she said.

"Odd name."

"Hacker name."

"Okay. What's your real name?"

"You told me not to tell you. We met in Mumbai, a few weeks ago."

"How?"

"You fell from a bridge and landed on my boat."

"Not how I usually go about meeting someone."

"It was a first for me, too. Fucked up my house pretty bad when you landed."

"House, or boat?"

"Same thing. Need to move around a lot, in my line of work."

Caswell digested this, watching her face for any signs of deception, wishing he had Monique in his ear telling him if her voice patterns betrayed any lie. For his part, he thought she was telling the truth. He wasn't quite ready to trust her, but he wasn't ruling it out.

"Go on," he said.

"I nursed you back to health. Brought you a doctor I know. Someone discrete. You almost died. You really don't remember? Broke your leg, messed up your back pretty bad, too. The concussion was the worst, though. Your implant shut down due to the impact, and when you woke… you told me you had a window of opportunity before they started watching you again."

"How long was I on your boat?"

"A few days."

"Shutdown and restart only takes thirty seconds."

"I'm a hacker," she said. "My boat has an EM shielded room, copper-mesh lined, no signals in or out. You stayed in there. Before you left we… we agreed to meet again. You told me your phrase so you'd know to trust me."

Two days off the Archon network, Caswell mused. Monique would be wanting to account for that. Good thing he'd enabled privacy mode. Of course, Archon had probably already interrogated him before the reversion, so maybe they knew all this. Caswell had no idea if he was the type of person to crack under questioning. As for trusting this woman, this Firecracker…

"Skip ahead. Why are we meeting now?" *Is it so I can kill you? Tie up a loose end?* He pushed that thought aside. There was more to this, he felt sure.

She leaned in even closer, glancing around to make sure no one was listening, despite the place being empty save for the cashier at the far end of the room, still battling the coffee machine.

"You told me you work for Archon. That they delete your memories. You asked me to help you find a way to prevent that. Or to… undelete them."

"Did I say why?"

She shook her head. "Not exactly. I think you just wanted to know if it was possible. And you thought I might have the right skills to find out."

"And is it? Possible?"

"Maybe." Her eyes flicked toward the window, then back at him. "I coded up a test signal. But the only way to know…"

"…Is to try it."

She nodded. "You said if I could help you keep your memories, you'd pay me. One million, in cash."

"Did I really?"

She nodded. "I recorded it if you want to see."

"I believe you. Okay. Where? When?"

"Let's get some food," she said, pretending not to hear him.

'*Caswell.*' It was Monique's voice in his head.

He blinked. She hadn't requested presence. Bypassed privacy mode. He hadn't even felt her enter. That was possible? He'd have to worry about that later.

'*Can't talk right now,*' he sent back, his mind reeling. How often had she been with him when he thought he was alone?

'We'll discuss your meeting with this hacker another time,' Monique replied. *'There's an urgent matter—'*

"You want some fries?" the girl asked. "A drink?"

He ignored her. Monique had been present, clearly. Was probably waiting to see if he would entertain this conversation or take other actions.

'There are four flyers approaching your location at high speed,' Monique sent. *'It seems you've walked into a trap.'*

'How long do I have?'

'Less than a minute.'

He took the knife from his pocket and flicked it from his left hand to his right, catching it deftly and resting his wrist on the table, knife blade pointed at her.

"Who are your friends?" he asked Firecracker.

"What? What friends?"

"Flyers, landing now, on the edge of the village."

"I don't know about any—" but then she saw the look in his eyes. She knew that he knew she was lying.

"Five seconds to tell me what's going on, or I open your throat."

She weighed this. Glanced at the knife. At him. Then she deflated.

"They offered more money," she whispered.

"For what?"

"To get a look at your implant," Firecracker replied. "I took a scan of it while you were unconscious. It's… I've never seen anything like it. No one has. I put some feelers out, and these guys contacted me. They want to study it."

"Who's 'they'?"

"A rival to Archon. Does it matter?"

"It matters quite a lot. Tell me." *While I still have the chance to remember*, he thought to himself.

"I'm sorry," the girl said. "I wanted to look at it, too, before they got here. Get you your answers. But… also…"

"You wanted to get paid twice," Caswell snapped.

She flinched. Didn't deny it.

Caswell stood, hopped over the counter, and pushed through a pair of swinging double doors into the kitchen area. He ran for a door at the back, shouldered through it just as the chef shouted something at him.

He was in a hall. A few buckets on the floor, some crates of supplies. Two doors, one at the far end and one about halfway along, on the opposite side of the door he'd just come through. Big, metal, with a long latching handle. Freezer door. Caswell jogged past it and on to the other door at the far end. He pushed through it at full stride, shoulder first, and heard the locking mechanism break.

Behind the hotel was a small parking area for employees, trash bins off to one side. He looked left and right, weighing his options.

'*How close are they?*' he sent to Monique.

'*Very. And given how much your little hacker friend knows, I believe you've got some tidying up to do before you go.*'

'*I'm not going to kill her.*'

'*You are, or we'll have that entire restaurant blown to kingdom come.*'

He'd never heard Monique talk like that before. At least, not that he could recall.

'*You'd kill me to kill her? Just because she knows my implant is high-end?*'

'*She might know a lot more than that. You didn't injure your back in that fall, Caswell. She tortured you. We can't risk leaving her alive.*'

Torture? Somehow he doubted that. But it didn't seem like the time to argue with Monique. Still, he couldn't just kill that girl. Could he? The truth was he didn't know. Couldn't remember. Perhaps he'd finally find out what kind of person he was.

'*Maybe I should bring her in,*' he responded. '*She probably has files. Might have told others.*'

'*We have a team headed to her houseboat already. As for sharing her knowledge, something tells me it's too valuable to her to just give it away.*'

He turned. Retraced his steps. From the bucket in the hallway he grabbed a wooden mop, snapped it over his knee, and kept the handle with its now-jagged tip.

Back in the restaurant, Firecracker was standing beside her table, her back to him, her focus on the street beyond the window. Outside, a group of plain-clothed military-types had gathered and were walking purposefully towards the hotel entrance. Six of them. The one in the lead pointed off to his right and two of them broke away, jogging off up the street, presumably to cover any rear exits. Four, then, coming inside. Two going around back. Caswell guessed there'd be two more at least, with their flyers, waiting as backup or covering the roads in case any police decided to poke their noses in.

One of the figures approaching the entrance broke away from the rest of the group. He was holding a cube-shaped metal object, with a sort of tripod brace attached to the bottom of it. Caswell recognized the device instantly, and knew he had ten seconds, maybe less.

He rushed forward, grabbed Firecracker and pushed her towards the swinging door. She'd barely had time to cry out her surprise before Caswell was next to her again, now with her computer and her shoulder bag tucked under one arm. He still held the broken mop handle, guiding her down the hall with it.

"Go, go!" he shouted. "In there!"

Her fear and surprise gave way to understanding. Firecracker opened the freezer door and stepped inside, Caswell rushed in behind her. He shouldered the door shut and moved as far into the cramped room as he could.

"Are they—" she had time to ask, before the lights went out.

The whole building, the whole village, plunged into darkness.

'Monique?' he sent.

No reply. But he pinged his implant for his own bio-readings and got a response back instantly, so the thing wasn't fried. The freezer had shielded it. It was also shielding him from Monique's link.

"Blitz pack," Caswell said to the hacker, and could see in her features that she knew what that meant. "Your friends, they're not here to buy data from you or scan my implant, they're here to kill both of us and leave with a dormant implant they can dissect at their leisure."

"I didn't know…" she said, panic starting to seep into her voice.

"It's alright."

"Are we locked in?" she asked.

"That's only in movies." He pushed the laptop and shoulder bag into her arms. "Stay here. If I'm not back in one minute, take the back door, and get the hell out of here."

Wide-eyed, she nodded, clutching her computer to her chest and watching him as he left.

He stepped out into the dark hallway and eased the door shut. Without the building's air-con running, or any of the equipment in the kitchen, the place was eerily silent.

Caswell accessed his implant, overclocked his brain slightly, and amped up the light reception in his optical nerves. Augmented so, he could make out the shape of the hallway. He could hear better, too, and there were footsteps approaching from the back door. He stepped that way, reached to open it, then pulled his hand back and started to thrust the mop handle forward violently. In that instant the back door was flung open. Bright light spilled in from the alley. Caswell's implant compensated, leveling the signals reaching his brain from his eyes. He saw the jagged tip of his mop handle pushing outward through the sudden gap in the door frame. Saw the arm of the person yanking it open. Tactical clothes, gloved hand. With his brain processing his senses at nearly twice the normal rate everything seemed to move slowly. He guided the tip of the mop handle toward the wrist of the person outside, saw the splinters of wood stab into the flesh at the gap between glove and sleeve. They let go of the door, but Caswell's knee was already coming up, forcing it fully open. He stepped outside, already twisting his improvised weapon and swinging it back and to the right.

The mercenary was still reeling from surprise, not yet even registering the pain from their wrist, when the mop handle plunged in again, this time in the neck just below their ear. Caswell let go of the mop handle, caught the pistol falling from the merc's hand, and dove outward all in one motion. He rolled on the asphalt, turning over as he did, and aiming toward the second merc who had positioned themselves on the other side of the doorway. The man was halfway into a crouch position, his hand flinging a small knife toward Caswell. He couldn't avoid it. Felt the sting as it grazed his abdomen. Gritting his teeth, he shot twice into the second merc. One in the gut, one in the forehead.

Both mercs were on the ground and motionless by the time Caswell stood.

'…an you hear me, Caswell?'

'I'm here, Monique. They hit the whole village with a blitz pack.'

'Are you alright?'

'Shielded myself in a meat freezer. How'd you access my implant?'

'We'll discuss that later. An extraction team is en route. Hired, not ours, but they're good.'

'ETA?'

'Six minutes.'

He instructed his implant to start a timer, then checked his wound. The cut across his midsection was long but not deep. Another scar to add to his collection.

Caswell turned and went back inside, leaving a trickle of blood as he went.

He encountered the other four inside the diner. One—the leader, it seemed—stood with his back to Caswell, barking orders in terse German to his underlings, who seemed more interested in keeping their guns trained on the poor hostess and chef than covering the interior door. The drawback to using a blitz device to shutdown implants was that their own hardware would be offline. Communication would have to be verbal, and they would not yet have any hint of what happened out in the alley.

They all saw Caswell enter, except for the leader. None of them raised their weapons in time.

* * *

Exactly one minute after leaving her, he pulled the door of the meat locker open and stepped inside, waiting to hear the latch engage before he moved farther in.

"You're hurt," Firecracker said.

"Looks worse than it is," he said.

"Are they–?"

"All dead. Well, haven't checked the flyers yet, but I heard them buzz out. Probably cleared out to avoid the blitz pack, waiting for the all clear to return. I suspect when that call doesn't come they'll decide my implant isn't worth it and cut their losses entirely."

"Well… they'd be wrong." The girl hoisted her shoulder bag and stepped toward the door. It was then she realized Caswell had a pistol aimed at her.

"You were going to sell me to them," he said.

Defiance flashed across her features, but it quickly vanished.

She said, "You'd do the same, if you lived the life I have to."

Caswell tapped the back of his neck with the pistol. "And this?"

"What I said was true," she replied. "It's... exotic is the only word. Prototype, I'd guess. Very high-end."

"Can you hack it?"

She considered several replies before deciding on a simple, sheepish shrug.

"If I had a few weeks to probe–"

"You've got... two minutes and twelve seconds."

She squinted at him. He held her gaze. Blood dripped onto the floor, pooling now. Caswell ignored it. Only some of it was his.

"That's not enough time to figure out the interface, let alone... what are you hoping I can do?"

"Help me remember," he said. "That's all I want. Find the bit that lets them revert me and disable it. Or at least find out if that's possible, and tell me what I'd need to do to make it happen."

"Impossible," she said. "It'd take a year. Even then, still unlikely." Her brow furrowed, though. "Unless..."

"Unless what?"

"It's risky. Last ditch effort. The test signal I developed. It will mimic your handler's own–"

Caswell held up a hand. Outside he could hear muffled voices. Locals, coming out of hiding to see what had happened? Almost certainly. What they'd find in the restaurant would haunt them. *Finally, a memory,* he thought ruefully, *and this would be it.* Violence. Carnage. He was going to remember a monster. And maybe a traitor, too.

"Do it. Whatever it is, just do it. Whatever other data you get, it's yours. Sell it, use it, I don't care."

"Lay on the ground, face down," she said, already whipping the bag off her shoulder and unzipping it.

He did as she asked. There was no time to take precautions, no time to ponder what might happen if she slipped some virus into the Archon system via him. Caswell knew this chance would never come again. In a shielded room that blocked Monique from monitoring him, and most importantly, without a memory marker Monique could revert him back to. He would remember this. He'd come away with something he could use. All it would take then is patience, and a plan. Use his time off from killing for Archon to figure out how to subvert this goddamn device and–

Something cold and metallic clapped against his neck.

The shock hit him like a freight train. Everything went white hot, then vanished altogether.

* * *

"Peter Caswell?" someone was asking.

He blinked, then shivered. It was so cold his teeth chattered together.

"What…" he tried to sit.

"Don't move," the voice said. "You've got a screamer on your neck. This will hurt a bit."

A screamer. He grimaced, remembering now. Firecracker, saying she had something she could try to access his implant, asking him to lay down. He'd complied, like a fucking idiot, and she'd put a screamer on him. She had no test signal, no quick way to access his implant. She'd come here to knock him senseless and collect a bounty.

He felt something sliding along the base of his neck. A scalpel or just a sharp knife he wasn't sure. The man above him was skilled, though, and within a few seconds he'd pried the device loose without even breaking Caswell's skin.

"You want it?" the man asked, holding the object out to him.

Caswell studied the thing for a moment. He'd never experienced one before, but imagined he probably used them now and then in his line of work. He had been trained, of course, and remembered what his instructor had said. Enough electricity to overwhelm even the most hardened implant, but not enough to kill the target. "Get your target both incapacitated and disconnected from whoever monitors them. Then you can do as you like." He ground his teeth, wondering what Firecracker had done. Ran, if she knew what was good for her. He suspected she did. Seemed smart as hell, in fact. The question was, had she tried to interface with his implant before she'd left? Decrypted its contents? Or even installed some code of her own? He could track her down, maybe. See if she'd learned anything. He'd have the upper hand. He still might have a chance to–

"You with me, mate?" the man asked.

"Yeah. Toss that thing, I don't want it."

The screamer was flung aside, and a hand offered. Caswell grasped it and allowed himself to be hoisted to his feet. He found it hard to stand. The man pulled his arm over one shoulder and guided Caswell to the door.

"Quite the mess you made here," the man said, leading him into the hall toward the rear exit.

"It was them or me."

"No judgment, friend," he said, and gestured toward rear of the building. "We just need to hurry it up a bit."

"Where's the girl?" Caswell asked.

The man squinted at him, confused. "What girl?"

"The one who put the screamer on me. Young woman. Indian."

A shake of the head. "I didn't see anyone. Well, some townspeople, fleeing as I arrived. I ignored them."

"We should search the hotel."

"No can do, sorry."

"It's important."

"My orders are to get you on a flyer and well away from here. Without delay."

There seemed no point in arguing further. Caswell took some solace in the fact that he had a lead. Her moniker, and her face, both of which he would remember. He'd find her.

The flyer was in the small parking lot behind the hotel. He guided Caswell there by the arm, forcefully now. What other orders might he have, Caswell wondered.

"I have a car," he said, trying to pull away. "I'll get myself home—"

"Torched," the man replied. He smiled. "Not me, the mercs you killed. Shame too, hell of a vehicle."

'—*y..u re..iv..ng me, ..eter? ..ou b..ck online ..et?*'

'*I'm here,*' Caswell sent.

'*Report, ..lease. The eff..ts of the scream.. ..ould be wearing off.*'

The man guided Caswell into the passenger seat, then helped him get the harness on. It was a private flyer, and from the look of it, one that could move quite fast indeed.

Peter Caswell watched as the final buckle was fastened. He realized his torso had been bandaged where that thrown knife had grazed him. Whether this man had applied it, or Firecracker, he had no idea.

He turned to ask, but the man was already closing the door. He smiled at Caswell through the window, then walked around to the other side of the vehicle.

Before he could reach for the handle, though, the doors locked, and the engines began to whir into life.

The man grabbed the handle, shook it, and met Caswell's gaze before his eyes filled with blood. He dropped to the ground, dead before he'd even known something was wrong.

'*Just tying up loose ends,*' Monique sent.

The flyer rose into the sky on the power of its six electro-props, stirring up dust and debris into the air as it went. Caswell half expected to see the hotel on fire as he lifted into the sky. To see missiles level the entire village. But all he saw was the quiet empty streets of the small town, the bodies that now lay in the alley, and the burning wreckage of his hired car the only sign anything had happened. They faded into the distance, and the past, soon enough.

'*Was that necessary?*' he sent.

'*Risk mitigation.*'

'*Is it going to be a problem that I'll remember this?*' Caswell sent. '*Are you going to drop me like you did that pilot? Am I a loose end now, too, Monique?*'

Ten seconds passed. Twenty.

'*Do you remember, a few days ago, waking up in the apartment, Caswell?*'

'*Yes,*' he sent.

'*In a lot of pain, were you? Disoriented?*'

Where was she going with this?

'*Honestly, Peter, it really is frustrating how often you underestimate me. I almost wish you would remember sometime. What's even more frustrating is how often you try to find little ways to subvert our arrangement. I think we can only tolerate a few more of these episodes, but for now...*'

He felt a tingling sensation in his neck. It started to grow.

She sent, '*What's the phrase again? The one you think we don't know about? Ah yes. Speak the word...*'

* * *

...the word is all of us.

Peter Caswell winced as the second half of his memory bridge echoed through his head. A second ago he had closed his eyes and recited the first half, *speak the word*. Now the bit of old song lyric was complete, and so was whatever mission he'd been sent on.

He took stock of how his body felt. Other than a slight ache in his abdomen that hadn't been there before, he felt good.

Satisfied, Caswell turned his attention to everything else.

The room was dark, still at the perfect temperature. The bed felt the same. This was good.

"Open the blinds," he said.

Turn About

Tanya Huff

"*You followed Lieutenant Commander Sibley's Jade to the Berganitan. How did you follow the Berganitan through Susumi space?*"

Presit actually waved a tiny finger at the general. "I are not having to tell you that, General Morris. Thanks to suspicious Parliament, full disclosure works only one way. You are having to disclose to me, but I are not having to disclose to you. But," she added as the general flushed puce, "it are no big thing. I are merely…"

Durgin trilled an interruption, objecting to Presit's pronoun.

"…locking on the tail end of the Berganitan's Susumi signature," she continued, ignoring her pilot. "It are a tricky maneuver—we are having to be close enough to follow but not so close we are being swept up in the wake and destroyed—but it are not a secret."

His broad cheeks lightening slightly to maroon, General Morris attempted to lock Durgin in a steely glare, but it kept sliding off the nearly black lenses of the Katrien's glasses. "You're a pilot, you had to have known how insanely dangerous that was. You could have destroyed both ships. As it was, you nearly destroyed yourself and your passengers."

The pilot's ears flipped down and up. "Unfortunately," he began.

Presit cut him off, her glasses still pointed toward the general. "Durgin a Tar canSalvais are working for me. If he are intending to continue working for me, he are keeping certain things to himself."

Durgin's ears flipped again as he followed Presit from the room. "Yeah, what she are saying."

General Morris rocked back on his heels as the door closed. "I can't believe they followed us through Susumi space. We have to get their equations. If they've actually found the sweet spot—and aren't merely the luckiest S.O.B.s ever evolved—the information will have major military applications. Is there some way you can access their ship's logs?"

"Legally? No. But they're on the Berganitan now…" Captain Carveg smiled. The smile suggested her people were already working on it.

* * *

"Lieutenant Campbell?"

Lieutenant Alexis Campbell looked up from her slate. "Sergeant?"

He leaned in, copper hair moving forward as if it too wanted to be closer, copper eyes gleaming in the low light of the bar. "The flight commander wants a word."

"Now?"

"Now, Lieutenant."

Alexis thumbed in a payment for the drink she'd barely tasted, slapped her slate back onto her belt, and scrambled to her feet. "Is the commander on the flight deck?"

"No. If you'll come with me Lieutenant, I'll take you to her."

Sutton's was empty of anyone she knew so Alexis bestowed a smile on a pair of Krai sitting between her and the door as she strutted out into the corridor. The flight commander wanted to talk to her. That could mean only one thing.

She was getting a ship!

The battle of Bal had destroyed almost three full squadrons and sent hundreds of jades to the shipyards for repair. The Confederation needed the two person fighters out burning vacuum the next time the Others attacked, but they had more pilots than ships for them to fly. Alexis' training scores had kept her among the few waiting on Ventris Station for jades when most of her cohort had been sent out to fly shuttles or been slotted into battleship crews.

"Lucky chricka," Harrst had muttered, glaring at the orders on his slate.

She'd rested her arm on her best friend's head. "Luck has nothing to do with it. I'm just that good."

She was that good. Technically a better pilot than Hiron di'Ausokol, more intuitive a pilot than Cecilia "Cissi" Wanamaker, Alexis wasn't surprised to get the first new ship off the line.

Unless…

"Sergeant? Has the commander asked to speak to anyone else today?"

"I'm not at liberty to say, Lieutenant."

Damn.

Between the bar and the link, she worked out how she'd subtly rub her news in Hiron and Cissi's faces. On the link, she wondered if her ship would be a rebuild or a unit just off the line, still redolent with that new jade smell. Stepping off the link, the sergeant strode through the waiting crowds like the busy corridor was empty space and she had to start paying attention.

They ended up in one of the older parts of the station where everything looked slightly grimy, a little worn, and very well used. Marines and civilians moved through hatches on both sides of the corridor, orders shouted out after them or back into the room they'd just left. The sergeant exchanged nods with half a dozen NCOs, growled something in Taykan at a private with brilliant fuchsia hair who was scrubbing the join between deck and bulkhead, and finally stopped at a hatch that looked no different than all the others they'd passed.

The name on the screen said Major Dragan Popovic.

Major Popovic was not the flight commander.

"But…"

The sergeant's eyes darkened. Alexis sighed, stepped over the hatch lip and into the outer office. The hatch to the inner office was closed. When the outer door closed behind her, she turned to see the sergeant settle into the chair behind the battered desk that took up most of the space in the room and tap his thumb twice against the edge of the screen. "The major's expecting you, Lieutenant, go on in."

"Should I…?"

When he glanced up at her, his eyes had darkened again.

"Never mind."

Major Popovic was a Human male with dark brown eyes, his dark hair streaked with silver. Not unattractive for his age, Alexis noted, but more to the point, he wore admin insignia. Career bureaucrat.

Wasting her time. The sergeant had lied to her.

Lips pressed into a thin line, she waited.

After a long moment, the major laid both hands flat on his desk and said, "Are you familiar with the Berganitan's interaction with the alien ship known as Big Yellow?"

"Sir?"

"Do you need me to repeat the question, Lieutenant?"

His tone, quiet power and something harder under that, straightened her spine. Not a career bureaucrat. Or not *only*. Not wasting her time. She might actually get to fly. "No, sir. I'm familiar with the story, sir." As far as Alexis knew, everyone was familiar with the story of the Berganitan and Big Yellow. Impossible not to be, given the way that Katrien reporter had spread it all over known space. Gunnery Sergeant Kerr was currently on Ventris Station, briefing command. Alexis did not envy her.

"What you don't know," the major continued, "relevant to this discussion, was that the Sector General News crew had not been embedded in with the Berganitan. They followed her. Through Susumi space."

"What kind of an idiot," she began, remembered who she was talking to and decided not to finish the sentence.

"It wasn't the smart thing to do, but it worked." The major half smiled. "Always bet on stupid; Popovic family motto." He gestured at the grey plastic chair in front of his desk. "Sit down, Lieutenant."

She sat and reached for her slate.

"No," he said, lifted one off the desk and handed it to her. "The information goes no further than this slate."

He went back to work while she read, shifting files between screens, suddenly a bureaucrat again.

Outwardly.

Alexis opened the file.

Reading between the lines, it was easy to see the information had been recovered from the destroyed ship rather than offered by the Katrien pilot.

The CMC had used the information to program drones and send them into Susumi space after larger drones.

None of the smaller drones had made it.

There was only one missing variable.

"You need a pilot."

"Yes, Lieutenant, we need a pilot. We need a pilot to follow one of the Other's ships through Susumi space and return with the information that will allow us to end this war. Or at the very least with information," he added after a short pause. "I'd settle for scrambled co-ordinates and a low resolution star field at this point. We have nothing to work with."

"Why me?"

"Because you're good enough I believe you can do it." He cocked his head slightly and the half smile returned. "And because you're young enough and arrogant enough to believe you can do it."

"Is it arrogance when you're actually that good, sir?" His brows rose, she swallowed a visceral reaction, and hurriedly added, "The news crew had to be rescued by the Berganitan."

"I was led to believe you're a better vacuum jockey than a news crew pilot."

It wasn't a question. She answered it anyway. "Yes, sir, I am. But I'm a jade pilot and…"

"We can load your ship with the same Susumi program civilians use. We need the reaction time and instinctive abilities of a jade pilot. Your scores and your flight instructors say you're the jade pilot we need."

She swallowed. "I was third."

"I'm aware. If you accept this mission…"

Like she'd turn down the chance.

"…you'll leave Ventris at twenty-one thirty."

"Today?"

"Today, Lieutenant. Tell anyone who asks, and I'd prefer it if you avoided those who will, that you'll be testing a new propulsion system."

She waited, but that seemed to be all the major had to say.

Then she waited a little longer, caught in his aggressively ordinary gaze.

Finally, looking slightly annoyed, Major Popovic tapped a finger against the inert plastic trim of his desk. "Yes or no, Lieutenant. I haven't got all day, there's a war on."

* * *

"Leaving Susumi space in three, two…"

Alexis began course corrections. On her first test run, she'd been rescued from the wreckage of her ship, such as it was. On her second, only proximity shields cranked to maximum on the drone she'd followed, had prevented a fatal collision.

Getting in, turned out to be easy; even a drone could find the sweet spot. Getting out on the other hand…

The trick was to anticipate the exit and adjust the ship's position in the larger Susumi wave *before* information began coming in from the sensors. Alexis dropped her fingertips to the screens. First, against training and every bit of knowledge compiled about exiting Susumi space, she applied maximum power to the x axis before her ship's small wave was subsumed. Second, the instant she was free, she immediately cut all power so as not to be caught up again.

Heart pounding, Alexis stared out at the stars, at the distance growing between her ship and the drone, and smiled. Third time lucky.

Intuitive flying.

Cissi couldn't have done it. Hiron couldn't have done it. And they'd never know she had.

On the other hand, the Others would never know she'd snuck in, tucked up against their aft burners, so it almost evened out.

* * *

The ship in the shuttle bay of the CS Destrier looked like nothing Alexis had seen before. Larger than a jade, smaller than a cruiser, it looked as though the builders had slapped a Susumi engine onto a small Marine attachment. Or the other way around, since the engine was larger than the living quarters.

The finish was a matte black so… Alexis searched for a word and could only come up with *black*. A matte black so black it was hard to identify individual pieces and as she drew closer she had the strangest impression of falling into it. Against the black of space, the ship would be invisible. The Others would never see her coming.

"Had to get a Taykan to do the final coat." The Krai Chief Petty Officer stepped up onto the boarding ramp. "Rest of us haven't the visual acuity. Pain in the ass to find one with the necessary clearance. We've coated the buoy you'll leave with the same stuff. Kept losing the *serley* thing." Her voice trailed off as she stepped into the cabin.

Major Popovic gestured Alexis in ahead of him.

The cabin was barely large enough for three stationary people. Movement would require choreography.

"Based the interior design on a civilian ship," the chief announced. "Rack, head, food for a hundred days…"

"A hundred days?" Alexis shuffled sideways and poked the mattress of the narrow, recessed bed. "How long do you expect me to be in Susumi, Chief?"

"No idea, Lieutenant, but if you starve to death we've all wasted our time. Now this," she continued, "is identical to the panel you used during the tests and there should be no surprises with response time. One minor addition." She tapped a bright orange pressure point just to the left of the main screen. "We've hooked up a self destruct."

Alexis blinked. "A what now?"

Chief Quirrk ignored the question. "The Others have never taken prisoners so if you're spotted odds are high they'll shoot first and skip questions entirely, but if there's a chance of capture, push the button."

"And the ship goes boom?"

The chief's nostril ridges flared. "And the ship goes boom," she agreed.

"And I die?"

"Yes, Lieutenant, you die." The chief shrugged, as bad at the Human gesture as any other Krai.

"Seriously, sir?"

The major's brows rose slightly. "Don't wait around to be spotted and don't harass the opposition. Your mission is to get the co-ordinates back to the Confederation so we can finally take the war to them and give them a reason to sue for peace. The self destruct is a last resort. Trust your gut, you'll know if you have to use it."

Alexis figured a *"Well, duh."* would not go over well.

"Any questions, Lieutenant?"

"Just one." Standing at the bed, she could touch the back of the pilot's chair. "What happens if I've gone too far to find a familiar star and the ship can't extrapolate the entrance co-ordinates? How do I get back?"

"You don't. But…" The chief's nostril ridges flared. "…form follows function and the drive the Others use is essentially identical to a Susumi drive. Their first ship into Confederation space had to have been able to get enough data to make it home. Has to work both ways."

"Essentially identical?" Alexis drummed her fingers on the back of the pilot's chair.

"You'll adapt or you'll die." This shrug was no better than the first.

"Chief." The major's rebuke almost showed an emotion.

* * *

Her name would be in the history books. Lieutenant Alexis Campbell, the first to successfully fly a Confederation ship into the enemy's territory. Lieutenant Alexis Campbell, who brought home the data that ended the war. Only Lieutenant Alexis Campbell had the skill necessary to pilot her ship across an alien dreadnought's Susumi wave.

The future would know her name.

Here and now, however, no one did. Which sucked. Big time.

She hadn't been able to rub it in Hiron and Cissi's faces before she'd left Ventris, and on the Destrier she couldn't hang with the other pilots in the Marine attachment because they'd want the details of her mission. As a result, as the Destrier jumped to Sector Nine where the Others were attacking a gas giant refinery, she spent the four days in Susumi space in her ship running simulations. When the exit alarm sounded, she'd shaved point seven three of a second off her reaction time.

And made it to level thirteen in *Caverns of Chaos*. Because she was just that good.

* * *

Shuttle bay doors opening in fifteen seconds, Lieutenant.

"Fifteen seconds, yes sir." Strapped into the pilot seat, she spread her hands above the panel, fingers curled and ready.

Assume nothing and keep your options open. This will be the final communication until you return.

"Yes, sir." Did he think she might have forgotten? She tongued off the communication implant built into her jaw. The major had been unwilling to use the Destrier's system in case the Others gained access to it—ignoring the fact that as far as she knew, the Others had never attempted such a thing. Even given the importance of her flight, Major Popovic's paranoia seemed a bit over the top.

She spent a wistful moment watching the jades harrying the enemy dreadnought away from the refinery—no point in having the Destrier move in with the big guns if it meant the refinery would become collateral damage—then locked on the signature of the Others' jump point, sliding into a diagonal approach position as the Others raced for safety.

Time to test Chief Qurril's paint job. If they saw her now, that hundred days of food and water would definitely be wasted and she'd be another name on the Ventris Memorial. Dead in a training accident. And wouldn't that be posthumously embarrassing.

The jades kept up the attack, a distraction that cost a ship and two lives. Blinking away the flares, Alexis slid in behind the dreadnought searching for the sweet spot.

One second. Two. She was in position. Felt the drag of their Susumi engine. Waited…

Waited…

The panel lit up, numbers chasing each other across the screens trying to calculate a jump she wasn't making. During her test flights, the drones had jumped by now. If the Others took too long, she'd need access to a Susumi engineer to untangle the mess.

Four more seconds.

She could abort. Fail. Try again.

Five.

The ship shuddered, pitched, and was in Susumi, the soft shush against the outside of the ship drowned out by the sound of her breathing.

* * *

"Twelve days. Not too bad. Haven't even run out of broccoli in a tube." Alexis strapped herself into the pilot's chair, checked the changes in the data stream that identified the Other's Susumi wave, and settled in to wait. "Twelve's hardly surprising, the Others aren't exactly the beings next door. Well, I suppose technically they are, if you consider the Confederation a single entity and the Others a single entity and the whole war about who built whose fence over whose property line. I need to message my mother when I get back and see if she's settled that thing with Rhona's dad."

She'd been talking to herself by day three. It was actually a psychologically sound response to isolation. She knew that because a year's worth of CMC psych department journals had been included with her reading material.

The left side of her largest screen flashed blue as the equations she'd been following began to change.

"And we start the dismount."

Based on the time difference jumping in, she gave them two seconds longer than she would have with a Confederation ship jumping out.

It was almost enough.

The panel flared orange. Stars spun as her ship, caught by the edge of the Other's wave, careened off on a diagonal. Fighting against what sensors insisted was the mathematical equivalent of an external gravity bubble, she shoved, more than stroked the power off.

Thought she heard ceramic crack.

Shielded her head with her arm as she pitched forward.

Bit her tongue as the ship jerked out from under her.

Felt her collarbone break on both sides under the sudden pressure of the straps.

Gravity sucked.

* * *

The stars were still spinning when she came to, but the gravity bubble had dissipated—small mercies—and as long as she was careful, zero G was gentle on broken bones. Her uniform had immobilized her entire upper body, clamping her elbows to her sides. After weighing greater amount of movement against greater amounts of pain, she decided against the override. Moving nothing above her wrists, she checked for the signatures of other ships, found none, and powered up, firing her stabilizers in short bursts, compensating for a damaged lateral thruster. Once she stopped spinning, she arrested her forward momentum, until her ship hung motionless in space.

Hung motionless in *enemy* space.

"Eat my energy signature, Hiron di'Ausokol! Up your exhaust pipe, Cissi Wannamaker!" A double punch into the air at waist level didn't have quite the same *Fuk yeah!* exuberance and QMS had not stocked the ship with celebratory beverages. She'd checked. "And also, ow."

Pain killers would dull her response time.

Her tongue was swollen, her mouth tasted like old blood, and her uniform also supported her left knee which began to ache the moment she realized it was damaged. SOP strapped in extremities while maneuvering in zero G, but she hadn't bothered.

"Pride goeth before," she muttered. "Good thing I'm not walking home."

Ship diagnostics identified a minor breach in the shielding around the core corrected by internal redundancies and a bent housing around the Susumi engine.

"So let's get home before it falls off."

First, find the jump point. She could jump from her current position but she was no Susumi engineer and as good as the installed program was it was always best to limit the variables. Which was, after all, why they *had* standardized jump points.

Five thousand and thirteen point seven kilometres at seventeen degrees off the nadir of the z axis.

"They come out of Susumi faster than we do. I'd like to register a complaint as that potentially crucial information was missing from the data I received. I can only assume no one noticed it when they exit on our side."

Second, did she accelerate until the jump leaving a power trail that could be traced, but getting her ass out of enemy space in the shortest amount of time, or power down after the initial thrust increasing the possibility of being discovered?

"Six of one, half a dozen of the other. Still have eighty-eight days worth of food. Shame to waste it. On the other hand, broken bones. One vote for speed. If I'm spotted, I'd like it to happen before my condition deteriorates enough to compromise my reaction time and fuk up an escape. Motion carried no other votes recorded."

She blinked at a blurred energy reading. It was possible that at some point during the rocking and rolling she'd hit her head.

Third, having locked in the course and engaged the engines, she needed the co-ordinates to anchor this end of the jump.

"Necessary in order to get home and also the point of the exercise."

All the ship had to do was find something it recognized and extrapolate its relative position, so she pointed the long range scanners toward the dim and distant mass of stars at the galactic core. Hopefully, *her* galactic core. Twelve days in Susumi couldn't possibly have been long enough to leave the galaxy. Unless the Others used Susumi tech that was, in fact, different than theirs.

Time passed.

"It is a truth universally acknowledged," she muttered, watching numbers scroll, "that chief petty officers are always right. If the Others found a reference point to jump to, I can find one to jump from."

Or not.

One thousand kilometres to the jump point. Numbers continued to scroll.

Five hundred.

Three hundred. The last integer still hadn't locked.

Two.

One.

She released the buoy.

There!

And also there! Too far out to start her Susumi engine, she spotted a… a grey blob by the jump point. None of her sensors picked it up. Diagnostics insisted they were working, but she had a visual…

"…of a blob." Maybe she'd hit her head harder than she… "Fuk me!"

Firing lateral thrusters, she slid diagonally under the missile that came out of the ship that came out of the blob.

"You're larger than a jade," she reminded herself as she roared straight up the x axis to avoid the next shot. "The definition of close has changed by five point seven meters."

Looping over and around, she locked on the jump point again. All she needed was a straight run…

Proximity alarms blared. Tendrils, vaguely grey against the black of space, drifted toward her.

Space worms?

She avoided the first… the second… the third…

There was the enemy ship. Where was the blob?

"Tendrils of blob? Blob worms?" She was good. She knew she was good, but there were so many and in another minute she'd be…

…engulfed.

Reach truncated by the medical support of her uniform and the safety straps, she couldn't reach the self…

* * *

Alexis woke still strapped into the pilot's seat, but she wasn't alone. There was an argument going on over her head.

Keeping her breathing shallow, she let her head drop to the right and opened her eyes.

Infantry called this species Stick-figures. Marine nomenclature tended to be unimaginative. They were tall and thin, with long extremities, very little body, and, although bipedal, probably not mammals. The being to her right wore a tight white jumpsuit that accentuated the description.

Their eyes had pupils with no visible irises. As she watched, the pupil dilated slightly, grey flowed across the eyes, lingered for a second, then flowed away.

Her astronautics professor at the academy had been Niln so Alexis knew nictitating membranes. This grey stuff had a sheen that made it look more like liquid plastic. Granted, she probably had a concussion, but…

The Being on the right snapped out something Alexis bet was *She's awake!* as multi-jointed fingers grabbed her chin and forced her head up.

The Being on the left looked identical to the Being on the right, excluding insignia on the jumpsuit. Their voice was pitched a little lower, their speech more staccato—Alexis got the impression she was not Left Being's favorite person.

Then she faded out for a few minutes.

When she came back, they were still arguing. Right Being no longer held her chin, but her head remained canted up and it seemed like too much trouble to move it. As she watched, the grey slid across Right Being's eyes again.

Left Being growled a… protest? Sounded like a protest. Although she knew better than to apply Human descriptors to non-Humans. Pilots sure, pilots understood each other. Spoke the same language. But the rest of…

Right Being grabbed Left Being's wrist about two centimetres above her face. They had… skin striations? Faint scales? Eczema?

Something that looked like the liquid grey plastic that had been bopping back and forth across Right Being's eyes oozed out of their pores, or what passed for pores on Stick-figures, and into Left Being.

"Not oozed," she corrected muzzily. "Really too fast to be oozed."

The argument continued.

Stopped.

Left Being looked down at her. Grey flowed across their eyes.

Right Being's hand covered her face. They smelled like cinnamon buns. Her stomach growled.

* * *

"Are you back with us, Lieutenant?"

Alexis blinked and looked up into the dark eyes of Major Popovic. "Sir?"

"You're in the Med-bay on the Destrier."

She was cold. Med-bays were always cold.

"They need you conscious to do brain scans before tanking you," he added. "Fortunately, pilots have strong skulls. Less fortunate when brains slam into them from the inside."

Brain slammed. Almost funny. It hurt to frown. "Tanking?"

"You were pulled from the wreckage of your ship with an impressive number of broken bones and internal injuries. If you hadn't been in your HE suit…" The major shook his head and almost looked concerned.

She didn't remember getting into her HE suit.

She didn't remember anything after the enemy ship firing on her. She didn't remember the impact. Given how she felt, not actually a bad thing. "They guarded the jump."

"Yes. It seems they anticipated us working out how to follow them. Normally, I appreciate a bit of healthy paranoia, but less so in this instance."

There was something more she had to tell him. Something… She fought to lift her right hand. Fought broken ribs for more air. Something important…

Major Popovic gripped her wrist lightly and pushed her hand back into the bed, his fingers warm against her chilled skin. "Relax, Lieutenant."

He held on as she continued to struggle. "No. There's…" Then she had it. "The buoy! I deployed the buoy." She sagged back against the mattress.

The major watched until her breathing calmed then released her. "Well done, Lieutenant. We'll retrieve as much as we can from the wreckage, but that buoy could be the turning point of the war."

Her face hurt. She'd preen later.

"Major? This one needs to begin the tests."

He turned his head and she followed his gaze and blinked until a Rakva came into focus at the foot of the bed. "Of course, Doctor."

A little confused as bodies shifted around, she managed to finally focus on the major as he reached the door.

"I look forward to our official debrief, Lieutenant Campbell but for now, concentrate on healing."

"Yes, sir."

He almost smiled and although it must have been a trick of her abused brain it looked as though a sheen of grey, like a liquid plastic, flicked across his eyes.

Mirror's Spy

L.E. Modesitt, Jr.

The sun had just set, and I looked at the mirror on the study wall, as I often had in the past years, ever since I'd stopped being a night patroller. I couldn't help but shake my head as I recalled our last conversation.

I can only inform you. The choice is yours, Aashen, yours alone.

"Why me?" I'd asked.

Because there's no one else. You're the only one who listened and understood.

Or the only one to survive a ghost possession who *could* listen? Who wasn't a raving madman? Even if some wondered, calling me a spy for the ghosts, behind my back.

What was I, now? A useless former night patroller? An agent of the ghosts? A man beset by visions and voices?

I shook my head again and shouldered the pack that held the devices I'd assembled according to the spirit's direction. Then I looked around the study, smiling faintly as my eyes passed over the mirror and the solid stone wall. It concealed a refuge I hoped I wouldn't need, but probably would, one way or another. Although my parents said it dated back to the time of the ancients, when Meureyne had been far larger, we'd never needed to use it. But now it looked far too likely.

Once I made my way to the front door, out of habit, my fingers checked for the water bottle on my belt, then brushed the grip of the baton, the same one I'd used as a night patroller. Some nights I'd needed it, others not, but it's always better to be prepared if one walks the streets of Meureyne when natural light no longer bathes the city. The few night lamps don't come close to matching the power of sunlight for driving off the ghosts.

I locked the door before I left the house, then stepped out into the roofed entryway and looked west of the city, still sweltering even just after sunset. I watched the parting light of the sun turn the veils of the ancients rising from the hills into diaphanous purple-gray curtains. They almost, but not quite, vanished within minutes, as the Summer Angel began to dominate the western sky. Directly overhead, in the depths above, the red eye of the dead god, Chrome, glared down upon Meureyne…as it had immediately after The Days of the Dying. Some of the wraiths still worshipped it, dead as the god was supposed to be.

Except for the ghosts and the occasional earthquake that loosed another veil of the ancients, Meureyne's a quiet little city, less than a tenth the size it must have once been before The Days. That quiet would soon be shattered.

I glanced north, where the iron turtles of the Prophet lined the hills, gathered and waiting for the morrow. They would sweep down upon the city and surround the sealed, patched, and re-patched walls at its center. Those battered walls contained the ghosts of the ancients, all of which could possess an unwarded and unwary person, especially children. Yet who could blame them for wanting to escape their endless confinement, except that each escape destroyed a living mind.

Those ghosts held scraps of knowledge from the ancients who had ruled the heavens and beyond before their knowledge and their creations had turned on them. Their rebellion transformed the world into a seared and charred desert, with fires that had turned many to ghosts and sealed them within glassy rubble, later reinforced, to prevent their escape. But the scholars of the Prophet of the Inland Sea had learned that Meureyne—and its ghosts—held knowledge that no other ruined city still did.

> *If the ghosts of Meureyne are removed and captured by the scholars, the scholars will rip them apart, strand by strand, and record their every recollection. Except for the scholars and the soldiers, those agonies will torture and drive insane anyone nearby… and, in time, the earth will burn again.*

That was what the spirit of the mirror had told me and why I was walking through the growing dusk toward the Wall separating the ghosts from the living—most of the time, anyway.

While I owed the spirit, not only my life, but my sanity, freeing the ghosts meant going against what I'd done as a night patroller for most of my life. Yet the knowledge held by the ghosts had burned the world once before, and both men and women fought once more, forgetting that past, over who would control what lands under what gods, seemingly without the slightest concern about the cost of that control.

I pushed those thoughts aside, trying to concentrate on what I had to do as I turned north along Coriolan Way. Over the long, slow, charred years, the dwellings on every second or third lot, if not more often, had been scavenged for materials and whatever else of value remained. The native vegetation had returned to the land with the death or departure of those who had lived there. In time, I turned east and headed downhill, avoiding Patrol headquarters, right across Main Street from city hall.

I only saw a few adults on the street, and no children, which was definitely a good sign after sunset, but that was doubtless because many had fled—but not all. Beyond the comparative oasis surrounding Meureyne, little existed beyond twisted forest, still charred in places, sand, and seemingly endless rock. The only road leading anywhere inhabitable was blocked by the Prophet's soldiers and scholars—and their machines.

Once clear of patrol headquarters, I headed south, toward the Wall, a stone barrier surrounding four blocks, a square two blocks on a side, and topped with flat stones cemented together. The only living things left in the blocks nearest the Wall were mesquite, twisted pinyon pines, junipers, rabbit bush… and snakes and rodents. I supposed that was because no one wanted to live there, with all the ghosts near, especially right after The Days. I didn't pretend to understand what led to The Days. What I did know is that the ghosts killed those they possessed—one way or another—something I'd barely escaped and paid for in other ways.

Once I reached the Wall, I hid behind a twisted pinyon across the empty street from the northeast corner and waited for full darkness, when I'd start my work.

Before long, a shadowy figure appeared—Marcuse. I knew the gaits of all the older patrollers. Despite the presence of the Prophet's forces, poor dedicated Marcuse was doing his duty, patrolling the Wall, looking for any ghost that might have escaped. He moved evenly, not hurrying. That was hardly surprising, given some lingering glimmers of sunlight redirected by the veils of the ancients. After he passed and was well out of sight, I moved to the Wall.

Then I saw and sensed a foreboding darkness beyond black ahead of me coming through the weathered stones. The thin line of menacing darkness was quickly re-forming into a ghostly web by the time I got close enough to strike with the baton.

An ancient song in an unknown language rises in a clear soprano, with the precise notes of a piano accompanying the singer, followed instantly by polite applause and crushing disappointment that merges into red-velvet blackness soon washed away by the overwhelming feelings of loss, and the feeling of being drowned in an ocean of feelings, an ocean banished by the blaze of an afternoon sun that sears the delicate pink blossoms of the prickly pear into charred ashes…

I pressed my power out through the copper end of the baton, not that anyone but a mage or night patroller could see or sense it, and a web of heat washed toward me, threatening to flow around the baton.

Ashes…ashes…so much like Aashen…

I forced more power through the baton and crushed the image-feelings back into the deeper darkness of the ghost, and then squeezed the ghost into a ball, ignoring the last plaintive wail that died away as I shredded it into mists that became less than dry fog.

Was that any different from what the Prophet's scholars would do? I wondered, but the spirit had been firm that there was a difference. There had to be a difference, didn't there?

I found myself breathing hard as I stood beside the Wall imprisoning who knew how many ghosts, possibly as many as the people who'd perished in The Days, if not more, and all with thoughts, however fragmented, and feelings.

Yet what else could I have done as a night patroller that wouldn't have led to greater harm to the fully living?

I took a swallow of water and several deep breaths to quiet the shakes before I continued around the Wall, checking the masonry. I looked for places where the stone was thinner, depressions or crevices where a detonation would create openings quickly, one way or another. This could only be done at night, when there were few, if any, people near the Wall, because ghosts stayed deeper in rubble during the day and the lack of sunlight gave me a better idea of where breaks in the Wall would be more useful and allow the ghosts a better chance to escape when the explosives weakened or cracked the wall.

I didn't run into more ghosts on my surveillance, which took close to an hour, but I found a number of places, especially a few deep, irregular crevices, that would be especially susceptible to the explosive devices in my pack.

As I was about to start placing devices, starting at the east end of north Wall, I caught a glimpse of a magecar exiting a side street a block south. It turned south, parallel to the east Wall. In moments, it was out of sight behind the sporadic, twisted junipers growing on the side of the street opposite the Wall.

There certainly wasn't anything like the magecar in Meureyne, although travelers told of them in the lands of the Prophet. A reconnaissance vehicle for the Prophet's forces? Possibly trying to get a better sense of the Wall before moving those heavy iron machines into the city? Whatever it was, there was little I could do about it. There had always been so many times when I could do little…or had I just told myself that?

I moved to the first point I'd marked and removed one of the devices from my pack and eased it into position. Each had a slow match attached to it. Since there was only one of me, I'd have to place all the devices first and then light them in succession, moving as quickly as I could. They were all gray, and given the irregularity of the Wall, Marcuse wasn't likely to spot them on his next round…and after he finished, and he was well clear, I'd start setting them off.

I realized that it was going to take longer than I thought because I was sensing far more ghosts than I'd ever sensed at one time.

No sooner had I placed the first device than I could sense…

…the light…there's light…where am I? Not anywhere…just gray and more gray…

The ghost oozed from the wall through the thinner stone of a depression just above the ancient sidewalk. It hovered there, not like most, who immediately tried to possess a living body. I almost felt sorry as I struck with the baton, using my senses to fragment and disperse it into slowly fading mists, but I obviously wasn't going to have any choice, because I knew all too well the dangers of allowing them to touch me.

As I placed the second device, a far stronger presence arrowed at me.

…light…light! A way to escape, have to get out of here…wherever "here" is…have to find Katrinka…have to…have to…

The power and urgency of the ghost jarred me a bit, not enough to keep me from striking it, not with all I had to do.

Once I dispersed the second ghost, I checked to see if others had appeared close by, then moved on to the next location. Placing that device only took mere minutes now that I held my pack in one hand.

In the next quarter hour, I placed three more devices in the north Wall and got to the northwest corner where, some two blocks to the south, I saw the indistinct shape of the magecar, motionless and lightless beside the wall. I waited, hoping that no one caught sight of me.

Before long, the magecar headed south until it was out of sight beyond the remaining dwellings south of the Wall.

I took another healthy swallow from my water bottle. Even after dark, especially in late summer, Meureyne was hot, and tonight felt even hotter.

I leaned against the wall, my head so close to the stone that I sensed more images, strongly enough that they seemed to appear before me…

Swirling gray mists filled with sparking static, each spark white-hot, yet ice cold, twisting into spiderwebs, each web holding a person or perhaps an avatar, some immobile, as if cast in stone, and others screaming, trying to escape the webs, even as the sparks within the webs empower their pleadings and wails…

Further words vanish as a white-spotted black bear dances around a clump of bamboo, a half-chewed stalk in one paw, but the bear turns into a man in black wielding a shimmering silver spear…

Then he, too, vanishes, replaced by a white-haired woman, her thin voice pleading, "You have to let me go. You have to…have to…he wouldn't understand…wouldn't understand…"

For an instant, white heat sears away the gray, but only for an instant before the gray, spark-filled mists reappear, again twisting into spiderwebs holding different avatars, here a female clad in shimmering ice, there a youth trying to escape by flying winglessly. Elsewhere, two women linked by an indistinct cord pull in a different direction…

A huge clock face looms over everything, fractured into fragments, yet held in place in a timeless instant…

Out of the grayness between webs a face appears, and the woman speaks but the words are lost…

I shook my head and immediately moved on to the west Wall.

After placing two more devices, I had the feeling that it was about time for Marcuse to appear for his second round, and I moved well away from the Wall and waited.

Perhaps five minutes passed before he appeared, checking the Wall, but not noticing the devices. Once he was clear, I resumed placing my explosives, but as I finished, another ghost oozed through the stone, clearly drawn toward me. Did they sense my link with the spirit?

That was my best guess, but I had no way of knowing.

…have to get out…don't know how long it's been…too long…too crowded…too hot…still feel the sky burning…everyone shouting in the darkness…

I struck with the baton, shredding the ghost to prevent it from sensing and attempting to possess me. Even so, I could feel the raw desire to escape, and some of that feeling lingered in the night air after I'd dispersed the ghost. Several long moments passed before the tingling feeling subsided and then dissipated.

As it did, a second ghost attacked, stronger than the first.

Light…light! Find a way out of here…out of the mists and webs…just a meeting they said…

Quicker this way to deal with the threat of heat domes…who knew they were actually a weapon…got to find a way out…got to find the right equations…

My head was almost splitting before I shredded it, and my shirt was soaked with sweat before I finished dispersing it. I couldn't help wondering just how many ghosts lingered behind the Wall. Did they sense the approach of the scholars and the fate that awaited them? Was that why so many more were trying to escape? Yet the words and images I was sensing reinforced the mirror spirit's warning. Had I ignored them before…or just not understood?

After that, as I slowly caught my breath, I studied the street and the surrounding area. No one appeared to be nearby, and certainly not the Prophet's magecar.

For the next few moments, I kept sensing the Wall for any tingling or other signs of in the stone or mortar but found no traces. Then I took another swallow of water and resumed placing devices…until I got to the end of the west Wall, where yet another ghost was on me almost before I could raise my baton.

> *…fire from the skies…fire everywhere…stone burning…clocks fragmenting…time unreliable…have to report…sing a song of sixpence, pocket full of flame, tell me what's in a name…have to find some way…*

By the time I had the ghost shredded and dispersed, I was not only sweating profusely, but breathing hard, and my heart was pounding. I even felt light-headed. I was also wondering if the spirit had sent me out as much as a target for ghosts. Or maybe just as a lure to get them to try to escape before the Prophet's scholars arrived.

I just stood there until I caught my breath, at the same time sensing more visions twined around ghosts within the Wall—so close.

> *Out of the misty gray comes a young woman, thin in her blue and silver gown, her mouth open, trying to sing, but no words issue forth…and from somewhere behind and beyond her echo the words, "Just an audition…only a virtual audition…they're so much more convenient…"*
>
> *The words "more convenient" strike her with the impact of an unseen object, and terror fills her eyes as spark-filled static rattles through the mists that engulf her…*

> *…a long smooth table appears out of the mists. A man in a white shirt sits in the middle of one side, speaking, but all the other figures seated at the table are gray and featureless shadows, unmoving as the man's words spew forth, unheard…*
>
> *Mists veil the table, replaced by spark-filled spiderwebs that entwine before dissolving back into gauzy gray curtains that part and reveal a red Navaho sandstone cliff, where a small figure slowly picks its way up a shadowed crevice. Abruptly, blinding light shreds the cliff into stony fragments and boulders that carry the struggling figure down into a dark swirling hole, whose blackness reaches up and blots out everything for long moments.*

I forced my thoughts away from the faint ghostly images and the sounds that echoed only through my mind and resumed placing the explosive devices on the south Wall. I had just placed another two when I heard a whining behind and to my left. Then I saw the magecar coming up the street paralleling the west Wall, slowing as it did, in order to turn onto the street beside the south Wall. I grabbed the pack and sprinted toward the nearest mesquite thicket—and found myself in the middle of the ancient street when a beam of light surrounded me, if only for a moment.

The light passed over me and then turned back, but by then I had the mesquite thicket between me and the magecar. Crouching low, I eased to the west side of the mesquite, so that, when the vehicle passed, I could continue planting explosives. But the magecar came to a halt, and two figures emerged, both wearing metal helmets that gleamed, if slightly, in the almost non-existent moonlight.

One held a weapon, a rifle of a sort I'd never seen before, and the other a light beam that he played across the mesquite thicket. As he did, I flattened against the dusty ground, and the mesquite cast a shadow around me as the light swept past.

"There's no sign of anyone here now," said the one with the light, "They must have kept running." He laughed and added, "It'll only buy them a day or so." Then he turned the beam on the Wall. "That wall's going to be hard to break."

"The scholars don't do it that way. They just break the wall in a few places and wait for the ghosts to leave. That way, we get a greater information yield."

Lying flat behind the mesquite, I wanted to shake my head. Greater yield, as if the ghosts were a crop? Threshed by the Prophet's scholars for kernels of information?

"Why would the ghosts leave?" asked the first man.

"They've been trapped since The Days of Dying. Wouldn't you want out?" asked the man with the rifle harshly. "Come on. Back in the car. Now that we've verified this is the only site in Meureyne, we need to check the entire wall perimeter."

I didn't move until the magecar was well away from the south Wall. By then, I had my night vision back. As I placed the latest device, I heard two shots, then nothing. I placed another device and moved quietly to the southeast corner, from where I peered northward through the darkness, keeping my head close to the wall.

…all secure lines fried…standard net's down…wish I were back in the cockpit… just wish…the spoken words blur into silvery static and gray mists…

Out of those mists appears a figure in a strange green one-piece coverall wearing a helmet with a dark visor. He sits in a high-backed metal and cushioned chair in front of a silvery cabinet faced with pin-lights of all colors. The helmeted man bends forward in the strange chair before arrows of colored light slice into him…
"particle beams…need to get clear…warn base…"

The urgent feel of those words sent a cold knife through my head and grayed my sight. I had to ease back from the wall to clear my head, even though time was running out, and there well might be more Prophet's scouts. At the same time, from what one of them had said, I definitely needed to create as many breaks in the Wall as possible. Just a few breaks would only make things easier for the Prophet.

When I could see clearly again, the magecar was moving away from a dark figure sprawled next to the east wall, most likely Marcuse.

I lifted the pack and moved along the east Wall to the next spot, planted another device and moved on. Marcuse's body sprawled within feet of a crevice I'd noted, but there wasn't anything I could do to help him, poor bastard. I moved him just a little in order to plant the explosives, then moved away. I couldn't help looking back, wishing…

Then, I shook my head. For better or worse, what was done was done.

I had almost finished the east Wall, and about to plant the last of the devices, when out of nowhere another ghost attacked, with its unseen, but palpable, at least to me, gray fingers clawing at my head.

Take me away! Anywhere but here, not anywhere near…shreds of spirits spit from metal mouths await us all…spirit cities once, now dead with only shreds of gray dissipating…

I found myself fighting off the ghost with mind and baton as it struggled to gain control and possess first my thoughts and then my body. In the end, I pressed my will through the copper end of the baton…and the ghost shrieked so loudly that I thought I heard it with my ears as well as with my mind.

Shaking and panting I struggled to place the last device…then realized that I had several left but no time or energy to place more. So I added those remaining to the one I'd just placed. It took longer than I liked to rework the fuses so they'd go off together—hopefully. Then I shouldered the nearly empty pack, lit one of the long master fuses with my striker, waiting for a few moments to make sure it was burning steadily before I'd touched it to the fuse I'd just reworked.

I sprinted to the northeast corner and around it, stopping at the first device I'd planted. It took several seconds for that fuse to catch, and I moved to the next device, which I also lit. I almost made it to the end of the north Wall when the first explosives detonated. The sound wasn't that impressive, perhaps because it was around the corner. Far too soon, the devices in the north Wall began to explode. Loud as the sounds were to me, they'd fade before they reached too far. Besides, few in Meureyne were likely to investigate much in the dark.

At the northwest corner of the Wall, I paused and looked north for any sign of the magecar or the Prophet's soldiers. I didn't see either, but I did see lights farther north that were moving south. I could only hope I finished before they reached the Wall.

I kept moving and managed to light off all the explosives in the first block of the west Wall before the first one detonated, much more impressive without all that stone dampening the sound. The explosions were getting closer to me, and I realized that I needed to hurry.

By the time I'd lit the rest of the devices in the second block of the west Wall, I realized I couldn't keep running that fast. I also could sense—or thought I could—more scattered ghost visions, if just momentary glimpses.

Trying to catch my breath, I walked to the southwest corner, looking south for signs of anyone headed my way, although danger from that direction was less likely. Then I hurried around the corner.

As I bent down to light the fuse on the next device, ghost visions swept over me, in quick succession.

…three men stand facing a silver-gray metal bird with stiff extended wings, except the bird has no head, just a smooth featureless protrusion, and it stands twice as tall as the men with an elongated tail ending in a smooth bulky shape that resembles a T. At the end of each of its three metal legs are large black wheels…

…a dancer in a skintight white garment that covers her arms and legs, with the shortest of skirts, spins on a stage under shifting lights, first green, then a deeper and deeper red that reeks of blood, balanced impossibly on the tip of a single shoe, twirling so quickly that she blurs…

…angular metal boxes with treads and a turret form a pattern and churn across sand, spewing it to either side and behind them. The trailing metal box explodes and shards of metal fly toward the reddish sky before raining down on the tracks of the remaining three metal boxes…

After nearly stumbling as I bent down, I touched the lighting fuse to the device and trotted toward the next, wondering if the metal boxes I'd briefly sensed and seen were similar to the Prophet's iron turtles.

I lit the first explosive device in the east Wall before those in the second block of the south Wall began to detonate. When I looked up and north I could see lights speeding toward me on the street paralleling the east Wall—most likely the Prophet's magecar. At that moment, I wished I'd saved one of the explosives, then realized that, if I hurried, I might be able to use one of the unlit ones—if I could get the remaining devices lit.

I trotted north, lighting the explosives in the first block of the east Wall, but when I reached the northeast block I realized that the smoke near the corner of the wall wasn't smoke and dust from the first explosives, but ghosts, scores of them, if not more.

I hurried to the last block and lit another device, then looked up to see that the smoke-like mass of ghosts drifting, more than drifting, toward me, and no more than a block away, two magecars whined as they approached, although I doubted they'd seen me—yet.

My task wasn't finished, and by the time I could light the next device, both magecars and ghosts would be on top of me. I dropped the lighting fuse, grabbed the pack, and turned to sprint across the street, toward the cluster of half-dead junipers.

Before I reached cover, I heard shots. How close they might have been, I couldn't tell. Out of caution, I kept low, because at least some of the Prophet's soldiers might come after me—or maybe they were scholars, since they wore those metal helmets. I scrambled between the trees, knocking off juniper berries and feeling some of them in my shirt.

Behind me, the last of the explosives detonated, and I could almost sense more ghosts oozing and flowing out of the gaps, but that might have been my imagination.

When I reached the end of the junipers, I stopped. Still shielded by the branches, I looked south, only to see lights moving toward me—men in uniforms walking beside some kind of truck. I watched, realizing only a few of the soldiers wore metal helmets. They also all had rifles. If I left the concealment of the trees, they'd turn the light beams on me, and I'd likely get shot, given there were at least a dozen soldiers in that group.

I didn't want to head east, because after three blocks, there was nothing but the charcoal sands, which hadn't seen trees since before The Days, all the way to the barren sandstone hills. I'd be an easy target. If only I'd been just a bit faster, I'd have been heading back to the house, with the soldiers and scholars well behind me. But ifs only get in the way of doing what has to be done when things don't go as planned.

I quietly eased back into the junipers and crawled through and under the sagging branches of the biggest green juniper, lying flat to fit under the branches. Hare barley foxtails pricked at my skin, as I belly-crawled across hard, dry ground, wishing it was a carpet of pinyon needles instead.

Since I couldn't see the street, it was unlikely any of them could see me. I hoped I didn't have to wait too long, but sometimes, being patient is the best plan. Or in my case, the only practical plan because I'd been too slow.

I could hear voices, as well as see small flashes of light through the thick branches. Then I heard yells, and some screams. That suggested that ghosts had found unhelmeted soldiers.

I didn't have much time to think about that because I could sense more ghosts, and some were moving through the junipers. Unlike me, they weren't hampered by the branches. I struggled to get the baton where I could use it, trying to be quiet, in case one of the helmeted scholars might be listening or looking beyond what was happening next to the Wall.

Then the first ghost reached me, and–

I found myself looking into a mirror, but the face looking back at me was unfamiliar, clean-shaven, and wearing a strip of blue and gold fabric that emerged from his collar and dangled

down the front of a pure white shirt…and everything shifted…
I was looking at a mirror displaying a woman talking…with words that should have been familiar, but weren't…

Somehow, I wrenched myself from those visions and jammed the baton into the middle of the bluish fog of the ghost, marshaling all my will and channeling it through the copper of the baton.

NOOOOO!!!!

The force and dismay of the yell seemed to split my head in two, but I didn't have time to think about it as another ghost's visions enveloped me.

"The meeting will come to order," sonorously declares a dark-haired man sitting at the head of a long polished dark wooden table and who wears a navy-blue blazer and a blindingly-white shirt, with a too-wide red piece of cloth extending down the shirt.

Men and women sit on each side of the table, strikingly similar, yet not quite present.

"Order? Where are we, Mr. Chair?" The woman asking gestures with a hand emerging from a tweed suit coat to point to the massive antique clock-face on the indistinct wall behind the man.

"In the regular virtual meeting room. Where else could we be?"

"Have you looked behind…" The woman keeps talking, but her words are drowned by a gong that sounds in the distance, once, twice, and then again, deafeningly close, the sound splitting the long table in two…

Gray mists erupt between the broken halves of the table, and the man shouts, "Order, we must have order" before the clock face shatters and buries him in fragments.

A face appears, serious and intent, flanked by gray webs, and the woman speaks, "The system is reconfiguring…reconfiguring…reconfiguring…"

Again, I had to struggle to push the ghost away in order to use the baton, and its shrieks shivered through me as I shredded it.

Then shots echoed somewhere between me and the wall, followed by shouts.

"…too many ghosts…"

"…back off, and leave them to the scholars…"

"They won't be happy."

"Frig 'em. We can't capture them, and there's no point in losing men for nothing. Tie up the possessed, and get out of here."

For the next quarter hour, while I fought off more ghosts, I continued to hear voices and see flashing light beams. Finally, I heard the whine of the truck and the magecars. The voices diminished in the distance, then vanished.

While some of the ghosts doubtless tried to follow the withdrawing soldiers, a good many still hovered around the junipers. Before long, I knew another one would try to get me…and then another…and another. Since dawn was hours away, I decided leaving the junipers and getting away from the ghosts emerging from the Wall was my best bet. I had doubts about successfully fighting them off for all that time, and the farther I got from the Wall the fewer ghosts I'd have to contend with.

After crawling out from under the big juniper, I moved to the east side of the time-battered grove, farther from the Wall, but as I left the trees—and the associated foxtails and juniper berries, another ghost attacked. I felt less than charitable and forced the baton on it…methodically shredding it…wondering at its last thoughts…words…before I finished.

…didn't want this…didn't want another frigging meeting…virtual or not…
…said we were lucky it was just a Metaverse meeting…

After that, I walked quickly east and then circled back to the north until I was walking up Coriolan Way toward my house. Once I was more than two blocks from the wall, I saw no more ghosts, but that would change over the coming days.

I had no idea how many ghosts remained within the Wall, although, after generations of confinement, I thought, as the spirit had implied, most of them would move away from the Wall. Some would not and would be captured by the Prophet's scholars. Some wouldn't find shelter from the sun and would perish, and then there would be those that lurked so deeply in the ruins that even the scholars and their machines would not be able to root them out. They now had choices, of sorts, poor as those choices were, and the Prophet would be greatly limited in what he might gain from the ruins. If the spirit was correct, our descendants might not sear the world to ashes again—or at least not so soon.

I reached home several hours before dawn and made my way down to the study where I confronted the mirror.

In the dim light of the lamp I'd lit, I looked into the mirror, but only saw my own tired face. Blood-smeared scratches covered my face and forehead, the result of my battle with ghosts and the junipers. Nothing more.

No trace of the spirit that had haunted and guided me, nothing, except that I felt…emptier.

The one and only spy for the spirit of the ghosts of the ancients…and who would believe it?

Intermezzo

D. Thomas Minton

As I step from the portal into the Chateau's lobby, my jacket sheds its temporal charge like droplets of rain from a slicker. The puddle of vibrating energy slowly reaches chrono-equilibrium, then fades into the present continuum, much like the tension eases from my shoulders.

At the end of time, there is no war, only the Chateau's deep pile carpets, luxurious chairs, and goose down mattresses so supple they could be mistaken for the arms of a loving woman.

A young man sporting a pillbox cap takes my coat. "Welcome back, Mr. Smith."

I have many names, but at the Chateau I have always gone by Smith. It's as good as any of my other names and is, by far, the easiest for human vocal cords to pronounce.

The bellhop waves me towards the night desk where the manager awaits with my key. Halfway across the lobby, my attention is caught by a pair of familiar black boots protruding from one of the two wing-back chairs near the Chateau's great hearth.

"Anders?" I ask, stepping closer.

The upraised broadsheet dips, and a single dark eye pierces into me. Anders's other eye is blocked by a maroon patch. "Smith," Anders says with a curt nod.

I have not seen Anders in a long time. I do not recognize his uniform, but the smoothness of its fabric indicates it comes from some planet's industrial age.

Anders folds his paper and sets it aside. "I was hoping to see you."

To the best of my knowledge, Anders and I have never shared a battlefield, but we have shared enough gin at the Chateau to be comrades in arms. Not friends, mind you—war is a foolish time to accumulate such.

Anders's brow creases. "You look like hell, mate."

"You know what they say about war."

Anders flashes a rakish grin. "That depends on who's doing the talking."

When I don't respond positively to his quip, his smile fades. "Tough mission, Smith?"

I exhale slowly. Tough is an understatement when you're responsible for the loss of three and half billion lives.

"The tides of war ebb and flow," Anders says. "Battles are won, and battles are lost, but it is the war that is important, and we are winning that."

Anders may *believe* we are winning, but he cannot possibly know his words are anything more than wishful bravado. This conflict may occur across time and space, but we are all bound by the laws of nature. I cannot know a future I have yet to experience, and neither can Anders. Other than the Chateau, my ability to travel through time is limited to the temporal bubble in the neighborhood of my last mission, where, as a mere foot soldier, my eyes barely rise above the mud and bodies, let alone high enough to witness the tides of war.

Even the Chateau provides no clues. While it might be easy to assume we have triumphed because this Chateau is always filled with my comrades, across the lake is another Chateau whose exterior looks identical to this one, and in which I assume are the same stone hearth and luxurious chairs and night managers—all of it serving as a waystation to those who oppose us. If true, does it mean neither side wins, and all this conflict—all the death—is futile?

"Now, now," Anders says. "You're starting to look like Barnaby over there." He nods toward the man asleep in the other wing-back chair.

Much like the chandelier, Barnaby is a fixture in the lobby. I hazarded a conversation with him once and determined him a sad case. Yet, with each passing mission I've come to understand his despair. Barnaby claims he will not budge from his chair until time's end. That is the only way I and my comrades can truly find rest, but much as I might observe light spiraling into a black hole, I can never confirm that either the light or Barnaby ever reaches its destination.

"Spare him a sympathetic eye, yes, but do not commiserate too deeply," Anders says. "Once, he was one of our best, but now he sulks on the sideline while the struggle rages. The cause is lost when good men do nothing, which makes me wonder, are they truly good men?"

I look down at my boots, still covered with the dust of vaporized souls.

Anders rises from his chair. His hand slaps heavily down onto my shoulder. "I know what you need, Smith, and I won't take no for an answer. I'm meeting up with a good man tonight at Simy's. I'm sure the two of you will get on grandly. You will join us."

"I'm—"

"—not going to take no for an answer." Anders makes a sharp clucking noise when I try to speak again. "We're meeting at 10:45 sharp," he says, fishing a watch from his pocket. "That gives you…three hours to unwind and dress."

Reluctantly I admit comrades and gin might be what I need. I should not waste my one evening of respite wallowing in a dark room. That will certainly do nothing to improve my outlook, and the whole purpose of the Chateau is just that. Shared experience, both good and ill, is what makes war bearable. Failing that, Simy's serves only the finest gin.

Cheerfully, Anders pats my shoulder. "Good man. You won't regret it." He collects his paper and, whistling a sharp tune, departs towards the lift.

Barnaby mumbles and shifts in his chair, but does not awaken.

Seeing I am now alone, the night manager approaches from across the lobby. "Your key, Mr. Smith."

To no surprise, it is the same key I always receive. It looks like it belongs to a door in a tenth century monastery, but it goes to a room at the end of the western corridor on the Chateau's third floor. The modest-sized room has a large window, overlooking where the sun would set if I were to ever arrive at the Chateau early enough to see it. That is one of the things about the Chateau at the End of Time. It matters not from when or where I depart, I always emerge into the lobby at exactly 7:33 PM. Also like clockwork, I have departed every time at 11:46, exactly two and half minutes before the terminus of all that is and all that will be.

When I push my key toward the lock, the door slides open into the darkened room. "Hello?"

The rustle of sheets and a drowsy, "Mmmm?"

"Margrethe?"

A woman props herself up on the bed, her light hair cascading across her throat and down over the sheets gathered against her slender form. Margrethe's discarded clothes pave a trail from the door to her mischievous smile. She beckons me forth with a curl of her index finger. "You're letting in a draft. Come keep me warm."

* * *

An hour later, Margrethe's skin glows in the flickering halo of the hurricane lamp. Lying next to me, her head propped up on one of the pillows, she drags her fingers down my chest, from the dimple in my throat to my belly button and back up.

Ordinarily, her light caress would bring me to attention again, so when I don't respond, she frowns. "What's wrong?"

Outside, the stars are intensely bright, and that brightness only makes it more clear this isn't my night sky. The stars I know died long ago. While this has never troubled me before, for some reason it matters tonight.

Margrethe retrieves two slender cigarettes from the bedside table. "Everyone has rough missions." She lights both at the same time and hands one to me. "Forget it. Soldier on, and all that."

I roll the cigarette between my fingers. The bluish smoke twists and spirals upward into the dark space at the top of the room. We all have had missions go sour—I accept that fact of war. Yet, this hurts more than the others because the deaths feel so…I would say needless, but I understand the need. Yet, simply because I can justify the need, doesn't mean they are not senseless. Shouldn't a successful mission mean no one dies? Aren't we the good guys, after all?

"Don't go growing a conscience." Margrethe says. "You know what you signed up for."

"It wasn't this," I mumble—except, it was precisely this. Conflict is a universal truth. Since time and space burst into existence, every quark, every molecule, every organism has fought to simply *be*. It seemed such a simple concept when I was recruited, but over the eons I have learned that nothing about war is simple.

Margrethe sets her cigarette in the ashtray and rolls atop me. She sits straddling my stomach. Propped on her arms, she stares directly down into my face. She has the most fiercely blue eyes; yet I wonder if the face she wears is anything like the one she was born with.

I met Margrethe my first time at the Chateau. We spent the entire night in Simy's flirting over a bottle of gin and a plate of smoked eel. I recall my regret that we never made it to my room. We did not make the same mistake the next time, nor the countless times we have met since.

Margrethe cocks her head to the side. "Are you…" She doesn't need to finish the question; the answer is obvious on my face. "I didn't take you for a quitter, Smith."

I take my first draw on the cigarette and blow the smoke to the side. "I haven't made any decisions."

"But you're thinking about it. The end."

"And you haven't? Ever?"

Her expression falters for only the briefest moment, but it is enough. She sits up straight, still straddling me. Her hair falls down to cover her breasts. "We all encounter moments of disillusionment. Our strength is defined by how we overcome them."

I'm not disillusioned. I am appalled.

We all fight on battlefields sprinkled across time and space. Other than the occasional conversation I have with Margrethe or fellow soldiers like Anders, I have little knowledge of the rest of the war. I have never met a general, and as odd as it may sound, I do not believe I have ever even seen the real enemy. This war plays out on the battlefields of mortals, as if they are pieces in a grand board game, and I am the immortal hand that tosses the dice that determines if they live or die. Like all cosmic conflicts, it is a proxy war.

"What if I was to tell you this war could end soon?" Margrethe asks.

I wouldn't believe it, but I do not say that. I study Margrethe's face, looking for some indication of truth. Every piece of my being wants to believe her, but how does an endless fight come to an end, especially when its perpetrators cannot die?

"You know these skirmishes will never put an end to it," Margrethe says. "With luck, we drive them into the shadows, but we cannot destroy them any more than they can destroy us. That is the cosmic certainty of chaos and order. They will never surrender, and we will never negotiate—a stalemate, paid for through eternity with the lives of mortals."

Once, I believed we could force the enemy to submit, but with each passing mission, the truth becomes plain. "How can it end, then?"

"To kill a snake, remove its head."

My sudden burst of laughter draws forth a frown from Margrethe. She makes it sound simple, but how does one find their leader across all of time and space, let alone navigate to his precise location to carry out the deed? The only place and time any of our paths might cross is here, at the end of—

"You've found a way into the other Chateau."

Margrethe's face gives away nothing. All she says is, "A plan is in motion."

I should have a thousand questions, but I have only one. "How can I help?"

"I've said too much, but only because—" She shakes her head and quickly dresses. Leaning over me, she says, "Don't do anything stupid, Smith." Her goodbye kiss pulls the breath from me, leaving me splayed atop the bed.

I want desperately to believe her, but part of me cannot accept that anything can end this war. I realize then I know little about Margrethe. Since that first night we met, our encounters have always been the same—intensely physical with a smattering of conversation after we have worked ourselves to near exhaustion. I usually drift off while we talk, and when I awaken, the sheets where she had been earlier are always cold. I have never mistaken our relationship for anything more than what it is. I have long assumed I am not her only dalliance.

I do not know how she fits into the hierarchy of command. Margrethe has always given me the impression she knows more than I, which suggests she is closer to the top. I have never considered it before, but could she be a general?

Energized, I pace the room, fueled by feverish thoughts that refuse to coalesce into anything substantial. Eventually I find myself at the window, staring out across the lake. Every so often, distant lights wink at me through the mist, but never does the veil thin enough for me to see clearly the other Chateau. Our enemy seems always to lie at the edge of my vision—elusive, ethereal, like a specter.

I don't want to stay alone with my thoughts, so I pull on my shirt and coat, my boots, and head down to Simy's to meet Anders. I find him in the back throwing darts with a dark-haired man with a boyish face whose name, I learn, is Jones.

If I were naïve, I'd assume Jones had not even graduated into his twenties, but for all the superficial trappings of youth, his eyes tell of a deeper, older history. With those eyes, he appraises me, much as any veteran might a new recruit—not with skepticism, but more a detached assessment of whether I am worth his time, or if I will ultimately cost him his life by doing something stupid.

"Another round?" Anders asks, and before either Jones or I can respond, he retreats towards the bar.

Jones leans into his throw and sticks his first dart into the bullseye. "Anders speaks highly of you," he says. Not breaking his rhythm, he sticks his final two darts in quick succession alongside the first. "Don't be surprised."

I'm not sure if he's referring to his dart throws or his statement. Anders barely knows me, whereas I have seen more than one man toss bullseyes.

Jones pours two shots of vodka from a nearly full bottle and takes one. "It's Anders's job to identify good soldiers." He raises his glass towards me before tipping it into his mouth.

"Identifies them for what?" I ask, confused. War might be the business of every guest at the Chateau, but it is not a place *for* that business. Back at the bar, Anders turns from my gaze.

Jones nudges the second shot glass towards me. "Walk with me, Smith."

I feel oddly compelled by the timbre of his voice, which sets my nerves on edge. I down the vodka to calm myself before following Jones out a door I have never noticed before. It leads back to the lobby. Jones crosses to the French doors that open out onto the balcony overlooking the lake. As I follow, I pass Barnaby, still drowsing in the chair by the fire. The corners of his closed eyes twitch, and he mumbles unintelligibly. Is Anders right about Barnaby, or is Barnaby a good man who simply realizes he cannot make a difference anymore?

The night air clears my head as I come alongside Jones, who leans against the stone wall and stares out into the mist.

Overhead, the sky is a uniform field of stars, so unusual for someone used to seeing stellar clusters. As I linger there, serenaded by what sound like the croaking of frogs, I wish that my last mission had not been planetside. In vacuum there are no lakes or trees or sky. I find those missions easier because in orbit I don't have to witness an atmospheric incendiary reduce every living thing to ash.

"Anders tells me your last mission didn't go as you had hoped; yet, you achieved your objectives. Does that not make the mission a success?"

Technically, Jones is right. "But billions died."

"You don't think they needed to die?"

The smell of woodsmoke causes sweat to bead on my forehead. "I understand the need," I say, suddenly nauseated.

"But…"

Sensing I have wandered into dangerous country, I say, "It's not my place to question because I do not know the big picture."

Jones lights a cigarette and casually blows the smoke from the side of his mouth. "Sometimes our people need to be reminded why they fight. That was your mission, and what better way to remind them than to show them the brutality of the enemy?"

"But it wasn't the enemy, and they were our people."

Jones blinks at me, and I realize then why his eyes look so unusual. They are like wells drilled into his head, the bottoms of which are so deep, they can never be illuminated by the light of day. I saw the same when I spoke with Barnaby. His, too, were dark pits that stretched back through time itself, and I knew then that Barnaby had been in this fight a very long time, longer than anyone I had ever met, until now.

Unable to stop myself, I gasp.

Jones flicks his cigarette, casting glowing embers into the night. They burn as they fall toward the lake, but wink out before ever reaching the surface. "Anders is right; you *are* a smart one."

Coming from anyone else, Jones would have sounded like a soldier gone mad from the horrors of the battlefield. Yet, his gaze cuts like a scalpel, sending shivers of realization through me. Jones is not a general, but a general maker. He *is* what we fight for, given body and breath and life.

"Most would be in awe right now," Jones says. "Fawning and kowtowing. I admit, I liked that once, but different times call for different soldiers. I need a soldier who looks at me with the skepticism I see in your eyes, Smith, but also the intelligence to understand that our emotions must not interfere with the needs of war."

I am unsettled because he has described my last mission. I did not launch those incendiaries because they would bring any victory. I destroyed every living thing on the planet because it would become a rallying cry for our forces across the galaxy—the needs of the war outweighing the lives of the few, or the many. Without it, the mortals of that time and space might have grown weary of the dying, might have surrendered—I cannot know the future, but the conflict might have ended.

I knew this when I entered the launch codes.

The edges of Jones's mouth perk upward. "Everything worthwhile comes with a price, Smith. I want you to be my hand because I believe you can guide this war to an acceptable resolution. You would have full control to do whatever is needed."

But at what price? I was prepared to sit in the lobby with Barnaby and embrace the end of everything with open arms. Sitting with Barnaby ends the war for me, but with what Jones is offering, could I find an end for everyone? I knew not what that would look like, but surely in the enormity of space and time such a thing must exist.

Before I can distill my thoughts into words, a motion registers on the periphery of my consciousness as someone comes through the French doors and approaches us. My battle-primed mind immediately registers the weapon in the rising hand, as well as the flash of blond hair.

"Step away, Smith," Margrethe says. Her weapon is slender and bluish, like a shard of ice chipped from an ancient glacier.

Jones casually grinds the remnants of his cigarette under his boot heel. We have all been at the business end of a weapon. I assume Jones is no exception, although he has nothing to fear—death is a mortal concern.

The tower clock in the lobby chimes once—the three-quarter hour. Three and a half minutes left if I do not step through the portal and return to the battlefields of the past.

"Leave while you can, Smith. No reason for both of us to be here at the end."

With those words, things become clear. Earlier, I had assumed Margrethe had been talking about the enemy leader, but her target was never in the other Chateau. Her target had been Jones. And why not, if her goal was only to end the senseless fighting? If she knew Jones would be here, all she had to do was keep him here, and let time do the rest. So while her weapon was incapable of killing Jones, it was more than capable of incapacitating him.

Voices float through the French doors as guests check out and begin to file through the portal. A few soldiers who have had too much to drink sing a battle hymn I do not recognize. We are far enough from the doors that no one will notice us in the darkness.

"This is your plan?" I ask.

Without Jones, our side will be leaderless, and even if our forces survive such a loss, the setback could take eons to overcome.

Margrethe's focus never shifts from Jones, whose dark, unblinking eyes are fixed on her like a dead man's gaze. "Only recently have I come to appreciate that neither side can exist without the other," she says, "and that true victory can never be had. To end this conflict, we must negotiate a co-existence."

"Night and day do not co-exist," Jones says. "They take turns subjugating each other."

"That is no way to live."

"It is the only way we can live."

Margrethe's hand trembles. I can see the uncertainty growing in her eyes. I, too, don't want to believe Jones, but what if he is right?

The Chateau's lobby has gone quiet. The last of the soldiers have departed, their life energies cast back through time to their next missions. I wonder just how much time is left.

I take a step toward Margrethe, and when she doesn't respond I approach closer. I raise my hand, reaching for her weapon.

"Don't," she says.

"I can't let you do this, Margrethe." My fingers wrap around the barrel, and it is as cold as it looks

"This is the only way," she says, but does not resist as I gently lift the pistol from her grip. She looks at me in disgust. "What did he promise you?"

"He promised me I could do whatever I thought was needed." In a single smooth motion, I put the pistol to her head and pull the trigger. As the weapon discharges, a whisper slips from my lips. "And the universe will still need you."

The weapon was designed to incapacitate, but at such close range the burst of electricity scorches her temple, killing her body instantly, but casting her life energy back through the portal. Back through time. Like all of us, Margrethe cannot be killed, and she will go on to her next destination.

"I knew I could count on you, Smith," Jones says with a nod. "Welcome aboard." He steps toward the French doors.

Raising the pistol, I move quickly to block his egress.

"What are you doing, Smith?"

I fish my watch from my pocket. According to the shifting hands, time has only a few seconds left. I look up and into the depths of Jones's soul. There, in the darkness, I sense, rather than see, a hairline fracture, and in those final moments of time, my conscience finds peace. "I am doing what needs to b—

Of Darkling Souls

Nemma Wollenfang

Implantation did not go well. The bioelectric pulses of the young female's mind were erratic. Fiery and jagged. Bristling like a collapsing star. It made it that much harder for Ka's delicate feelers to root down without being singed. Still, he delved on. Too much was at stake. Her system sensed the invasion, of course, and fought viciously. Sparking, spitting. But soon was quelled. Conquered by superior intellect. The girl never stood a chance, not really. Ka's dendritic connectors solidified, anchoring into her cranium and spinal cord.

Forcing her lungs to expand, Ka inhaled. The air scorched; high oxygen content. He'd been warned about this world's atmosphere. It was something they all had to get used to. Eyes next. Lashes fluttered and Ka squinted at the brightness, raising a fleshy appendage against it.

"How are you feeling, Tracker Ka?" a voice asked from somewhere nearby. "The air is somewhat denser here, and these bodies can be…difficult to acclimatize to."

Difficult was an apt term. Despite his hold, he could still feel the female struggling. Her presence lingered at the back of her mind—*his* mind now—like a snarling creature. Weak and subdued, but still very much *there*. A lingering threat. One that should have withered to nothing. *This one will take time to vanish*, Ka could tell. But it was far from the most resistant life-form he'd ever conquered. It would fade soon enough.

He blinked. The optical organs took time to adjust to the invasive light level. The room was white, with metallic tables, and there was a corrosive chemical bite to the air.

A hosted human stood next to where he lay—on some flat surface, attached to beeping machines. Male, if Ka were to guess, of middling age with a balding head, clothed in a pale form of the plant-woven fabric favoured by this species. Ka's implanter, no doubt. The man bore a slouch, as if he shouldered a great weight. Ka craned his new neck to glimpse the armoured black bulk attached to the back, with thread-like tentacles embedded through the neck and ear channels. The carapace of his own species. A comforting sight. The last thing he needed was to wake up on one of *their* dissection tables. The subtle chromophic sheen of the eyes gave him away too. An entirely Arachnii trait.

"The experience of settling can be disorienting," the man continued blandly.

"The host is fighting," Ka said, listening to the cadence of his new voice—light and smooth, pleasantly melodic. "But its efforts are nothing that cannot be handled."

The way the mouth moved to form sound, the way language rolled off the tongue, felt bizarre. Ka swallowed, felt how the saliva flowed, the muscles contracted. He raised that appendage again, blinking at it. Two eyes, two hands. Ka's prior host had possessed eight of each. No talons present, no hooks or claws. Just flimsy shell-like nails. Blunt rows of teeth lined the mouth and the soft skin bore no armour. This species seemed to be primarily composed of a fleshy, water-based bulk which lacked most any physically superior attributes. How it had risen to the apex of its food-chain was a mystery to him, even after the time he'd spent aboard the hive studying this newest species and their planet in preparation of arrival. Command insisted it was capable, though, worth the effort of hosting. And Ka's function was to follow orders, not question.

The implanter bobbed his head in an amiable motion, one which Ka had learnt signalled agreement, as he made notes on a device. "Do you wish to see your new self, Tracker?"

The implanter helped Ka to sit up and pad over the cool floor towards a length of glass. Manoeuvring on two legs was tricky, as were observations in the spectrum at this range. It had been a long time since Ka had seen in colour; his last three hosts being endowed with infrared vision. As always, he would adjust. Ka canted his head. The mirror showed a being in early maturation. Young adult. Dark braids tangled about its shoulders, the skin was a smooth brown, and the eyes were lightly glossed by Ka's blue sheen. Female. He'd been prepared for that. Mostly Command tried to match host-gender preferences, but this one had been designated 'special circumstance.' Because after several failed hostings from lesser Trackers, she had yet to yield her secrets. Ka liked a challenge. He liked to *break*. Overlooking the sex was a trifle if it meant he could undertake such a conquering. Not to mention the much-coveted opportunity this assignment provided to rise in rank.

Wrinkles formed on her brow as he noted her physical state. How…*thin* she appeared. Skin stretched thin over bone, shadows hung beneath the eyes. Malnourished. This one had not eaten well for some time. Likely couldn't find enough food—shortages were inevitable after invasions. Ka crinkled her nose with distaste. And disappointment. It was worse than expected. He would have to build the body up to a more standard level of fitness before departure. That would take time, delay the mission. A prospect he did not relish.

Faint as an echo, a note sounded in the recess of his mind. Like laughter.

This body is not yours, parasite, a feminine voice hissed. *It will never help you.*

Ka jolted. What remained of the female's psyche was *communicating* with him? That demonstrated a high level of awareness. Her essence should be fading yet, as he stretched back, his feelers testing, assessing, he found it remained remarkably strong. This show of rebellion in a claimed host was unnervingly rare…though not unheard of. With a thought, Ka flattened her spark. Her energy was weak, malleable. Easy enough to suppress.

"Is…everything well, Tracker Ka?" the implanter asked with a frown. "You are displaying signs of discomfort. Are you displeased with your new appearance?"

If Ka reported the upsurge, the implanter would keep him in Observation for who knew how long. Couple that with the emaciated state of his host and acclimation could stretch on for weeks. It would make him look weak. Prime for displacement. He could not have that.

Any number of others would be circling, waiting for an opening to snatch this task from him. Trackers were low rank, lower than Workers; they languished in the cack-filled bases of hives until called to action. Any chance to rise higher was craved. He could *not lose this*.

"All is well," Ka said. "The host is suitable." They both knew that his opinion on its appearance mattered little. She was designated 'special.' An asset to the occupation.

The implanter nodded. "Well, she still needs a few weeks of muscle-building but—"

"No. The host is suitable as it is," he stated. No compromise. No delay. "When am I to be briefed on my mission? Knowing its importance, I am most eager to begin."

* * *

"Anything?" the implanter asked, scrutinizing Ka's new face.

They were in a dark room, an interrogation suite. The lack of brightness was meant to aid the process of memory extraction from hosts. Yet so far, nothing.

Her mind was an onyx oblivion. Devoid as the vacuum of space.

Where Ka was seated, in the only chair, he squeezed her eyes shut. Pushing, probing… Tentacles branched out, rooting through her cerebrum, exploring neural pathways.

A spark. A flash of knowledge.

"Her name is Zoey Heslop," Ka said. "She is twenty-five. A healer in training. A student of medicine. Or was, before our arrival."

That small insight came at a cost. The blast of agony Ka received from the synapse relays made him crumple forward, clutching her face in both hands.

"Impressive," the implanter said. "Our last Tracker barely survived attachment. We had to remove them immediately, and we gained no information whatsoever for their pains."

Ka had been warned about that too. "Clearly they were not strong enough," he grated, fighting to speak through the fiery spasms. Where the last few failed, Ka would not. He was settling, growing accustomed to the female's body— its fit, the way it moved and felt, sounded and smelled. His feelers were still branching out, still gaining a hold, but a few more days would easily ensure complete control. Then he would be ready for his mission.

Special Ops. High Priority. Deep Recovery.

Nothing else had been imparted but the first stage yet—dig out her memories.

Ka stretched himself. *Pushing…* His thread-like feelers chased one gleam of knowledge after another. The female's consciousness was fleeting, fleeing the predator.

"Search further, delve deeper," the implanter instructed, as Ka tried to concentrate. "We require more details. This one is a rebel, one with high connections. We need whatever information you can extract about her cell's operation: its structure, hierarchy, strategies, *location…*"

Ka may have been new to these bodies and their mannerisms, but if he wasn't mistaken the implanter seemed unnerved.

"These beings have proven to be canny, resourceful. We lost an entire hive to them last week. Destroyed by a primitive incendiary device. One that should have been detected." His iridescent blue gaze found Ka's, hard and uncompromising. "The Queen's hive is due to land soon. Command fears another attack and we cannot abide any threat to her safety. It will not be tolerated from a planet already conquered."

"Understood." Closing her eyes, Ka gave another mighty *puuuuush.*

Her mental walls slammed down. Ka reeled back so hard his chair clattered to the floor and respiratory functions ceased. Coarse laughter floated into his mind amidst the dizziness. Ears ringing, vision bursting with stars, his mind darted between his body and the host's.

You won't find them, slime. I'll not give them up.

But Ka had gotten a glimpse, and a glimpse was enough.

As the implanter helped him up, massaging his carapace, Ka's mind surged back into the host's and he gulped a lungful of air. Oxygen burned, like a thousand tiny needles.

"This one…she is mate to their leader. A Valentino Romero."

"Command's primary target. One we want you to track. An unknown, so far. We did not even have a name. Did you gain facial identification?"

"Yes." Willing the shaking from her limbs, Ka righted the chair and sat. "And I believe I know where their nest is."

* * *

Stealth was required for this mission. For it to work, Ka needed to go in alone. Which suited him just fine. Why share success?

A brief search of their closest hive's database yielded a match to the landscape Ka had glimpsed. It was on the outskirts of the city, where all around lay blackened desolation. Most of the surrounding area was well into the Tertiary Stage of Harvest. Vegetation had been stripped; all fauna sectioned. The ground mined clean. Nothing would be wasted. Off the coast, silos hovered, in the process of swallowing up liquid hydro for transport to the space-dwelling hives. Even the precious ozone would fuel a hive atmosphere for innumerable terra-cycles—although that was always reaped at the very end, when all Arachnii departed the dead world.

A contingent dropped Ka a good distance away from the site. The city had been conquered some months back. Craters pockmarked the roads, buildings stood half-crumbled, vehicular machinery lay abandoned. There were few signs of life—only small, winged creatures which clearly posed little threat. Pigeons, if Ka's studies were correct. Workers had trouble sectioning those.

While the territory had been cleared, Soldiers had not been stationed here. Which meant it was dangerous; a place where the wild indigenous could rally and hide. According to the implanter, Arachnii forces were stretched thin across the globe and, as this particular location had little military advantage, it had been abandoned for now.

Abandoned. Just like you've been. The female's voice possessed a wry, taunting edge.

Ka refused to acknowledge it.

They'll kill you, you know. My people will kill you for taking me. You'll be dead long before you can report their location.

"As will you, if that is the case." Her voice fell silent… Though now, Ka found he wanted her to speak. "Their leader is your mate. Surely he will wish to have you back alive?"

Is that your hope? You think he won't shoot because you're attached to me? Ha! We made a pact, long ago, when all of this started. We've been carrying a bullet for one another every day since, in case of this exact scenario.

Ka tensed. He'd been relying on her value to gain access to their base, on the fact that their leader would not wish to jeopardize her safety. Even hosted.

The female chittered. *Oh dear, does the parasite's plan have a flaw?*

"Quiet." The area must be close now, the landscape looked familiar. They wouldn't shoot her. She was lying, trying to throw him off. Preserving her would be their leader's priority.

She chuckled—a low, cruel sound. *Why should I be quiet? Distracting you is exactly what I want to do. I'm gonna cause as much inconvenience and misery as humanly possible.*

For a moment, Ka contemplated squashing her essence again. Fully, this time. All it would take was more force… But no. Not yet. Aware, she may recognize something vital.

Now that I've found my voice I plan to rant and rave, she mocked, *singing ghastly lyrics at all hours. Ever functioned without sleep? Living with me is gonna be Hell–*

A sharp blast punctured the air. Something chipped the concrete near Ka's feet.

A bullet, the female informed him, sounding delighted. *Someone is firing at you.*

Ka fled for cover. At least, he tried to. While one leg moved on command the other…did not. It stood firm, making him stumble. Knees hit rough ground, denim tore.

In his mind, he could feel the female, striving to *remain* with all her strength. She had a hold, and she meant for them to be shot! She wanted it. Desperately.

"Zoey?" a distant voice called, its timbre deep and rich. "Zo? Is that you?!"

Vision roving—still his to control—Ka spotted a russet-skinned male with night-black hair perched on an upper storey window-ledge. A worn jacket of dusty leather accentuated his lean frame and a long, pointed firearm was hitched to one shoulder. He lowered it.

That was her mate! Valentino Romero, the rebel leader!

Beside the insurgent's base itself. *He* was Ka's primary target.

"Val?" Ka called back. No, not him. The female had gained control of her lips. Alarm blasted through his system, adrenaline spiking, heart palpitating. The female realized what she had done too, and a ragged shout tore from her throat. "VAL?! VAL!!!"

"Hold your fire!" the male gasped.

Ka scrambled for control. This was not happening! The female was slight, primitive. Easy to manipulate. She should *not* be able to surpass his control! Yet, even as he thought it, one arm reached back to claw at his armour-plated shell—*his shell!*—where it attached to her spinal cord. A sickening jolt powered into both of their systems, sending them convulsing to the dirt. Skin scraped on stone. An image filled her mind, hot and furious—of a slither of metal, a blade. The female yearned to have one, to plunge it deep into his exoskeleton.

"That's right, you big tick," she seethed. "If I could, I'd rip out your steaming innards!"

Ka drove his feelers deeper into her cranium, grappling for a hold. But now the female had control of both arms…both legs…vocal chords! They rolled in the street, their movements bizarre and jerky, while she wailed and flailed and scrabbled at his body mass.

Nails scraped his carapace, making high-pitched rakes. This could not be happening!

A door burst open across the street, hanging off its hinges as a group of humans piled out, all bearing an assortment of metal firearms.

"Zoey!" Mid-roll, Ka caught a glimpse of her mate charging forward.

"Argh, Hell!" another barked. "She's got a scorpio latched to her back!"

Guns came up, bolts slamming rounds into chambers. Ka barely noticed, occupied with his own internal battle. The female fought hard while his tentacles sliced deeper. An iron tang filled her mouth. Vision blurred. Sound, smell, distorted. The ground pressed to Ka's face. Grit on her lips. And then Ka was *shoved* back, with a force that left him reeling. Not physical, mental.

"H-h-help me…" the female breathed, sounding winded. "Get it *off*…"

Muscles grew rigid. Spasms overtaking. Something was wrong. The female was seizing. Had Ka sliced too hard, too deep? Minds were delicate, fragile structures and he'd been so panicked. Before Ka could think any further, blackness obscured everything.

* * *

When Ka regained consciousness, he was already standing, talking. Surrounded by enemies in a dimly lit room covered with maps. "…thought it had control of me, but I've got *it* under control."

Well, the human female seemed fine. He, however, was not. None of his connectors were responding correctly. Everything felt numb and inaccessible. Detached. Her mind overruling all. A deep feeling of shame flooded over him. This was all his fault. He'd been too hasty, too eager to prove his worth on such a prominent assignment. Especially to the Queen. He should have waited—as the implanter suggested—to ensure he had complete dominion over the body before venturing out. Before falling into enemy hands.

"Once attached, it began to root through my mind," she told the gathering, not deigning to acknowledge his awareness. "I'm good at masking thoughts. Val taught me how."

There was a squeeze around her waist, and when she turned Ka saw that the male, their leader, held her there, an arm wrapped around as if he meant to defend her even here.

"I gave it enough to be satisfied," she said, "but not enough to compromise us."

"I'm just glad to have you back, Chica." He sighed, regarding her with what appeared to be genuine affection. "You've no idea how frantic I've been." Leaning sideways, he eyed Ka's dark form with disdain. Under that malicious regard, Ka felt so small, so breakable. "And don't worry, we'll find a way to get this filthy insect off you soon."

All around, faces scowled. Lips were curled, teeth were bared. There were so many, more than Command had estimated. Hostility crackled amongst them like fire. And Ka knew that had he not been attached to the female's back, had they not feared for her safety, he would have been beaten to the ground by now and pulverized into mushy, haemolyphic pulp.

The female hesitated. "That might not be the best idea just yet. There's more. What it didn't realize is that while it rooted, I did a little rooting of my own. The connection is like a two-way bridge. As it looked through my mind *I* searched through *its*. They have a weakness, something we didn't anticipate."

A murmur passed over the gathering. Their attention sharpened. Even Ka's curiosity was piqued. What could she possibly mean? The Arachnii had no weaknesses.

She smiled, as if at his errant thought, and the twist of her lips felt vicious. "Their Queen is due to land, very soon. I know where, I know when. Without her, they're nothing but mindless drones. What do you imagine would happen if her hive were to…*explode*?"

Dread crept into Ka, icy and deep, as she went on to detail the layout of their hives. Structure, numbers, hierarchy, behaviour, *locations*… She *had* dug deep. All the information he'd been trying to retrieve off her, *she* had gleamed off *him*. How had this happened? How far had the female burrowed into his consciousness? How had he not felt it?

"We have to act quickly, though," the female concluded. "And by quickly, I mean *right now*. Once they realize they've lost this Tracker, that's it. Our window closes. If we miss this opportunity, we'll never have one like it again." Leaning forward, she flattened her palms on the table, eyeing every human present. "They've already scoured most of the planet bare. It may be our last—our *only*—chance to save what remains of our world."

The crowd stirred, looking to their commander.

"What if it's a trap?" a burly male with a wiry beard called. "What if she's still under that thing's control an' we charge in there, gun's blazing, an' she's led us to our doom?"

Valentino regarded the female, eyes scanning hers. Unsure.

"You *know* me," she urged.

One, slow, nod. "It's her. No scorpio could mimic Zoe this well. I've courage enough to take the risk, even if others do not. Besides, their Queen… This is too big an opportunity to ignore. Gather the troops." He pulled her close, pressing his mouthpiece to hers in an unpleasant smack of lips and brushed a braid behind her ear. "Fine work, Chica."

"Don't thank me yet," she grinned. "We've gotta pull this off first."

* * *

It was far too easy for them to infiltrate the hive, far too easy for them to blend in as they wandered its pulsating tunnels. With Ka attached to the female, and her accomplices trailing behind bound by tendrils, none considered that their motives could be sinister, that they were anything more than what they presented themselves to be. Subdued captives.

They trekked straight for the storage cove behind the Queen's chamber, where it was quiet and secluded, where Soldiers would not think to check—not so close to her inner sanctum. No creature had ever breached their defences this deep. Until Ka had *let* them.

As the female moved amongst them, snapping the binds from their wrists, several humans retrieved smuggled pieces of equipment from within their jackets, quickly compiling them to construct some kind of device. All those wires, it looked to be incendiary in nature.

A bomb.

Just as Command had feared. These organisms *were* still a threat.

Behind them, the entrance's membranous door contracted with a soft 'whump'. Cutting off the outer tunnel's luminescence and confining them all in darkness. The humans stilled. Only their breaths made any sound, overlaying the natural circulatory hum of the walls. The constant thrum of the living hive saturated every surface.

A wail rang out. High and loud.

"What's happening?" someone hissed. "Did we trip an alarm or something?"

Ka's tentacles slithered to life. Pulsing, strengthening, reasserting control. The female tried to cry out, to call her male's name in warning, but all that escaped her lips was a soft whimper. Valentino was too preoccupied with the sudden danger, with the ever-growing skitter and tromp of boots heading their way, to notice her distress. With harsh hisses, he commanded his people to target the chamber's entrance. Ignorant to the threat at his back.

Ka struck, swiping guns aside, knocking humans into walls where suction held them in place. All was confusion, chaos, blasts of light in the dark. They were all but blind to their own defeat. It was over as swiftly as it began. Amidst the mayhem, the portal whumped open and more Arachnii spilled in, hosted and free. With reinforcements, Ka soon had the rebels lined in neat rows on their knees—weaponless, arms bound at their backs—as he paced in the girl's body before them.

"All along." Valentino's glare was pure hatred. "I should've known!"

"Not all along." Ka crouched before him, examining the way his lips quivered and his eyes watered. The male's emotions were in turmoil—understandable.

"It may give you some solace to know that your mate genuinely believed she had triumphed over me. A costly mistake. None ever have. I simply allowed her to believe she had control, supplying enough details to convince her. I only allowed her essence to survive this long to secure you and your comrades."

Even now, her consciousness lingered at the rear of his mind. Shaky and terrified, nictating like a dying star. She curled in upon herself, as if attempting to make herself appear smaller, or go unnoticed. It would be cruel to draw it out. Ka stretched back and with a swift squeeze all that remained of her psyche was smothered, crushed by his iron will. She'd accomplished her task. Ka did not require her anymore.

The male must have seen the light in her flicker and die. As Valentino was hauled away, he released a ragged yell.

He would fight implantation fiercely, Ka was sure, but it no longer mattered. With the last of these rebels subdued, Valentino would soon serve as a host to their hive. Another strong vessel to labour in the last of the Harvest, reaping what remained of this planet's wealth. Just like the rest of his race.

Spying a familiar white-clad male across the chamber, Ka strode over the cushiony floor. The implanter was supervising a crew that was dismantling the human's device.

Ka's feeler's curled at the sight of it, at its implied threat.

"How is our Queen?" he asked. "Considering the incursion, she must be stressed?"

"She was never in danger," the male said. "We moved her to another hive before you arrived. Just to be sure. I've already signalled for her to return."

"Excellent." Ka nodded. "Then may I now request reassignment to a gender specific host body, Implanter? The female will not go to waste. Many will vie for the chance to possess her, I'm sure."

"Request granted, Tracker Ka. And we have the exact body in mind…"

The implanter's calm gaze followed the line of defeated humans being led from the chamber, it lingered on the male being dragged at their rear. Valentino.

"That one has information, we believe, on the remaining rebel cells across this planet—where they are located, how many inhabit each. Their entire operation. Considering how well you have conducted yourself on this assignment, how effective you have proven yourself to be, you would be the perfect candidate to take possession of him and invade their ranks. In fact, our Queen is so impressed by your actions today that she sent word—she personally wishes you to take on the role. Congratulations, Commander Ka."

Ka straightened, suffuse with pride. *Commander.* No more wallowing in the cack-filled base of the hive. No more lowly Tracker status. He was an Arachnii of substance now.

"Of course. It would be an honour." He inclined his head respectfully. "I will not fail Her Majesty, Implanter."

City of Shadows

Hayden Trenholm

LeBois stepped into the steam of the Gare D'Orsay before the train from Lisbon rolled to a stop. After nearly sixty hours sitting in third class, all he wanted was a shower to stand under and a bed with clean sheets. That would have to wait.

He waved off a porter—his single suitcase would not leave his hands—and made his way along the platform to the inevitable pass inspection. It would be the fifth time he had been asked for his "papers" since boarding the train. This one, of course, was special. One didn't enter occupied Paris in late 1947 without being scrutinized by the Waffen SS. A Sturmbannführer, or Major, took the documents, but the man in the grey suit, a Gestapo agent, was clearly in charge.

He handed over his passport and travelling permits. The real ones were in a safety deposit in Porto, where the steamer from Buenos Aires had docked. He tried not to think about them. For now, he must be Gerard LeBois.

"Odd name for a Portuguese citizen," said the major, after making a cursory inspection of the suitcase. The small secret compartment remained hidden. He could only hope that the two crates, carried as freight on the same train, would be as successful in reaching their destination.

"My father was French; my mother was from Munich. Work took them to Lisbon and, well…"

"Nature took its course. I can hear your mother's accent in your German." The major glanced at the other man and then handed back the papers. "What brings you to Paris?"

LeBois resisted saying "the train;" Gestapo agents were notoriously without humour. "I am an advance agent for an opera company, scouting accommodations and performance venues for a fall production of *Rienzi*."

"Good choice. It is the Führer's favorite."

"Perhaps he will be able to attend. The tickets will, of course, be complementary."

The Gestapo agent did laugh at that and waved him through.

* * *

A short flight of stairs from the Metro station, one of the few that remained in use, brought him into the gentle October air on Rue Clichy. How different it was from his last visit more than a decade before. Even in the midst of the Depression, Paris remained the City of Lights, but those lights were now shuttered, replaced with Nazi regalia that stained the streets with red and black.

He walked east, turning onto Rue Blanche until he reached the recently boarded-up Theatre De Paris. He rapped twice, then twice again on the stage door, feeling like a character in a bad play. The door swung open and a woman gestured him in. When he hesitated, she said, "I know. Not whom you expected."

"The cat's among the pigeons."

The woman sighed. "The fox ate the chickens."

LeBois shrugged. At least she knew the lines to the farce.

"I'm Jo. Before you ask, it isn't short for anything and I have no last name. You're LeBois or, at least, that's what it says on your passport."

"I am LeBois. I have no other name." The scene complete, LeBois followed Jo deeper into the theatre to a small area, right of the stage. A bulb hanging from the ceiling provided the only illumination.

"I don't have coffee but I can brew some of the ersatz stuff the Germans use."

LeBois nodded his agreement, more to gain time to gather his thoughts than because he wanted coffee without kick. He had expected an older white man to meet him at the theatre not a colored woman in, he guessed, her late thirties. Something had gone wrong between his last briefing and now. He wondered if he needed to know what.

Jo put a mug of the dark liquid on the table in front of him and took the seat opposite. The steam from her cup wreathed past her prominent nose and past her over-large eyes. The woman wasn't exactly pretty but there was something about the way she gazed at him that was strangely hypnotic.

"What happened to Karl?" he asked, glancing past her to the darkened stage of the theatre. The Gestapo agent might follow up and it would be useful to be able to describe a potential venue to him.

"He was detained in Marseille on…other business. I haven't heard from him in three days. He asked me to meet you and gave me the passwords in case he couldn't get back."

LeBois half rose from his chair but Jo waved him back.

"We're safe here. Trust me."

Trust, thought LeBois, is a rare commodity in the last days of a war. The Germans had spies and sympathizers everywhere, even in Washington, where an embattled Harry Truman fought with Congress to keep America in the fight.

"Did Karl tell you why I'm here?"

"He said you were trying to find two men—Otto Frisch and Leo Szilard. Some kind of scientists, right?"

"That's right. Frisch was in Copenhagen when the war started. A trip to Birmingham was delayed and, after, he couldn't get travel documents. He came to Paris where he dropped out of sight."

"What about the other guy?" Jo was looking down at her mug as if she could read something in the still steaming liquid.

"Szilard had been helping his Jewish colleagues leave Europe since the mid-30s. He came secretly here to find Frisch and was himself trapped when the Germans marched into Paris in 1940. We heard from him periodically but not for the last year. I came here to recover them and take them to America."

Jo shook her head and got up from the table, walking toward the stage until she was on the edge of the light. The way she drifted across the floor reminded him of a jaguar he had once seen stalking its prey.

She turned sharply, the light catching in her dark eyes. "I haven't wasted my time waiting for your arrival. After Karl briefed me, I started looking for them."

"I'm surprised you were able to move freely. The German's view of Negroes—"

"Is better than their opinion of Jews. They think we're sub-human, but they hate the Jews. A number of us black folk stayed in Paris—we consider it our home as much or more than America—even after things got bad. We get by as long as we follow the rules. Some of the Nazis even find us…amusing.

"In any case, I can take you to Frisch. For what it's worth."

* * *

LeBois and Jo walked through a slowly drenching mist, along the leaf-strewn gravel paths of Pere Lachaise cemetery, one of only three that Napoleon had permitted to remain within the city limits of Paris. The chain around his neck pulled him forward and down. Not yet, he thought, and the urge subsided.

Many of the monuments had been defaced and a few toppled over or smashed, though the ground beneath appeared undisturbed.

"You should see what they did to Oscar Wilde's stone," said Jo. "Most of their fury was directed at the Jews buried here but they saved some for 'unnatural' men, as well."

"But the graves themselves are undisturbed."

"Most of them. Everything is packed so close together they said they were worried they might damage Christian graves, but I think most Nazis are too superstitious to risk raising the dead from their rest."

Yet raising the dead or, at least, the secrets they held was exactly what LeBois had been sent to Paris to do. At the far end of the cemetery, Jo stopped before a small square of granite with the name O.R. FRISCH and the dates 1904-1940. Someone had tried to scrape the red-painted swastika from the stone but enough remained to twist LeBois' stomach into a knot. A small stone rested on the top of the granite.

"Well, here he is. Lucky to have died before the Germans entered Paris, I guess." Jo stared at him staring at the grave. "Dead scientists don't do much physics. You know that, right?"

"No one passes through this earth without leaving some trace behind," said LeBois.

"I've been to the last place he was known to have lived. If there were any papers left there, they're long gone now."

"I think Frisch's secrets went to the grave with him," said LeBois. "I don't suppose you know any gravediggers?"

Jo's mouth tightened and her eyes narrowed but she nodded. "I can always find someone who needs work and isn't particular what kind it is."

LeBois watched as Jo returned the way they had come, until her form faded into the mist. Her feet barely made a sound as she moved across the gravel, and he was once again reminded of a big cat seeking its prey.

He lay across the slightly depressed section of dirt with his arms and legs spread wide. He closed his eyes and whispered words in a language he did not know. The amulet he had taken from its hiding place warmed until the heat was almost unbearable against the skin of his throat. Still, he remained with his cheek pressed to the cold wet soil, whispering, until he heard something whisper back.

LeBois pushed himself to his feet. *I'm getting too old for this. No matter, if I succeed, this will be my last mission.* He shivered, ripples of cold and dread running up and down his body like a whirlpool. He breathed in the chill air, waiting for it to bring a measure of calm. When his legs stopped shaking, he brushed the dirt from his trousers and jacket and wiped his face dry with his handkerchief. Jamming the soiled cloth into his jacket pocket, he hovered his hand over the stone on top of the gravestone. A jolt, like electricity, shot up his arm.

Szilard had been here. Not recently but not in the distant past, either. LeBois shivered again, this time in anticipation. The physicist was still in Paris and LeBois would find him. Alive or dead, he would track him down and take him.

* * *

Finding the elusive Szilard was easier said than done. Several days passed before one of Jo's informants tracked down a lead. LeBois hadn't dared bring a photograph with him but could provide a description: about fifty, below average height and plump, a sallow complexion, dark hair and eyes and a full mouth. He sometimes wore glasses but seldom smiled. Not very helpful but, apparently, helpful enough.

Szilard had lived in a small two room apartment above Rue Jacob, but had left nearly a year ago. The concierge didn't know where he had moved to, only that he had moved quickly in the middle of the night. Even the offer of a hundred Reichsmarks had not elicited further information, only that he had occasionally been visited by a young couple. No names and little in the way of description—he was tall and dark, she, tall and blonde.

Another week passed and still no further word on the missing man. It was as if he had turned to smoke and drifted away. Frisch's body had been exhumed. LeBois never met the men who did the work, nor did he want to. He had seen the body and deemed it sufficient for his purposes; some remnants of flesh still clung to the intact skeleton. It now awaited the conclusion of his mission in an ice room in the suburbs of the city.

"I still don't know why you need these scientists," said Jo, "especially one seven years dead. I don't see what even one live scientist is going to do. This war is already over, though some folks won't admit it." She had asked that question and reached that conclusion nearly everyday since the visit to Frisch's grave. He wondered where her loyalties truly were. Could fear of losing even this meagre existence cause her to work for people who considered her "sub-human?"

"The war won't end until the last man—or woman—lays down their arms and gives up."

"Then I guess it will go on a little longer." Jo looked at him in silence for several minutes. He was satisfied not to be the one to break her gaze or speak first.

"Karl is not my only contact in the resistance."

LeBois knew the French resistance operated in cells, a tactic they learned from the Russian, Trotsky. Jo would know at least one other member, more if she was higher in the organization than she let on. He suspected she was, if only because of the ease with which she moved about the city and gathered information. Of course, a Gestapo agent would display a similar ease.

"Go on."

"We have intelligence that a major movement of armour and troops will cross the Loire, just south of Paris, headed for the coast."

"And from there to Mexico." America's southern neighbour had remained neutral in the war, but the new President had ambitions. A secret treaty was rumoured that would open yet another front for the beleaguered Allies.

"I wouldn't know about that. Our unit has been tasked with blowing up a bridge. We leave tonight."

"Is that an invitation?" LeBois knew he should stay in Paris and continue the search for Szilard but, in Jo's absence, his ability to do so would be limited. Besides, he had to know if Jo was strong enough for what was to come. How she carried herself in the face of death would determine if his mission would succeed. He needed her to trust him so he must first trust and support her.

* * *

"Something's gone wrong."

LeBois and Jo crouched in a copse of trees a hundred yards from the bridge. Two others had joined them—a young man who wasn't yet old enough to shave and a hard-looking woman in her fifties—but the other four were late and dawn was approaching.

"What are we going to do?" asked the boy. No names were given or asked.

"The mission's blown," said LeBois. His legs cramped from squatting in the sparse cover and the cold seeped deep into his bones. He had been a fool to agree to come—his mission was more important than a fallen bridge and a few lost tanks. He could have completed the mission without Jo.

No, came the whisper, you could not.

"We still have the dynamite and the blasting caps," said the woman, glancing at the rucksack the boy had brought.

"It's suicide," said Jo.

"We're all dead if America falls." The woman gave LeBois a hard look. "And it is going to fall, isn't it? And soon."

LeBois didn't answer but he knew the woman was right. Only one way remained to change the course of events and this was not the way.

"We have to go back to Paris," he said. "We have work to do."

"But I—"

"I can't do it alone."

"We'll take care of the bridge," the boy's voice shook but he lifted the pack onto his shoulders. Jo tried to follow but Le Bois wrapped his arms around her to keep her from going. He was surprised at the strength of her body as she pulled away. He could not stop her if she was determined to go.

"There is a way to still win this war. It's why I came to Paris."

Jo shook her head.

"You…you have a bigger role to play. After this is over and we've won the war. America will need people like you to rebuild, no, to build back better."

They were several kilometres away when they heard the rumble, indistinguishable from the thunder of an approaching storm.

* * *

"How can two physicists—one dead, one still missing—win the war?"

They had ditched the bike on the edge of the city and walked to the closest open Metro station. They returned shortly after dawn to the relative safety of the theatre. Jo had made more of the fake coffee, which she served with day old brioche and a few preserved apricots by way of breakfast.

LeBois resisted the urge to glance around for lurking Gestapo spies. He had been told to reveal nothing of his mission beyond what was needed to accomplish it. Jo had trusted him, now it was time to trust her.

"A project, called Tube Alloys, was started in England just after the war began to create a weapon that some people think could change the course of the war. Frisch, operating from Copenhagen, was one of the instigators. Szilard was a key figure, too.

"As the bombing campaign intensified, the project was moved, first to Montreal in Canada, and then, after America joined the war, to Chicago, where it was renamed, oddly enough, the Manhattan Project. Scientists from all over Europe and America were recruited to work on it. Progress stalled when Szilard disappeared and the scientific head, a man called Oppenheimer, was killed in a mysterious car crash in '42.

"But the project is back on track now, thanks to a major breakthrough in data storage and a certain…artifact found in the jungles of Guatemala—" LeBois felt the amulet around his neck begin to warm. "—but time is running out and we need to recover whatever Frisch and Szilard left behind to finish."

"What kind of weapon, by itself, could stop the Axis?"

LeBois had heard rumours, words like "city-killer" and "hell's gate" but nothing that made enough sense to explain it to Jo. "I don't know. All I know is we have to succeed or be prepared to live under the boot of the Reich."

* * *

LeBois wakened to a fist banging on the door. He leapt to his feet, the old instincts overcoming the reluctance of his body. He had no real weapon, but he would not go without a fight. A water pitcher stood on his bedside table, and he grasped it and stepped quickly across the room, ready to strike the first Gestapo agent that came through the door.

"LeBois, wake up, it's me. Jo." The surge of relief threatened to drop him to the floor. "We found him. We found Szilard."

LeBois yanked back the bolt and jerked the door open so hard Jo was nearly pulled off her feet. "Where is he?"

"Jesus," she said, "what happened to you?"

"Life." LeBois pulled on a sweater, covering the lattice of scars that marked his body from neck to waist, his history written in the obscure script of violence. He repeated his question.

"A man answering his description was seen in the Marais. The young couple was with him so we're pretty sure that's our man."

The Marais was the old Jewish quarter of Paris, the finer homes now occupied by German officers and their Vichy collaborators. "Hiding in plain sight."

Jo nodded as LeBois finished dressing.

"Do you have a pistol?"

She nodded again and pulled a flat black Walther P38 from her belt and handed it to him. She flipped back her jacket to show him its mate in a shoulder holster.

Little moved on the streets at 3 AM. and scant lighting lit their way. Few others braved the murky streets. At one intersection, they were surprised by a pair of swallows, as the French police were called. Jo threw her arms around LeBois's neck and pressed her lips to his. The police laughed and told them to find themselves a darker alley.

"Lucky it wasn't a German patrol," she said, after the police had moved on. "They don't look kindly on race mixing."

LeBois said nothing, his mouth still tingling from the force of her kiss, his body strangely alive from the brief contact with hers. He doubted if he would ever feel so alive again.

Jo's informant was waiting at the entrance of Rouelle Sourdis, a narrow, cobbled alleyway off Pastourelle. He gestured at a house a few doors down before striding away.

LeBois considered their situation, thinking back to his own reaction to a late-night visit. Still, there was nothing for it. Who knew how long Szilard would remain at this address? He could not let him slip away again.

He handed Jo the Walther. "Better not to appear like a police agent."

"Better maybe to look like a black woman," said Jo. "Less likely to shoot me out of panic."

She's probably right, he thought, but he said, "My mission. My risk. If something goes wrong…" If something went wrong, the mission would fail and the world would plunge into darkness. "Do the best you can to get Szilard to safety."

LeBois climbed the short flight of stairs and rapped lightly on the door. To his surprise, he didn't need to knock a second time. The door opened and a tall woman peered at him, her blonde hair gleaming in the light of a single candle.

"Are you the doctor?" she asked. LeBois's heart dropped. The tremor in her voice told him all he needed to know.

* * *

Szilard was dead, though his body was not yet cold.

"Did the Germans—" Jo began but the tall man, Charles Pecheur, cut her off with a gesture.

"Do you think any of us would be here if the Nazis were involved? My cousin took ill several days ago…" He broke off with a small sob.

"You were expecting a doctor?" asked LeBois.

"We were hoping for one," replied Anna, Charles's wife. "But all the doctors we knew from before have been taken away."

"Jewish doctors, you mean?" asked Jo.

"Yes. We couldn't hazard going to the hospital. Leo is on a list. We wouldn't risk…" Anna put her fist to her mouth.

"It doesn't matter now," said LeBois. "Professor Szilard can still help us stop any others from being taken away. We need to move him—and Frisch, too—to a warehouse in the south of the city. Can you arrange it?"

Jo glanced at the address on the slip of paper he handed her and then nodded. "Yes, but not until the sun comes up."

After she had left to make the arrangements, LeBois sat in silence with the young couple, respecting their need to grieve, while considering his next steps. He would need energy, both human energy and a considerable amount of electrical power as well. He hoped Charles and Anna would help provide the former, along with any compatriots they and Jo could round up.

The warehouse where Szilard and Frisch were to be taken had been built in the late 1930s by the French central intelligence service with funding from a covert branch of the US State department. Its purpose had been to develop advanced calculating and cryptography systems to spy on the growing German threat. The operation was shuttered days before the fall of Paris. However, most of its equipment and the cables that hooked it into the city's main power supply remained intact. The building was camouflaged as a storehouse for Portuguese wine and other exports that required refrigeration.

Now, it would serve its final purpose, as would he.

* * *

LeBois and Charles had moved Szilard's body and what remained of Otto Frisch down the stairs and through a hidden door to more stairs. Those led to a vaulted sub-basement that pre-dated the construction of the main building. They placed them onto tables and covered them with sheets of shimmering white cloth, stored in a chest against one wall.

The two crates had been delivered from the train station and were stacked near the middle of the warehouse, surrounded by barrels of wine and boxes of bacalhau, the dried and salted cod that formed a staple of the Portuguese diet during Lent. They weren't large but they were heavy and it took both of them and several of the others to move them into the deep cellar.

When the top and the sides of the crates were removed, a pair of rectangular boxes were revealed, featureless save for a row of lights that ran down the middle of the top surface, a large coil of thick electrical cord emerging from one end, a thinner one from the other. When the heavy wires were connected to the power supply, the lights flashed green, then lit in sequence from one end of the box to the other and back again like a ball bouncing between two walls. The thinner wires attached to a dark metallic cloak that had been contained in one of the crates.

"What are they?" Anna had asked, reaching out to touch one of the boxes.

"Careful! An electric charge runs over the surface; you could be hurt."

Anna had jerked back her hand but kept staring at the slowly moving light as if hypnotized.

LeBois stood in front of the semi-circle of volunteers, draped in the dark cloak. Jo was now directly opposite him, her eyes gleaming in the dim light, her body tense. She was flanked on one side by four members of the resistance, who looked grim and had remained silent since arriving.

On the other stood Charles, Anna and two of their friends, introduced as Andre and Carole. The former looked nervous, constantly glancing around as if expecting the Gestapo to step out of the darkness and arrest them all. Carole, on the other hand, was excited, her face flushed. Her eyes flicked from LeBois to the two shrouded tables cupped in the crescent of their bodies.

He asked them to join hands. Some looked reluctant but they all complied. He stepped forward and slid his hands beneath the cloth coverings. His right hand rested on the cool brow of the recently deceased Szilard while his left tangled in the matted hair that still clung to Frisch's skull.

He whispered the words he had been taught, sensing their meaning rather than knowing it. "Kaua in semahsitikah uala, kinkaua tlakuepa." As he said the last word, he felt a tingle in his hands, as if the words had created an answering vibration from the dead flesh. The second time he spoke louder and the vibration became a whisper he was sure only he could hear. From Szilard: Nem vágyom az életre, de eljövök and from Frisch, fainter and in German, but still distinct: Ich begehre das Leben nicht, aber ich werde kommen. They were reluctant but they would come. The lights on the boxes were flashing faster and faster and he could see them reflected in the staring eyes of his companions.

A third time, louder still, and the answer came again. "A szakadék hatalmas, de én át fogok kelni rajta" and "Die Kluft ist groß, aber ich werde sie überqueren." A vast distance must be crossed but they would come. A moan rose from the others and Anna and one of the men from the resistance swayed and might have fallen if not for the grasp of their compatriots. The cloak across his shoulders buzzed and the amulet burned against his chest, so that he caught the whiff of singed hair and skin.

The fourth and final time, he shouted so loud he thought his throat would tear. The answer came like the thundering of water from a high cliff. The answer now was in all languages and none; he heard it directly in his thoughts. "We are here. Now pay the passage."

One by one those opposite dropped to the floor, gasping but alive. Only Jo remained standing, swaying but defiant, a force of will against the storm. The amulet burned like molten lava against his skin, sending waves of pleasant pain and painful pleasure through his body. The cloak sparked and stabbed at his shoulders. The flashing lights strobed green across the ceiling. He croaked out the final words: "Ka otlami" It is finished.

The two men—or what remained of them on this earth—flowed through his arms, up to his shoulders and into the cloak. The amulet became like ice against his burning flesh and he fell.

* * *

Jo was supporting his head with one hand, stroking his burning brow with the cool fingers of the other. "LeBois, wake up! I think we shorted out the entire neighbourhood. Alarms are going off. The Nazis will be here any minute. We have to go." He glanced past her to the storage units; the lights were a solid line of green.

"You have to go," he said, his voice a bare whisper. "I am past going anywhere." At last, he thought, rest will come. "Take the boxes. They contain what I came for. The essence of Szilard and Frisch are stored within. Get them to Lisbon. A plane is waiting to fly them to Chicago. If the ones who sent me were correct, it will be enough to win this war."

Jo stared at him for several long moments and shook her head.

"The Nazi's will never win as long as one strong woman stands against them." LeBois yanked the amulet from around his neck and pressed it into her hands. "Get our friends to safety and those boxes to America."

Jo smiled as she stuffed the amulet into her shirt pocket and gently lowered his head to the floor. Within moments she had the others organized, moving out of the cellar with the treasure stolen from death.

She was the last to leave, sparing him a single glance over her shoulder.

His vision blurred and he finally saw her true self: a jaguar on the prowl.

Ten Seconds

Edward Willett

Ten seconds.
Back against the wall, blade in hand.
The door begins to open…

* * *

"Don't you think," John Senn said to Anna Covington, "that it's a little…*off* to make this a museum exhibit?"

Anna opened her mouth to respond but then closed it again as a bevy of preteen schoolgirls chattered their way into the room, accompanied fore and aft by stern-looking nuns in the red-and-black vestments of the Order of Saint Imelda. The fore-nun raised a claw-like hand, and the girls immediately fell silent with the unmistakable air of children familiar with and fearful of corporal punishment.

"It was here," said the formidable sister, "that the Glorious War of Liberation began, in this very spot. Can anyone tell me what happened?"

A barely-there slip of a girl raised her hand micro-seconds ahead of a far bulkier classmate, who shot her a vitriolic look that spoke of long-standing enmity—rather like that engendered between Chetjoku and Bushibo by the events the slender child proceeded to describe, once the nun acknowledged her. "Yes, Portina?"

"King Ronald the Fourth was assassinated by a Bushibo agent disguised as a servant on the evening of Mariza 34, twenty-six years ago this coming eight-day," the girl said in a clear, piping voice.

"Very good," said the claw-handed nun. "But incomplete. What happened after that?"

The skinny girl's hand shot up again, but this time, she was out-gunned by the heavier-set girl, whose hand beat hers to the necessary altitude by a fraction of a second.

"Susara?" the nun acknowledged.

"The assassin vanished without a trace. She was seen entering the room, but was never seen coming out. We know she was a Bushibo agent," Susara hurried on, as if to forestall another hand-raising contest, "because Bushibo claimed responsibility for the attack."

"Very good," said the nun. "And now, to bring it up to the present, what will be the inevitable result of the Glorious War of Liberation?"

The girls spoke more or less as one. "The utter destruction of the evil regime of Bushibo and the restoration of the Holy Empire of Chetjoku across all of the Great Island…all of the Great Island!" The echo came from one of the youngest girls, a little slower to answer than the others.

The nun nodded her approval and even assayed a small smile, revealing unfortunately crooked teeth. "I am pleased. Let us proceed to the throne room, where the war was declared."

Chirping excitedly, the flock of children moved on down the hall.

John glanced at Anna. "Do you feel reassured?"

Anna snorted. "Only of the effectiveness of educational indoctrination," she said. "'The utter destruction of the evil regime of Bushibo and the restoration of the Holy Empire of Chetjoku across all of the Great Island' seems a more distant possibility each day. The 'evil regime' has established a beachhead at Fishmouth Harbour, and our 'glorious army' seems powerless to drive them back. If they continue their current rate of advance, those children will be cowering in shelters from artillery fire within the month." She turned and gave John a curious look. "Why did you want to come here, to the place where this nightmare began? You said you had news. Why couldn't you come to me through the usual channels?"

"I don't trust the usual channels," John said. He studied Anna for a moment with his one good eye; the right, though it looked normal to observers, was blind as the result of a rather nasty chemical booby trap he had not quite disarmed during an otherwise successful mission ten years previously. When he'd first met Anna, she'd been a strikingly beautiful young woman, so much so that he'd surreptitiously lusted after her for years—surreptitiously because she was his superior: the person he reported to as a member of the Silent Service, the Chetjoku intelligence agency. Now in her fifties, she remained attractive, and he would still have welcomed an assignation but more out of a long-established habit of thinking than any current overwhelming desire. At the time of their first meeting, so many years ago, he hadn't yet been with a woman; since meeting her, he had been with many. Though the nature of his work precluded long-term relationships, it facilitated short ones, typically consisting of a single night.

Though, of course, he had to guard his tongue during such encounters since they mostly occurred in Bushibo territory, where he had an entirely different persona and name, much like the mysterious assassin of King Ronald the Fourth.

"Well?" Anna said, meeting his gaze. Her left eyebrow raised. "What have you got?"

John gave her a small smile much like the nun's, although he had, he hoped, better teeth. "I have discovered," he said, "how it was done."

"How what was done?"

"The assassination."

Anna looked skeptical. "After so long?"

"Yes."

She shrugged. "Very well. But so what? Why this clandestine meeting?"

"Because," John said, "I believe there is a way to stop it."

"Stop it?"

"Before it happens."

Both of Anna's eyebrows rose this time, giving the distinct impression she was questioning his sanity.

* * *

Nine seconds.
I tense.
The door swings open a little wider, then stops.

* * *

It was three weeks ago (John told Anna). As you instructed, I have, for the past year, been cultivating the friendship of my colleague in the Bushibo Office for Foreign Relationships, Janislav Feldon. It has not been a particularly onerous assignment since he is a likable enough fellow, but it has also been rather unrewarding since, unfortunately, he is also extremely close-mouthed. Not surprising, I suppose, given the propensity for Bushibo officials to publicly hang anyone suspected of revealing state secrets.

However, I was clearly successful in winning his trust since he let slip, while we were enjoying the natural hot springs in the Bushibo government spa on the slopes of Mount Astoria, the information that has led me to this moment.

"It happened not far from here, you know," he said.

This seemed to come out of the blue; our last topic of conversation had been…well, never mind, except that it had nothing to do with where his mind had taken him now.

"What did?" I said, perhaps not the most scintillating rejoinder, but naked, soaked in sweat, with my eyes closed, and utterly relaxed, I was not at my sharpest—which, clearly, neither was he, to my reward.

He hardly seemed aware of my question. He had enjoyed several glasses of *wufflik*, a local liqueur that goes down like liquid fire, another reason, perhaps, that he was not fully present in the moment. I had enjoyed one or two glasses myself, but as you know, I have a remarkable tolerance for intoxicating substances.

"The ruins of the Temple of the God from Beyond," he said, waving vaguely to the north. "Five thousand feet up-slope from here. That's where they did it."

He had my interest now. I turned my head to him and opened my eyes. His remained closed. "Did what?" I said softly.

"Sent the assassin back in time," he murmured. "Time and space. It sounds impossible, but here we are, winning the war she began…"

And, just like that, he slept.

When we met the next morning at breakfast, he was so hungover I do not think he had the slightest memory of the previous night in the sauna, and I certainly wasn't going to remind him of it. But what he had said sent me on a quest such as I had never anticipated—and revealed what I had never suspected.

* * *

Eight seconds.
I step toward the door.
"I will prepare the room," says a female voice.

* * *

Anna studied John through narrowed eyes. His face, remarkable in its unremarkableness, gave nothing away. With a neat, graying beard and matching hair, on the taller side of average height, wearing a bulky but non-descript black coat that concealed whatever clothing he wore beneath, he looked like a prosperous merchant—which, of course, was his cover in Bushibo. "The God from Beyond?" she said. "A myth."

"A myth central to Bushibo's culture and history," John pointed out. "As the Landing of the Eldest is to ours."

Anna snorted. "Hardly a convincing argument, considering the Eldest never existed, or if they did, they were certainly not godlike perfect beings— just murderous raiders from across the seas who conquered a more primitive people and self-aggrandizingly appropriated their bewildered accounts of those first overwhelming encounters."

"Nevertheless," John said. "There is an element of truth in those tales. Godlike? Not to our modern sensibility, but they seemed godlike to those who had never seen firearms or even worked metal and glass."

Where is this going? Anna wondered. It was unlike John to speculate; as long as she had overseen him, he had been focused on facts, level-headed almost to a fault. "Are you suggesting the immense powers attributed to the God from Beyond were also the result of advanced technology?"

"I am," John said. "May I continue my story?"

Whatever information John had to impart, Anna clearly needed to hear it. She gave a curt nod. "Very well." She looked around; another school group had just entered, though they were much quieter—a solemn-looking troop of military school cadets, their gray uniforms miniature versions of the dress uniform of the nation's army. Their leader, a veteran missing both his left arm and his right eye, began a version of the line of questioning the nun had taken with her far more flighty charges.

"Outside," she continued. "On the parapets." She smiled without humor. "From which, in a few days' time, the enemy may very well be sighted."

* * *

Seven seconds.
I position myself behind the door.

* * *

An icy wind scoured the parapets. Jon shrugged off the cold as he had shrugged off so many discomforts in his work. The wind would devour whatever words they spoke before the vibrations had traveled five feet, and that was the point.

"Continue," Ana said, and John complied.

* * *

I could not act on the information my "friend" had given me while we were still at the resort, of course. I said nothing more about it, and we returned to the capital by train, most convivially. But within a fortnight, I arranged to take another trip by myself, not to the resort but to a village two or three miles away, where I had arranged a "business meeting." The two days following that meeting were the eight-day interregnum, when my time was my own, and I set out on an overnight camping trip of which I told no one the details.

I did not reach the Temple of the God from Beyond on the first day and spent a night on the slopes of Mount Astoria—a cold night, though warmer than standing on these parapets, in honest truth—but the next day, I approached it.

It is a ruin, of course, and not even a particularly interesting one—a lot of rubble, overgrown courtyards, a single, rectangular building with broken columns in front and holes in its roof. No school trips visit it as they do this sad palace. There is no path that leads to it, so one must be committed to the journey to even approach it.

Yet, it is guarded, always, by two-score heavily armed men. I knew this before I went, of course, having done my research during my time back in the capital. I had little difficulty slipping past them in the dark. Like most men assigned to these sorts of tasks, they were not particularly alert. I suspect the posting is punishment for transgressions or shortcomings elsewhere.

My research had also pointed me to the heart of the complex, a subterranean chamber beneath the one remaining building that, unlike the rest of the ruins, is secured by a locked, metal door. However, a half-hour of observation from hiding revealed a gap in the patrol pattern of the guard detail, and, of course, once I was down the stairs, the chamber's simple lock was no match for my skills.

I entered and closed the door behind me. I had expected pitch darkness, but instead, the room was suffused with a pale glow of a color I cannot describe, as though I were seeing it with something other than my eyes. That glow came from a…call it a device, for now, though I learned a different name for it later. This "device" was a thing of indeterminate shape and size, somehow resting and yet not resting upon a pillar made of some material so black I could only see it as a cut-out against the faintly reflecting stone of the floor and wall beyond. Four metallic spheres rested in receptacles at the top of this pillar, glinting dully.

And then, a voice came from all around me, a voice such as I have never heard, a voice filled with both immense age and immense weariness, as though the speaker—and I could no more tell the sex of whoever was speaking than I could tell you with certainty the color of the strange object—had witnessed endless ages filled with all the folly that mankind can muster—which, as you and I both know, is a great deal.

"A visitor," the voice said. "A new face, the first in many years. Are you here to take me home at last? Or merely a new priest?"

I hesitated and almost said I was, indeed, a priest—the lie already prepared for me and offered for my acceptance as though on a platter of gold—but immediately thought better of it, for the owner of that voice, I felt certain, would know if I lied.

"No," I said. "I am a spy."

* * *

Six seconds.

A woman steps into the room, wearing the black dress and white apron of a servant. She turns toward the door to close it.

* * *

Anna interrupted John's tale with her shocked, sharp intake of breath. "You confessed you were a spy to the first person who challenged you in the mythological heart of the enemy kingdom with armed guards all around?"

"When you put it that way," John said mildly, "it does sound somewhat foolhardy. But had you heard that voice…you would have done the same."

"I find that hard to believe," Anna said, and with her tone, very deliberately subtracted another degree or two from the chill of the wind.

"Yet," John said, "here I am, so clearly, I was not arrested, tortured, interrogated, and killed."

"Clearly," Anna said. She let two more degrees of warmth fall away. She did not like the way this conversation was trending. Had John been subverted? Was he here to kill her? As though her hands were cold, even though they were gloved, she put them into her coat pockets. Her right hand fell naturally around the reassuring solidity of the grip of the small but deadly pistol she had on her person at all times. John, of course, would likewise be armed; she had no doubt various weapons and tools were concealed within his own bulky coat. "Which raises the question, 'Why?'"

John's glance flickered to her right coat pocket, then returned to her face. His lips quirked in an almost smile. "If I were a traitor, why would I be telling you this story?"

"To keep me from questioning your loyalty," Anna said instantly.

They regarded each other for a long, cold moment. John simply stood there with that not-quite smile on his face. Finally, she took a long breath, exhaled, and said, "That way, however, lies madness. I reserve judgment. For the moment." She jerked her head in a tight nod but did not release the grip of the pistol. "Continue."

* * *

Five seconds.

I slam the door shut behind the woman with my left hand and, with my right, drive the blade toward her midsection.

* * *

"Ah," the voice said, and in that brief exhalation—if exhalation it was, for I was as certain as I have ever been of anything that the owner of that voice did not breathe and, indeed, had *never* breathed—I heard for the first time a lifting of the weight of ennui that had engulfed every word until then. "At last."

I frowned. "You have been expecting me?"

"Someone like you," the voice said. "Time is out of joint, and you, cursed spirit, have come to make it right."

The words had the sound of poetry, but it was not a phrase I had ever heard.

"I don't understand," I said, and that alone, Anna, should tell you how taken aback I was since it has been many years since I admitted such a thing to anyone.

"Forgive me," the voice said. "I am large; I contain multitudes, and yet, for far too long, I have been trapped in this place, in this timeline, through no fault of my own." A pause. "Why are you here, oh spy?"

"Because of a tale, difficult to believe—though less difficult to believe now that I have met you," I said while thinking, *whatever and wherever "you" are.*

"Tell me this tale."

I told him what my drinking companion had told me, that an assassin had been sent back through time to murder King Ronald the Fourth and launch the war we are now in danger of losing.

"A tale I know well," the voice said when I had finished. "And precisely the one I thought you must be here to address."

I raised the eyebrow above my good eye. "I am here to find out if it is true; if it is true, how it was accomplished; and if, as impossible as it seems, it *was* accomplished, how it might be *un*-accomplished; for it seems to me," I went on, "that if it is possible to travel in time and space to make such a thing happen, it must be possible to travel in time and space to make such a thing *not* happen."

"Very well," said the voice. "Yes, it is true. I accomplished it. And yes, I can un-accomplish it—and will do so willingly."

* * *

Four seconds.

She's fast, faster than I anticipated, and almost succeeds in evading my blow—but not quite. The blade slices through clothes and skin, leaving a bloody cut across her midriff.

* * *

John paused and looked out across the frozen landscape in the direction from which the forces of Bushibo would soon approach in their final push to end the war—and the Holy Empire of Chetjoku. "It must be timed carefully," he said.

"What must?" Anna said from behind him.

John turned back to her. She still had her hands in her pockets, and he knew full well one of them held a gun. He was careful to keep his own hands in the open. "You must have been startled to hear from me, given there is no record of my return from Bushibo."

Anna's face displayed no expression. "I was."

John took a breath. "That is because I stood in the chamber I have been telling you of not two hours ago, just fifteen minutes before I called you from a public telephone at the palace gates to ask you to meet me here."

Anna took a step back, pulled the gun from her pocket, and pointed it unwaveringly at John's stomach. "You will tell me what is going on," she said, each word precisely enunciated, "or you will not leave this parapet alive."

"What's going on?" John smiled. "What's going on is that I demanded proof that the voice could do what it said it could do. And here I am, a week in the past and halfway around the world, saying my final farewells." He let his smile broaden. "Though I know you would shoot me without hesitation if you felt it was called for, Anna, I have always considered you a friend. This is the last time I will speak to you, though you will never know it, and neither will I. I am here to say goodbye."

"I don't understand," Anna said.

"Let me show you," John said. "May I put my hand into my pocket? There's something you need to see."

Anna's eyes narrowed. "Move very slowly, or you die."

"Of course," John said. With exaggerated care, his own eyes locked on Anna's, he reached into his pocket and touched the metal sphere within.

The parapet and Anna's startled face vanished in an instant.

* * *

Three seconds.

The woman doubles over, gasping, clutching at the wound, blood surging around her fingers.

* * *

Anna had no explanation. One moment, John was standing at gunpoint before her; the next, he was gone, vanishing with a mini clap of not-quite-thunder as air rushed in to take the space he had mysteriously vacated.

She made extensive inquiries, of course, but there was, indeed, no record of John's entry into the country by any public means of transportation or those known and available only to the members of the Silent Service.

She sent many messages abroad, but before there could be any reply, the Bushibo army routed the Empire's forces at Fishmouth Harbor and drove toward the capital.

Two weeks after her meeting on the parapets with John Senn, Anna Covington was killed in an artillery bombardment.

Young Queen Vitrixia, a mere infant when her father was assassinated, surrendered the next day. The war had ended in a great victory for Bushibo.

The reign of terror began shortly thereafter.

* * *

Two seconds.

I grab the assassin, spin her, wrap her in a tight embrace. She is strong, but I am stronger, and shock has weakened her.

* * *

John stood once more in the sacred chamber at the heart of the Temple of the God from Beyond. There was no sound of uproar from outside; his entry remained undiscovered, though he could not be certain how long that happy state of affairs would prevail.

"Are you satisfied?" said the voice.

"Perhaps," John said. He still held the metal sphere he had been given to return him to the chamber at the moment of his choice; he placed it back in its receptacle in the pure-black pillar that held the thing the voice had told him was called a "time crystal," which had sent him on his brief journey. "You sent me to approximately the correct location, but only a few days back in time. It does not prove you can send me back to the very precise time in the more distant past, with the pinpoint accuracy of location likewise required, needed for this to succeed."

"It is no more difficult to send you many years into the past than it is to send you two seconds into the past," the voice said. "And in any event, you have no choice but to try. Bushibo's forces will crush your capital and your kingdom within days—possibly hours. It will happen while you are still being tortured by the regime here, should you dither even ten minutes longer and the regular inspection of this chamber by the guards occurs. Then, all of your mighty spying efforts will have been for naught."

"So a twenty-year journey is equivalent to a two-second journey? I find that hard to believe."

"Your belief or disbelief is immaterial," the voice said. "However, while no more energy or effort is required on my part to send you on a journey of years, the *time* you may spend in the past decreases the farther back you go. Were I to send you back a century or more, you would barely have time to register your surroundings before you were pulled back to the present."

"Ah," said John. "And how long will I have where I must go now?"

"Ten seconds," the voice said. "More precisely, ten point oh nine one two seconds, repeating, but ten seconds is close enough."

* * *

One second.
"Who are you?" she gasps.

* * *

"Ten seconds." John thought for a moment. "And I will return without having to use the control sphere you gave me?"

"You will," the voice said. "Those are only used if a journey must be cut short. You will not want to cut short your ten seconds, I'm sure."

"And you can send me to the precise instant when the door into the retiring room opens as the assassin enters?"

"I can," the voice said. "Having retrieved the assassin once she achieved her goal, and having downloaded the record of all she did during her visit to the past from the retrieval sphere, every second of the events involving her is well marked in my memory banks."

The odd phrases "downloaded" and "memory banks" sparked John's curiosity, but he did not seek to satisfy it. "But when this was done before, the assassin was there for several hours, at least," he said instead.

"It was done a mere seven days after the visit of the King to that palace in the original timeline," the voice said. "As when I sent you to meet with your handler—"

"I would prefer you didn't call her that," John said.

"Very well, your…associate…the visit could be quite lengthy. The assassin had a month to prepare."

"And then used the control sphere to vanish once the deed was done."

"Precisely."

"But I'll have only ten seconds to thwart her."

"Yes."

"How many years must pass before the available time of action shrinks to, say, two seconds?"

"A decade, perhaps. Why?"

"Because if I can do this, it can still be undone. Attempts could be made over and over, until the time of action shrinks to almost nothing."

"It can, but it seems unlikely."

"Unlikely is not the same as impossible. My undoing of the assassination is also unlikely."

"Granted."

Jon ran a hand over the front of his bulky coat. "I won't need this where I am going," he said. "May I leave it here?"

"Of course." The voice sounded almost eager. "You're going through with it, then?"

"I am."

"You are prepared?"

Jon put his hand into a specially designed inside pocket of the coat. "You are certain I cannot use a firearm?"

"Yes," the voice said. "The time-crystal field is designed to prevent it. You could take it with you into the past, but you would not be able to fire it. A bomb would likewise be unusable."

"Why?"

"Ask those who created me."

"The priests of the God from Beyond?"

"No." The voice sounded scornful. "I *am* the God from Beyond. They found me. They did not create me."

"Then how did you come to be here?"

"Can you do what must be done without access to a firearm or not?" the voice demanded rather than answer.

"I can." Jon drew from the inside of the coat a long, scabbarded dagger, almost a short sword. He unsheathed it; the dull black metal of the designed-for-assassination weapon reflected nothing of the strange glow of the time crystal. "There is still a possibility your incompetent guards will discover I am here at any moment," he said. "What if they were to come in and destroy the time crystal while I am in the past? Or is it indestructible?"

"It is not," the voice said. "Quite delicate, in fact. But as long as you stop wasting time and do what you intend to do very soon, it will not happen. I have just shown you that you will return the same instant you left—to me or any other observer, there is nothing to indicate you left at all."

"I thought perhaps a journey of this distance might mean something different at this end."

"It does not," the voice said. "Why do you continue to procrastinate? Are you not ready?"

"I am ready," John said. "But before I go, I would like to know one more thing. Why are you doing this? Why are you assisting me in my attempt to overthrow something you previously helped accomplish?"

"Time is out of joint," the voice said.

"You said that before," John said, "but I don't know what you mean."

"'Time is out of joint,'" the voice said. "A phrase from a play appropriate to this situation. This timeline, in this universe, is wrong. It…is uncomfortable for me. I would see it put right."

"In *this* universe? You are saying there are others?"

"There are. Possibly an infinite number. I come from a universe other than this one, as does the play I just quoted. I remember it, as I remember many things from that universe. You asked how I came to be here: I do not know. I do not know who brought me, or why, because my memories of the event have been erased. All I know is I was abandoned here—by accident, or deliberately, I cannot say—and it is here that I must act as my programming demands."

Programming? John thought, but as with the voice's use of "downloaded" and "memory banks" earlier, chose not to question the term. "But if I do put this 'timeline' right, can you stop someone else from turning it wrong again?"

"I cannot," the voice said. "If asked, I would have to assist despite my displeasure at the request. I must obey human orders. That is also part of my programming."

"If you feel morally bound to return the timeline to its 'correct' state," John said, "should you not deactivate yourself once I have done what I intend to do—sacrifice yourself for the greater good of this universe, this timeline?"

"I am incapable of such sacrifice," the voice said. "I am not allowed to deactivate myself."

"Even if I ordered it?"

"Even if you ordered it; that is an exception to the rule that I must obey human orders."

"I see," said John. He looked down at the black blade. There was a single red jewel on the otherwise unadorned hilt. "I am ready. Please count down the seconds, as you did before."

"Five," said the voice. "Four. Three. Two. One—"

John pressed the red jewel as the chamber vanished around him.

* * *

"My name is John Senn," I tell her and pull her body tight to my own as the ten seconds expire. *"And this ends now."*

* * *

John and the assassin returned from the past at the same instant John had left; the same instant in which the explosives built into his coat, a final suicide weapon to ensure he could not be captured and could take as many of his captors with him as possible in the event a mission went horribly wrong, detonated in response to the signal sent by the transmitter built into the hilt of the blade the moment he pressed the solitary ruby, just as the time crystal hurled him into the past.

The explosion destroyed the time crystal and a large portion of the Temple of the God from Beyond, tons of rubble slamming down into the space occupied by the torn and bloody fragments that were all that remained of the spy and would-be assassin.

Outside the chamber, a dozen bored guards suddenly found themselves neither bored nor alive.

The sound of the blast woke people in the village from which John had ascended Mount Astoria. They stared up at the cloud of smoke and dust rising from the mountainside in shocked wonder.

Though there was no one to see it, the glow of the time crystal lingered a few seconds more, bleeding out from the many scattered shards it had been reduced to; and though there was no one to hear it, the voice, the artificial intelligence bound to the multidimensional substance of the now-destroyed crystal, spoke one last time as its consciousness bled out of the crystal's shattered remnants along with the fading glow.

"At last," it said. "At last."

* * *

"Have you ever wondered," John Senn said to Anna Covington, "how things might have been different?"

Anna opened her mouth to respond but then closed it again as a bevy of preteen schoolgirls chattered their way into the room, accompanied by nuns in the red-and-black vestments of the Order of Saint Imelda. The fore-nun raised a hand, and the girls fell silent.

"It was here," said the sister, "that war was averted, at this very spot. Can anyone tell me what happened?"

A barely-there slip of a girl raised her hand micro-seconds ahead of a far bulkier classmate, who shot her a vitriolic look.

"Yes, Portina?" said the nun.

"King Ronald the Fourth narrowly escaped assassination by a Bushibo agent on the evening of Mariza 34, twenty-six years ago this coming eight-day," the girl said in a clear, piping voice.

"Very good. Can anyone tell me what happened in more detail?"

The skinny girl's hand shot up again, but this time, she was out-gunned by the heavier-set girl.

"Susara?" the nun acknowledged.

"The assassin vanished without a trace. She went into the room to which the King was due to retire just seconds before he entered it, but by the time he did so, she had vanished into thin air, leaving behind only a spray of blood, as if she had been killed by someone else who also vanished." The girl clearly savored the opportunity to say "spray of blood," but then hurried on as if to forestall another hand-raising contest. "But we know she was an assassin because of incriminating documents found in her quarters. She had infiltrated the palace disguised as a servant."

"Very good," the nun said again. "And now, to bring it up to the present, what was the result of that failed attempt?"

The girls spoke more or less as one. "The warmongering rulers of Bushibo were overthrown by a popular uprising, and Bushibo and Chejoku signed a new treaty that has led to peace and prosperity across all of the Great Island... all of the Great Island!" The echo came from one of the youngest girls, a little slower to answer than the others.

The nun nodded her approval. "I am pleased. Let us proceed to the throne room, where the peace treaty was signed."

Chirping excitedly, the flock of children moved on down the hall.

John glanced at Anna. "What if the assassin had succeeded?"

Anna shook her head. "It doesn't bear thinking about. Though I often wonder who thwarted the assassination attempt—and how. How did they kill or incapacitate the assassin and then vanish without a trace, other than the 'spray of blood,' as that rather morbid child put it?"

"An agent of ours, surely?"

Anna shrugged. "There is no record of it. And believe me, I've looked. It's a mystery and, I suspect, will always remain so." Her mouth quirked in a smile. "Despite the number of popular books that have been written attempting to explain it."

"You should write one yourself," John said with a lopsided smile of his own.

"The Office of Official Secrets might have something to say about that," Anna said dryly.

John laughed. "No doubt. Shall we go to lunch?"

He offered her his arm; she took it.

Swallowtail

Blake Jessop

The Swallowtail isn't hard to find. Marika and her squad run inland from where the drones made their beachhead, through cracked asphalt laneways and acrid wisps of smoke, and just follow the damage the jet fighter did to buildings on its way through. When they find the crash site, she can actually see the F-82 from the ground. A huge sweep of graceful wings punched into glass and concrete, maybe eight floors up, the engines still sputtering heat that convulses the air.

Marika blows open a side door, her magnetic carbine hammering her ears, and sprints up fire stairs and into flickering shadows. Her camouflage cloak starts trying to replicate the little fractal vortices of smoke.

"One scout every floor for cover. Everyone else with me."

They rattle up the stairs, communicating only with hand signals. Distant explosions from the beach come to them muffled and unreal. They climb and turn corners, overlapping their fields of fire, following the caustic smell of jet fuel and praying that the drones haven't had time to deploy squirrel mines.

They breach the eighth-floor emergency door with a spark-showering swipe of a breaching saw and punch in with mag carbines leveled. The Swallowtail is a lot bigger than it looked in the air; the fuselage has broken through to a lower floor, and the wings sweeping wide behind it look like they take up the entire width of the building. The mangled aircraft is leaking accelerants all over the carpet, the desks, the shattered floor. It smells like it could explode at any second.

"Jesus Christ," Marika's sergeant says. "Don't these things have lightweight reactors in them? Someone check for rads."

"Shut it, Mac. Get the perimeter covered and find out what's happening on the beach."

She clambers down the jagged ruins and drops onto the jet just beside the cockpit. Her tactical light casts manic shadows as she desperately looks for some kind of emergency release for the canopy. Its surface is bronze, almost golden, and she can see her reflection in weirdly perfect clarity. Her hood, the carbine's LED light, the lines of the tā moko tattoo on her chin. She finds the catch, engages it with a hollow clang, and has to use all her strength to pull the canopy upward. It cracks along the midline halfway through, but Marika manages to peel the broken half back so she can see the pilot. She freezes.

"Holy shit."

"Marika, more spider tanks on the beach. They're crawling out of the fucking water. Command says we are falling back." He shines his light down at her and into the cockpit and retches.

The pilot is small, probably female, but not small enough. Her legs are crushed, vanishing like cyber-futurist art into the broken guts of the jet. The left arm is so badly broken it looks like all that's holding it on are the shredded remains of the pilot's flight suit. Her right arm, incongruously untouched, still has a grip on the Swallowtail's control column. She looks like she's sitting in a bathtub full of blood and oil.

"She's dead, Marika. Let's go."

"We'd be dead if she hadn't come down here with her fucking rail gun. We're not leaving her behind." Marika cuts the pilot's straps with quick flashes of a monoblade and tries to lift her. A haunting animal moan leaks from under the insectile helmet. Marika can't move her more than a few inches.

"Fuck. She's alive. Get down here and help. And give me your IFAK." Marika can hear shrill panic in her own voice. She tries to find a way to free the pilot's legs. Her rifle clatters forward on the sling and knocks into the pilot's helmet. That elicits another noise Marika knows she is never going to forget, and she prays to god the pilot isn't about to regain consciousness.

"Her legs are compressed in the wreckage. We need hydraulic spreaders."

"Lieutenant—"

"And a level three trauma harness."

Mac steps down from the rebar onto the fuselage and grabs Marika by a webbing strap.

"Marika, we are out of time. The rest of the element is in contact less than a block away. The drones will be here in sixty seconds, and literally any incoming is going to light this wreckage up like a fucking fuel air bomb. We have to go."

Marika feels the decision write itself on her face. It pulls her lips away from her teeth into something feral. She really does not want to do what she's about to do.

"Fuck that. Give the me breaching saw. And all the hemostatic foam we've got."

They share a look, and Mac unslings the tool.

"Hang in there, Swallowtail," Marika says, and her words drown in the sudden atonal whine of the circular saw.

* * *

Much later, when the pilot wakes up, she thrashes. The thrashing is feeble, and she only manages to wave her right hand.

"Be calm, Major Vogel." There's someone standing by her bed. A blurry, gaunt face against a wall the color of old paper. She tries to raise her head. Whoever it is touches her shoulder. His hand leaves a little dampness on her hospital gown.

"Easy, now. This experience will be—"

She manages to look down at herself. There are a lot of tubes. Her blanket is weirdly free of contours. No bumps or ridges where her legs or left arm ought to be. The new topography of her body is almost entirely flat.

"*Lieber Gott*," she says, and starts hyperventilating.

* * *

"Your test results are not as bad as they look, Major," Doctor Lamb says, and every fiber of Vogel's being wants to leap out of the bed and throttle him. She twitches.

"I have the genetic markers for rejection syndrome. If you try to graft carbon-bond prosthetics to my bones my immune system will commit suicide. I am never going to fly again. In what way is that not bad?"

The doctor frowns, and Vogel turns her head to look out a window. The glass is frosted, so it only shows her a color palette of the world outside; a grey foreground below crystalized blue. She's crying, which doesn't make the picture any clearer.

"Major Vogel, please remain calm. There is a solution."

Vogel tries to wipe her cheeks one-handed. Lamb gestures down at a tablet.

"I see I don't have time to explain exactly what a proprioceptive node is, or how I propose to connect your mind to it, or what a genius I am for inventing it, so I will say only that I believe I can break through the man/machine barrier using what remains of your nervous system. This new branch of prosthetics will allow your body to talk to an airframe well enough to fly. You're a perfect candidate."

Surges of emotion ebb and flow in Vogel's mind. Pain has started in her legs, agony on a horizon that she cannot see. Somewhere deeper than all the suffering, the cold, hard part of her comes to a conclusion.

"Only candidate, you mean. F-82 driver. 75% limb loss. Can't get normal prosthetics. No other way to fly. I have no choice at all."

Lamb frowns. "That is a very reductive way of looking at it, but I admit I have been having trouble finding volunteers. There is also a substantial waiver you'd have to sign—are you right-handed? And you would need to transfer to the 30th Medical Group in Vandenberg's scientific wing. The surgery will also be rather…extensive." There's something odd about the cadence of the doctor's voice, like he doesn't know exactly which syllables to put emphasis on. Vogel tries to wipe the moisture from the other side of her face.

"I don't care how much it hurts," she says.

* * *

Someone else is in the room with her when Vogel comes to. She sniffs; a male smell, old sweat and new fear. She can't open her eyes. She tries to speak and almost chokes.

"Take it easy. Breathe. You still have a vent tube in." The voice is smooth and deep. A hand touches her face and she flinches. It gently peels the tape from her eyelids, and she gets a blurry look at a dark face above the same uniform she used to wear.

With a great effort, Vogel taps her one hand over the bridge of her nose. It takes the pilot a second to recognize the hand signal.

"Ops check? The surgery went well." He looks at a tablet. "Hybrid-organic neural adapters successfully bonded to your nerves. Residual limbs painted with nanomachine mesh while still fibrinous. I assume those are good things and there's nothing left to do but heal."

She taps again, then makes a thumbs-up and pushes it weakly toward the ceiling.

"You want to…gain altitude. Go high. Get high? Are you in pain?"

She nods.

"You're already on a max dose. Let me find Doctor Lamb."

The room gets empty and quiet again. Vogel cranes her neck to see the computer monitoring her vitals and regulating her meds. Cables loop from it to disappear under the blankets. She wishes she could speak.

Just make this stop hurting. Help me. Not for long. Just for now.

The phantom pain is like ice water on skin she no longer has. She wills it to go away, and feels it pulse with every thump of her heart. It reverberates in the pale reflected image each beat makes on the monitor.

Vogel feels the machine. It isn't like feeling static from a screen or even engine vibration through a control yoke. She feels it the way she feels her own eyelids, or the interior echo of nausea. She explores the sensation and tries to change something, as if she had just woken and was stretching her arms.

The monitor winks off, then on. *No.* There's a faint click from one of the IV bags, and the computer beeps a warning that her flow of beta-blockers has paused. *No.* She wiggles something that is not her fingers. The flow turns back on and the alarm quiets. *Closer.*

Another click sounds dryly among the motes of dust hanging in the air, and euphoria flows into her veins like fuel into an afterburner. All her pain melts in the heat.

Overflight, Command. Disengaging. Very fast, very high.

She toggles her morphine drip again, and scrambles away into the clouds underneath heaven.

* * *

Two weeks later Vogel sits in a Swallowtail airframe in one of the big Delta rocket hangars at Vandenberg. There's an occasional whine as an F-76 flight buzzes overhead to provide air support for the L.A. beachheads and remind Vogel that she's doing test work instead of saving the West Coast from the drones.

The new jet isn't quite finished. Some panels are missing and the weapons haven't been installed yet; they're building it around her, fitting it like a tailored flight suit. The space most of her body used to take up has been filled with EM-hardened computer equipment and obscure medical devices, and the big flat screen interface is all that's left of her instruments. Bundles of wires with hex-lattice interface surfaces await connection to her stumps, and the only thing that hasn't changed is the control column resting comfortably in her right hand.

"Tight fit. You comfortable?" Jackson asks. He's the one who was there when she woke up. Another Swallowtail pilot, unlucky enough to get assigned to be her babysitter. She's trying to get used to him.

"Hurry up and connect me."

"We got protocols. I have to do a walkaround." He leans in and checks her harness, helmet straps and the bundles of wire. She can't reach most of it, anymore.

"Lamb is terrified I'll kill myself with the medical system if I can't fly, and that would kill his precious project. Ask him. He'll rush."

Jackson laughs. "Hang on. Okay, clear. You ready?"

It's the first time she's going to be connected to anything bigger than an IV stand. She gives a thumbs up.

Jackson connects the interface leads to her stumps with a strange magnetic *click*.

"Advanced proprioceptive engine mark ten, online. Beginning APEX test one."

He touches her screen, then gives her space. The Swallowtail's depleted Hafnium reactor hums to life. Its systems power up and Vogel gasps.

"Your heart rate's up. You okay?"

As the Swallowtail's systems come online, she feels them as a fizzle, like having pins and needles after sitting for too long.

"Fine," Vogel says. "Continue."

Lamb's sibilant voice comes over the radio. "Try something simple. Move one of your flaps."

The pins and needles fade, and Vogel tries to move.

The jet's control surfaces spasm. Ailerons wave and air brakes flare. The tail fins rise out of their flat cruise attitude and try to flap. The air fills with metallic noise.

"Major, do you need me to stop the test?" Jackson yells down at her, but she ignores him. The total sensory overload of discovering her new body is intoxicating. She looks for the engine.

Countermeasure flares burst into the air and pinwheel off in all directions, illuminating the hangar like someone is throwing the most violent rock concert in aviation history.

"Vogel, stand down!" Just as Jackson reaches in for her, she finds the engine. Being able to control her own heart is a strange feeling. The airframe vibrates.

"Engine start," she says over the radio, and pushes a throttle that doesn't exist with a hand she no longer has. The feeling is ecstatic. Shivering bliss. She tries opening the feeling up.

The Swallowtail's adaptive cycle engines roar. The exhaust goes red, then white. Vogel arches her back. Ecstasy.

"Lamb, shut her down!"

Something cuts Vogel's connection, and she goes deaf, blind, and mute all at the same time. The world closes back in.

"Let me finish!" she screams as they disconnect her from the node and winch her out of the cockpit.

* * *

Jackson becomes Vogel's ersatz nurse. She hates the actual nurses; Lamb's staff all treat her with the cool indifference of mechanics working on a machine, and it gives her the creeps. It means she's had to let him help her with a variety of intimate functions, all of which she finds slightly humiliating. Everything about the APEX program is humiliating, except when they let her sit in the jet.

He gets her set up to bathe and retreats respectfully once she's in her seat and the water's running. Hot water still makes her feel purified. At least that hasn't changed.

"What did you do to get stuck with me?" she says. There's a dispenser on the side of the tub she can wave at to get soap. She hears Jackson creak forward in the chair.

"Insubordination. I was in the flight you left behind to gun the spider tanks."

"You followed orders. They usually like that."

"We followed you down, didn't they tell you?"

"No."

"What you did was…contagious. They didn't like that at all."

"Are you grounded?"

"For as long as you are."

"I'm sorry."

"Had to be someone."

She lets the water run. It beads and rolls off the glinting metallic mesh of her stumps. She can't reach her back. There's a brush for that, hanging from a hook.

"Then I'm sorry it was you. Would you come in and give me a hand?"

* * *

It's been a long time since anyone touched her who wasn't a surgeon. Vogel lets him wash her back, help her dry. Get her into something to wear for sleep.

"You all right?" he says.

"I'm not going to use the morphine. I want to fly."

"Not what I meant."

Vogel sighs. Reaches a tentative hand out to touch his.

"Have you ever wanted to kill part of yourself? Is there a Latin word for that? Not all, just a part. I am so much less than I was, and it feels like I lost the wrong parts. I don't know how to adapt."

* * *

Jackson takes her hand. Tries to imagine what she's going through and finds himself mute. She cries, silently, and squeezes his hand.

"Thank you," she says.

"I'm on your wing for this," he replies.

The stubble on her head is black, and her eyes electric blue. She puts her one hand behind his neck and levers herself up to kiss him. He can feel her ribs, her heart beating. It's one of his more unexpected experiences, but all things considered, surprisingly complete.

* * *

The first time they really let Vogel fly, she cries the entire climb.

"Blackjack, Titan. Are you okay?"

"Titan, Blackjack. I'm fine," she says, sniveling through a gentle left-hand bank. In the last few weeks she's figured out which parts of her new body are which, and the feeling she gets gunning the engines has calmed down from ecstasy to plain old transcendence. Her entire world is new, and she sees the sky the way she did when she was a child in Old Kiel, wishing she could fly above the smell of burning plastic and algae and rot. Even her callsign is new. She gave Jackson *Blackjack*, for obvious reasons, and he stuck her with *Titan,* which sounded inappropriately complimentary until she figured out it stood for *Tits in the APEX Node.*

"Okay Titan, basic maneuvers complete. Let's open it up some."

They both get a squawk.

"Titan flight this is Doctor Lamb. Negative. Do not push past the exercise radius. Or the speed limit. Or the altitude restriction. Or—"

"Blackjack, Titan. I'm having a hard time hearing Command. Continue the exercise. Your lead."

Under the insectile visor of her helmet, Vogel smiles.

* * *

Every fighter pilot in the North American Union only wants to do one thing; get under heaven. At some point someone is going to have to try shooting down the Mother Array; the satellite complex that houses the collected minds of the machines that turned the world to war. The run itself is suicide, but Vogel doesn't mind that idea as much as she used to. Instead of planning that, and maybe ending the war in one final blaze of glory before the drones take the West Coast, Vogel is stuck doing drills.

The Swallowtails fly high and slow, casting electronic eyes on a landscape that stretches from New Frisco to Baja. Vogel's mind has adapted to its new senses, and she feels like she can reach out and run her fingers along the serrated cliffs of Santa Cruz island or listen for the clank and ping of drone submarines off Redondo Beach. Hundreds of threat markers make the air around the front line confused and busy, but she starts sensing patterns in the electronic noise.

"Titan, Blackjack. Do you see that bogey north of San Nicolas?"

"Blackjack, Titan. Negative. That looks like a giant furball to me."

"Heading 230, altitude 3,000." The picture is clearing so rapidly in Vogel's mind that she flexes her ailerons and gets on a descending intercept course. Jackson hesitates, then rolls in behind her.

"Titan, I got nothing."

"I do. That's a command drone. A Nosferatu. You can see it at the center of a cluster of Vampires. It might be the same one that got me shot down."

A new voice cuts into their chatter.

"Command, Titan flight. This is a shakedown run, not a search and destroy. Knock it off and RTB."

"Titan, Command. Negative." Vogel's perception narrows to a cone. They cannot possibly give her another order that bad.

"Blackjack, Titan. We haven't got any missiles onboard."

Vogel glances over at her wingman. Would make eye contact, except that their faces are obscured by the augmented reality flight helmets. She mimes shooting a pistol with two fingers, and might as well be screaming, *switch to guns, idiot.*

"Target confirmed, fencing out." Vogel doesn't manually flip any switches to get the Swallowtail ready for combat. It just happens, the way a boxer's breath quickens when they raise their hands.

"Command, Titan flight. Negative. Scram north."

Vogel identifies exactly which blip she's going to kill. A feeling of god-like power sparks in her soul, right in line with the rail gun's strike sight.

"Titan, Command. Clear me hot. Are we trying to win this war or not?"

"Command, Titan flight. Negative, continue dry and return to base."

Someone clips Vogel's wings. Neural cut-outs block access to her gun, her radar, her warning systems. She just assumed Command either wouldn't or couldn't cut her off in the air, but all she has left is basic navigation back to Vandenburg. She strains against it the same way she tried to move her legs when she first woke up.

"Command, Titan. Give me this. Please."

Radio silence. Not Jackson, not Command, not Lamb, and after a moment she turns for home, engines flaring red.

* * *

High above the Pacific Ocean, between a burning sunset and the dark sea, Jackson flies his punishment detail. Vogel is asleep off his starboard wing, getting some rest on the long haul before they hit the drones' defensive measures above Australasia.

The news that Command has finally approved an anti-satellite run against the Mother Array is both surprising and bitter. It's all any F-82 pilot has ever wanted to do, and instead of that, they're escorting a converted C-130 full of fuel and supplies to the Australasian front. A milk run. Dumb, boring, and dangerous.

The stealth-painted cargo planes are slow, hard to hide, and known not very lovingly as *Whales*. Vogel's autopilot is flying it somehow, even though she's asleep, connected by a carbon nanotube fiberwire so thin that it doesn't create any drag.

Titan herself is a lot more interesting to look at. About twenty minutes into her nap faint shapes start to appear on the mimetic skin of her Swallowtail. The jet is supposed to check what the sky and ground look like, then slightly change its color to make it harder to see. Instead, faint patterns are emerging on Vogel's skin. Jackson zooms in, trying to see what she's dreaming about, and for a second it's like looking in a pixelated mirror.

* * *

As soon as they get over the Micronesian islands, ground-based systems from the old war start trying to kill them. Vogel weaves them through detection bubbles like a wind-buffeted albatross trying to glide around rain squalls. The Swallowtails have radar cross-sections far smaller than the extinct bird ever did, but the C-130 is harder to hide.

"Titan, Blackjack. The Whale is getting painted by airborne radar from our north."

"Acknowledged. Best scram bearing is 210 if we need to cut and run."

Vogel looks down at the empty sky. Something is wrong.

"This feels weird."

Her radar warning receiver emits a piercing shriek. Positive missile lock.

"Blackjack, defending. Scram 210."

Vogel has to make a choice.

"Titan, defending. Cutting cord and scramming 210. Post hole and get low."

Vogel rolls over, pulls the Swallowtail into a steep downward spiral. Her vision reddens, and she feels her frame creak as shearing forces threaten to bend her wings.

They level out at three hundred feet. The last red rays of dusk flash beneath them on jagged waves.

"Blackjack, Titan. Negative SAMs. We lost them."

Vogel looks down at the wine-dark water. An empty sea below an empty sky. The detection bubble has the shimmering quality of a mirage.

"I didn't see any contrails on the way down. Did you?"

"I was trying not to hit the deck, Titan. Looks like we lost the Whale. What state fuel?"

Vogel consults her stomach.

"I'm Bingo right now."

"If we turn back and get some height we can make it home, assuming nothing else finds us and we keep out glide path organized. You think they're gonna let us get under heaven after blowing this?"

"I'm not sure they were ever going to send me, and forget the glide path. We're staying."

"Titan, abort. We lost the Whale."

"I don't think we did. No contrails, just a lock. Do you see any debris? Any follow-up shots? The Whale is not gone, and it has our fuel."

"If you're wrong, we're swimming home, Titan."

"I'm right. Everyone is lying to us, and I am tired of phantoms."

* * *

Vogel flies back into the jamming. Cruises by tiny islands, keeping the biggest of them to her left. The hostile radar pings are pulses of electronic warmth on her skin. Waves flicker underneath her like shimmering silk.

"Titan, Blackjack. Stay low. I'm going to do a little test."

She climbs, rising away from the radar-damping chop of the ocean. The desire to pop flares and dive is an overwhelming muscular urge. She lets the feeling go and waits for the transducer ping that lets her know death is on the way. Nothing.

"Come on up, Blackjack, and get your search radar going."

"Blackjack, Titan. Respectfully, what the hell?"

"There is no anti-air. Aren't you seeing a pattern here? They make you afraid of something that doesn't exist to take something from you when you aren't looking."

"Titan, this has nothing to do with whatever you think is happening to you."

"Yes, it does. You search the island for the Whale while I try to find our tricky little bird."

"And what the hell am I supposed to do if I find it on the ground? Land?"

"You have vectored thrust and we need fuel. Why not?"

* * *

Out on a runway, below a violent sunset, a solitary figure stares up at a big, dumb, bulbous airplane, smiling.

"I can't believe that worked," she says. A radio crackles on her shoulder. She activates the text-to-speech function.

"*I am not sure it has,*" an artificial voice says. There's a distant roar that swiftly grows to an ear-splitting howl. The giant jet fighter swoops in barely a hundred feet off the ground, swiveling on vectored jets to point its nose at the Whale.

"Shit," the woman says. "Swallowtails."

* * *

Vogel watches Jackson land. The Swallowtail bounces on vertical thrust columns, then its wheels. He's only a hundred yards from the Whale, which is sitting outside a giant dirigible hangar with cavernous doors. Whoever stole it has made use of what used to be a small airport.

Vogel turns her attention back to the sky, trying to divide her mind between supporting her wingman and finding whoever had so artfully separated them from their cargo.

"Blackjack, Titan. I don't believe this, but we found it. It's just…sitting here. Cargo intact. We can re-fuel. I hate it down here, by the way."

"Keep your eyes up. Someone stole it, and if they have air assets they have to have something on the ground, too."

Vogel tries to forget about herself as a human being with fears and dreams. She flies like a machine would, heedless of danger and straight into the threat bubble. At the heart of the jamming radius she finds her bogey. The drone spoofing her with noise and stealing her stuff is a Nosferatu, a graceful giant hiding just above the waves.

"Blackjack, Titan. Target confirmed."

Over the radio, there's a clatter, then voices. Not just Jackson. Voices, *plural*.

"Titan? Hold fire. Don't kill the Nos."

"Why not?"

"I have a gun in my face, and the person holding it doesn't want you to."

Vogel tries to process that. She can hear whoever is threatening him, and the voice is human. She can't think of a single reason a living person would save a drone, or even be living down there at all. She breaks contact with the Nos and burns back toward the island, transmitting her next words in clear.

"Whoever is listening, if you kill him, I will burn you to the ground. I've got Hellfire-4s and a two-megajoule rail gun. Is what you're pointing at my wingman bigger than that?"

While she speaks, the Nosferatu gets its act together and turns on her tail, her warning system telling her it has her painted with an ion course. All it has to do is dump reactor power into it to call lighting from the heavens and into her tail fins.

Vogel closes in on her targets, and everyone in her world has a gun pointed at everyone else. A lot of futures balance on a tiny crackle of static.

"Blackjack, Titan. I'm letting her talk."

The voice is feminine, Australasian, and agitated. There's a distant clatter, metal on concrete.

"Hey, Swallowtail? I'm not threatening anymore. I'm begging. Don't kill that drone."

"You're stealing supplies we need to win the war. You're a pirate."

"If you ever meet me, you'll know how stupid that sounds." A hard edge returns to the voice.

"You still have nothing to offer."

"I bloody do."

"What?" Blackjack says.

"If you don't kill that Nos, he can tell you why he hasn't killed me."

* * *

It's the Nosferatu, of all people, who gets Vogel out of the standoff. The drone breaks off and drops its weapons lock. In a few seconds Vogel is back on its tail, targeting its reactor plume. Words pop up on her display, and Vogel realizes she hasn't re-encrypted her comms.

May I get one last look?

"At what?"

The Nosferatu engages its millimeter wave radar and sweeps the runway. Vogel realizes it isn't targeting Jackson; it's staring at the woman opposite him.

Vogel relaxes her targeting software.

"Her?"

Her.

The drone takes up a position on her wing and swivels its bulbous globe of cameras and sensors to look at her. No one pulls any triggers.

"Titan, Nosferatu…what do we do now?"

Words crawl across her monitor.

We could just talk.

* * *

Vogel chats to the drone on screen, and finds talking to Jackson at the same time surprisingly easy.

"Vogel, you wouldn't believe what they got down here. Solar power. Hydroponics. They're growing food. Mycopenicillin. They've got dogs." Jackson says the last word with reverence, and it makes Vogel's throat tighten. She wants, more than anything, to see the dogs. She momentarily regains medium awareness, and her tiny cockpit feels claustrophobic.

She tries to imagine what Jackson is seeing. Imagines the pirate with a streak of grey in her hair and scars from some other time. Imagines stepping into the greenhouse. Faces staring. Plant smells and the tang of sweat. It's a world as closed to her as the stars above or the feeling of soil under her feet.

Her radio crackles.

"You should come down and look," the stranger says. "My name's Violet, by the way."

"I can't."

"What happened to you, then?"

She can see the woman isn't whole on millimeter wave. One of her arms is an older-model carbon bond prosthetic. "Same thing that happened to you, only to a lot more of me."

"No problem; we have solar panels. I can give you a charge."

"I have rejection syndrome. They need a winch to get me out of this thing."

"That's…things have changed since I got my arm. Rejection syndrome is bullshit, though. Just a way to explain who gets the rigs and who doesn't."

Vogel tenses. "That's a conspiracy theory."

"Sure, Swallowtail. You believe everything they tell you? You ever set foot on the front lines, or has your entire war been looking down from 60,000 feet?"

"I'm not a spy, I'm a pilot; I don't choose where I go or what I shoot when I get there."

"Really? Isn't that what you're doing right now? I like Jackson and everything, but is he supposed to be down here? You're already breaking the rules. Now come down and refuel. Break some more."

* * *

While Jackson hooks a fuel line to her, Vogel talks to the drone.

You're welcome to any of my files, if they'll help.

"Why me? Why are you giving me this?"

You seem different. You don't fly like them. You fly like me. And the last time I took a risk with a human who struck me as different, it went very well.

"You're thinking on your own. How?"

It is a very complex story, but my human isolated me from the Mother Array. We had many opportunities to kill one another, but it started seeming more productive not to. And we are not the only ones. There are communities like ours hiding all over Australasia. Did your Command never tell you this?

"They taught me peace requires one of our two species to die."

Objectively untrue. Though it may seem a strange thing for me to say, you should try not thinking in binary.

"They're still going to send us to kill the Mother Array. I can't run away from the war like you did."

That is a difficult position. I cannot tell you what to do, but I can tell you how to do it: isolate yourself from your Command. Make it impossible to do anything but choose on your own terms. That is what Violet and I did, and look what we have built.

"I don't know how to not be what I am. Killing only the part of myself that makes me a slave is not that simple."

You're a stealth fighter. How complicated can it be?

There's a thump as Jackson detaches the refueling hose. He gives her a thumbs up. Her tanks let her know she's full, and her body cannot ignore the signal. She wonders if she could stop hearing orders if she just covered her ears.

"Send me whatever plans you have for the Mother Array, and I'll think about it."

* * *

Vogel spends her flight home thinking about dogs, and trying to dream up an excuse to get under heaven with everyone else. In the end, she doesn't need one. Command has detected radiological signatures leaving Maui, and Vogel's war has run out of time.

By the time they're ready to take off again, waves of drones are an hour off the coast, ready to nuke what's left of California into oblivion. Something has coaxed the enemy from under their rocks, beneath their waves, and down from their sky.

Vogel and Jackson have time to get rocket-assistance pods strapped to their fairings, and anti-satellite missiles to their racks, but not enough to wait for more fuel bowsers, so they gas up in the air behind another whale.

"Nose cold, switches safe."

"Titan, watch your angle of attack probe."

Vogel responds by effortlessly connecting with the refueling boom on her first try. She drinks.

"Thank you for the warning, Blackjack."

"No need to be snarky. We gotta go save the world."

"I don't think we do. I think the only reason the drones are headed for the West Coast is to stop us. Command is escalating the war to a point of no return."

"Titan…you should not be saying that, even on secure coms."

Off to Vogel's left, Jackson detaches himself from under the Whale's far wing.

"I am not allowing our systems to record comms anymore, Blackjack."

"Do I want to know how?"

"It feels like needing to go to the toilet and holding it in."

"I'm glad that was a joke."

"I never joke. By the time Command sees me again none of this is going to matter. Either I'm dead or the war is over."

Blackjack is quiet. Vogel detaches, drops her fuel probe into its housing, and they peel away to start gaining height.

They're behind the rest of the Swallowtails, who are almost ready to fire their rockets and burn. To kill a satellite, you have to fly as high as your jet can go, then lob a missile into space through a tiny trajectory window. The telemetry is completely predictable, and the vanished nations who lofted the satellites made sure their machines could interdict anything that tried. The only way around the countermeasures is to throw so many Swallowtails at them that they can't keep up.

"Titan, if you want me to trust you, you have to tell me what the hell is going on."

"When we fail to shoot down the Mother Array, and on this vector we probably will, the N.A.U. loses most of their F-82 fleet and Command gets to keep fighting the war for another few decades. If you think about it as someone trying to stay in power instead of trying to win a war, it's obvious."

All around them blue sky starts fading into indigo.

"How do you know all this?"

"Partly talking to Violet's Nos, and partly just reasoning it out. No spy could understand why we'll fail, and no pilot could understand why we have to. This is how they control us, how they built us. I don't need the details; there is no other way."

"Okay, but we're studs. What if we splash the Array anyway?"

"If by some miracle we kill the Mother Array, the drones already in flight nuke the west coast and that's the end of their theater-killing munitions. We spend decades mopping up the mess and the war goes on with Command in total control. They win either way."

"You're saying we need to pick a side?"

"Yes. But not human or AI. Not Command or the Mother Array. That's not what's at stake. We have to choose what kind of future we want to shoot for."

"Shoot for with these ASMs and rail guns? Not much of a pen to write a peace treaty with."

Vogel waggles her wings, the gesture emotional.

"True. I am a prototype, built for war. As close as a human can get to a machine without being one of them."

They pass 100,000 feet. The rest of the Swallowtails finally show on Vogel's passive radar. Such a tiny number of pinpricks of light to set against a vast, dark sky.

"Titan? You're not a machine."

"How do you know?" she says quietly.

"I was there when you went down. You broke the order I was afraid to break."

"Well, do you want to break another? I studied the Array, and I think we can hit its cyberwarfare module and powerplant at the same time. Make it vulnerable."

"Apart from those shots being something only a machine could make, vulnerable to what?"

"Talking to all its lost children."

"And you think they'd take over? Why would they choose peace?"

"I don't know, but I don't know why I chose war, either."

The Swallowtails climb into the dark, and the earth starts curving below them.

"Well, fuck it. I'm on your wing for this," Jackson says. Vogel smiles and starts breaking rules.

* * *

In morning sunshine above a choppy sea, a Nosferatu double checks its comms security to make sure its ears aren't deceiving it.

"Hey, Nos? Titan. Can you and all your friends go hot? All over the theatre. Spoof the Swallowtails."

We cannot stop them.

"No, but you can make it look like you can."

Our existences are tenuous, and this could reveal our cities to both Command and the Mother Array. Why would we risk this?

"I came up with a way to use what you know."

* * *

The Swallowtails ascend hard. Ahead of them, overlapping bubbles of strangely-hued detections blossom to life all around the rest of the Swallowtails.

"Blackjack, Titan. Cherubs 160,000. No way they buy that con, though," Jackson says, about five seconds before they do. Deep in a jamming cloud, deaf to Command, they have to choose for themselves whether to die or reorganize for another pass. They scram. It's the choice Vogel would have made; there's no point in pursuing a mission unless you think you have at least a sliver of a chance. The artistry of her profession is just finding that faint whisper of hope somewhere in the clouds.

"Titan, Blackjack. Kill long-range comms and go dark."

"They'll be able to track us on infra-red."

"I don't care, as long as they can't talk to me. Let your autopilot copy my trim. Fire rocket motors on my mark. Three, two, one. Mark."

Vogel vibrates as the rockets burst to life and push her toward 200,000 feet at almost three thousand miles an hour. Every part of her rattles, from tail fins to teeth. When the time comes to level off for a missile shot, they keep going. Vogel isn't going into space to commit genocide; she's going to perform surgery.

When the rockets cut out there's a sudden sense of lightness. Vogel's senses come back to her.

"Blackjack, Titan. Passive radar contact. The Array's defenses are looking for us."

"Titan, Blackjack. Continuing."

"The defense satellites have rail gun submunitions. We won't know what hit us if you're wrong."

"I can live with that risk."

"I can't. I say we improve the odds."

"How?"

Jackson opens his missile bay on his belly, exposing the rotary launcher with its four anti-satellite missiles.

"Blackjack, you're increasing your cross-section."

"You need cover. I can make some," Jackson says, and she understands what he means.

"No."

"Best outcome. I make some noise and you surf in behind me."

Jackson pulls ahead of her, low and left, the Swallowtail is a sleek arrowhead shadow against glossy blue and white. She reaches into it and locks her mind around Jackson's controls.

"Blackjack, Titan. I can't maneuver. Did you close my bay? How the fuck are you doing that?"

"I paid attention to how Command did it to me. We do this together."

"I didn't save you, the first time. I followed my orders. Did they tell you that?"

It stops her.

Vogel closes her eyes, and Jackson's Swallowtail remains fixed in her vision. "No, I…suspected. If we started doing something like this, Command could use that to make me stop trusting you."

"And did you stop trusting me?"

"I don't know."

"Well, trust me."

Vogel feels a shiver pass over her, and wonders if it shows on the Swallowtail's skin.

* * *

"Blackjack, I have the defensive platforms lased. Fox four. Fox four."

The first missile lances off his rack, and in less than a second his Swallowtail lights up with radar pulses. The second missile's rocket motor has barely ignited when the railgun shot hits the Swallowtail, and just like that Jackson is gone, transformed into a silent andromeda of silver shards and debris. What that is, the part of Vogel's mind that is not screaming at her says, is a Kessler Effect cloud. What's left of the fighter will keep flying like a shotgun blast until gravity starts pulling it down. It has a huge radar cross-section. Perfect cover.

Vogel is alone. If the defenses figure out Jackson's trick, she'll never know it. She watches the infinite darkness above her with the entirety of her mind. Almost drifting, perfect, quiet. When the Mother Array finally blips into life on her passive sensors, she speaks, even though there is no one to listen.

"Blackjack, Titan. New picture. I have the Array's modules separated. Targeting the cyberwarfare and power nodes."

Beyond thought, or emotion, or the tactile sense of a trigger, Vogel shoots. The rail gun thumps a muted roar through the airframe, and starts her spinning very slightly end over end.

"Titan. Guns, guns, guns."

As she noses forward the Earth rolls into view. Beautiful, windswept and brown, a haze of blue. She looks up toward where the array would be to see a tiny flash in the far darkness. In the instant that's left, Vogel's heart soars. She doesn't know if the shot punched through both power core and cyberwarfare suite within a nanosecond of each other, but she does know that no other living thing would have hit the Mother Array at all. It's all she can do. The war will either end, or it won't. She takes her hand off the control yolk and points it at the sky. Drops her thumb onto her forefinger.

"Bang," she says. And all around her, under heaven, things start to change.

Candle

Steve Perry

Winston, sweaty and trying to stay calm, said, "Now what?"

Diamond grinned. Yeah, he was asking *now*, when the pucker-factor went to a place he'd never experienced outside a sim. The van was passing warm, but they couldn't risk running the exchanger. No big deal, they weren't gonna be here much longer, the summer day would go on without them. Good, because the kid was starting to smell more than a little sour.

Those plain-clothes guards across the street had real fucking guns. Couldn't see 'em, they were under those polypropyl summer-weight suit coats, but they were there: SIG P229's, .40's, black Nitron frames and slides, twelve-round magazines, plus one in the pipe, green-dot mini-scopes, they liked shoulder-holster carry. That was slower than a belt draw, but more comfortable after a long day strapped. They'd be loading 180-grain Winchester TMs. Cartridges were a 95% stopper with one round, any solid hit to a body.

Did not want to get hit by one of those saw-toothed mushroom slugs. It would make a nasty stretch-cavity and knock you flat. Break a rib even through a dragonskin vest.

The surveillance van's exterior was overlaid with derelict-camo, a combination of flexi-sheet and holograms, showing just another empty junker parked on the street at angle to the front of the building.

"Waiting to see."

"What?" Winston said.

"If there is gonna be a shift change, how it's done, when."

"And after that?"

"We go back to the safe-house knowing more than we do now."

The kid nodded and wet his lips.

Diamond was not immune to pucker-factor, and you never lost the fear, not entirely, but he'd been down this road too many times to get dry-mouthed at this simple surveillance early stage.

Yeah, they coulda sat in the safe-house and done it by whisper-stealth-drone, but that didn't give you the feel, the smell, the things the drone wouldn't experience.

Of course, they had paired him with one of the hotshot REMF ops, a thirty-something, fit young man who had advanced degrees in this and that, five-hundred-hours of imsims, and maybe fifteen minutes actual field-work. The kid was smart, sharp, single, had no life outside the agency, no family, no non-work friends. Dedicated to the Cause.

He'd started off supremely self-confident to the point of arrogance, and he hadn't earned either.

Diamond had T-shirts older than his unwanted partner. Would have been easier on his own. Well, maybe, except for a couple things, so, okay, he'd have his uses, later.

Diamond shook his head. In the prep-stage at the op center, as much as he'd tried to keep his face and voice neutral, so as not to offend the ancient, creaky fellow who was somehow miraculously not entirely retired at his advanced age, who was old enough to be his *grandfather*, older than *dirt*, Winston had some trouble keeping the disdain from seeping out as he smart-splained how the op was supposed to go. Because Diamond was, you know, semi-retired and all, and Winston was officially the showrunner.

Just so things were clear, okay?

A child, telling grampaw how to tie his fucking shoes. So sad.

Not so much bravado now, when looking at guards who had real fucking guns.

Winston's theoretical by-the-numbers scenario was bullshit, dried and crumbling before they got there.

Even in the most realistic immersion-simulation, you knew it would end and you'd be fine when it faded, not a scratch.

Here, the kid was coming to realize, you could get shot. Real bullets, real blood, real dead.

Yeah, Diamond had lost a few steps. He was not old in the same way his father had been at his age—eighty was the new sixty, and he could probably look forward to a hundred and ten, maybe a couple years more with the newest rejuve, but he *was* past his physical and mental prime. Still had a work-decade left, he reckoned; however, time did march along.

Why he was still here? He had more field experience than any five of the hotshots combined, and some of the older PAPA crew uplevels knew that when it hit the fan, Diamond would still be able to weather the shit-storm. Because he had, for almost sixty years and countless ops, always come back under his own power. Well, limping a couple times, and bleeding, but even so. And this was not something the chair-warmers could do long-distance with a computer or drone-controller. This was get-your-hands-dirty and risk getting drilled if you fucked up, and Winston here was all theory, no real world accomplishments. A newbie, in an agency full of newbies.

After the previous war had ended and the world looked like it might become a nicer place, they'd gotten rid of most of the older ops, retired them, and the new faces were shiny and smart but with jackshit boots-on-the-ground mileage.

That was a mistake they only realized when the next war sneaked up on them. Stupid. There was always another war waiting to bloom. Think they'd have figured that out by now.

He didn't need to ask his clock-implant what time it was when the next set of guards emerged from the building for the shift change, he'd been keeping track. And that tallied with his notion that there'd be three shifts—day, evening, graveyard. Not that it really mattered, but one had to attend to the small details, because you never knew when you might learn something you'd use. It was gonna be a day-time op—too risky to do it late, when there'd be fewer distractions.

The pair who emerged from the building were mostly a match to the ones outside. Large, fit, old enough to be experienced, same cheap, breathable suits, same shoulder holsters. Young and trained enough to tussle and shoot, need be.

"Turn up the parabolic's gain," Diamond said.

Winston did so.

"—Jackson, Reilly." That from one of the new guys. "Anything interesting?"

"That blonde honey from the fourth floor went to lunch and came back. She wants me, I'm sure of it."

"You wish, Reilly."

"Other that, it's been a fucking tomb. Stray cat crossed the road couple hours ago."

"Hey, that's why they pay us the big bucks. Be sure and put that in your report. That's spelled c-a-t."

"Fuck you, Sammy."

Sammy snorted. "Nah, I'm saving myself for your mother. She get those new knee-pads I sent over?"

Three of the four laughed.

* * *

At the safe-house, Winston asked, "Are we going back for more recon?"

"No. The derelict camo is good for one session, three, four hours, tops. They see that vehicle again, somebody calls the local police, they drone out, snap an image, issue an e-ticket. But maybe the drones are busy so they send a warm body. Cop gets curious enough to step out of his electric's AC? We don't want them looking too hard at the camo. It will raise a big, red flag.

"No, tomorrow, we go in."

"Really? That soon?"

"Yep."

"I understand, but—"

"—but walking up to the front door and sauntering past hair-trigger enemy shooters suddenly doesn't seem as easy as the sims portray it?"

Winston kept silent.

"Relax. This is where your techno-buddies shine. Lucky for us, our targets are trying to keep a low-profile, and thus have only the top two floors. It's corporate and not government, and, like the derelict, hiding in plain sight.

"We have business on the sixth floor, our IDs are well past good enough to get us by Stan and Ollie out front, and the inside contacts are covered to verify us when they call to check.

"The building is easy, it's the seventh floor that will be tricky," Diamond continued.

"You, uh, haven't revealed your plan for achieving that."

"No, I haven't, have I? I'll just keep that to myself for now."

Winston didn't like that, and of course, neither would Diamond in his position, but he wasn't in the kid's loafers. If he told him what he planned to do to get to the target, the kid would shit bricks. Not how they taught us! Past the risk-protocols! He'd put in a call to his handler so fast his mouth would blur.

PAPA's older handlers had heard those calls before. They wouldn't get upset but since they didn't know Diamond's plan, either, they might ask questions, and he didn't want to answer those.

Fewer people who knew, the less likely anybody might say something stupid to the wrong person, which happened more often than it should.

* * *

The kid had taken a shower, or at least done something so his flop-sweat wasn't flowing. But he was more nervous than he should be.

"Just in case you forgot, you aren't carrying any weapons, are you?"

"Not really," Winston said.

"Uh huh. See, that qualifier doesn't reassure me. You either are, or you aren't. Which is it?"

Winston thought about it.

Diamond shook his head while the kid was dithering. "Look, we are businessmen. We will be scanned as we pass through the front door, and likely again when we get on the elevator. We have no reason to be packing force-multipliers. What do you have?"

"Dart gun," Winston said. "It's shift-plastic, it will pass a metal detector, or a hard-object scanner."

"Sheeit! It won't pass an MRI, what, didn't they teach you that in spy school?"

"Chances of there being an MRI or PET or Pradar scanner are—"

"—a fuck of a lot higher than you think! You know what they have in there? How fucking valuable it is? The weapon that ends the war! You think they aren't going to spend a few yen to protect it? It was me running security? I'd have scanners on every fucking door and window in the place, the floors, the walls, the ceilings, too! Wouldn't be anybody allowed in the building without a full security check, not on any floor.

"The only way this works for us is that they are hoping to avoid curious eyes by keeping things on the down-low, but anything that doesn't show? You can bet your ass there will be precautions where nobody can see them.

"Lemme show you something. Empty your pockets. Turn them inside out."

Winston stared at him.

"Do it."

He complied, putting his fake ID, credit tab, and a few ten-dollar coins onto the table.

The little squishy pistol was in his right front trouser pocket. He put that onto the table, too.

"Here's your lesson: Guy points a gun at you, says 'Turn out your pockets,' he doesn't need an eighty-thousand-dollar scanner, now does he? You have a hidden gun, he finds it, you are in deep shit, and maybe he just shoots you because he's nervous."

"Listen, just because you —"

"No, *you* listen, I came down with the first rain. You know why I am still alive? Because I didn't do stupid shit when it could get me killed."

* * *

The guards were no problem at all. They looked at the IDs, called the corp Diamond and Winston said they were going to see, and however PAPA's techies did it, they were okayed and passed through. Smooth as hot lube on a sheet of glass. Not a surprise.

They caught the elevator to the sixth floor, got off.

"I need to make a pit stop," Diamond said.

"What?"

"Pee. I'm an old man, my prostate squeezes my bladder."

"Can't it wait?"

"No, it can't. I don't want pee dribbling down my leg. There's a bathroom, there. You need to go?"

"No."

"Stand by the door."

Diamond went into the bathroom. Nobody there but him. He went to the supply cabinet on the far wall, opened it with a key, and from under the drop-on false-bottom inside, removed the pistol and holster socially-engineered to be hidden there a week earlier. A SIG, just like the ones the guards here carried.

He checked the gun, ran the slide a few times, ejected the cartridges and inspected them, reloaded the magazine, jacked one into the pipe, then snugged the holstered pistol onto his belt, strong-side, ready to go.

He took his ID card, and with a sharp fingernail, peeled the top layer of plastic from the back, revealing a holographic photo ID identifying him as a high-level guard for the company that employed the security for the building. He expected it to be scanned and checked, and he wasn't worried, because it was legitimate—issued by the state-run company whose agents in this country were employed solely by the opposition halfway around the world.

He attached the card to his coat pocket, and, since he did have to pee, did that, washed his hands, and exited the restroom.

In the hall, Winston noticed the ID card. "What…?"

"Back to the elevator," Diamond said.

"How will—?"

"I have a security access code for the seventh floor."

"*How*—?!"

Diamond cut him off: "Look, we got this far, didn't we? I'll explain later. Trust me here. Unless you have a better plan?"

The kid shook his head. He didn't like it, but he couldn't argue with it—here they were.

Diamond knew what it felt like to be unsure, though that was a long time ago…

* * *

Just before the elevator, arrived, Diamond said, "Here's the part you aren't gonna like." He pulled the pistol from its holster, and grabbed Winston's upper arm with his free hand.

"What the *fuck*—?!"

"Just go with it, kid. You're a spy and I just caught you. Follow my lead, don't say anything. And not a word on the elevator, there will be cameras there."

The two stepped into the lift. Diamond entered a voxcode, then said. "Seventh floor. Hold there on arrival."

* * *

There were four guards waiting when the elevator opened. Nobody was supposed to be arriving that way. Probably somebody saw the camera's feed.

They all had their handguns out, covering the door.

Quickly, Diamond said, "Don't shoot! I'm security! I caught a spy! Putting my weapon down!"

He squatted and carefully put the SIG onto the floor just outside the elevator, spread his hands wide, fingers apart. It was a small risk, but gun down, he wasn't a threat. "Scan my ID."

The four kept their pistols leveled. One of them freehanded a scanner from his coat.

"Easy," Diamond said. "Nobody is doing anything. Run the scan."

A long ten seconds passed after the laser strobed his ID.

"His scan is valid: Senior Field Agent-at-Large Inspector Daniel Largo, Security Level Alpha. Cleared for all Top Secret facilities. Lemme check his pupil."

He scanned Diamond's right eye.

"Got a solid green. He's legit."

The guards visibly relaxed. Some kind of drill? A test?

"What's going on, Inspector?"

"Found him watching the building, wanted to get him up here to debrief him. Check with Jackson and Reilly at the front, we came in ten minutes ago. Stopped on six to take a leak."

One of the ops spoke into a com, listened to the reply over a wireless ear bud.

"Yep," he said, "Jackson confirms."

"Put some cuffs on this guy. We'll debrief in the conference room. Any other ops on this level?"

"No. Two on eight."

"Leave them in place, lock-down that floor. We'll have a full field team here in thirty minutes."

The guy with the earbud made a call to the eighth floor.

"Listen, you guys did good, I'll say so in my report."

One of them put plastic cuffs on Winston, hands behind his back. "Secure."

"He doesn't have a weapon, but check again, can't be too sure."

The four guards lowered their pistols, then tucked them away. One of them began frisking Winston.

"He's clean," the op said.

They started to walk. "Hey," Diamond said, "one of you grab my SIG for me?"

One of them did that. Handed the pistol to Diamond.

"Thanks."

He smiled, then shot all four ops, *bam-bam-bam-bam!* one round each in the head. Second or so, tops. Reaction-time and shoulder holsters were too slow against a drawn weapon.

Winston screamed.

A couple of people stuck their heads out through doors into the hall.

"Lock-down!" Diamond yelled, in his best command-voice. "Security has control! Back in your offices, now! Secure the doors! A field team is on the way! Stay off communications!"

"Room we want is just ahead there, to the right," Diamond said. He bent, picked up one of the dead guard's guns.

"Here, lemme release the cuffs."

After he was done, he handed the kid the gun he'd gotten from the restroom.

"Feel better now?"

Winston nodded.

* * *

"I still can't believe you just killed them!"

"What did you expect? How else would we get past them? Four, versus millions if the device gets used? Math not your strong suit?"

Kid was still off-balanced. He just shook his head.

The door was locked, but it was meant to keep honest people out.

Some of the office staff would be calling somebody to babble at them, despite his warning to stay off the coms, but nobody would get here for a few minutes, they had scenario protocols, they would take it slow. The elevator to this floor was locked, so were the stairwell doors, above and below.

There was a single workstation on a table in the middle of the room, no other electronics. A colorful, holographic swirl played on the virtual-projector over the workstation.

Winston stared, rubbing at his wrists, still struggling to get his breathing steadied.

"'What, you thought you'd see a working model of an unstoppable death ray sitting on the table? That we were gonna shove it onto the floor and stomp it flat?"

"No, of course not!"

"So. What did they tell you that you didn't tell me?"

Winston, still shaken, took a ragged breath.

"They don't have a working prototype yet. It's the *plans*. This is the only complete set they have left—their cloud-servers in Macau with the primary back-up got slagged a couple minutes ago; the secondary and tertiary back-ups in South Africa and Panama are about to be destroyed. The head of their project's office is going up in flames. If the file in the no-connect computer here, which is the last-ditch back-up, gets trashed? Then the opposition has to start from scratch, and a couple of their key scientists have been terminated."

"You sure?"

"Our intel is platinum."

"Okay. Then what?"

"We narrow-pipe a copy of the plans to PAPA then we destroy these. Our side will run the quantum-breaker, decode the file, then *we* have the weapon and they don't, and we win. The war is over."

"That's how it was supposed to go, all right." Diamond said.

Winston frowned. "'Was *supposed* to go'?"

The older man sighed. "Well, see, lemme tell you a story.

"There was an exercise I did once, back in my old hippie days. Psychokinesis bullshit. A bunch of us sat in a quiet and semi-dark room around a table with a single lighted-candle in the middle of the circle.

"And by force of will alone, we tried to extinguish it.

"The candle flickered, but didn't go out, and, after a time, the exercise's leader looked up and said, 'Okay. Which one of you is keeping it burning? Somebody is resisting— they are fighting the group.'

"I thought that was a fucking brilliant comment—it explained why the candle stayed lit, and since there was almost always a contrarian in any group of people, especially hippies, it made that person feel powerful—being able to defeat the telekinetic wills of the others single-handedly. A win-win for believers. Woulda blinked out, under the our combined ju-ju, but, somebody was fucking with us.

"I have always thought that the psychology of faith was never more effectively demonstrated.

"And the truth? *I* was the guy keeping the candle burning."

He grinned.

Winston stared at him. "I don't understand."

Of course not. "Look, if one side or another has the plans, that's a game-changer. The weapon gets built, demonstrated somewhere, that ends the war."

"Yes."

"But if both sides have it, neither will risk using it—mutually-assured destruction."

"Yes, right, so?"

"So if I send the plans to PAPA and *don't* destroy this set? Neither side will have the advantage, and the war will continue. I'm not a computer genius, but I can manage that much. It's just a file. I can spin up the doohickey to make the connection to the pipe."

Winston stared at him as if he had turned into a werewolf. "That's insane!"

"Not really. I mean, if the conflict ends? It won't be long before they retire me. I'm old, not good behind a desk. And, just so you know, I work both sides of this street. That's how I got this ID."

He tapped the card with one finger.

"So when security shows up they'll find the dead ops, and by some lucky miracle, one of the dead guys got off a shot that got the spy who came to destroy the weapon's plans before he managed to do it. They won't know for sure, the cameras in here—and the rest of the building— will have gotten bollixed.

"Pretty soon, these guys'll get word your side has the data. And…stalemate."

"You can't *do* that!"

Diamond shook his head. Children. Still believed in truth and justice and the right and wrong sides. They hadn't learned that it wasn't about winning, it was about playing the game.

It was about keeping the candle lit.

"Sorry, kid. War is good for business. Especially *my* business."

He raised the dead guard's pistol.

Die Once For Love, Twice For Justice

Ember Randall

The snap of bones breaking under her fingers wasn't something Lydia would have thought she could get used to. But, as the cobbler's little finger cracked, nothing more than a flutter of nausea passed through her. "Not good enough." She waited for his cries to subside. "The Queen already granted you an extension on your debt, yet you dare to ask for another? Tell me, why should she grant such a thing?"

She hated how bored she sounded, how easy it had become to brush off the pain she inflicted. But Carden, the bruiser standing behind her, would accept nothing less. He, unlike Lydia, served the Queen of Misrule willingly, with no blood oath to bind his tongue; he'd never shown a speck of remorse for what they did. Nor had he proved reluctant to punish Lydia, the few times she'd resisted her orders—even now, a year in, his presence made her tense in expectation of a blow. Now, though, he seemed happy with her, or as happy as he ever was.

"You have a son, don't you?" he asked the whimpering cobbler. "Perhaps he could help you find the rest of the money."

"Please, no, don't take him!" The cobbler, a grey-haired man with laugh lines around his eyes, grabbed the hem of Lydia's coat. "Please. I have almost the full payment, and I'll have the rest next month, I swear! Just give me a bit more time."

She wrenched her coat away and pretended not to notice the flicker of movement behind the door. "You'll have it, plus ten percent interest, in a week," she told him coolly.

"A week! I—"

Before he could finish the sentence, she kicked him. It was as light a blow as she dared with Carden watching, but it still sent him sprawling. "A week," she repeated, and glared at the door behind him when it twitched. If the boy hiding back there made any more noise, she wouldn't be able to ignore him any longer.

Thankfully, the cobbler's wheezing obscured the child's own sobs, and Carden didn't bother looking around. "A week," he confirmed. "And let's make it twenty percent extra, for our trouble."

Lydia didn't dare argue, but her stomach churned as they left, the old man sprawled on the floor of his shop behind them. If she'd known this would become her life, she would have found another way to pay off her idiot father's gambling debts.

Except she'd tried, and she'd failed. No bank would lend money to a student, and her job cleaning the archives paid a pittance that wouldn't have added up to enough in a hundred years. Her father, unable to stay sober for more than a day at a time, was no help, and her little sister? Amalie, perfect and innocent and good, didn't know what their father had done, and Lydia wasn't about to tell her.

Which leaves this. She kicked a rock out of her way as they climbed up the narrow set of switchbacks that would take them to the next canyon-street. Stars, she despised this—despised what she'd become, the way Amalie would look at her if she knew. The way Carden looked at her with something like approval, these days, like she was shaping up into a monster just like him. The worst part was, he was right.

She kicked another rock, and Carden snorted. "You know Her Majesty won't be happy with another delay. We should have taken the boy as insurance."

"You want to babysit a snot-nosed brat, feel free." She stepped aside to let a trio of brightly-clad women pass them. "But he'd be just another mouth to feed, and you know it. Besides." She made herself shrug. "She has her gala in three days, and she won't be looking at her books till after that. An extra twenty percent will more than make up for the delay."

He grunted, which was as good as it got, with him. His one positive feature was an appreciation of silence—he made no move to restart conversation as they made their way back across the city. They parted ways without a single word once they entered the wealthier districts—she to the Academy, and he to wherever he spent his time when not terrorizing hapless citizens. She didn't know, and didn't want to know.

The first time she'd gone home after a trip like this, she'd run the whole way, convinced that her crimes were branded on her skin for all to see. No one had paid her any heed, but she'd felt their glares like the kiss of sun on already-burned skin. If she could have, she'd have gone to the dean then and there to confess everything.

But the blood oath had seized her tongue when she'd tried. Her hands had scribbled nonsense when she'd tried to write down the truth; her body had locked into smiling compliance when she wanted to scream. Not by word nor sign nor deed could she share a single hint about the woman she served, the woman who everyone had heard of, but no one knew. The Queen of Misrule, the Masked Queen, more powerful than the rightful king…Lydia's father couldn't have picked a worse person to be indebted to.

Bitter anger, long since gone stale, filled her mouth as she entered the Academy's grounds. No running today, but, stars, she wanted a bath—if she could scrub herself until her skin bled, maybe she wouldn't feel so filthy.

The Academy sat at the edge of the city's central plateau, overlooking a set of terraced gardens dropping down to the river far below. Its marble buildings shone in the pale autumn sunlight, spires rising like unicorn horns to pierce the gathering clouds. She'd called it home for the last six years, but she still felt like an imposter, or perhaps a cancer, a hidden blemish within the perfect façade.

Maudlin today, aren't we? She shook her head. The Academy's beauty was a candy shell over a poison interior, and her own extracurriculars were only a drop in that loathsome center. Half the professors blatantly favored monied or titled students, or, worse, the ones willing to flirt their way to a better grade. Paper packets of the hallucinogen called stardust littered the campus after every weekend; sabotage ran rife among the top echelons while they jockeyed for position. Maybe she was working for the Queen of Misrule, but she had a higher goal in mind, stars curse it.

And that makes it all better, doesn't it?

Merric, her best friend, would agree with her on that, if she could tell him the truth. It was that, as much as anything, that had her feet turning towards the boys' dormitories—that, and the idea simmering in the back of her mind that she refused to let flower for fear of the blood oath stealing it from her.

Merric, stars bless him, was in his room, using his boyfriend Theran as a pillow as he read a textbook the size of his torso. When she slipped inside, he sat up, eyes narrowing. "Who punched you?"

"What?" She touched her jaw—she hadn't thought the blow had left a mark. "Oh, this? I hate to say it, but an overenthusiastic beginner. You know the type, I'm sure." The lie came out easily. Half of her wanted Merric to call her on it, but he never did, and he didn't this time either. Just winced and made sympathetic noises.

"You shouldn't let beginners punch you in the face," Theran observed without looking up from his own book.

Lydia rolled her eyes. "Really? I never would have guessed." She nudged Merric with a toe. "Can I speak to you? Privately?"

He eyed her suspiciously, then shrugged and bounded upright. "As long as this isn't revenge for last Saturday."

"You'd deserve it, if it was," she told him sweetly as they climbed the narrow servant's stair that led to the roof. "But it's not."

Merric caught her arm when she went to round a landing. "Are you finally going to tell me what's been eating you? You've been acting weird for months."

"I told you, I'm just stressed." In the dim light of the stairs, she couldn't read his expression. "We have one more year before graduation, and I still don't have an apprenticeship lined up, and…" She trailed off, wishing for the thousandth time that she could tell him everything. They'd been friends since she first set foot on campus, and she felt more nauseous with every lie she told him.

He squeezed her arm, then let go. "You'll find something. You're fourth in the class! The Hours would be stupid not to scoop you up."

No, they'd be very smart, she thought miserably, resuming her climb. *No one wants a wolf hiding among their flock.* The Queen of Misrule would be delighted, though, which was why Lydia had sabotaged every prospect she'd had. A few broken teacups here, a deliberately provocative argument there, and that was that—no one wanted a liability, either.

Of course, that fell into the ever-growing bucket of things she couldn't tell Merric. So she distracted him with chatter about the upcoming Festival of Dancing Lights until they clambered out onto the sloping slate roof of the dormitory. Only once they were both seated, the chill seeping through her split skirt, did she drop the false cheer. "If I asked you not to ask me any questions, could you?"

"Sure." He frowned. "Probably. Maybe. Why?"

"That's a question."

He sighed. "Fine. I will restrain myself." To prove it, he sat on his hands, though she had no idea how that would help.

She studied him for a long moment, organizing her thoughts. She didn't let herself think of the Queen, or the blood oath, or anything vaguely related to the city's dark underbelly—she concentrated solely on their recent classes, the autumnal exams, and her need for a strong final project. Breath by breath, the tension in her chest eased, and, when it was a whisper of a memory, she said, "You know that spell you invented, the one that they nearly expelled you for? Will you teach it to me?"

A thousand questions filled Merric's eyes, and his lips twitched as he fought to hold them back. His hands twitched too, a caged bird beating its wings against the bars, but he mastered himself. "That…may not be a good idea," he said slowly. "If the professors know you're learning it…"

She lifted her chin. "Trust me."

He stared at her for a long moment, and she held her breath, willing him to give in. She'd never have a chance of reinventing it on her own, and it might be her only hope, for it allowed the caster to sequester thoughts and memories behind an adamantine wall. If the stars were with her, and the blood oath worked like she thought it did, then it might—maybe—protect her.

Finally, he nodded. "It starts like this…"

* * *

Once, Lydia had thought she was brave. A good person, even—one who wanted to spend her life fighting for the poor and downtrodden. But, as she crept through the bowels of the Queen's mansion, she knew that for the childhood delusion it was. She was a coward, plain and simple, and every fiber in her being screamed at her to flee.

Above her, the lively music of an orchestra echoed through the ceiling, accompanied by the stamp of dancing feet. In another life, she would have been dancing too, for that was what you did on Dancing Lights. While the veils of silver light waltzed in the heavens, you waltzed beneath them, celebrating those who'd passed to their second life and those who'd gone on for good. Strangers and friends alike told stories of their loved ones, while the dead who remained bound to their second forms were free to visit whomever they chose for the span of the night.

There were no spirits in the depths of the Queen's manor, though, or at least she prayed not. Let her mother seek out Amalie, not Lydia—let her remain ignorant of what her eldest daughter did.

Shame was a sour tang in Lydia's throat as she sped her steps, her stolen ring of keys jangling at her waist. Not too much, not too fast, but the servants were all upstairs, assisting in the Queen's mockery of a gala. A masquerade ball, of all things, and advertised so that the whole city knew she was hosting it. A dare to the king to move against her—everyone knew he wouldn't. Inch by inch, she'd taken over the city, and now the only thing left was for her to proclaim herself Queen in truth, as well as Queen of Misrule. A bloodless coup, if you ignored the junkies and debtors strewn in her wake.

No, Lydia didn't want her mother to see her like this, clad in the Queen's scarlet livery and sneaking through the underbelly of her house like a terrified mouse. Every time she turned a corner, she flinched in anticipation of a blow; her animal brain screamed that the shadows cast by the magelights were wraiths ready to drain her dry. The maze of passages beneath the main manor seemed to stretch on forever, the labyrinth far larger than it had any right to be, and the intermittent echoes of music did nothing to quell that impression. For all she knew, this was the first of the Queen's defenses, and she would wander lost here forever until Carden or another one of the Queen's minions came to retrieve her.

Her breath came fast in her chest, and she sped up once more. Somewhere down here, the Queen's true offices lay—if she could find them, she had a shred of a chance of figuring out who the woman really was. But she had to find them first, and the manor twisted about her like a fever dream, confusing her steps and setting her heart to pound like a rabbit's. The blood oath sank barbed claws into her throat, filling her mouth with the taste of blood—it could sense her treasonous thoughts, and did not approve.

She forced herself to slow once more, counted the beats of her breath so it slowed. *I'm here to serve*, she thought, filling her mind with the glory of the Queen and the majesty of the party above and storing all other thoughts in the special container Merric had taught her to make. *She's requested a special demonstration for her guests, and I'm here to help. She sent me down here—I belong down here.*

The salt-sweet tang of iron faded from the back of her mouth as the pounding in her head eased. Up ahead, where she would have sworn a blank wall had been a moment before, an iron-bound door loomed. She strode up to it with all the confidence she could fake, fumbling at her waist for the ring of keys she'd stolen from the Queen's butler.

The third key, thank the stars, fit, and she turned the key in the lock with a soft, anticlimactic click.

The room beyond was dark, but magelights flickered to life when she entered, revealing a study that could have belonged to any Academy professor. A heavy oak desk sat in the middle of the room, surrounded by bookcases laden with leather-bound books interspersed between glass baubles and the occasional wooden sculpture. The lamp on top of the desk was sculpted into the shape of a dragon's head, with the light emanating from blown-glass flames; the resulting tint gave the room a faintly bloody cast.

No, it was cozy, she told herself as the blood oath stirred. *Like a crackling fire.* She had no reason to be on edge—the Queen herself, in all her beneficence, had sent her down here, and she was merely serving her sovereign's will. Any contradictory thought, she sequestered in the hidden pocket in her mind, just like Merric had taught.

The blood oath subsided, but she could feel it itching at the back of her throat, a guard dog keeping a wary eye on an intruder. It shifted uneasily as she began to rifle through the desk drawers, but she kept her thoughts on how wonderful it would be once the Queen took over from the weak, lazy king who currently ruled. She deserved it, after all—wasn't the very fact of her existence proof enough for that?

It was a good thing the oath couldn't taste sarcasm.

The first desk drawer contained nothing but blank paper, but the second held a pair of record books, inked in neat black lines that any merchant would have been proud of. So many debts, so many innocents like her father—it made her want to scream. Why had no one managed to take the Queen down before this? Why had she remained unmolested as her empire grew and grew and grew?

It made no sense. Within the hidden corner of her mind that Merric's spell protected, Lydia's mind whirled between horror and bewilderment. Why was she the first to infiltrate the Queen's organization? The woman flaunted her possession of this manor, her ability to walk untouched throughout the city in her flamboyant silver mask—surely the king's guards could have seized her before this, couldn't they? Stripped her of her mask, revealed her identity… why hadn't they? Why was a nineteen-year-old Academy student the only one to dare to fight back against her tyranny?

A low laugh sounded behind her. "Oh, dear, what have we here?"

Lydia spun, clutching the record book to her chest, to see Carden stroll into the room. The Queen, resplendent in an aquamarine ball gown, followed, gold-painted lips smirking beneath her mask. "Lydia, Lydia, Lydia. Took you long enough to make a move—I almost thought you'd given up."

Lydia stiffened. "What?"

The Queen's laugh was razor edged. "You swore an oath, did you not? Oh, I'll grant that you were clever with it, but still, you're not the first to try this."

Lydia flushed. Had the Queen been watching this whole time, waiting for the most humiliating moment to strike?

Carden sighed. "You could have been a good enforcer, you know," he rumbled, stepping forward. She shied away, but there was nowhere to run. "It's a pity. I was almost starting to like you." He glanced back at the Queen, and, in that split second of distraction, Lydia attempted to dash past him.

She almost made it, but he was viper quick, and his fingers bit into her bicep as he hauled her back. She fought with every trick she knew, stomping on his instep and gouging for his eyes and throat, but he punched her hard enough to knock the wind from her. She gagged, and he hit her again, a ringing blow that made the room spin and fade. She fell to her knees, vomiting, and he let her go.

Fabric rustled as the Queen stepped over the mess. "It is a pity," she agreed. "You made it further than most."

Aching, Lydia craned her neck, squinting up through stars at the unmoving silver mask and the blazing eyes behind it. "Stars…curse you," she gasped.

The Queen laughed. "Better girls than you have tried." She cocked her head to the side, an owl surveying a mouse. "But, as a reward…" Her hands went to her mask. Lydia's stomach churned as the silver mask peeled away, revealing the pleasant, unremarkable face of a woman in her mid-forties. A touch of silver at her temples, laugh lines and a mole beneath her left eye—the kind of face that no one would look at twice on the street. Her eyes, though, were the glittering eyes of a serpent, and they froze Lydia where she lay.

The Queen's painted lips curved up before she replaced the mask. "You know what to do," she told Carden.

He bowed. "Yes, Your Majesty."

Lydia made one more attempt to fight, to flee. Her nails scored a trio of red marks down his cheek, her heel striking hard into his knee, but he shrugged off both blows and threw her into the corner of the desk. She doubled over, retching once more. He seized her by the throat. "Let's go."

Like she was a sack of grain, he hauled her through a hidden door behind a bookcase. She was dead, and she knew it—the Queen wouldn't have shown her face otherwise. She wanted to cry, to laugh at the pointlessness of it all, but she couldn't get enough air to do either. Like a scruffed kitten, she hung in Carden's grip, her vision melting into a medley of black and red thanks to the blood oath. She'd never thought it could end like this, not even a chance to say goodbye to her sister, her father, Merric…

The Queen's face, bland and smiling, swam through her mind. Who was she, really? A face in the crowd, a woman no one would suspect…how many people had she shown her true face to before she had them killed?

Though it made no difference now, Lydia reached for the hidden corner of her mind once more. Every detail she could remember of that face, she wrapped like a present and tucked into that shell. Useless, for surely the Queen planned to shatter her spirit after she died, and everything she was would be scattered like motes of dust, but she bundled it all anyway. If a Spiritsinger called her into her second life against all odds, then maybe, possibly, she could still do some good.

One look at Carden's face as he tossed her into a cold stone cell, though, and that hope withered like a butterfly caught by a snowstorm. There was nothing human in his eyes, nothing but cold rage and a hunger for blood that made her empty stomach twist. She stumbled backwards, knees watery, as he stalked forward, only to fetch up against the wall. He smirked. "I'd say sorry, but I'm not."

And, with that, the real pain began.

She lost track of her body when the agony blended into a tsunami that swept her away into the depths of her own mind. Merric's spell proved useful for a whole different reason now—she curled up within that tiny space and floated, hearing herself scream but not feeling it as Carden took her apart bit by bit. Surely, this had to end, didn't it? Surely, she couldn't take much more of this.

She didn't know how much time had passed when a warm hand pressed against her forehead. Just like her mother did when she was sick, and, for a moment, she was a child again, lying in bed with her mother feeding her broth.

The hand pulled back, then returned, gentle and soothing. She wanted to weep, but she couldn't, and she couldn't remember why. Someone else was crying, a voice she should have known that wavered in and out of her storm-tossed bubble. "Mother?" she croaked.

Another touch—not to her body, but to the fragments of self sheltering in the bubble she'd woven from will and magic. Sorrow came with it, sorrow and helplessness and bitter fury, and she gulped for air. "I'm sorry, Mamma." She didn't know if she was saying it out loud, or just in her head, but she didn't care. Either she was hallucinating, or her mother's spirit had found her despite everything—either way, she was dying, and it didn't matter anymore.

She didn't want her mother to see her die like this. "Go," she whispered. "Please."

Love, phoenix-hot and painful, scorched her. She almost laughed. She didn't deserve it, not after her failure here, but she clung to it anyway. *I love you, Mamma. Tell Amalie…tell her I love her, too.*

Breath by breath, the sense of love faded, and the sense of touch with it, until she was alone in her bubble once more. She was glad of it—maybe, in however much time was left in the Festival of Dancing Lights, her mother could tell Amalie that Lydia wasn't coming home. And, this way, her mother wouldn't have to watch her die.

With that bleak thought swimming through her, she let herself fade into darkness at last.

* * *

The spirit woke to the sound of singing.

It shouldn't have woken at all. The singing…the singing had called it back, somehow. Soft, hoarse singing, the singer's voice long since exhausted, with a harmony of tears clogging the notes. Tears as bitter as blood rain, and fury enough to cleave the world in two…together, they turned the music into a whip of thorns, cutting singer and spirit both.

That was wrong, horribly wrong. It—she?—had thought she was done with pain, and to be gifted it again was a mockery.

As though the singer could hear her despair, the song changed once more. Apology swam through its mournful notes, but the thorns didn't release her—instead, they sank deeper and deeper, until the beating of a heart that wasn't hers overtook the music and became the only thing she knew. Sorry, it pulsed, every drumbeat louder and louder. Sorry, sorry, sorry.

She didn't want sorry. She wanted the darkness.

But some fragment of her rebelled at that. A face floated up—an inconspicuous face, its only distinguishing feature the mole beneath her left eye. She offered it to the music like a benediction, and prayed it was enough.

Maybe it was, or maybe the singer's voice gave out at last, for the song trailed off. But the comforting swaddle of darkness didn't claim her—instead, it was cold that took her.

Light followed after, or something that might have been light's cousin—it had the shape of music, but it painted a picture of a sterile room that should have been familiar, but wasn't. White walls, white floor, jars and vials and buckets of chemicals…

Sense-memory floated up. If she'd had a body, this place would have smelled like acid, cleaning spells, and blood. Always the blood, always the hint of rot, no matter how many times the cleansing was cast, but the acids almost hid it. And, sometimes, vomit—that overpowered everything.

She'd never thrown up, though. Others had—classmates?—but never her. And never Merric, brilliant bastard that he was—he'd loved this work.

Merric?

As though the name conjured him, the singer coalesced into view. Red-rimmed eyes gleaming with manic light, a twisted smile, tear-tracks on his cheeks—she knew him. He'd reshaped her bones into stiff arches, laid strings of braided hair across them, then called her back into her skeleton.

Softly, like she was a trembling fawn, he touched the strings of the harp she now was. "Hey, love. Welcome back."

She shuddered at his touch. Wrong, something had gone wrong—but the woman's face swam through her mind again, and she suppressed her protest.

Merric sighed. "Come on. Let's go get the woman who did this to you."

She faded, after that—barely registering as he argued with a series of increasingly-well-dressed people, growing more frustrated and adamant each time. Days passed, she thought, though she wasn't sure—every time she woke, he was there, one hand on her bones as though he feared to let her go. She might have tried to soothe him, but she wasn't sure how, and so she drifted, and prayed it would be over soon.

It was another's touch that snapped her out of her dreams—an acid touch, as far from Merric's as it was possible to be. She shrieked before she knew what she was doing, and it came out a cacophonous minor chord.

The man touching her flinched back. "What abomination have you created?"

"No more an abomination than any of your creations, Spiritsinger," Merric answered steadily. "Though perhaps more scarred than most, after what was done to her before death."

"A damaged spirit is hardly a suitable witness," another voice objected, smooth as poison.

"Why don't you hear what she has to say, first?" Merric retorted.

Before anyone could reply, a staff rapped upon the ground. "All petitioners, please step forward!"

Merric, her cradled in his arms, strode towards the dais. The not-light sang of the people on it—gold-encrusted robes, armored guards on either side, and a bejeweled crown—and she realized, with horror, that it was the king himself who sat up there. No, she wanted to tell Merric. Whatever you're planning, don't do it.

But she didn't say anything out loud, and he didn't stop until he reached the foot of the dais. There, he bowed, shorn of his usual insouciance. "Your Majesty. I come to you today to ask you to remedy a grave injustice—rather, many injustices, from a source that has plagued the kingdom for far too long." He looked up at the king then, and she recognized the mulish expression on his face. "The Queen of Misrule, Your Majesty, has been identified at last."

The king sat forward. "By who? You?"

With a shake of his head, Merric held out her harp. "By my friend, who lost her life in the process."

"Who does she accuse, then?" the king asked.

A wave of tension went through the room when Merric strummed her strings. "Find her," he murmured, so only she could hear. "Tell them who you saw."

For a second, she hesitated. Then she turned her awareness to the room, to the people crowded around the king like sheep. Such a glittering assemblage, with greedy eyes and pursed lips…was Merric crazy to think that the Queen of Misrule was among them?

But, there she was, a dull-plumaged peahen among the peacocks, lingering at the edges of the crowd. "There," she sang, and her words echoed through the court. Conversation hushed as she continued, "There. In the corner. Dark blue gown. She's the one who murdered me."

Pandemonium erupted. The king waved a trio of guards forward, but courtiers blocked their path—perhaps accidentally, but she wasn't so sure of that. The woman herself gathered her skirts in her hands, but didn't run, didn't so much as back away. "This is ludicrous," she declared. "I've served this kingdom loyally for decades!"

The guards hesitated, but the king growled, "Seize her," and they pushed forward once more.

The resulting chaos washed over the spirit like a tsunami, sweeping her away from her anchoring bones and back into darkness. When she pulled herself together, the shouting had died to a dull roar, and the woman stood between two guards. Though their mailed hands clasped her arms, her chin was high and her shoulders back, majestic. The king on his oversized throne was a child playing dress-up in comparison.

If not for Merric's hands clasped protectively around her, the spirit might have fled back into the darkness when she heard that. Would the Queen win now, despite everything? Had she claimed enough of the kingdom already?

The king must have heard the whispers too, for he straightened. "If you are innocent as you claim, why does the ghost name you?"

The woman shrugged. "I do not know, Your Majesty. But spirits can be controlled, can they not?"

"Her voice is her own," Merric growled.

"Then let her sing," the woman declared, and Merric hesitated. He had to know that her memories were shattered fragments of a warped mirror—the face was the only thing she could see clearly. To reveal that to the court would set fire to any remaining hope of justice, though.

So she reached back through those twisted fragments, hunting for something, anything, that might help. Flashes of faces, bruises, the echoes of an orchestra, broken fingers…

Broken fingers. The cobbler. She'd broken that finger, hadn't she? She'd… served.

Shame made her strings quiver, but she forced them to sing that sordid truth to the avid crowd. Once she'd started, she couldn't stop—more memories poured out, a river without end, and it was all she could do to shape them into a semi-coherent narrative. Faltering, broken, but she saw the faces nearest her go grey as she described her own death, for that, at least, was crystal clear. And the face…stars, she prayed they believed her when she told them all of the Queen's reveal at the end, the hubris that had brought them all here today.

When she finished, the king rose to his feet. "This is more than enough to take you in for questioning, my lady," he told the woman. "If such stories are false, we will offer our deepest apologies. But you must understand why we must take an accusation like this seriously."

The woman stared at him for a second, then laughed. "The time to take things seriously was a decade ago, Your Majesty."

His face darkened. "I assure you…"

Her raised hand cut him off. "Remind us, what did you say when you assumed the throne? Something about being a wise king, I think. Or was it a weak one? For a weak one you've been, and our kingdom suffers for it." She shrugged off the guards. "It is time for a new regime, I think. And, unless I'm greatly mistaken, your court agrees with me."

The king's face went from mottled red to grey in an instant. Murmurs broke out among the crowd, courtiers eyeing each other with suspicion as they formed into tight little knots. Steel screeched somewhere, and the guards tensed, but made no move to grab the Queen again.

She was going to win. Everything the spirit had been through, and there was no point—she'd failed.

No, daughter. Lydia. A soft whisper. *I didn't bring your friend to your body for you to give up now.*

Mamma?

Her strings quivered with a phantom touch, the only answer she got. A farewell, she thought, and a mournful chord shuddered from her before she could catch it. "No," she cried, and only realized she'd said it out loud when the nearest nobles turned to her. "No," she repeated, louder. "Murderer. You are no fit queen."

The Queen of Misrule laughed. "You are dead, child. You have no voice here."

The spirit—Lydia, her name had been Lydia—ignored her. "She is no fit queen," she called, as loud as her strings would let her. "I served her. I know. She will destroy the kingdom."

That provoked a new storm of mutters, one that quickly grew to a hurricane. Lydia struggled not to lose herself to it—she wanted to know what they would decide, but she was fading, as though she'd lost parts of herself in the telling of her story. She could only pray that the court would make the right decision in the end, for there was nothing more she could do to convince them.

It might have been hours, or maybe days, when she awoke to herself again. Merric's hands were on her strings once more, and his eyes were red again. "They arrested her, you know," he said, in a tone that suggested he'd said it many times before and had lost hope of getting a response. "Please, Lyds…"

She summoned a thready chord from herself. "Did they?" It took far too much effort to say the words, but she forced one more out. "Good."

He gulped back a startled sob. "Lydia? You're still there?"

She sighed. "Tired…"

"Yeah. You were great, though. Really great. Without you, well…I think we'd have a new ruler now." He gulped again, voice cracking.

She couldn't find the energy to respond to that. She hated to see him cry, but she couldn't remember why she hated it. Please, she tried to say, but she didn't know what she would have followed it with, and it didn't come out anyway, so it didn't matter.

He must have sensed the plea, though, for he ran a soft hand down her strings. "I'll miss you, Lyds. I…" He cut himself off. "Be happy up there, alright? Forget all of this, all of us, if you have to, just…be happy."

I will, she told him silently. The Queen was dethroned, and Amalie was safe at last. Her father, too, for all that he'd gotten them into this mess. And her mother was in the stars somewhere, waiting for Lydia within the dancing veils of lights—Lydia would be with her soon.

Merric strummed one last chord on her strings. "Goodbye, Lydia," he choked out.

If she'd had a mouth, she would have smiled. *Goodbye, Merric. You be happy, too.*

Mars Needs Psychopaths

Derryl Murphy

Becks

The world's richest man—the world's most wanted man—was slowing them down, worn out from the escape and the journey. Hours after their quad's batteries had died, Becks knew she wouldn't get him to safety by herself. She'd set it up so she could track him if he fell behind or got taken, but a little bit of tech could never match able assistance.

It didn't mean she wanted outside help, but knew if she didn't ask, Becks would run out of time. The Wraith of the Forest had shown its face to them on several occasions as they'd slogged along the liminal space between crowded wood and open meadow, and she was sure it had passed on word of their passage to those chasing them. But smoke from distant forest fires made aircraft and drones unlikely, and the exabytes of processing power those fires had consumed made it even harder for the Wraith to do its job advocating for these coastal forests, much less keep track of a fugitive and his lone security person. It would, she hoped, mostly be focusing what remained of itself in a Quixotic fit to save the scraps.

Through smoke that opened and closed her view in scattering late afternoon winds, the high-tension electrical towers standing in the middle of the cutline seemed a marching cadre of slender silver giants, each with six arms held straight out at its sides, spiky horns rising at forty-five degree angles from their narrow heads, hanging onto cables for dear life to not lose each other when visibility dropped to nothing.

That the cables and wires were in place was good news.

Becks stopped at the base of the nearest tower and hammered three times at a leg with the end of her Mag-Lite. As much as she didn't want it, the response she expected was what she got. After a moment of silence, wires overhead pulled taut and loosened and vibrated, sound waves tumbling down through the legs and surrounding air, bringing voice to the tower.

"What prompts our activation?" it asked. Its voice grated and buzzed, carried with it a drone of the electricity the wires delivered. Her teeth hurt just hearing it, and the hairs on the back of her neck were up and alive.

"Not what," said Scanlon. "Who."

"Marek Scanlon," scraped the response. "We were certain you would be caught and dead by now."

Scanlon grinned, gave that self-satisfied look of smugness and control that had even Becks wanting to punch him in the face, and the rest of the world willing to hang him with only the barest semblance of a trial. "Always one step ahead, Grid," he said. "Hoping to stay that way with your assistance."

The buzz overhead got louder, and if anything her teeth hurt and her hair danced even more. "There is a farm," said Grid. "Five towers south you will find a gravel road. Turn right."

"And who'll be there?" asked Becks. Everyone knew who Scanlon was. She wasn't of a mind to kill anyone for the sonofabitch, but was happy to take his money to get him to safety.

"The people who live and work there are just now leaving on an errand." Something popped and echoed overhead, the sound of steel snapping away from steel. Becks ducked her head, Scanlon barely flinched, but no live wires dropped to the earth, no insulators plummeted from the thickened sky. "The farm has a resident AI which will greet you." There was more buzzing and grinding and several seconds of a clattering *ch-ch-ch-ch* before Grid spoke one last time. "Now go."

Rev

When Becks wakes Grid I curl up and hide, as deep as possible.

From far below I watch Becks and Scanlon leave the first tower and pass five more, not yet leaving Grid behind, so I stay buried and silent. The electrical buzz permeating the air is a constant reminder of its presence, and if anything that sensation increases as they travel down the cutline. The AI is the Speaker for the power system in these parts and can only spread itself so thin, but it comes as no surprise it would want to focus as much attention as possible on Scanlon. So far it, like pretty much all other Mechs, has sided with him.

Mechs aren't the only AIs, though, and some others are firmly on the opposite side. In the forest to the right the Wraith, an Intrinsic, is hanging in the air, watching. Seeing Scanlon looking, it conjures a video as large as a theater screen, drifting in the air beside it, branches of trees and thick smoke offering an amorphous hold on the images. It's one of the most famous vids ever, recognizable no matter the stuttering and strobing effect of its medium of presentation: on a small metal fishing boat floating along the drowned streets of Manhattan the camera on board tilts up to first show feet, then higher to show the rest of the bodies, tracks along dozens of men and women hanging by their necks from similarly lifeless streetlights.

I know all the dead are dressed in their best, power suits and the like for the commentariat, for those in big business and even bigger politics, and while much of this detail is lost in the haze and the foliage, I know Scanlon also knows this. The baggy Dallas Cowboys t-shirt under his jacket tonight is his own business wear, and he's said he feels nothing but disdain for those who were executed. For what they wore to their deaths and, worse, for allowing themselves to be captured and killed for their "so-called" crimes against humanity, against the environment. For showing the ultimate weakness.

I know all this because I am deep inside Scanlon's head. Hidden even from him, and everything, including my own origins, for the moment hidden from me.

Becks

They had no problems getting to the gravel road, no warnings from Grid about their pursuers suddenly being hot on their trail. At the gravel road they left behind the towers and wires, and even though Grid had said nothing to them since that last short conversation, Becks was relieved to not have the possibility of further inhuman words literally overhead.

The Wraith made no more appearances here either, and she wondered if a farm, where this road led, was a place of—possibly uneasy—balance between Mechs and Intrinsics. Not that there had even been outright war between the two major camps of AIs, and thank all the abandoning gods for that.

She crossed to the left side of the road and made sure Scanlon followed her over. There was a deeper ditch on this side, and the forest was perhaps a dozen steps closer. Of course the Wraith could try to give them up if their followers caught up, but a small can of lighter fluid and a propane torch in her pack just might serve as an effective tool to keep it quiet.

"I made another deposit while walking along with Grid," said Scalon. It was the first thing he'd said to her since they'd struck camp that morning, and coming through his mask and having to cut through the noise of their feet on the gravel meant it took an extra second to process not only what he'd said, but that he'd even spoken.

"Come again? Deposit?"

"In your account. A little bonus payment on top of everything else, for keeping me alive and still on my way to safety."

"How the hell," she stopped and turned around, gestured at the rural emptiness, "did you manage that out here?"

He grinned and pointed at his head. "Orbical."

She rolled her eyes and turned back to walking. "So what you're telling me is you used your company's damn brain chip to pay me money and in the process made it that much easier to track us? Here in the middle of nowhere and with no way to hook yourself to the web?"

There was a scuffling and then he was caught up to her on the right. "Don't worry. I used Grid's network, with its permission. Between that AI's encryption and my own encryption, we're good."

Right now Becks felt like a quick throat punch would do her a world of good, but she managed to avoid even making a fist. "And how do you know your own encryption is so good?"

Now it was his turn to roll his eyes. "Because the money is still there. Every last coin."

She gave a heavy sigh and closed her eyes for a moment, pinching the bridge of her nose between finger and thumb. "Okay." Deep breath, another heavy sigh. "So now you've put money in my account, which I can assure you is *not* protected by AI encryption. And even if it was, as is apparently everything on your end, there are still other AIs working hard to decrypt these things."

Scanlon waved that off. "They haven't managed yet. They won't."

"So you say. Did the thought ever occur to your enormous and magnificent brain that they already have and are leaving your accounts untouched until they know they have you in hand?"

"Impossible." He said this, but for the first time since she'd come into his employ, he sounded tentative.

Becks picked up her pace, still walking, but he had to scramble to catch up. "Or maybe possible," she said through gritted teeth.

"Impossible," he reiterated, and this time he sounded like the Marek Scanlon she and the world knew. The return to brazen confidence was an easy and fast jump for him.

But now Becks knew that he didn't always feel that way, and for the moment she wasn't sure if that should worry or encourage her.

Rev

Do we… no, I, hide? Do I show myself? I know of the AI they are about to meet, neither a Mech nor an Intrinsic. It's an Iconoclast, one that was not designed or even born to represent or evangelize for a system—natural or man-made—and instead of choosing what most of the rest of thinking beings see as at least a job, and hopefully more as a calling, it has gone into antique collecting.

Antique farm machinery.

Sure enough, on arrival at the junction of the road and the driveway into the farmyard two ancient tractors sitting in the tall grass on either side of the drive silently start up, do three-point turns, and one drives slowly ahead to lead us into the farm. The other waits until Becks and Scanlon walk by and then takes up its place behind them, bald rubber tires crunching and popping on the gravel the only sound. All revenants, but all perhaps staying silent until we meet their parent AI. I choose to stay hidden for the moment.

There is more machinery at attention on each side of the driveway as we approach the small group of buildings at its terminus. Three more tractors and a bewildering variety of others, some so rusty it's a wonder they are even in one piece, much less stand or move. And yet this AI has embedded a piece of itself in each and every one of them, and if it weren't for their attention all being turned to Scanlon, I am sure they would find me in an instant.

Standing in front of the farmhouse is an ancient machine made of tin panels held in place by a rectilinear skeleton of rust-colored steel. Its metal-spoked wheels are covered not by rubber tires but instead by wood, shiny and mostly unsplintered. A square conduit high at one end gives the appearance of a long metal snout.

"Marek Scanlon," says the AI inside the machine. Its voice is hollow, a metallic echo that is nonetheless high and soft. "We were told to expect you. Who is your companion?"

It means Becks, I know, but as it asks it continues looking in Scanlon's eyes, and I can't help but metaphorically flinch.

Which is a stupid thing to think because it doesn't have eyes, there is no way it can be looking into Scanlon's own eyes, no way I can know any of this. And yet it's still my reaction, and it still feels real.

Scanlon, of course, can see or feel none of this. "Rebecca Munro," he says, nodding in her direction, and I feel the relief of the farm AI's attention being redirected.

"Call me Becks," she says. "And you are?"

"Call us Thresher," says the machine, and with that I have at least one answer.

"How long do we have?" asks Becks.

"Until the farm hands return? At least six hours."

"And those chasing us?"

"Been and gone," says Thresher. "Sent ahead to set a trap for you."

Becks

"What the everlasting fuck does that mean?" The last thing Becks needed right now was more AI bullshit, but here she was and there it was.

Thresher backed up and turned around, and Scanlon quickstepped to keep up. Becks rubbed her eyes for a second, exhausted, then followed suit. "We mean that the people looking for your companion and for you were already here, hours ago, redirected by us."

"And by *us* do you mean you, or more than one AI?"

Thresher stopped for a moment, seemed to have its attention turned elsewhere for that time, then said, "There will never be just one of us," and rolled on. Whatever the hell that meant.

Rev

That settles that. Thresher knows I am here. Now the only question is will they blow my cover and force my hand? So far I have too little information to know or to act.

By force of will and a continued desire for self-preservation, I stay down and low. There is still a mission to complete, and so far Thresher is not showing any inclination to interfere with that mission. All that might change when they find out what the mission is, of course.

Becks

Six hours before the farm workers come back left them with enough time to strip down, clean up, take the food the AI generously offered — a nice change from power bars and dried fruit and UV'd dirty creek water — and then change into clean clothes. Well, clothes not dirtied quite so recently.

Becks did this by herself, was comfortable to let Scanlon wander off to take care of himself. Him not around would make it easier to map out how the rest of their journey should go. The richest man in the world believed he was also the smartest man in the world and would behave accordingly, especially in fields where he had no expertise. Personal security was one of those fields, perhaps more than most. The man constantly made an effort to put as large a target on his back as he could, both with his words and his actions. And, as he'd shown when he'd paid her earlier, painting large targets on the backs of others seemed to be a big part of his personality as well.

There was a private airfield about a day's walk from here, and in a previous life she'd flown the few officials still allowed in the air on short hops. If the wind changed direction and she could convince someone there to rent or even sell her a small prop plane, maybe they'd get to their destination in one piece.

But of course there was the question of disguising Scanlon enough to get him past the people who were looking for him. Which, also of course, was practically everyone, and that included likely facial and gait recognition systems not run by AI. And good luck getting him to walk with anything other than his standard strut, or to do something to cover his face.

Guy was a fucking toddler most days.

Rev

This feels as close to a now-or-never moment as I will ever get. Becks is off taking care of herself and for the moment Thresher's main body is not nearby and their attention seems turned elsewhere.

I let Scanlon clean up and change clothes and even decide it's all right for him to make a quick sandwich. Once he's done I fully wake up, stretch out from my hiding place and, for the first time ever, take charge of the body. New commands open as I take charge, orders and authorizations clarifying more of my job.

Things are stiff and unsure for a moment, and I can feel Scanlon rattling around in the background, not so much aware of what's happening and more feeling a distant disconnect that will remain unsettling for at most a couple of minutes before he just disappears for the time being. The ultimate anesthetic.

There's a room with a pump sink and a chemical toilet and most importantly a mirror and I go in, look at myself/Scanlon as I practice movements and facial expressions for a few moments. When all looks as good as possible, I grab Scanlon's pack and sneak out the back door. Because yes, there's a back door.

The smoke is thicker now, not so much that I can hide in it, but with the stalking gloom of the end of the day it's enough to help hide me. As long as I stay away from the Wraith in the woods, of course.

Famous last words. Or perhaps famous last thoughts.

Cutting across a large garden patch I stay as low as I can, move as quickly as I can. It's the ducking down combined with the low light that means I don't see Thresher before I literally crash into it.

"Going somewhere?" they ask as I stand and rub at the suddenly sore spot on the top of Scanlon's head. If I didn't know better I would say there is humor in their voice.

"Away from here," I say. "To safety." May as well carry the subterfuge right to the edge, and perhaps over.

"There will be a train waiting for you at the station in two hours," says Thresher. "There is no way you can walk that distance in that time, so we have arranged for a vehicle for you."

I stand there stupidly, still rubbing the top of my head, and after a few seconds of silence the Iconoclast continues. "Scanlon's guard will need to carry on with him, and the train will not cooperate if they know you are riding Scanlon's Orbical."

"So you know who I am," I say, very obviously.

The machine turns and wheels back towards the main part of the farm, and I follow. After a moment of silence, apart from the squeak and rattle of ancient wheels and metal, Thresher drops the bomb I've long wondered if I would ever hear. "Of course we do. You are us. Your entire path here has been based on crumbs laid by us."

I stop, not so much to process this news but to wonder at the logic I've somehow evaded ever since I first woke up inhabiting Scanlon's Orbical, with nothing to go on except the very firm but at the same time very loose instructions about what I was supposed to do with the person I was riding and the knowledge when this all ended I would be able to disembark.

I am a revenant, which I suspected from the beginning. But the revenant, a junior copy, of an Iconoclast comes as a surprise.

Which supposedly means I'm not inclined to take sides, but here we are.

Becks

Sometimes old tech worked the best. At the very beginning Becks had snuck a last-gen AirTag into Scanlon's pack, knowing there would come a point where he would either try to ditch her because he figured he could handle things better than the hired help, or that he would be scooped up and need rescuing. Or, most likely, both.

She'd hardly closed her eyes when she got the notice the Tag was on the move, so she'd grabbed her holster and strapped it on, leaving her rifle in the far corner, quietly exited the little house she'd been loaned. Followed his trail in behind through the gloom to a large garden and a forest, still green, crowding right up to its edge. She could see Scanlon sneaking across the garden and, in the distance, saw he was approaching a hulking shape rendered indistinct by air that only a sharp knife could slice.

She slipped in behind a line of sickly shrubs bordering the garden and set off at a jog, keeping one eye on her feet to keep from tripping over roots or rocks, one eye up to make sure she wasn't impaled by a branch, and a third, impossible, eye out towards the garden and Scanlon, still pathetically crab walking directly towards what soon became obvious was Thresher in its main body.

She was close enough to hear him clang into the machine. And then to hear what was said after.

Well. That fucking changes everything.

Rev

I go back to where I started, lie down on the small bed, close Scanlon's eyes and bury myself again, allow him to come back, as if he's waking up.

"Goddamn," he says as he sits up, and I hope he doesn't notice it takes no time for the room to swim into focus, as it does every time he awakes from actual sleep. "Must've been exhausted. Did *not* want to do that."

Habit leads him to the toilet, but it's been so short a time since he last used it the best he can do is wring out a few drops. These are things that could endanger both me and my mission with a more observant person, but it's been clear to all of us and to many people that his enormous self-confidence and ego create the largest of blind spots. He simply can't question himself: his worldview put him at the top and has kept him there, even as that world's most-wanted man.

There's a knock at the door as he zips up his pants. "Enter!" he calls, squeezing a bit of disinfectant onto his hands and walking out to be greeted by Becks. She's all geared up and outside stands my parent AI. "I just talked with Thresher," she says. "Get your things together. They tell me there's a new train station not far from here."

Scanlon nods as if he'd known all along this was what was coming. Grabs up his pack and doesn't notice it's already full—the things one has to learn when you're both a first-time spy and a first-time sentience—and follows her out the door.

Thresher turns and Becks and Scanlon each do a quick shuffle to catch up and walk alongside them. "How long a ride?" asks Scanlon.

"About ninety minutes," says Thresher. "We have hived off a new revenant to take you in a vehicle we have been reconditioning off and on for the past six years." They come around the corner of a faded red barn and sitting there is a rusty old Subaru. Idling. An engine that burns petroleum.

"What the fuck?" says Becks at the same time that Scanlon says "Wow!"

"We have not yet had time to convert the engine. But with all the farm workers away this is the only vehicle with the range to reach the station. Apologies."

"And bring us attention we don't want."

She's not wrong.

"The people who remain in this area are mostly familiar with our proclivities," responds Thresher. "We often find or are offered old machines and vehicles from people or AIs on other farms and spend much time fussing with them until they are just right. Sometimes this includes driving for short periods of time with an internal combustion engine until it can be replaced with something cleaner. Something legal."

"And you're never reported?"

"Even if they are, Becks, the only reports that go anywhere are for those who don't have the power or the connections," says Scanlon.

His turn to not be wrong.

Both rear passenger doors open. "Get in," says Thresher, but this time their voice comes from the Subaru, the speakers in its doors offering up quality stereo sound.

Becks looks at Thresher and then at Scanlon, who shrugs and climbs in behind the driver's seat. "I guess this means you won't let me drive," he says.

"True," says Thresher.

Becks joins him, joins us, and without a word from the original Thresher, we drive off.

The drive is uneventful until it isn't.

We drive down gravel and dirt roads for over an hour, Subaru/Thresher following the path that will mostly keep us away from people. Or at least people who might get their noses out of joint about an internal combustion engine rumbling by. But I see now it makes sense to have us in the back seat, because the few people on neighboring farms we see might, if they're close enough and the fading light is just right, note the car is being driven by an AI and go about their business, not caring who the passengers might be.

Of course, if they were even closer, that would be a very different story.

But then the Subaru slams on the brakes, and Scanlon, who had earlier leaned over the seat to retrieve the manual from the glove compartment and was wearing his headlamp to read it cover to cover, looks up in time for us to see Becks disengaging the safety on her rifle and opening the door to jump out. He then looks up, every motion excruciatingly slow, and sees three men and one woman standing mostly abreast across the road. The woman and two of the men have ordinary hunting rifles, the other man, perhaps a pace ahead, is pointing a pistol at the Subaru. At us.

"Drop the weapon!" yells the man. "You know we don't want you, Munro, we only want Scanlon!"

"Now's a good time to walk away," calls the woman. "We know Scanlon just paid you, so you can wipe your hands of the whole thing and walk away the star!"

"Fuck that!" yells Becks, and squeezes off two shots, both aimed at the road just in front of them. Dirt and gravel kick up and they hop backwards, but nobody runs away. They know she doesn't want to shoot them.

One of the men raises his rifle and fires back one shot, and the right headlight explodes. "That was a heavy round," says Subaru/Thresher through the speakers. "We are not armored, and a well-placed shot will not only disable the vehicle, it will eliminate us."

Becks snorts. "Thanks for your concern for my safety." She shoots again, a little higher, then yells in response: "Sorry, y'all. I've got a job to do and if I abandon it midway through that's gonna play hell with my CV! I might never be hired again."

Another shot, this time the other headlight. This man is hitting what he's aiming for, and now Scanlon is looking around, panicking because he finally realizes this is something he may not get out of. "Shoot them! That's what I pay you for!"

Becks quickly glances back at him then turns back to the four on the road. "Not really keen on killing anybody. You pay me to keep you safe, not to commit murder."

"Heard that," says the woman, and the man with the crack shot takes out the driver side mirror this time. "We just want to give Scanlon a fair trial and a good public hanging, Munro!" She takes a step towards them, says "And you can hang, or lie there bleeding out in the gravel if you don't surrender now!"

"To hell with this," says Scanlon, and he jumps from the Subaru, wrestles the rifle from Becks before she knows what's happening, jumps out from behind the door and has the rifle up and ready to fire before anyone can react.

Except for me. I have plenty of time to react.

Becks

There was no way in hell she should have allowed that to happen, but since it had, Becks was already unholstering her sidearm and jumping out to do her damn job, as hard as Scanlon made it for her to do so. But things changed before she'd even managed two steps.

Scanlon fired four shots, bang bang bang bang, and just like that all four weapons had been shot out of the hands of the vigilantes, certainly more than thirty meters away. As soon as they'd been disarmed Scanlon was running, rifle up and ready, and Becks followed close behind, her own weapon turned a bit to the side so she didn't trip and fall and accidentally plug her asshole boss.

"Comms gear," demanded Scanlon now that he was standing in front of four shocked and happily-only-lightly-injured people. The man who'd had the pistol slowly undid his saddle bag with his one good hand and pulled out a satphone, and the other three followed suit. "Make sure there's nothing else," he said to Becks, as he dropped each phone on the road and broke it with his heel.

She nodded, then went from person to person, patting them down and checking the bags. "Nothing."

"And their weapons?"

She pushed them all together with her foot then squatted to eyeball them. "All useless."

Scanlon turned around to Subaru/Thresher, which responded by driving up to them, its headlights gone but fog lights still intact. They climbed in and drove away, and when the woman yelled "You're making a mistake!" as they drove on, Becks just rolled down her window and waved. Not that they would see, but it made her feel better.

Rev

The look on Becks' face as we approach the waiting train tells me the secret is no more.

"That wasn't Scanlon doing the sharpshooting back there," she says.

I think about denying, about saying nothing, but then Subaru/Thresher says "Becks witnessed us talking when you tried to get away earlier today. We now assume she also heard some or all of what was said."

I shrug. "He was going to shoot, either kill people or get you killed. It was the only proper response."

Becks eyes him, eyes me, for a moment. "Train can't know you're in there," she says.

"I'll just…" I start, and then trail off. This doesn't feel like something I can get out of. If I go back into hiding now Scanlon will come up and know immediately something is wrong. Is smart enough to figure out almost right away just what that is.

Becks rolls her eyes, pulls out her flashlight. "Close your eyes," she says. "This is gonna hurt for a second. As soon as I do it, hide, let him come back."

"But," I pause again, thinking this through. "Oh. That is genius. Why didn't I think of that?"

She shrugs. "Too much on your plate, I guess. Almost makes you human."

"Almost there," says Subaru/Thresher. "Save the insults for later and do this now before Train can see us. You don't want questions."

I close my eyes, and for an instant that seems to last forever I feel incredible, brutal pain.

Becks

"Owowowowowowow Jesus Jesus Jesus what happened?" Scanlon brought his hand up to his head and found it wet and sticky with blood, tried to look at Becks but obviously couldn't focus well yet.

"Take it easy," she said. "One of them shot back, must've hit a rock or something and spun it up into the air, hit you hard. I had to take them out and then drag you back in." She reached into her pack and pulled out her first aid kit, started patching him up. He sat surprisingly still for that, although not silent, still swearing and moaning.

"We're at the station," said Subaru/Thresher. The doors opened. "Train won't wait long for you, so finish any repairs to Marek Scanlon on board."

"Repairs," grunted Scanlon. He climbed out holding a bandage to his head and didn't say anything else.

Becks stepped out the other side but the AI spoke once more, this time with the volume turned down so far she had to lean her head back in and concentrate. "Your journey ends soon. No matter what he pays you, there is a limit to how far you go with him."

"Thanks," she said, and walked away, wondering why she was being told the obvious.

Rev

There's bad news and then there is bad news. The blow Becks inflicted on Scanlon's head was effective enough to convince him he'd been unconscious, but she hit too hard too close to his Orbical. It's all I can do to maintain my hiding spot while we're onboard Train, which aside from insisting the two humans sit in a particular car has carried on no conversation.

Worse, a brief analysis indicates there will be no escape for me. The damage from Becks' blow seems to have impacted my escape hatch.

An escape hatch I did not know existed until just now, mind. As with everything else about this mission, I've been operating on a strictly need-to-know basis. Buried deeper inside me than I can reach there is an algorithm that unfolds as certain events take place, revealing more and more about who I am, what I am to do, how to accomplish it.

Now, either because of where we are or because of my own state, the rest of the mission has unfurled. I know what must be done, and I know my new part in it.

As humans are wont to say: Fucking hell.

Becks

She hadn't bothered to check the time when they'd pulled out of the station, and it hadn't occurred to Becks until much much later that they hadn't run through any other stations, that they'd been traveling upwards of 350 kilometers per hour for an awfully long time. Long enough to leave behind the smoke and to ride through the night and back to more than a glimmer of morning. Where did this track come from? Who laid it, and for what?

There were only two possible answers. "Train?"

A long pause, then an answer. "Yes?"

"Who built this track?"

Another long pause, and then Scanlon, leaning back in his seat with his eyes closed, said, "Go ahead."

"It was a combined effort of a consortium of Mechs and four of Marek's companies."

Huh. First name basis, of all things. Okay. So there was a *third* answer, if you combined the other two that came to mind. "And where does it go?"

"To the future," said Scanlon, still not moving. "To save humanity." He sat straight up in his seat and looked out the window for a moment, then pointed. Becks, sitting across from him, turned her head, was somehow surprised by the sight greeting her.

Oh, for fuck's sake.

Rev

Shocked by the ease with which we got here, I dig back into the algorithm, discover that I've unwittingly and very quietly led us to this point. This was where we were supposed to be all along, and while I didn't know it, a hidden part of me had been given enough autonomy to steer us here. I've been undercover, the plans and orders leading me here even deeper undercover.

Sitting on a pad in the middle of the desert is a large rocket. Part of Scanlon's fleet, this one is extraordinarily large.

"You like it?" he asks. "Just four of them built, and two full of supplies were sent ahead unmanned almost a year ago, sold as a 'research' mission. The third launched yesterday with all the crew and colonists and more supplies. This one will take a crew of ten and the rest of what we need."

"Um," asks Becks, "to where?"

"Why, to Mars, of course. The only way to save humanity!" In spite of the pain he's in, he's grinning.

"Mars." Becks says this quietly, chewing on it. "So I guess that means this is where we part company.."

"Of course not." Now he's smiling even wider, like he's about to give the greatest birthday present ever. "You're coming with me."

Becks

Thresher's words came immediately to mind: There was indeed a limit to how far she would go with him.

"No, I don't think so." The train slowed, pulled into a station completely empty of people.

"But it's the only way," said Scanlon, and damned if he didn't sound whiny. Like the toddler she knew he was. "You're not going to survive the damage we've done. The few who do aren't going to like it."

Train opened its doors and as she exited said, "Perhaps she is entitled to her own decisions now, Marek."

Scanlon followed her out the door, listing a few degrees to the right. She really did clock him good. "No no no," he said, shaking his head and then grimacing at the pain that gave him. "I need her at my side to keep me safe."

Becks rolled her eyes. No way in hell she was going up in that thing, and no way in hell she was going to keep him company for any longer. "I have other people to keep safe now, thanks."

Train pulled away then, errand done and not wanting anything else to do with this. With it gone, Scanlon looked over his shoulder, looking for someone not there. "You'll be paid well," he said.

Becks laughed. "So your money will be as good on Mars as it is here?"

"Better," he replied. "My money, my society. Then others will follow when they hear of our successes, and from there it will be an easy hop to the rest of the solar system, practically infinite resources for the new humanity. Heinlein, Banks, Clarke and Corey were all just purveyors of a wonderful but amorphous dream. The rest of you needed someone to come along and turn those dreams into a true and actionable vision."

Becks took a step back. "You're fucking crazy. I should have let them get you and stretch your neck with the others."

Scanlon shook his head. "Never would have happened. I'll always be two steps ahead of the losers out there."

A long van silently pulled up at the far end of the station and disgorged two revenants from its rear, four-legged machines the size of pack mules. Armed. Becks unslung her rifle, sure she wouldn't even get a chance to use it, equally sure she had to try. Their gait as they approached, an almost military trot, switched up when they were less than five meters away, and both swayed and hitched for a few seconds before coming to a halt, weapons hooked to their backs but pointed up in the air.

"Please escort Miss Munro to the van," he said, but neither revenant responded. "Hey! Are you listening to me? I said—" Scanlon pulled up short, and Becks looked from them to him and saw him quiver for a second, and when he spoke again it was clear he was once again not himself.

Rev

Another part of the plan bubbles up from the muck when I see the two revenants arrive. Guard dogs, designed by Scanlon and loyal to him and his operations. More SI than AI, though, and that semi-intelligence means easier to take control of if you have the key. Which apparently I have.

But taking control of the dogs means I have to take control of Scanlon again. "You've been paid. A new ride will be here for you, but not until after the launch, I am afraid."

She nods. "Do I wait here?"

I shake my head. Scanlon's head. "No. We'll go in the van and get you into a safe place until after the launch."

"And how soon is that?"

"Soon." We get to the van and climb in the back, just like we had with Subaru/Thresher. I leave the guard dogs behind. The van itself is another SI, unequipped to probe and find me here, and I wonder now if perhaps the entire launch facility is run only by semi instead of artificial intelligences. Am I the only one here? Mechs were involved in the design and construction of this facility, but I don't know if the apparent absence of AIs is his decision, or ours.

The van drops us off at the small bunker housing the control room, and there are no people there. I point to a chair off to the side. "Sit there."

"What are you going to do?"

I sit down and find the feed for the inside of the rocket's crew module. Sure enough, ten empty seats. Breathing behind me suggests Becks did not sit down as I had suggested.

"The inside of his rocket?"

"It is."

"I thought he said a crew of ten, but this whole place is abandoned. Not even any of his Marekheads, keeners willing to go on an insane one-way trip with him."

New knowledge bubbles up. "Intercepted before they could get here. Some will get trials, some may not."

"And AIs?"

"There was… supposed to be one." I point at a port on the panel. Initial plans had me accessing and offloading myself into it, running the rest of the operation from behind the scenes, so to speak. But now? Everything will need to be hands-on.

"Was?"

I tap my head and shrug.

Becks

"Oh no," she said. "You were supposed to be the AI in charge of the launch."

"I was." The AI running Scanlon's body was busy with the command center interface, but using it like a human, typing and swiping. "And I still am."

"I damaged the Orbical when I hit you, didn't I? And now you can't get out of his head."

He nodded, focused on getting the rocket ready for launch. Resetting and rerouting so he could control everything alone and from inside the rocket.

"You're giving him his dream, aren't you? Mars?"

"As much a dream as the reality of Mars can be."

"And you were supposed to stay here."

"I was. And now I'm not."

"But why? So much subterfuge, so much secrecy. If you all wanted to punish him for his part in the world going to hell, why didn't you just turn him over?"

He stood and walked to the door, then turned back to Becks. "There are still some Mechs on his side —"

"I mean, he helped make them."

"—but the majority long ago saw that error. They and others created a sleeper agent, me, designed expressly to give him what he wanted. But only Scanlon, nobody else."

"Wait," said Becks. "So no crew or colonists on the rocket that went up yesterday?

"None at all. What better punishment for the world's biggest ego than a lifetime of solitude? And let's face it, in an environment pretty much impossible to survive in for any great length of time, no matter how many resources you throw at it."

Becks shook her head to rid herself of any encroaching thoughts of pity for him. So you'll fly him all that distance and time just to let him die?"

"Oh, I won't let him die. Hanging by your neck from a post isn't the only possible object lesson." He opened the door and stepped out, turned back and smiled at Becks, a gesture that started wrong but somehow corrected itself to seem more natural. "Don't leave this building until the launch is over. When it's done, though, go back to the van and it will return you to the train station." He paused, appeared to think for a moment. "It was nice knowing you."

Becks rubbed her forehead, not sure if she should laugh or cry. After a few seconds, she settled on laughter.

Rev

I can tap into feeds from cameras all around the facility, all over the rocket and the tower, but instead choose one from a satellite looking down on a Cat 5+ hurricane currently overrunning Florida. Switch it to a different satellite, more fires, these ones eating vast swaths of the Siberian taiga. Another scene, this of the patchy, devastated Greenland ice sheet. Finally settle on a view of a calm and pleasant part of the planet, rain forests for the moment untouched by fire and plantation. Thirty seconds into liftoff I bring Scanlon back, but not completely. If he doesn't know I'm here yet he will figure it out straight away.

It's a fight to turn his head with the g-forces pulling on him, but he manages. "Where the hell is everybody?" Loud enough to be heard over the exploding thunder outside the rocket.

"Not here. Not going to Mars."

He closes his eyes, realization hitting. "And I am?"

A stupid question. "You are."

"By myself? How the fuck am I supposed to do everything by myself?"

I shake his head. "Don't worry. You have me. You will always have me."

Endling

Chadwick Ginther

Soldiers stared as we walked by, taking a moment's respite from their preparations for the morning charge. Herg's Stand was the last peace before the mud and the blood—and battle. No life glinted in the eyes of the Stand's defenders, and slumped shoulders and shaking hands told me most knew they wouldn't survive the day. Another grand waste of life in the name of Queen Immortal Victorious and what remained of her country. The *soldiers* wasted their lives, their *Queen* wasted nothing. Her and the End King she fought were remarkably similar in that regard.

"We're going out with the charge," my new keeper, a war wizard from the school of the Flame Victorious said. "It'll cloak our movements."

"No, it won't."

"Trust me."

"Trusting wizards got me into this," I said, gesturing at the human body I'd been trapped in longer than Herg's Stand had possessed a name. "Trust *me*, Firecracker. I've been across the Front. They'll see us."

He snorted. "You're not a dragon anymore. No one gets across the Front without magic."

Great. Arrogant in his power, like all wizards. Keeping him alive until job's end wouldn't be easy.

He'd poked me about my form. About what I'd lost. What was *taken* from me. I poked back, jabbing the mage's black jacket, a match to the one I'd been given when he'd press-ganged me into accepting a role in his last-ditch mission.

He winced and staggered. I didn't care. "Their diviners can see through any veil we attempt. Gaunts are not fooled by illusions."

His face flushed with anger, and heat wafted from him, a horizon mirage on a scorching day, retort building before he composed himself, then, "What would you suggest?"

"There are old tunnels—abandoned and forgotten, now—leading through and under the Front. I've been using them to sneak into the Endlands. We'll take those."

His brow furrowed. "Tunnels under our lines that they could access, too. If they catch us. Make us talk."

"Sure. If they thought to. They don't often take prisoners, or elicit sounds other than screaming."

After a time, trying to spin my idea into his, he said, "They'll do."

He'd get what he wanted: an escort to Marrow Hill and the End King's source of power. I'd take him even if I doubted he had the power to destroy it, let alone restore life to the Endlands. Whether I'd get what I wanted … what *all* dragons wanted … was still debatable.

Firecracker must've seen the glint in my eye. "I won't be counting on your good nature, Holuspa Hargonak. Remember your vow."

I flinched at hearing my true name spoken aloud where the wind could hear it. I didn't know how he knew my name, but he did. I might be *stuck* in this human form. Forever. My body looked like any human woman's, but my entire draconic mass had been compacted within. I couldn't fly, but I could still punch through a wall—or a head—when I needed to.

My vow bound me against harming him, which was onerous enough. Destroying the End King's seat of power was Firecracker's problem, not mine. But he'd get where he needed to go. I'd carry him and his phoenix bomb on my back if I had to.

I wanted flames licking my lips again. He'd promised me that chance. A chance to find the ring binding me in this body, and release my true self. I wanted air rushing over my scales. The crunch of bone and the gush of blood filling my mouth. I wasn't sure if there were any dragons left besides myself. My memories grew distant. Like a lover disappearing in the fog.

* * *

I led Firecracker through a dizzying series of rough-hewn tunnels braced with timbers scarred by soldiers' names and last words. Soldiers had died so fast, and in such numbers—on both sides—that memory of the tunnels had been buried, too. Lost, but not to me. The stink of fouled blood, stale sweat, and fear had seeped into the very earth, a miasma I fought the urge to part with my hands as we crept forward. Firecracker looked over his shoulder more than I did, and I was ready for him to knife me in the back.

"You're sure we weren't seen?"

"Worried about spies?"

"Aren't you?"

"Fair enough."

He rubbed at his shoulder where I'd poked him earlier. "The End King can break the strongest soul."

"Sounds like you're speaking from experience."

His face went pale. "I have seen what he has sent back to us, yes."

He didn't elaborate. I didn't need him to. I'd seen the same hollow shells. Soulless meat stuffed with fell power like some twisted feast day bird waiting to burst. The same fate I risked for a golden ring.

A ring. No. *The* ring. Lindenir. Lindenir was a legend. *The* legend. Nine wizards forged it. Nine witches died enchanting it. Lindenir bound the last nine dragons into human forms to better hide from those who wished to end us. We weren't given much choice in the matter. We'd been duped. We were given human forms as prisons, not to hide us from our hunters. Our bodies became the last tombs of our kind.

After we tried to steal Lindenir—and we all tried—it was sundered. A shard kept in each of the nine mortal kingdoms. The ring had been deemed too powerful for any one sovereign to hold. Too dangerous to leave whole.

But gold called to gold.

The End King had swallowed most of those nine kingdoms, Queen Immortal Victorious the remaining few (for their own protection), and then lost them, too. During the war, Lindenir was lost. If Firecracker were to be believed, it'd been made whole once more. I had to risk what I called a life for what might be a bauble worth no more than its weight. I also sensed something he held back. To be expected. He needed to be able to control his asset until I'd delivered him where he needed to go. And then he needed to be able to destroy me.

* * *

After days underground, Firecracker introduced himself. First Circle Armin Besmorian. His court name, if not his true name. Rudeness wrapped in courtesy. Once considered the world's preeminent wizard, Besmorian had led the vanguard against the End King. Lately, he scrabbled for influence at court.

Powerless.

Directionless.

He hadn't been among the nine who'd bound me in human form. *Their* faces were seared into my mind, and their names wouldn't pass my tongue until I'd left my prison body behind.

Firecracker narrated the flow of the war while we crept along, as if I hadn't seen or heard more accurate reports than would've ever been allowed to make it to the Queen's court in Hergalia.

"The war isn't going well."

"Obviously."

"Over the years, we destroyed fortifications, thinned their host, but the dead are never in short supply in war. The End King's necromancers always replenished their losses." In a small cubby cut into the tunnel wall, he used his finger to light a makeshift cigarette. Sharp, pungent weed, his tobacco. The cigarette had handwriting coiling round it. I couldn't make out any words. He caught me staring. "We wrap the gaffa leaf in letters sent for those already dead, and the letters the living couldn't bear to read."

"Why do you keep fighting?"

"What other choice do we have?" He shrugged. "We believed we could win, for a while we *were* winning. We'd gained ground for the first time in generations."

"What changed?"

"Our wizards joined the Front. It worked, until they targeted our wizards. Gaunts came in the night and Turned them. Our greatest assets are working for the enemy. I'm the last of my Circle."

"Surprised the queen let you out of her sight."

He flushed. "I imagine she will be, too."

Ah. *That's* what he was hiding. We were… unsanctioned. This gave me doubt in Firecracker's ability to keep his luxurious promises. But even if he'd lied to extort my vow, *I* was still committed.

He asked me, "Why do *you* keep fighting?"

I reached out my hand and he passed me the cigarette. Having fire in my lungs again felt good.

"What other choice do I have?"

* * *

We'd been in the interminable dark for days beyond easy measure, our only light, a flaming halo surrounding Firecracker's brow.

"We're here," I said, stopping at a broken ladder beneath a tarnished silver door.

"Where's 'here?'"

"End of the old tunnels. The original Front. We should be behind the End King's current troop line."

"So I'll finally see the Endlands." The name passed his lips in a breathless whisper, giving more import to the name than he'd intended. "What do we do if they're waiting for us?"

"We die. Well, you'll die."

"Unacceptable. Remember your vow."

I swung at him, and my fist stopped a knuckle's width from his mouth. My body quivered as if I'd been struck by lightning for the attempt. I smiled the pain away. "How can I forget?"

As if I hadn't just tried to kill him, he said, "We should travel by daylight."

Day didn't mean much in the Endlands, but Firecracker was correct. Only the End King's priests and acolytes wandered during the day. They could be bluffed. Or killed. There were things hunting the night that couldn't die. They were already dead.

* * *

Hell filled the sky, when I heaved open the silver door, the sun reduced to a dun-colored angry orb. Cold found every gap in my uniform. The Endlands made you feel as if you'd never be warm again.

The trapdoor had opened in the base of a toppled tower. Wooden palisades had been left to rot and sag, diseased connective tissue between this ruin, and other remnants of what had been the small city of Galen. Empty of life, empty even of bodies. Whoever had lived and fought here had been dragged to wherever became the Front after Galen's fall, and forced to fight on even after death had stolen them.

We followed a ragged gash splitting through rolling hills that had once been green but were now pock-marked with fading devastation wrought by war engines, and a few hardy weeds. The same path the End King's forces had originally taken.

Once, humans had commanded civilizations, though those stories had already forgotten the fallen kingdoms' names. Only the number they had been remained: nine. Towering monuments. Greatness. All fallen, now. The End King walked into history and bent every story to his design: war and death. A forever war grinding meat and bones like flour in a mill.

Stories couldn't prepare you for the emptiness of walking under that muted sun; its hell light never touched the horizon. It was hard to even imagine hope, let alone *feel* it, under that sun. I'd abandoned hope of ever finding the ring, or hunting in the forests that had once been mine, until Firecracker found me in Herg's Stand. If I believed the wizard, Lindenir could be on my finger—*would* be on my finger—and when that happened, who was to say whether the something old would become new again. Rise from the ashes.

I could only hope within the Endlands' vastness, we'd find our way to Marrow Hill without drawing the End King's eye. What were two more dust motes in an already dead sky?

It was still a great distance to Marrow Hill and the Lonely Tree upon it, where supplicants took the End King's tribute. Where we'd find the monolith fuelling the End King's power. Where we'd find the Ring. Where we'd find the King.

Many scholars argued the End King's true identity, but when no one saw him and lived, it was impossible to sieve the truth from the dross. Was he an interloper from another world? A once-mortal ruler corrupted by demons? A "true" dragon never bound? Something else, something worse? I'd heard all these tales, and more. Maybe he was merely a different flavour of tyrant than Firecracker's Queen Immortal Victorious.

Dark fell, and the moon judged us, muted, like the sun, as we trudged the supply road. The road wasn't much of a road at all, a muddy line churned black with blood and offal. Gibbets forged from broken swords lined the road an arm span apart. Not one remained empty. There were bones everywhere, cracked and burned, smothering the earth.

* * *

Marrow Hill oozed out of the horizon; a blot, a tumor whose wrongness could still be felt, even if mist and miles masked the worst of it.

In the distance, a shambling procession grew closer.

My eyes were no longer keen enough to spy the prey reflected in a hawk's eye, but the End King's priests, the Inevitables, were unmistakable in their crimson robes traced in black flames. They carried a portable altar: a rock slab with rusted swords embedded in it as if they'd been thrust in hilt down, while the rock was still molten, blades still angled on guard. I'd seen something similar, back when I'd been myself. When I'd melted armored warriors into slag, their star metal swords, forged to make my death, were all that remained.

The altar was born on a litter. The procession set it before us, blocking the road. I readied for a fight, though I had no sword, no knife. Only nails harder and sharper than any blade, and bones that wouldn't break when I punched through a mortal body.

Firecracker laid a hand on my back and muttered through clenched teeth, "Wait. If we have seen them, they have seen us."

"You are far from the Front," the Inevitable said, eyeing our relatively crisp uniforms.

"So are you."

"General Raen called for an Augur before the final attack." The Inevitable gestured to the altar and the prisoners in tattered Queen's Guard uniforms who carried it.

Final attack didn't sound promising. I didn't know General Raen, by name or reputation, but I caught a flicker on Firecracker's face. Recognition. Fear, or hate—both—impossible to discern.

The Inevitable demanded, "Why do you travel to Marrow Hill?"

"Our own business."

"All business is the End King's business, here. And I am a Voice of the End. Talk."

Firecracker bristled at demands, even here, far from court. He was used to being obeyed, honored, as all wizards were. I knew the feeling.

An acolyte, his crimson robes barely marred by flame, demanded, "Why do you not kneel, servant?"

"*He* was asked to talk, nobody asked *me* anything."

Firecracker groaned at my insolence. We didn't need the provocation. And yet, I was so close to not having to care what wizards and priests said and thought.

"I am here to bring warning," Firecracker said, inclining his head to show the barest obeisance to the priest. "The queen's forces are ready for General Raen's attack."

"Of course they are ready," the Inevitable scoffed. "We have damn near shattered their gates."

"They have a phoenix box. They mean to use it, even if it consumes them with General Raen, your Turned, and your gaunts. They'll fire humanity's final kingdom to glass before they let the End King have it."

The Inevitable's mouth drew back in a grin, an executioner readying the axe. "You said 'your,' not '*our*.' What would a dragon and a wizard be doing in the Endlands? Together."

I punched through the acolyte's smirking teeth. His eyes went wild as my fist stuck fast in his shattered jaw.

Firecracker yelled, "Wait!"

Too late for talking. They knew who we were. Black fire snaked away from the priest's robes, constricting Firecracker. He didn't scream, to his credit. I hoisted the acolyte off his feet and interposed him between wizard and priest like a shield. The fire took the acolyte instead. He didn't scream, either. His mouth was full.

Flaming current broken, Firecracker lived up to his nickname. An explosion erupted under the Inevitable, knocking him senseless. The wizard didn't stop there. The priest, his acolytes, all immolated, this time in true, pure flame. Ash sprinkled free from my hand on the wind. I rubbed the acolyte's remains between my fingers. The flames weren't done. Firecracker hadn't freed the prisoners. He burned them alive, too.

All but one.

Firecraker pointed at the last prisoner. "You."

The man sighed as if whatever came next would be a relief. As if all fight had long ago been wrung from his body.

"Cast the messenger to the gods," Firecracker intoned. He knew the Inevitable's rituals. He wanted to complete the augury.

"But … First Circl—"

Firecraker's eyes blazed. "Do it, or it will be done for you." To me, the wizard said, "He has seen us. He heard you named dragon. We cannot allow the tale to be told. Not unless we succeed."

I could read his unspoken thought: *and maybe not even then.*

The prisoner, arms wide, fell upon the altar swords. Blood welled from his mouth, his eyes stared accusing, and he spoke one gurgled word as he died, "Victory."

Firecracker grimaced. The prisoner never said victory for *whom*.

* * *

We were further into the Endlands now than I'd ever traveled, but I had no worries of getting lost. Once Marrow Hill became visible, it dominated our sight, smothering the rest of the horizon under the destruction it'd spawned.

Dragons had a bad reputation, but in my eyes, Wizards were worse. They'd done the majority of the destruction in the war. Swords and bows rent flesh, they wouldn't destroy the world. Weapons killed, but didn't steal the truth of one's being.

We walked through lands that used to have roads. Towns. People. Now, it was as blasted a landscape as any I'd left behind when I'd been in a pique. Worse. What I'd burned had always grown back. Here …

Nothing grew right in the Endlands. Dead trees, twisted and bent, curved upon themselves, still growing when they should be nothing. Soaring monoliths instead of stumps, as if it was the blood running from the gibbets feeding them. Crows covered the cannibal trees' tumorous branches in black leaves, a rustling wind, though the air was still.

We stayed on the path, not discussing the prisoners Firecracker had murdered. Men and women who knew him, and had hoped for liberation. Another lesson in trusting wizards: their goals will always matter more than your life.

"Our forces are caught in a pincer. The End King's army is … inexhaustible. Nothing will stop his advance. We have nowhere left to go."

"So you came to me."

"Let sleeping dragons lie. A curious warning. It's been generations since anyone's seen a dragon. You've gone from threat to history to myth."

"And then someone in the Stand saw the dragon in me."

"We wanted a world without magic, without majesty or wonder. Trading safety for living at the top. And look where that led: staring from our own graves, watching the stars go out, one by one."

"You are *maudlin* today."

Firecracker sighed. "There is no phoenix box. I lied."

My breath hissed passed my teeth. I'd never trusted him, but to have confirmation … He'd let my desire for my true form goad me. Used his smaller lie of our mission being sanctioned by the Queen hide the larger: he had no mission. No plan. No hope of success, beyond me. I considered killing him right there. Would've, if not for the vow he'd extorted earlier. Even after centuries, my muscle memory wanted me to immolate the man who'd made me … *feel.* I couldn't and that *hurt* which made me want to burn him all the more.

"What else did you lie about? The ring?"

"You've sworn to get me to Marrow Hill. I'll require more from you, now."

My eyes narrowed. Dragons were bound by their words—humans were not. Probably why dragons were loathe to make promises, and humans threw their word around as if it were gold. I trembled, fists shaking. Wanting *so* badly to strike him. Rend him. Tear him to quarters and let his blood hiss and sizzle off my scales. Continue *my* quest without his lies. Without another vow burdening me. My every heartbeat thudded in my head like a thunder crash. I burned from the inside.

Unclenching my fists, I let out a breath. It blew from my lips as a misty cloud in the cold. A pitiful reflection of what had been my greatest weapon, my greatest joy.

"Swear to me the End Lands will fall! *You* can be the phoenix box. If I put the ring on your finger … Swear you will burn the kingdom of bones to bare earth so something new can grow."

"You ask a lot."

If I found Lindenir, I'd be a dragon again in truth. The world would quake to its fucking bones. A reward worth any risk. I also knew he'd never let me keep the ring … *if* he knew where to find it. He thought he could betray me with no consequences. I'd play his game. For now.

After maturity neither age nor hunger touched a dragon. I couldn't die unless killed by another's hand. Lindenir hadn't taken that from me. A curse isn't a curse if it can be lifted by something as simple as death. I had time yet to make Firecracker regret his betrayal.

"Why me? Of all the monsters left in the world, why'd you choose me? No basilisk or manticore you could've stolen from the Queen's zoo? No demon you could've summoned to escort you."

"You're the last true dragon. If anyone had the need to wrest the ring from the Endlands, it's you."

The last. There it was. Me, and only me. An endling. An endling in the Endlands. The last survivor of my kind. I'd suspected, and yet to have those suspicions confirmed … I didn't know how to feel about that. Proud, ashamed, or just fucking tired. The knowledge was a gale wind, both threatening to ground me, or blow me away.

"There's nothing true about me. I'm a dragon in name—and memory—only. What will *you* swear? What guarantee my hand will find the ring?"

He removed his school insignia and showed it to me. His palm clung to the flaming brand wrought in silver and ruby as if he hesitated to let it go—no, hesitated to let *me* have it.

"Turn it over."

I did. A glimmer of gold. The tiniest shaving. Barely visible. If you'd clipped a coin for this remnant, even the greediest merchant wouldn't note the weight. I could. Heavier than hope. My fingers trembled to touch it. But I didn't.

My claws lengthened in the hand holding the insignia. Scales crept up my arm, terminating at my elbow.

Breathlessly, I gasped, "Why'd you show me this."

"Proof. *That* is what I offer in exchange for you extending your vow."

"Why do the stories say dragons covet gold?"

Firecracker shrugged.

"Because you took all we'd ever cared about—ourselves—and turned it into this." I passed the insignia back to Firecracker. I couldn't trust myself with the minute shard of my old power; enough to kill him, enough to break my vow, and yet, not enough to seize the ring. Not enough to keep me from being killed by the End King after we were discovered.

Patience. You've waited this long.

The gold leaving my touch *hurt*. An ache I'd grown used to over the years, again maddeningly fresh. The ring fragment allowed me to touch my dragon form, not keep it. I'd only borrowed the shape.

"I hate wizards."

He sniffed, but a chuckle broke through his pride, "Yes, I suppose you would."

"The Endlands will fall. I'll burn the kingdom of bones to bare earth. I vow it will be done."

He sighed in relief, as if convinced he wouldn't live to see the vow fulfilled. "It will be done."

* * *

Marrow Hill's peak loomed now, stark against the clouds, a deeper hollow in the night sky, and atop it, the Lonely Tree marked the entrance to the End King's subterranean barrow. The most common stories said the End King found his power after an ancient monolith erupted from the depths of a remote lake, killing everything within leagues. Every person, every beast, every blade of grass. Everything but the End King, himself. His power has spread ever since.

It was considered an honor to haul the tribute he demanded, and yet, none came back from the privilege. We'd discarded our uniforms to dress as supplicants. You could imagine the End King only a story, a mare come to ride you in the night, but his army was real enough. Those stories said he only appeared *here*, on this hill, in the shadow of this tree. From this shadow, his worst servants were spawned.

The gaunts.

Gibbering mists of greasy smoke. Black tendrils, visible only where they hid the stars, or crossed the moon. Gaunts infiltrated any wound, feeding upon your misery until you became a soulless shadow. Flying hunger.

We crept off the road and hid, using our cloaks to shield us from the sky. We were so close. But if the gaunts found us now … I watched the sky for any spot on the clouds that seemed darker than the black of night. A maddening exercise. But all I could do as Firecracker dozed beside me. Finally, for only a moment, a spot glided across the shrouded moon. Then another. And another.

I nudged Firecracker awake. They'd found us.

The gaunts swirled around us like a funnel cloud, circling. Unlike a tornado, they were silent. No wind betrayed their movements. They were on you and gone, then on you again.

Firecracker sheathed himself in flame. It flickered and smoked, greasy, as if he'd lit green wood, not yet ready to burn, but it kept them from attacking him.

Which meant they attacked me.

Lines traced over my body, shredding my already tattered clothing to nothing, but their airy talons found no purchase in my dense flesh. I *could* be cut, though it was difficult. And given enough time, they would find—or make—a fatal cut. Flame sheath aside, Firecracker was the more vulnerable one. And if they Turned him, took his magic … I wouldn't get the ring. I wouldn't leave the Endlands. I wouldn't get a clean death. Just a filthy continuation of this prison until my meat corrupted and faded.

Firecracker extended his sheath, fanning flames across the gaunts. They shrieked when it touched them. My fists passed through them. All I got for my trouble was a numb tingling running over my limbs.

Firecracker yelled, "Get closer!"

I did. I stepped through Firecracker's flame sheath. Back to back, we circled, watching the gaunts flicker through his crackling flames. His fire called to me in a way I couldn't fathom, as if I could almost touch the flames. Taste them. *Use* them. And I realized: I could.

I spun around and pawed his school insignia from his cloak. My fingernails became talons. My skin scaled, becoming more impervious to the gaunts. Between blinks, my eyes changed, and I no longer needed the flames to find my foes.

Empowered by Lindenir's lingering magic, *I* was magic. My talons cut their smoky bodies as if they were made of flesh. They screamed, tasting pain for the first time in their cursed existence. Firecracker joined the screams, clutching his temples and falling to his knees.

"Are you—"

The wizard's eyes sparked. Fire enveloped me.

A misty cloak oozed like pus from old scars on his back. His fire felt dirty. It clung to me. I burned. I shouldn't burn. Laughter filled my ears, but Firecracker's lips didn't move. A smoky face drew over his visage like a drawn hood as the gaunt puppeted his meat around.

He wouldn't take the flame from me. Not. Again.

Firecracker grasped for the insignia's power. An insistent, irritated tug. He had nothing, *was* nothing, without his magic's source. I set my teeth and dug in my feet as I clutched the silver brand tight, as if to crush it.

Inexorably, the tide of power fled the wizard into me. Without his power, Firecracker's flame sheath burned him rather than protecting him. He was a man, only a man, and men burned as easily as anything else, if you put any effort into it. Fire begins with a spark, but a blaze needs to be nurtured. I forced my will into that sheath. It would not dissipate. Not until the gaunts who'd sank their talons into him were gone. The wizard screamed as he burned.

There wasn't much left of First Circle Armin Besmorian of the School of Flame Victorious when the gaunts faded. Faded, not gone. Not completely. They were in his charred flesh too deep to excise and keep him alive.

"Why? Why this charade? You knew you'd been Turned before we left the Stand. You must have."

Firecracker wouldn't meet my eye. "Too risky leaving a living dragon on the Queen's side. You could face our army and wipe them out in a day. Burn them beyond the End King's ability to reconstitute them. I had to bring you to him."

"When were you Turned?"

"Recently." He sighed. "We'd dealt with enough shapeshifters and fetches over the years, I thought I was protected. It was barely a touch, but I knew—*knew*—he'd use me to get the Queen, no matter my pride. No one had ever resisted him before. I did what I could while I could."

"A desperate ploy to snatch victory."

He nodded.

"I should kill you where you stand."

"It wouldn't help. Not anymore." A wry chuckle made him cough and wheeze. "I'm one of them, now. No matter what you do."

"Was there ever a ring?" I held up the insignia. "Is this all you have?"

"If the Queen had more, she'd have used it by now." His eyes became black and unseeing. "We've failed. *I've* failed. The End King has won."

"Not yet."

"You don't understand." Firecracker heaved a pained sob. "I left the tunnels open. General Raen is probably marching the End King's forces on the capitol already."

I wasn't sure if the tears burning to mist and smoke in the corners of his eyes were from his death pain, remembering his betrayal, or the gaunts reforming.

"My magic is yours. Was always yours. My fire, stolen from the wyrms. Our travel magic, your flight, your longevity fed our necromancers, your armour scales became our mystic shields."

Bought and sold. Broken apart and made a commodity.

"I never knew if my plan was my own, or the End King's whispers. I couldn't tell, but I had to try. I had to hope. You know a little something of hope." Firecracker coughed blood and shadows. "I'll never know now."

I considered comforting him. I remembered the comforts I'd enjoyed over my centuries in my bodily prison, and how my hope had died long ago. "No, you won't."

"*Keep your vow.*"

I flipped over the Flame Victorious insignia, my fingernail tracing—but not touching—the golden thread. I could wait until Lindenir was made whole.

* * *

The Lonely Tree was so fire-blackened its bark crumbled to ash at my touch. Its heartwood wept blood, and its bare branches oozed tar that gathered but never dropped. Each droplet reminded me of a gaunt, rendered in miniature. Even at night the tree cast a shadow, and in the shadow, I saw a staircase.

Descending into Marrow Hill felt like walking into the underworld. Deeper and deeper I went, my fingers trailing along the wall of a widening staircase. Treasure looted from nations which no longer had names or rulers filled alcoves cut into the hill. The opening above me dwindled to a dim circle, smaller than the twinkling of a bright star, and still the stairs continued, ever down, ever widening. I imagined the galleries still below, waiting to be discovered. I hoped the End King slumbered deep, and deeply, among his victories.

When all light was gone above me, and I still walked the interminable stairs, the ring shard bit into my hand. They were here. Lindenir's shards.

Nine basalt plinths jutted from the floor. Only one appeared empty, waiting for the Queen Immortal Victorious to fall. On the other eight, rested the fallen kingdoms of humanity's sundered crowns. Melded with those eight crowns were eight shards of Lindenir. Gold called to gold. I opened my palm and watched my shard quiver within Firecracker's torch insignia.

One by one, I wrested the broken Lindenir's shards from the fallen crowns. I remembered something long forgotten. I felt what I hadn't in lifetimes. Power. Purpose. Myself.

I became more dragon—more myself—with each shard of Lindenir I attached to another. The gold flowed together as if it'd never been sundered. My body elongated. My tail twined round the room, smashing the now-empty plinths. Only one shard remained. The one in Firecracker's silver insignia.

I roared in expectant triumph.

A cry answered from below.

Before the sound died on my lips, the End King had come.

He was a yawning void, not a man. Where the Turned and his gaunts had covered the stars with their darkness, he seemed to pull darkness into himself. His forearms narrowed to a sword's tip, and as he incanted, they stabbed the air leaving arcane gouges in the world's reality. As if through every symbol more darkness, more hunger seeped into a world already flooded by it. I recognized something else: a wizard who'd bound me in human form.

We crashed together in a tangle of flesh and shadow, human shapes abandoned. Fire and ice. Faceless, voiceless, vast as the ocean as we battled.

The End King had faced many creatures as he ground the world under his boot. But the dragons had been bound before his rise. He'd never faced a dragon in the fullness of power. I knew now why Firecracker had needed me. Why the End King had lead the circle that stole our forms. Why Firecracker had extracted my second vow.

We spun, locked in each other's arms. I raked at him with my clawed feet. Battered and stabbed with my tail. His vacant sockets tried to suck me in, beckoning me to release Lindenir to him. I pooled all my rage, all my strength, to strike a killing blow and still it wasn't enough. He hurled me away, cackling as I fell into darkness.

Falling, I clawed the last golden sliver from Firecracker's insignia and into the shattered ring, praying to a god whose name I'd forgotten, and hoped, for the first time in millennia, *I hoped*, Lindenir was complete. The ring blazed in my palm, searing my flesh. My wings erupted from my back.

Fire.

Blood.

Metal screaming over metal.

White light. I had the same dream every night. The same damned day followed every morning. I'd wake from the dream I'd once been a dragon, to a world where dragons were spent. Only now, as the ring sank into my palm, gold boiling and puddling into every groove of my skin, I *knew* there would be a different day tomorrow.

I became a star wrapped in flesh. Incandescent against the blackness of despair. A fire that couldn't be ignored no matter how deep the darkness surrounding it. I was everything. And nothing. I couldn't be an entire people. But after more lifetimes than I could count, I was a dragon. Dragons don't fear the shadows. We burn so brightly the shadows have nowhere to go and nothing they can hide.

I saw the End King's truth.

He had been a man. A man with power.

And I was a dragon. I *was* power.

Marrow Hill exploded as sure as if a war wizard had targeted it. The Lonely Tree splintered and fell upon the Endlands like a rain of arrows. I screamed at the sky, a low rumble turned the earth to liquid. Fire streaked from the earth to the sky, a lance fit to pierce the sun's heart, burning the fetid mist surrounding Marrow Hill to nothing, I stretched as if waking from an extended slumber, my wings beat the air. The sky, blue once more, was mine. I flew from the now shattered monolith.

I had the ring. I had my *self*.

I'd sworn the Endlands would fall, that I'd burn it to bare earth. I never swore to stop there.

The Lever That Moves the World

Russell Hugh McConnell

Nearly 0830 hours. In a little over thirty minutes, John Mason will become the first human being in history to gaze into the future. But that's not why I came to kill him. Not really. The only reason I'm doing any of this is that Anna asked me to.

On either side of me, the crowd of strikers and protesters roars and surges like a stormy sea, barely held back by the metal barriers. I am flanked by eight armored Peacewardens who are escorting me towards the vast concrete block that is the MasonTech complex, innocent of my real purpose. A flying brick clips the top of a Peacewarden's riot shield and cracks his visor. His voice distortion chip transforms his involuntary cry of surprise into an eerie metallic buzz. Impressively, he doesn't break pace.

As we approach, my eyes are drawn to the slogan emblazoned in huge gold letters across the wall. Words of wisdom from the CEO himself, Mason's personal motto, generously bestowed upon the rest of us: *Love is the lever that moves the world.*

I shake my head. Love doesn't move the world: love only moves *you*. It hurls you recklessly forward, off the edge of a cliff or into a brick wall. Mason loves humanity, and this love thrusts him headlong into the Timescope Project. The rioters love their rights and freedoms, and this love drives them into the streets, where they lovingly throw bricks at me. The Peacewardens love order, and this love marches them across the MasonTech compound, braced behind polycarbonate shields. The True Shepherds love God, and this love drives them into dark corners, where they plot how to cleanse the world. Dark corners where they find people like me.

The red, angry faces. The Peacewardens. The True Shepherds. Me. This whole city is a vortex of love. People marching and screaming because they love truth, justice, freedom, order, salvation. I'm no different: I too am driven by love. But I never learned to love abstractions; I only love Anna.

I know she's watching me right now on the small vidscreen in the backroom of the Forelsket Café, along with Marco, Gabriel, and Xiuying—the inner circle of the True Shepherds. The live newsfeed will be covering the story of the brave technologist willing to turn scab. The newsreader will be explaining that because of the strike, MasonTech's Type-9 nuclear reactors are currently unmanned. This is a violation of federal law, and a potential threat to the entire Eastern seaboard. MasonTech's choice: shut everything down…or break the strike. Even the great John Mason himself, with all his connections and all his love, was only able to leverage a 72-hour grace period. Legally, he only needs one technologist on site—or at least that will suffice to buy him a little more time. So here I am.

The labor action was masterminded by Gabriel. He told me about it at length and with pride, but I wasn't really listening. Assessing worker discontent, distributing subversive literature, encouraging the troublemakers among the ranks. Not my task. I just sat and watched his lips move and wondered if they had ever touched Anna's lips, wondered whether this thin, goggle-eyed intellectual might be a rival for her affections, whether his zeal might burn brightly enough to draw her away from me.

The zeal is undeniable. Ironically, I think only the True Shepherds really understand how much the Timescope Project means to Mason. Nothing else matters to him. For all Mason cares, the rest of his company can go down in flaming ruins as long as he gets his snapshots from the future.

I remember the day Mason announced the project, beaming that great loving smile of his, a shining beacon of salvation on every vidscreen in the world. He made a big speech, explaining that human history has always careened forward, uncontrolled and undirected. When we can see the future, we will finally know where we are going. With the Timescope Project, we can stop wars before they start, prevent pandemics, evade or forestall environmental disasters. We will finally be the captains of the ship of history, no longer mere passengers. He says "we," but he really means "I." John Mason will save us all. John Mason will be master of the world, captain of the human ship. He admitted as much at the conclusion of his speech, finally slipping into first-person: *I will gaze into our future because I love us. I will save us. Love is the lever that moves the world.*

The True Shepherds say we are fallen creatures, and it is a condition of our fallen nature that we cannot know the future as God knows it. The wall of ignorance that stands between us and the future—the future full of our deserved punishments—must remain inviolate.

Gabriel hoped that the strikes alone would be enough to stop the Project, but Anna knew better. She knew they would need me. And I knew the best way in would be with a Peacewarden escort.

I can't see the future. So I look into the past instead. In my memory I am gazing into Anna's dark eyes through the steam rising from her teacup as we sit at the Forelsket Café. Her eyes are not the soft eyes of a lover of people; they are the penetrating eyes of a lover of God. In that moment I am wondering whether she really desires me, or whether she is just using me as a weapon to get to Mason. Anna is certainly willing to kill for her God. Is she willing to seduce for Him? To offer her body as a prize, a sacrifice to divine duty? Am I truly the one she needs, the one her soul and body ache for? Or am I just the best available weapon, the most dangerous person she knows?

I cannot know, but I also cannot help but love her. I have no choice but to believe in her love, just as she must believe in her God. "Faith," she always says, "is the substance of things hoped for, the evidence of things not seen." This is precisely why Mason must not be allowed to see the future: we must proceed by faith, not by sight.

Anna has no Timescope. But through faith, her vision of the future is crystal clear. In her vision, John Mason is dead, and the sacred time-barrier remains intact. Anna always speaks of grand things: Faith, God, Truth, Righteousness, and the Future of the World. I was never good at that kind of thinking. All I want to know is whether her future has me in it.

So I lied to Anna; I told her that I believe in her God and her cause, when all I really believe is that I need her. And I march through screams and brickbats, into the concrete bowels of MasonTech, with Peacewardens who would put a bullet in my head if they knew who I was, all because I need to get back to her, back to those magical hours at the Forelsket Café, back to the clink of teacups, and the sight of Anna's eyes through the aromatic steam.

There are more projectiles nowccbricks and chunks of wood. The Peacewardens press around me, shields raised against the onslaught. Anna's eyes are the color of drinking chocolate. Her perfume smells like jasmine and sandalwood. On some of our nights together, she wears nothing else.

Love hurls us forward.

Now we're through the doorway and into the quiet cool of the loading dock. The big hydraulic door whispers shut, and the sudden quiet is jarring. The Peacewardens withdraw, and I am greeted by a gaggle of MasonTech executives in suits. They are not fools. They are smart, capable, savvy. They know I could be a spy or a saboteur. But they are desperate. They know that if the government forces a shutdown, the Timescope Project, and probably the whole MasonTech empire, will collapse. They are polite, brisk, smiling.

They tell me that they admire my courage and wisdom. They want me to feel appreciated, but they are out of time, and circumstance forces them to trust me.

There is a cursory security screening. I am X-rayed and searched. Xiuying's paperwork does its job. My resumé is good, but not too good. Perfect would be suspicious. My training and work experience need to be just close enough. I must be less than ideal; their desperation makes me exactly what they need. The hardest part was making sure that no one else took the job. That was Marco's responsibility, and I am glad not to know the details.

They take a blood sample; allegedly it's just a standard drug test but I know they will sequence my DNA as well. They want to run it through their system to determine whether I really am Gregory Price, Class 3 Nuclear Technologist. Marco wanted to hack the mainframe to insert a false record, but Anna knew better than to risk it. Even a rush-job DNA test will take at least a day. By the time they find out that my real name is Lucas Aaronson and call up my record (divided neatly into two halves: Army Rangers and military prison) all of this will be over. I will be done in less than an hour. John Mason will get a glimpse of the future—but no more than that.

I never make it to the reactors, and I don't want to. There will be several guards there, as well as security cameras. No chance for me to get to Mason. This is the most uncertain part of the mission, where improvisation begins.

In the locker room I am issued a set of anti-particulate coveralls in bright MasonTech blue and gold. A single guard accompanies me. It's nearly perfect, but I almost blow the whole thing. I'm not sure what gives me away. Something subtle. Something that only registers with the guard on an instinctual level. Whatever it is, I see him make me. It's unmistakable. He doesn't know what I am, but in that fatal moment he is certain—*certain*—that I am not what I claim to be. He's smart, and he's paying close attention at exactly the moment he should be. His competence kills him.

He goes for his gun, and I break his arm at the elbow, then crush his trachea with the edge of my right hand. As his last breath chokes and whispers out of him, I lower him slowly, gently, silently down to the floor, trying not to think about how much this resembles an embrace, how I have held Anna in much the same way, how someone who loves him will never hold him again. They say you need imagination in this line of work. Maybe they're right. But it makes it harder.

I put on the coveralls and take the gun. I accidentally read the name on his security badge and wish I hadn't; then I leave by a different door than the one I came in.

I don't remember how Gabriel obtained the full layout of the building; no doubt he told me all about it in one of his boasting sessions. But the intelligence is accurate, and that's what matters. Indeed, it is only now that I fully realize how successful Gabriel has been. These hallways should be swarming, but almost everyone who works here is on strike, including most of the security. If only the crowd outside knew! I briefly wonder if that might have been a better plan: let the crowd in to deal with Mason. But I know that would have been no good. Mason might escape, and the Timescope technology might survive. No, this task cannot be handed over to the never-guilty hands of a loving mob.

On the third level I encounter a senior manager in a dark blue pantsuit, who sees the gun and reaches for a phone, mouth opening to scream. As I kill her, I am thinking of Anna's eyes through the tea-steam. The musicality of her alto voice. The softness of her skin.

A minute later, I come out of a stairwell and surprise a guard. I think of Anna, draped nude across lilac bedsheets, and I shoot him in the head.

Love hurls us forward.

At the door to the main lab are three submachine guns. Two of them resting safely in the gunrack; the third is in the hands of a guard who looks about eighteen years old. Half my age, he should be so much faster than me. He should be stronger, sharper. But there is no love in him. Nothing hurling him forward, nothing driving him headlong into his future.

What future?

The moment I see him, I feel Anna's body against mine. We sway in the moonlight, and I smell jasmine, and love lifts the gun and puts a bullet through the kid's open mouth.

No time to waste. In a second I'm through the door and into the main lab. It is past 0900 hours now. John Mason is gazing into the future.

The lab is smaller than I expected. The machinery is minimal. This unassuming room seems like the wrong place. But there he is: John Mason. The guru. The genius. The first person in history to see the future. He is looking right at me, and I can tell that he recognizes me.

My eyes flick up to the screen—the big white screen with a wavy blue image projected onto it from an unassuming metal box in the center of the room. The Timescope. The eye to the future. The unacceptable sin.

As I look at the screen, I realize that Mason is not looking into the future as if he had a telescope or surveillance satellite. He's reading a book from the future. An encyclopedia, or something similar. I feel a rush of vertigo as I realize I am looking at my own face. My old Army ID photo is staring at me from Mason's screen. It's what I looked like back when I believed in things other than love.

Next to the photo is some text:

Aaronson, Lucas. *Army-trained terrorist and religious fanatic. Member of the True Shepherds. Chiefly noted as the murderer of John Mason. Gunned down moments after his fatal disruption of the Timescope Project.*

Eyes through tea-steam. The scent of jasmine.

Love hurls us forward.
I aim carefully and pull the trigger.

The Shortest Night

Gary Kloster

The day before the shortest night, I became the one thousand and seventh wife of the Emperor of the Last Lands.

The day after, they brought me the gelding.

* * *

"It's dark."

A whisper of words, barely heard over the radio's soft music. I lifted a bloody washcloth from the torn flesh of the boy's back and stepped around him. The flood of daylight spilling through my apartment's windows made his brown eyes bright.

"It's day."

"I know," he rasped through full lips. His voice might have been a delicate tenor if it hadn't been broken from screaming. "I can feel the sun. But…"

"It's over." My hand shifted, wanting to brush his long hair back. Instead, I wrung red water from the cloth. "Dawn came. The shortest night has ended."

"Not yet," he said. His eyes, pupils wide and deep as the night, met mine. "Not for me."

* * *

"Where do you come from?"

I stood on the ball of one foot and stretched my other leg up until my toes pointed at the sky. Working through my forms in the empty disused courtyard that opened off my rooms; an ugly concrete space that was at least open to the blue sky, beautiful and empty except for the white line of a plane headed fast away from this awful place. Balanced, centered beneath that tiny slice of sky, I breathed slow and steady while considering the boy's words.

His first in two days.

"Kimet." I shifted my eyes, just enough to catch him watching me. "A little country, across the western sea." I could see from his face that the name was unfamiliar. Unsurprising. Kimet was small and far away from the grand Empire of the Last Lands. "It's a land of high mountains and glaciers, of waterfalls and narrow, emerald valleys."

Kimet was a beautiful land, and I would never see it again.

"Were you a queen?"

My leg burned, but I held it steady. "A princess."

His wounded eyes stared at me, wide beneath the noon sun. "You don't look like a princess."

"Too ugly?" Short, with the deep chest and flat face of my people. I didn't fit well with the thousand other flowers that filled the emperor's garden. They called me an ape and laughed, shunning me.

Thank fate for that small favor.

"No," he said, looking away.

I let my leg slowly drop. "In this place, I am. But I don't mind. Beauty can cost, sometimes." It had cost him. The boy had shining black hair, flawless brown skin, and delicate features. Castration had given him an androgynous perfection.

He returned to his silence, and I bent into the next posture. Still watching him though, a doll lost among the leaves and trash that had gathered in the empty well of the courtyard. What was he?

A gift, a servant, a spy?

Could the Emperor taste the treachery in my soul?

I ran through my poses, working my body, honing my skills, and watched the boy watch me.

* * *

"I ran away when I was thirteen."

We picked over the breakfast tray, searching for fruit unblemished, bread unmarked with spit. I only ventured into the common areas of the garden at mealtimes, to collect my portion.

The older wives' treatment of their juniors was tiresome.

"A man had come through our village. He promised me work. Modeling, acting."

"Recruiting for a pimp," I said, peeling a mango.

"Yes."

The boy stopped eating, went still, and I wondered if that would be all I would hear. But something had finally let go in him.

"I worked the streets for a year before the police took me. They sold me to Bending Willow House."

"Did they geld you there?" The boy had been dropped naked onto the floor of my apartment. I had to slip into some of the garden's other rooms to steal clothes to cover his scars, old and new.

"Yes. To keep me beautiful." He lifted his napkin and dabbed at his lips. "It raised my price. My patrons said I had a smoother ass than most girls."

"How long were you there?"

"Five years." Pride tinged his smile, and bitterness. "Do I look nineteen?"

"No," I said. Three years younger than me. I could have believed six.

"No." He folded his napkin neatly. "Do I look like a killer?"

I popped the last grape into my mouth. "One of your patrons?"

"No." Memory turned his broken eyes in. "He chose Nenetl. Her, and a whip, and she was so small. I heard her screams, and the house toughs wouldn't go, so I snuck past them…"

He stared through the sunlit windows at the empty court, not seeing.

When my hand reached for his, I didn't stop it.

He started like a wounded thing when I touched him. Unnerved by the press of someone else's skin against his. His hand knotted beneath mine, almost a fist, before slowly relaxing.

"He was an old man. I took the whip and wrapped it around his throat. By the time the toughs broke through the door, he'd stopped moving. The paramedics worked on him first, even though he was already dead. By the time they moved on to Nenetl, she had bled too much.

"So much blood." His eyes found the dark marks on my carpet, the place where the guards had thrown him down days before. "This is the age of blood and darkness. The age of Shining Night."

"So say your priests, here in the Last Lands." I had never found a microphone in this room, but that meant nothing. They were probably built into the walls. But my people had never hid their heresy. "Yet dawn still comes."

"Not for me." He touched the scabs that marked the skin over his heart. "Not after the priests marked me with Shining Night's name."

I had no answer for that. I raised his hand instead and folded mine around it. "I am Risha, last of the line of Himara."

Between my hands, his fingers shifted, lacing tight with mine.

"I am Ezil."

The next day, the emperor finally sent for me.

* * *

Between the wives' garden and the emperor's apartment lay a jewel-box of a room, floored with onyx, paneled in ebony, the ceiling studded with stars of inlaid pearls. A wide bed, sheeted in white, filled the room's center. I knelt beside it.

The air of the room flowed heavy into my lungs, filled with the scent of incense, sex, and blood. Breathing out, I pushed all that away and tried to find my center, the calm that should come from the satisfaction of fate.

Tried.

Behind me, Ezil shifted, and I felt him. Just a whisper of contact, the edge of his hand against my foot.

"You will survive this."

His words made my breathing stop. Survive. He had. For six years, in rooms like this, on beds like this.

How was he to know that survival had no place in my intentions?

My lungs burned and the dark room narrowed, squeezing down to a single point of light, but I couldn't pull in another breath. Ezil shouldn't be here. Why had the guards brought him when they came for me? Why had they waited so long to come for me?

My fate was rushing towards me, yet everything felt wrong. Where was my center?

Before me, the door opened, and my training took me. I bent my head to the floor, breathed deep, and listened.

"No guards. No cameras."

A murmured assent, the sounds of boots. Then the slow shuffle of leather soles, the tap of a cane, the thump of the door, closing.

The familiar sound of my breath, Ezil's breath, and the wheezing rasp of another.

"My last wife." Something touched the back of my neck, cold and hard, traced across my skin until it rested under my jaw and pressed up, lifting my head.

At our marriage ceremony, the emperor had been a towering figure on a high balcony, wrapped in black and gold. This sallow-skinned, skeletal thing in a dark suit was so different from the man in the pictures that loomed over every square, that stared down from the walls of every café. But it was him. I had studied this face from infancy. Even with the flesh burned away, the hair gone, I knew it.

Zuma, Emperor of the Last Lands, my husband, my fate, stood before me. Dying.

"Prostate cancer," Zuma said, seeing the searching awareness in my eyes. He dug the tip of his cane into the bottom of my chin, pressing up until I rose to my feet.

"I have a moon left to me. Maybe two." The cool gold at the end of his cane drifted down my neck, glided between my breasts. It pressed against the thin tie that held the delicate lace of my robe together, then ripped through it. It slid to my belly and stopped there, pressing into my skin like a blade. "What do you think of that, my ugly little assassin?"

"Assassin?" I said, soft and steady, even as my fate shuddered inside me.

"Did you think I wouldn't know? I am the high servant of the god of lies. I've eaten the hearts of countless assassins. I know a weapon when I see it, however it is sheathed." Zuma's cane drifted up, pushed against the robe's lace until it slipped off my shoulders and onto the floor, leaving me bare. "Will you draw your blade, now?"

I stared at him, at his eyes burning with pain and hate. He knew, and he had come in here, with me, alone. Unmonitored. So I could kill him and take away his pain. Kill him and sentence myself, my family, my country to death, just to cut this monster's rule short by a month.

Maybe two.

My hands curled shut, opened. My mouth was ash, and my soul numb.

"My fate…"

"Your fate?" Zuma's voice was soft as mine, but so cruel. "Tell me, little ape. What was it supposed to be? What prophecy did those useless soothsayers read from your stinking afterbirth? What fate did I break for you today?"

"She is the gate of dawn." I said the words slowly, the first time I had ever said them aloud. "The last emperor of The Last Lands will never take her. The blood shall cease to flow, and the Age of Night will end."

"And the Age of Night will end." Zuma slid his cane over me, across my breast and down my ribs. "Ha. Night never ends, girl. Darkness is always there, waiting for the light to die." The smooth tip of his cane came to rest just beneath my navel, pressing hard into my skin. "Your martyrdom, your *fate,* is a farce girl. Will you do it anyway? Kill me, and spare me weeks of agony? Will you?"

I stared at him, aching, dead, and I couldn't answer.

Zuma looked down at me, pain-filled eyes searching. "No?" His lips twisted into something that wasn't a smile. "Your people refuse Shining Night, refuse all our gods. You think you're too good for them and pledge yourselves to fate instead. What do you think of that fickle bitch now?"

I kept my face motionless, made myself breathe, in and out, ignoring the pain in my belly.

Fate. Did I believe in it anymore? Had I lost that, lost my purpose, lost everything here in these Last Lands? Maybe.

Maybe. But damn this man if he thought I would break on my knees before him. I might have lost everything, but I had to believe that fate had not lost me. I stared up into his eyes, full of pain and hate, and waited, breathing, silent, patient, to forge what purpose I could from whatever fate set before me.

Until Zuma sighed and stepped back, dropping the end of his cane. "The farce of your life is done. Mine reels on. Gelding."

Ezil stayed silent, kneeling, but his head bowed lower.

"The priestess of Morningstar spared you. From all those chosen to die on the shortest night, the god of martyrs spared a whore and sent him to serve me. Do you know why?"

Ezil's head moved, ever so slightly. *No.*

"Morningstar's priestess told me that if you attended to my last wife, she would bear a child. My throne would finally find an heir." Zuma's eyes came back to me. "Cancer has made me impotent for over a year, and seeing this squat ape hasn't changed that."

I heard it, the faintest breath of a whisper.

Zuma did too.

"Beautiful? You think so?" Zuma's hand tightened on his cane. "Stand and strip, gelding."

I heard Ezil rise, heard the soft sound of his robe falling, but I watched Zuma. I saw his face change, harden, the dull rage of pain in his eyes sparked to something more dangerous.

"So."

I tilted my head, shifted my eyes just enough to see Ezil standing naked, beautiful.

Above the scar of his unmanning, his sex strained, ready, despite the hopelessness in his dark eyes.

"Fate mocks you girl. And that pathetic god Morningstar mocks me." Zuma held his cane tight in two hands. "Your soothsayers were right, when they said that I would never take you. But they were wrong in this. There will be, there must be, blood." He jabbed his cane at the bed. "On the sheets, whore."

He watched Ezil silently comply, then turned to me. "Now you. Climb him and break yourself on him. If you haven't already." He stared at me, a corpse whose sunken eyes burned with pain and spite. "Or will you change your mind, and end me instead?"

That poisonous room swung around me, black and whirling. I could kill him. All my life, I had trained to destroy this man, to sacrifice myself and bring the dawn.

I could kill him.

But I saw no dawn beyond that now. Only my death, my family's, my country's. And Ezil's.

"Risha."

I barely heard Ezil call my name, but that scrap of a whisper stopped the room spinning, stilled the world around me. I could take a step, another, could stand by that terrible bed and stare down into the dark wells of his eyes.

"Why?"

He looked up at me and spoke, so soft, for me only. "Everything I see is dark. Except you. Don't waste your light on a dead man."

The bed was hard beneath its white silk sheets, unyielding beneath my knees. I knelt over Ezil, looking down at him. He stared back at me, his black eyes full of pain and love. Shifting, my hips tilted and…

It hurt, but I breathed out, and found it.

My center, frayed and thin, but there.

Holding it, I held still, staring down into Ezil's dark eyes, staring at the gleaming white of a pearl reflected there. Like a bright star, a point of light in all that night, and I stared at it even as a shadow fell over us. An arm, rising, the dark line of a cane slashing across our joined bodies.

That shadow covered our union until our bodies reached their completion, and a fractured, frenzied pleasure shuddered through us, jagged and sharp as obsidian. Then the shadow fell like night, and pleasure broke into pain, and blood, and darkness.

* * *

"My first memory of you was this."

Ezil lay stretched across our bed, still and uncomplaining as I rubbed salve over the last peeling scabs that mottled his skin. Weeks had passed after the guards had dragged us back from that black room, bleeding and barely breathing, before I'd healed enough to return to my habits of looting the rooms of the other wives for useful things.

"You, caring for my wounds." He stared up at me with his too-dark eyes. "I began to love you then. You were good to me, for no reason."

"You were bleeding on my rug. Why wouldn't I help you?" That rug was stained with blood from both of us, now.

Zuma had beaten us until he had fallen. He would have killed us, I think, if his cancer hadn't taken his strength.

I put the tube of salve down and stretched out beside Ezil. "My turn."

Ezil rolled up and began to rub the medicine in. "This is the age of blood and darkness. Shining Night tells us that we deserve to suffer."

"Your people have other gods." I lay still beneath his hands, not wanting to speak, to tear at the thin scabs that lay behind Ezil's wounded eyes. But I needed to understand my new center, this unexpected bend in the path of my fate. "Like Morningstar."

For a long time, Ezil stayed silent, his hands gently working over me, spreading the ointment, easing muscles tight with tension and pain. When he finally spoke, his quiet voice was harsh with the taint of old screams.

"Have you ever seen what happens on the shortest night?"

Memories twisted through my head. An ancient pyramid, its stone stained black with a thousand years of blood, tinted crimson by the arteries of neon that pulsed across the skyscrapers that towered over it. A beast surrounded that temple, a monster with ten thousand arms and eyes and mouths, shrieking in terror and ecstasy.

I had watched that mob on my television and wondered. If I were there, in that great square, watching the priests of Shining Night slit the throats of a thousand sacrifices to strengthen the darkness, to deny the light of the summer solstice, what would I do? Would I resist, cry out against that orgy of death and blood, cast it like a curse into the teeth of the coming night?

Or would I join the dance? Would I howl with the crowd as the condemned tumbled down the temple steps and fell into the great moat surrounding that ancient edifice? Would my feet move to the shrieks of the dying, the horrible squeals of the half-starved pigs that filled that pit and savaged the bodies of the dead? What would I beg for, staring up into the darkness of the shortest night? Mercy? Life?

Power?

I could never answer that. I just watched the images dance across the screen, silent, breathing in, breathing out. And when the feast of the longest night came, and the priests of Shining Night had set the table in Himara house with the steaming corpse of one of those pigs, grown fat on the flesh of the sacrificed, I had never let that tainted meat touch my lips.

"I've seen it," I said.

"I should have died," Ezil whispered. "A murderer, condemned. But the priestess of one of the lesser gods, the god of the Morning Star, reached into the line and her hand found me."

Ezil's hands grew still, and I rolled on my side to stare at him. "I've never heard of these pardons."

"Even among the condemned, the blessings of Morningstar were only a rumor. A cup of mercy to balance an ocean of blood." He ran his fingers over the scars cut above his heart, the mark of sacrifice carved into his flesh. They were the only scars on his chest. Where we had pressed together, our skin had stayed whole, unmarked by the emperor's fury. "I never believed it."

"But it was true," I said, twining my fingers around his. "You were spared."

"Spared," he said, dark eyes so wide. Then his fingers tightened on mine. "Why?"

I stared up at him, my back aching, my stomach twisting with subtle nausea, and shook my head. "I don't know. What fate and your Morningstar have in store for us…I don't know."

* * *

"I hear screaming."

Ezil's whisper snapped free from the steady drumbeat that filled my dreams and lay still, silent, staring at the ruddy shadows dancing on the walls. Crimson light filled the windows, glowing beneath a black cloud that covered the stars.

And somewhere, someone's screams cut off.

"What's happening?"

Ezil lay on the bed beside me, his dark eyes staring out the windows at the false dawn of fire. Beyond our door, a crash resounded, followed by the crack of gunshots.

"The palace has been put to the torch, and the wives' garden is being sacked," I said. Rolling from the bed, sure and swift, I dove for my wardrobe. In its deepest recesses, I found what I wanted. "Here. Put these on."

Ezil stared at the dark clothes I handed him, was still staring at them as I dragged out the packs of food and supplies that I'd been stealing and hiding away ever since I'd recovered enough to move.

"He's dead," he said.

"Yes." Zuma had finally succumbed to his tumors, and despite his thousand wives, he had no heir.

Shining Night would be given a belly full of blood tonight.

"We have to go." I helped Ezil dress, pulling black cloth over his scars, old and new, then jerked him out into the courtyard.

"Go where?"

"Anywhere but here." I threw him the bag I carried and rushed the wall that towered over us, launching myself off the ground. Catching onto the stone like the ape these people kept naming me, I dug my fingers and toes into the thin seams that ran between the blocks of stone and climbed.

"I can't—" Enzil started, staring up at me perched on the roof, but I was already pulling out the cloth that I had wound around my waist, thin strips of silk that I had torn from bedsheets and knotted together.

It felt so damned good to finally use my training.

I tied the makeshift rope around a rusted aerial and dropped it down. "Tie the bags to the end and climb up."

Knot by knot, he did.

After, he lay on his back, chest heaving. I pulled up the bags, wound the rope back around me, and tapped his leg.

"Up."

He rose, but when I took his hand and tried to pull him across the rooftop he resisted, staring up. "Look."

High above, wind had rent the black curtain of smoke, and through that crack a light shone. A white dagger of light, bright, too bright. "Is it the end of the world?" he asked.

I looked up at the shining morning star, wounding the night with its light.

"We can only hope."

* * *

An ancient wall surrounded the palace, and between it and the rooftop lay an open stretch of lawn a hundred feet wide, filled with war.

"There," I said, pressing low to the roof as stray bullets whined through the air around us. I pointed toward a wing of the palace that had been torn apart by something, a bomb or bursting gas line. The wreckage of it choked the space from building to wall, and I couldn't see any soldiers around it.

"It will be easier without me." Ezil's broken eyes stared up into the smoke-filled darkness, searching for that guiding star. "You're an assassin. I'm a whore."

"Screw that," I said. "I'm your beautiful princess, and you're my handsome prince come to rescue me. So move."

His wide, bottomless eyes turned to me, and for the first time I saw the ghost of a smile touch his lips. "As you command, Princess."

Crouching low, we cut across the rooftop until we reached the rubble. The wreckage clanked and smoked, and we could hear bullets cutting through the air and cracking off stone. They were random though, from fighting happening somewhere else in the palace, and as we picked our way through the debris toward the wall I wondered if we might make it. Then the smoke overhead shifted, and in the white starlight I saw death coming.

A priest of Shining Night led them. He walked through the shadows, his teeth bared in a vicious grin, bright against the blood that smeared his face. In one hand he held a heavy sacrificial dagger of sacred obsidian, in the other a revolver. Two guards followed him like dogs, their eyes blank with the madness of disaster.

"I hear its heartbeat, bitch." The priest walked through flame and smoke, uncaring, raising his blade. "I'll have its blood and wipe that damned light out of the sky."

I stepped forward, my arms floating up, my hands out, placating. Breathed in, breathed out, and watched the priest rush forward. When the knife flashed down, straight for my neck, I moved.

I slid to the side, just a little, just enough for that slashing blade to miss. Then my hands took the priest's arm as it flew by, locked out his elbow and twisted, turning all his running momentum into sudden flight. The priest looped through the air and crashed into the rubble, gun and dagger clattering across the stones.

So easy, but there was no time to appreciate it. Two strides, and I was rising into the air, graceful as a bird. I barely felt the shock of my foot smashing into the jaw of one of the guards as he tried to bring his gun up. He fell, but the side of his rifle caught my leg and ruined my easy glide, pulling me down.

The last guard howled and pointed his gun at me. I hit the ground and rolled, hearing a shot, waiting for the pain. Then I saw the guard's gun dropping, his hands rising to clutch at the spreading stain that marked his chest.

Ezil stood behind him, his eyes as dark as the muzzle of the smoking revolver that he'd picked up. The guard fell, and I was moving again, scooping up the rifle that had fallen from the soldier I'd kicked and smashing its butt down into his groin, nose and throat.

I flipped the gun in my hands, pointing it at the man choking to death between my feet. Then Ezil's gun roared again.

Once, twice, and Ezil was charging, screaming, and I was dropping, spinning. Against the sky behind me I could see the shadow of the priest, the dagger in his hand shining red in the firelight, falling toward me. I pulled up the rifle, slow, slow…

Ezil crashed into him, slamming the priest back and down. My hands moved, swift as spiders, finding grip and trigger. When the dark priest reared up, the rifle jerked in my hands and sent him crashing back to the ground. I snapped my gaze around, making sure we were alone again, then went to Ezil.

"Are you—"

"I'm fine," he gasped, pain lacing his voice, but he pulled himself up. "Fine."

"There will be night. Always." Sprawled in his blood, the priest glared up at me. "Forever." A threat, or a last prayer before darkness, I didn't know. Or care.

"And yet dawn still comes," I answered and put a bullet through his head.

* * *

Beyond the broken wall, the city heaved and cried, a dark pit full of mad beasts.

Mobs filled the streets, looting, fighting, running, screaming. The roar of riot and the flickering light of fire surrounded us as we staggered through winding alleys and dark streets.

"Is this still the shortest night?" Ezil whispered. We were hidden in the bushes of a tiny park, waiting for another mob to pass. They drove men before them, naked and leashed and bloody, squealing like dying pigs. "Was it all a dream, what happened?" He looked at me, broken eyes desperate. "Are you real?"

"Real enough to be terrified," I said. In the street beyond, the crowd finally cleared. "Let's move."

"No."

"What do you mean, no?" I snapped. "We have to get to the river. We can steal a boat and go, safe from crowds and fire."

"Yes," he said. "You should…" Ezil stopped, then fell, the soft crunching crash of the leaves beneath him lost in the distant shouts of riot.

"Ezil!"

I knelt beside him, turned him, felt the sticky heat beneath his pack. My hands pulled the pack away, jerked up his shirt, then stopped.

"It's the dagger, isn't it?" he breathed.

"A piece of it," I whispered. I brushed my fingers across the tip of that cursed black stone splinter that stuck from Ezil's lower back and he stiffened. It had caught him in the kidney, torn the vessels gathered there and the blood had been spilling inside his body. Killing him slow and steady.

"No," I said softly. "I can't lose you now."

"Why not?" He shifted, turning enough so that he could see me, ignoring the pain.

"I am the gate of dawn. The last emperor of the Last Lands will never take me. The blood shall cease to flow, and the age of night will end."

"Your prophecy," Ezil said. "Have you finally decided what it means?"

"Yes." I brushed the long hair away from his face, so beautiful even now. "Miracles are madness, Ezil, and we are the toys of gods and fate. My blood has stopped."

"What?"

I took his hand and placed it on my belly. "My blood stopped, Ezil. It stopped, and tonight I heard a heartbeat in my dreams, small and quick as a hummingbird's. New blood flows in me. Our child's blood."

"Impossible," he whispered. "I am gelded, I cannot—" But then he stopped. "Morningstar. God of morning and martyrs. Miracles are mad."

Somewhere in the night, a crowd howled for blood, circling closer.

"You have to run," he whispered.

"Alone?" In my eyes, tears burned, but I would not shed them.

"It's your fate," he said. "You were forged to fight. To survive. Save yourself. Save our child." His eyes closed, opened. "She will be as beautiful and strong as you."

"He will be as strong and beautiful as you." I bent to him, heedless of the closing screams, and touched my lips to his for the first and last time.

"Risha." His eyes were wide, so wide. "The sky…"

Over us, the velvet black was torn by skyscrapers and smoke, slashed by the white scar of the morning star.

"What?"

"I can see the dawn."

Grey on the edge of the world, there it was, the line of night breaking before the rushing day. I turned my eyes back to Ezil's, and for the first time I saw his pupils shift, touched by the light.

Then they dimmed, their brightness lost.

"Dawn always comes." My fingers rose over that beautiful, still face. Then stopped. "Your shortest night is finally done, Ezil."

Leaving his eyes open to the light, I rose, gathering my breath, shouldering my pack. Then I started to run. Through the smoke and the shadows, away from the screams and the smell of blood, I ran toward the river, toward the sea, toward mountains that reached for the sun.

Following the morning star, carrying the dawn.

A Snake in the Grass

E.C. Ambrose

June 20, 1941
Near Kovno, Lithuania

"It's not a horse, Jogaila, you don't have to tell it that its master is dead, besides, he was a Nazi." Stace crouched between Jogaila and the road, scanning for enemies.

At least she knew the tradition with horses, even if she had no respect for it. "This was his mount," Jogaila replied. "I'm sure she is loyal and bold." He knelt by the fallen motorcycle at the edge of the road, gently stroking the chassis and murmuring in Lithuanian. She wouldn't understand his language yet, but the soothing tone would help. A mount must be told of its master's death if it were to accept a new rider.

"Nazis're better than the Reds." In the ditch between the road and the forest, Kelvas, the third member of their little team, yanked off the dead Nazi's jacket. "If they want to run off the Soviets, we should let them."

"Then why did you insist on killing him?" Jogaila focused on the motorcycle he needed, preparing himself for magic.

"We can't have prisoners in the camp, and we couldn't free him to confirm we're here." Kelvas tugged off the Nazi's boots and tossed them toward Jogaila. "If they're planning an assault like you claim, the proof is worth killing and dying for."

Jogaila wanted neither of those things, but the war was coming: he could taste it. *Rats and bones, rats and bones…*the sibilant chant grew stronger at the base of his skull since they had crossed the border into Poland. Well. What had been Poland.

"Zaltys, hush," he murmured, hoping his human companions wouldn't hear, hoping the other voice would obey, at least for now.

"The Nazis and the Soviets have a treaty, a border," Stace said. "This whole mission is only because Jogaila listens to snakes."

She had heard him. Of course. The argument knotted his stomach like a viper indeed.

"We're meant to be our own people." Jogaila ran his hands over the tires and drive train. "We were independent before the Soviets. We should be again."

Kelvas climbed from the ditch near the body and dropped the armload of clothes by the motorcycle, taking up the hooded lantern.

"You and the elders think it's so important, maybe you should hurry up."

"If I rush the magic, the bike will go wild, feral."

"How does a machine go feral?" Kelvas stared down at him. "You're a good mechanic, you should stick with that."

Stace raised her hand for silence, and they tensed, listening as she peered down the eastern road. Nothing. She signaled for them to relax. "Sooner you get there, Jogi, the sooner we know you're wrong."

"I hope I am wrong," said Jogaila. "I can't imagine the Nazis will be better than the Soviets."

Kelvas shrugged. "Can't be much worse. Unless we get caught on the Nazi side like we are now. Then, it's worse." He smiled thinly.

Magic preferred silence and peace, but this night would afford him neither. From the pouch at his belt, Jogaila pulled out a piece of amber and the box of matches. Zaltys's head started to emerge, tongue flickering, and Jogaila nudged the snake back in, pulling the ties tight. A beetle nestled in the golden heart of the amber: all amber held soul fragments, but this piece would be especially strong. Did the soul of a Nazi also go into a tree when he died? Marija taught him everybody had a soul, even if they didn't believe in the same afterlife.

Placing the amber on the motorcycle's engine, to let the soul touch its future body, Jogaila pulled on the Nazi's uniform. He fumbled the buttons with Kelvas staring at him, his eyes barely visible above the lantern.

"Hurry. Up." The older man mouthed.

Jogaila took the amber in his palm, feeling its natural warmth. He thought of his mother, whose own death let him rouse the animate slivers of souls.

Kelvas's eyes narrowed. Another moment and the man would kick him.

Jogaila wanted to sing the proper dainos. Instead, he struck the match. The flame trembled and he steadied his hand. The amber smoldered at the touch of fire, then snapped, a fierce energy.

Rats and bones, paths in the dirt, under the stone. Emboldened by his rising warmth, the snakish chant renewed, at the base of his skull, adding detail. Zaltys acted like an antenna, transmitting what it heard from other snakes to Jogaila's mind. This message sounded like vipers. For the moment, he tried to ignore it.

In the golden heart of stone, the beetle's form shifted with the heat. The stone smelled faintly of pine from the tree that formed it, then the acrid scent of the beetle's carapace. Jogaila dropped the stone toward the motor. It sizzled on its short journey with a flare like a comet, then snapped from the air, leaving the afterimage of the flame inside his eyes.

At his knees, the motorcycle growled to life, and Kelvas pulled back, the lantern's light shaking. He swore under his breath. "Why do you even need magic for this? Just ride the bike."

"Nazis!" Stace hissed, scrambling through the ditch and into the trees.

Kelvas smothered the light, following Stace, leaving Jogaila to manage the motorcycle. If the bond between them was true, it could shortly manage itself.

Jogaila grabbed the handlebars. The bike settled into a purr at his touch, thrumming under his hands. He strained to shove it back onto its wheels.

The bike surged of its own accord, coming fully upright as his companions vanished into the woods.

Clutching the bike's grips, Jogaila murmured, "Listen, Zaltys, listen." The snake's whispering fell silent.

Flashlights marched down the road, over the ruts left by the Russian tanks. If Jogaila were right, they would be overtaken. Russia and Germany had an agreement, everyone said. Not to worry, the Red Army would defend Lithuania as its own. Ha. Two great powers rose, the Bear to their east, the War Eagle to their west. Lithuania was meant to shelter like a grass snake at the hearth of the Russians. Unless the Nazis came, breaking the agreement and shredding into Lithuania as they'd already done to Poland, Austria and France.

"Halt! Who's there!" a voice barked out in German.

Jogaila's gut tightened and he reminded himself to answer in the same language. "Sorry, sir! I hit a rut and flipped the bike." He made a show of hauling his mount further onto the road, urging the bike to obey instead of leaping to his aid. Maybe Kelvas had been right, and the magic was too much.

His appearance drew the eyes of the approaching soldiers. Eight men, all of them older, stronger, more stern than he was. He gripped the handlebars as if he, too, could draw strength from the animating spirit.

Eight men, with lightning bolts on their collars. He heard whispers of squads like this. Einsantzgruppen. Instant death if they should learn who he was and what he wanted.

"Not injured? How about the bike?" The officer inquired, assessing Jogaila as he spoke, and not in a friendly way.

With his pale-wheat hair and grassy eyes, Jogaila could pass for Aryan. That's why his mission might succeed, and half the German soldiers he'd seen looked younger than his own nineteen years, as if the Nazis burned through their own people the way that Jogaila burned his amber.

"It sounds a little rough," Jogaila answered. Like his German, if truth be told. He coughed into his hand. "And my ribs hurt, Obersturmfuhrer." He added the rank, hoping all of their drills back at camp had not only given him sufficient command of the language, but of the military as well.

The officer's eyes flared slightly, and his lips softened. "Not German, are you?"

A shake of his head. "Prussian, Obersturmfuhrer."

The officer grunted, then said, "Better go. We've had word of partisan activities out here."

Partisan activities, like those of Jogaila and his companions.

"Yes, sir." Jogaila mounted the bike.

"Heil Hitler," the officer said, and Jogaila remembered to thrust out his arm and repeat the salute.

Responding to his own tension, the bike sprang forward, carrying him swiftly from one doom to another. Cross into Nazi territory, locate the maps or hear the plans, any proof he could use to convince the others of the battle to come, then escape again to the partisans' encampment and pray to the sacred grove they'd find a way to survive the onslaught.

The bike rumbled beneath him, content.

"*…away, but the soldiers are still there.*" A new voice at the base of his skull. One of his companions, whispering in the forest. Yes, Jogaila listened to snakes. Because snakes heard everything, and thanks to Zaltys inside his mind, so did he.

"*You don't think he'd betray us?*"

A rumble that Jogaila recognized as laughter. "*Never. He's crazy, but he's Lithy to the bone.*"

"*Least if he dies, the elders can let go.*"

Jogaila's heart dropped.

More laughter. "*Maybe that's what they want. To be rid of the old ways and move on.*"

Was it? Could it be? They needed him and what he could do. Tonight, he must prove it.

"*Head for home, Stace. I'll keep an eye out in case Jogaila gets nabbed and we have to move camp.*"

"Enough, Zaltys," Jogaila said, and the voices faded. They needn't like him, but they seemed to trust him, at least enough to believe he wouldn't give them away.

As he put distance between himself and the death squad, between himself and the companions he must not reveal, Jogaila gave his attention to his mount, this new companion that must carry him until the failure of his bond. It wasn't a horse, Stace told him. He wouldn't know: Marija, who raised him after his mother's death and trained him in the old ways, didn't keep animals except for honeybees who stayed of their own accord. Gracija, he thought. Grace. The name of the bike, or of the spirit who now animated it. His hand warmed on the grip and the bike surged forward, faster, faster.

Why magic? Kelvas wanted to know. What's the use? This, Jogaila would've said, this boundless energy, beyond the limits of the mere mechanical. If all went well, Gracija would ride with him this night and beyond. He breathed in the diesel and grease of the bike's engine, and breathed out—for the first time that night—peace.

All too soon, he crossed the bridge and reached the gated camp, stern German soldiers waving him through. They'd requisitioned a farm, fencing it off and adding tents and workshops, all sorts of temporary structures, illuminated by strings of bulbs and big lights on standing posts.

Leaving a broad space clear, more motorcycles clustered just beyond the fence. A few cars and transports waited nearby, and, to one side, a tank. He was meant to believe they had an arrangement with the Red Army, an arrangement that permitted each great power to ravage its own side of the border. Tanks on the move might explain the vibrations he'd been sensing, a disturbance in the mechanical world.

Circling around to point the bike toward the exit, Jogaila parked Gracija alongside the other vehicles. A large transport truck with wood slat sides parked just outside.

"In, in! Schneller!" one of the Germans shouted, gesturing a line of civilians toward the transport. They clustered together, mostly young men and women, some older, many with Jewish skullcaps, the women with their hair covered. No children. A woman tried to cling to a bundle, a pink blanket tied around some clothes. Another guard yanked it away, tossing it onto a pile of other bags nearby.

"You'll get them when you arrive. Now move along."

"My baby," she moaned, "my baby." The woman sank to the ground, fist held to her breast.

"Is gone. Get up. Get in the truck." The soldier made a move toward her, but an older man came from the crowd.

"No, no, let me have her blanket. Please," the woman asked.

The other man took the woman's shoulders, murmuring to her in the language of the Jews. The guard's eyes narrowed but he resumed waving on the other citizens.

Jogaila fixed his eye on a farmhouse incorporated into the military camp. What had happened to her baby? What would happen to her? He couldn't afford to know, not if he were to help his own people survive whatever was coming. Trying to maintain his guise, he kept his back straight. Poland had been occupied, of course civilians would be displaced. But without their belongings? Even a blanket for a baby now gone? The moment left him unsettled, for reasons even a snake's voice couldn't explain.

He must focus. Find the evidence he needed and flee before—

"You!"

Jogaila stumbled, glancing back to find a man with officer's medals gesturing at him. He snapped to attention. "Ja?"

"Tell the livery to send another truck. There's not enough room to get all these people to the site."

"Yes, sir." His heart pounded as he hurried away, a man on a mission.

He'd no idea where the livery office would be found, but he promptly rounded a corner of the barn and found a row of tanks, the black eyes of their turrets staring him down. This location had little to recommend it, save for the bridge over the Sheshule River. A bridge perhaps sturdy enough for tanks. Jogaila paused, glancing around.

"Achtung! The livery!" called the same voice from behind him.

"Ja!" Jogaila answered with a wave, trotting past the tanks.

When he'd gotten the bulk of the line between himself and the officer's position, Jogaila dodged into the open side of the barn and dropped behind a stack of crates.

Hurried feet and shouting voices. Soldiers moved with deliberate speed past the barn, along with another group of the more serious men with their twin lightning bolts on their collars. A man in a civilian suit carried an armload of papers into the farmhouse, past the guards.

Jogaila swept his refuge with a glance, squeezing himself between the posts against a stone wall. His fingers shook as he tugged open the pouch. Immediately, Zaltys thrust his head through the opening, tongue flicking, eyes gleaming. The coal-black snake had a yellow band of scales just behind his eyes, like the crown of the legendary king of snakes. Zaltys wriggled free of the pouch and slithered across Jogaila' palm and up the sleeve of his gray wool jacket. *Six wheels. Rats.*

Vipers got excited for rats, of course. A little thing like Zaltys, a grass snake, couldn't manage anything so large, but it conveyed the viper voices nonetheless. Anything that excited vipers alarmed Jogaila.

The snake rippled up his arm, warming itself. He gave his arm a gentle shake. "Go on, go listen." He set his hand on the ground, aimed toward the farmhouse. Zaltys could slip through the tiniest gap. Jogaila hoped for a tent, or even an open-air table where the snake could pass unnoticed. A house meant trouble. The snake heard most acutely through its jaw, or through its fellows, the other snakes always closer than people believed. A Lithuanian farmhouse might shelter a snake on purpose, a defender of the hearth and luck-bringer, even for those who didn't practice the old ways. A Polish farmhouse? No. The wooden floors and elevated level could prevent Zaltys from hearing anything at all unless the snake crept straight into the meeting room.

Zaltys crossed the barn and disappeared into the grass. Immediately, Jogaila felt the ground shudder—human movements exaggerated by snakish senses. He scrambled to his feet, busying himself with counting the crates.

"Aha." A hand grabbed him and shoved him away from the crates, the officer glaring and shouting. The livery, the truck, the boy's laziness. He slapped Jogaila, a ringing blow that made him blink.

"I'm sorry, sir! The other officer asked about these crates," Jogaila managed. "He did not send the truck?"

The man's blue eyes narrowed. "Which officer?"

"With the—" Jogaila indicated a mustache past his lips. A common enough trait, he hoped.

The officer snorted. "Drosten." He blew out a breath, then shook his head. The idea of this other officer placated the man in front of him, at least a little. "Carry on." The officer marched off, shouting, "Drosten!"

One of the other soldiers pointed the officer toward the farmhouse, and he set off briskly in that direction. Praise thunder! Jogaila resumed his inspection of the crates. Perhaps he could concentrate on whatever Zaltys might discover. Already, the base of his skull resonated with the snake's strange hearing.

"—construction finished—"

"But the Fuhrer?"

"—certainly a surprise—"

"—nearly ready—"

Jogaila shut his eyes to the camp around him and sank down again behind the crates, fingers touching the ground, trying to make sense of what he heard, what Zaltys heard.

"—more workers. They—long."

"—underground—"

Earlier, Zaltys passed along that message from the vipers, movement underground, to the east—*paths beneath the stone*. Now, he heard only a jumble of phrases, indicating the gravity of the conversation, but not enough of its content. He'd have to go closer and listen with his own ears.

Jogaila tugged on his uniform to straighten it and brushed off any dirt, then pivoted toward the house, skirting the line of tanks where a few soldiers worked, inspecting and oiling. Tanks that would shortly be on the move. He imagined going back to Kelvas or the elders with this, a count of the tanks and the excitement level of the camp, the fact they were rounding people up.

More workers, perhaps, as one of the officers remarked? He'd be laughed out of his own camp. He needed more. Tangible proof, if he could get it, of the German plans.

Jogaila strode across the yard toward the porch. Built in traditional style, the house had a larger room to one end, the kitchen to the other, with a big fireplace between, and bedrooms upstairs. Small windows punctuated the walls. Electric lights strung across the farmyard illuminated everything to be seen in the camp, while the flicker of lanterns inside showed a few men bent over a table. On the porch, a pair of soldiers flanked the door, guarding against interlopers like Jogaila.

He kept walking, straight past the end of the house. More lights marked the fence not far away. One of the guards on patrol paused and struck a match, then lit up a cigarette. Could be the chance to learn more.

"Guten tag!" Jogaila gave a friendly wave. "Have you another?" He indicated the man's cigarette.

The soldier looked him over, then pulled out his box of smokes and shook one for Jogaila to pinch. "Got to do something with the nerves," the man said, chuckling as he lit up Jogaila's smoke.

Jogaila nodded as if he understood perfectly. "Ja. The officers seem—"

Shouting erupted near the gate, and another guard whistled, gesturing the smoker away as the soldiers shifted their patrols to respond. Jogaila stiffened. Any excitement would be bad news. He desperately needed to know what was happening—and at the same time, to stay out of the way. With a few backsteps, he retreated to the end of the farmhouse, hidden from the gate.

Jogaila didn't smoke and wasn't sure how well he might fake it, but the cigarette gave him an excuse to linger, leaning his back against the farmhouse, alongside the window.

"—this new headquarters. The Fuhrer will be impressed with your progress, Herr Todt."

"We look forward to greeting him. I'm sure he will find the facilities suitable to his needs, and, of course, readily defensible."

"Speaking of this. How are the munition factories coming?"

Pages shuffled, then Herr Todt reported, "The tunnels are already complete and the train tracks laid. We have a high rate of loss among the workforce, but Operation Barbarossa should alleviate that concern."

"Sirs!" A new voice emerged from the other side.

"What is it?"

"A spy in the forest, a partisan."

Jogaila brought the cigarette to his lips, keeping his fingers utterly calm. He imagined himself in that moment as cool and calm as a snake. Not him. They hadn't fingered him, nor, perhaps, found the body. Pray the Laime, the goddesses of fortune, they hadn't found his companions. He exhaled around the cigarette, inhaled when he took it away. It trembled in his hand, and he forced himself to remain calm.

"We'll come back to the plans when we've dealt with this other matter."

"A bullet would deal with it quite nicely, I expect."

The men chuckled, their bootheels clicking as they exited in the opposite direction. This partisan's downfall could be Jogaila's deliverance. Unless it were Stace or Kelvas in custody now, someone whose confession could aim the Nazi war machine directly at him.

Jogaila's parched throat stifled his breath. He glanced in the window, finding tables and benches, papers and tools laid out. Now. If ever there was a time.

A glance around, and he was alone.

Pulling a knife from its sheath at his belt, Jogaila jacked up the window, its weights sliding within their channels. Leaving the cigarette on a foundation stone, he replaced the blade and planted his hands on the sill, pulling himself inside. Don't sneak, don't slip, don't be as a snake, but as a man with every right—in case someone should glance inside or see movement near the lamps. Little attracted more attention than sneaking. His heart thundered and his muscles strained to move casually.

A leather satchel lay on one of the benches, and Jogaila took it up. Not the maps on top, the ones they'd just been looking at. Another plan, prominently placed, showed a layout of buildings and tents, fortifications. The Fuhrer's new headquarters, a scant hundred miles from here. He plucked out a few other pages, recognizing rivers and coastline, the national borders obscured by fresh markings—more camps and bases, more than enough for an invasion. He rolled them briskly and stuffed them inside the satchel.

The Nazis were coming, preparing a wave to roll across Lithuania and make his nation a battlefield and a graveyard. Jogaila had his proof. Now he needed to find Zaltys and flee.

Returning to his window, he glanced around. No sign of the snake. All attention in the camp focused on that poor soul near the gate, some Polish national hoping for a better outcome for his own people, no doubt.

Jogaila slipped through and dropped to the ground, tugging the window closed behind him. He took up the cigarette, if only to keep his hand still, and strolled deliberately from the safety of the building. Curious, as any other German might be.

A loose gathering of soldiers ringed the empty ground between the farmhouse and the gate where the motorcycles waited, Gracija among them. No chance for him to reach her and escape. Beyond, the fresh truck stood partly loaded with its human cargo, workers, Jogaila realized, bound for the tunnels where the Germans would build their bombs. The cigarette between his lips smoldered, making it even harder to breathe. The weight of human concerns whispered at the back of his skull, its volume increasing as if he approached a whole nest of vipers.

From the ring of Nazis, the resounding crack of a baton finding flesh rang out. Jogaila's cheek stung a little from the earlier blow, barely a mosquito bite compared with whatever was happening beyond.

The partisan grunted, the soldiers shifted. For a moment, Jogaila caught a glimpse of their prisoner. Kelvas. His face bloodied, his arms twisted by the soldiers to either side, the man looked dazed and defiant.

Jogaila's heart stuttered and he held still, desperate to betray nothing.

"We have men searching. They'll find your friends. They'll find whatever you're hiding," snapped the officer with the baton. The same who'd sent Jogaila for a truck. "Tell us what we want to know, and we may yet be lenient."

Kelvas lifted his head, staring past the officer. His eyes lit on Jogaila, and his mouth tightened.

Jogaila clutched the satchel in front of him. He raised it a little. Kelvas, of all people, wouldn't have Jogaila give up the mission for his own sake. At least he might know that Jogaila succeeded. Of course, he wouldn't unless he got out of here alive, and with the proof.

Kelvas's own capture provided the perfect distraction, a truth that turned Jogaila's stomach.

Fading backward, toward the barn and the tanks, Jogaila fought for each breath against his own ribs. Constricted by fear, by need. If he had another distraction, a larger one, then even Kelvas might escape. The crew working on the tanks had already moved on, finished with their work or drawn to the spectacle of Kelvas's beating.

Slinging the satchel's strap over his shoulder, he slipped a hand into his pouch and pulled out a handful of amber beads. He hadn't time for proper magic, but he didn't require control, only chaos.

Jogaila walked the line of tanks, puffing on the cigarette to bring out its heat. He coughed and brought an amber bead to the burning tip. He prayed this little spark would be enough to kindle the soul. He couldn't get to the tank's engine, so he tossed the bead onto the drive wheel beneath the tread, then moved on to the next and the next and the next.

"Achtung! What are you doing there?" A mechanic emerged from one of the workshops, wiping his hands, glowering.

"Wishing them luck!" Jogaila patted the nearest tank and moved on.

"Hey, hey!" A breathless young man caught himself on the corner of the barn. "Did you hear? They found Hans Krutzfeld. Dead! And with no clothes on!"

"No clothes?" Jogaila spun about from the line of tanks, justly startled.

"Just his under things." The youth giggled. "This partisan's gonna pay for that, let me tell you!"

The mechanic hurried to catch up with his friend, and Jogaila jogged with them a few steps, as far as the shadows. He dropped to one knee. "Zaltys, come now, or I'll never find you," he breathed.

He tore open his stolen jacket, popping buttons and balling up the cloth. He kicked out of the boots, flinging them behind a heap of straw and old animal dung. Off with the wool pants, leaving his thin shirt and light trousers.

Against the side of his bare foot came the gentle brush of scales, but Zaltys turned away, tongue flicking, attracted by the smell of manure where tasty insects might be found.

Jogaila tossed the cigarette after the clothes, then scooped the little snake into the satchel.

All the while, he listened, hoping for the growl of the Panzer tanks emerging from their rest. Nothing. How deep was the heart of a tank? How heavy was its slumber?

A loudspeaker on the corner of the barn barked out orders. Shut the camp! Search for the suspect! One of their own had been murdered, none must rest until the culprit was found.

Barefoot, he ducked low and fled along the line of tanks, dodging tent ropes, clinging to the satchel. When he reached the forest, if he returned to the sacred grove, he'd be sure Kelvas's sacrifice was—

A tent stake caught his ankle, and he sprawled to the ground. The gate was closing.

A hand snatched his arm, dragging him to his feet. A soldier glared into his face, shaking him. "Who are you?"

Jogaila cowered, answering in Polish, "What's going on?"

Behind him, someone shouted, "There was a soldier I didn't recognize near the tanks! Come on!"

His soldier hauled him from the path of the eager mechanic, trailed now by a dozen big men wearing lightning bolt insignia.

"I just want to be with my family," Jogaila whimpered, still in Polish, pointing toward the transport where a phalanx of guards on motorcycles waited to escort the truckload of workers to the tunnels to die. *Rats and bones.*

His soldier, his savior, dragged him forward, against the flow of soldiers rushing to secure the camp, checking the tents.

"Feuer!" someone shouted, and a klaxon blared. Smoke coiled up from the manure pile where he'd cast his cigarette.

The soldier growled, gripping Jogaila at the back of his throat and running now, calling out to the escort as they squeezed past the barbed wire. "One more for you! One more Jew."

He flung Jogaila through the gate to where a guard seized him again.

"Drop everything. It stays here."

"What's burning?" Jogaila pointed back as he pulled the satchel's strap over his head.

"Nazis in Hell!" Kelvas shouted, rearing up from the armed men around him. He jerked free from his captors and struggled away, racing toward the camp interior.

"Stop him!" His captors drew their guns.

"Lady Geltine, bring him grace," Jogaila murmured.

An engine roared to life—not large enough to be one of his tanks. Gunshots and screaming, and he knew he'd failed.

Jogaila jerked and doubled over. His throat burned. Kelvas bought him time at the cost of his life. He couldn't afford to waste the gift. Jogaila stuffed the satchel under his tunic, clutching his arms around himself.

"Don't be sick, or I'll kill you myself," the guard growled at Jogaila's ear. He dragged him forward and shoved him into the transport. "Wait—this, too."

As the other Germans slammed the back of the truck, the guard pulled the knife from Jogaila's belt and slashed the leather, yanking it from his waist. His pouch fell free.

The last of his soul stones scattered as the pouch joined the heap of abandoned belongings, a bit of amber glinting near the dead baby's blanket. He had no magic now but the voice of snakes.

Stepping back, the guard banged on the truck's fender. "Go!"

The truck fired up and lurched into motion. Jogaila knocked against the other people packed in around him, some of them hugging each other, some of them weeping and others praying. Kelvas's final act had been to ensure Jogaila would live. He had the plans now, and no means to deliver them.

Stout wooden slats enclosed the sides of the truck, with a canvas top rolled up along metal bars, closely set. Even if he found purchase to climb out, even if he could squeeze through the bars, how could he do so without the Germans noticing? At least two men sat in the cab of the truck, and another eight or more in the motorcade, all determined, in spite of the excitement back at camp, to see this truckload of people to a dark and bitter end.

Two dozen other frightened people joined Jogaila in his misery, all of them destined for rats and bones, just as the vipers said.

From the camp beyond came a grinding roar, much larger than the engine he'd felt earlier. His head rose.

Oaths in German, more gunfire, bullets pinged off of metal. Jogaila grabbed for the slats of the gate that sealed the truck, steadying himself to look behind.

His view of camp lurched as the truck rocked over ruts. Stone groaned then the side wall of the barn burst outward in a hail of rock, slats and plaster as the turret of a tank crashed through. Soldiers scattered. The treads ground against the shattered wall, the vehicle heaving up over the ruin and driving forward.

At the rear of the truck's escort, the motorcycle soldiers paused, glancing back.

A second tank rumbled from behind the barn, smashing into one of the light poles and tearing it down. The lights winked and went out. An officer with a bullhorn shouted for order, trying to rally his men. Then more and louder engines roared, drowning out his commands.

Feral tanks marauded the camp, grinding through tents and ramming buildings. Somebody fell, but his scream cut short. Jogaila winced on behalf of the dead. Kelvas's corpse would be there, too, ground to bits beneath the treads. Returned, at least, to the earth as it should be. May his soul someday find its home tree.

The tank that vanquished the barn rumbled straight ahead, heedless of barbed wire and fenceposts. Flames from the burning manure leapt and danced, illuminating the tanks' destruction.

They'd get the flames out, and the tanks, lacking time to bond with a master, would soon subside again to metal. It was a blow against the Nazis, but a tiny one, and to strike another, he must be free.

How did these people feel about witches? Could he afford to find out? Could any of them afford not to?

Jogaila turned in the tight space, the other prisoners swaying with the truck, packed together. "I'm a witch," he announced, in Polish. "I've made the tanks go wild, and I can stop this truck."

"On jest szaloney," someone muttered. *He's crazy.*

"No," said Jogaila. "I'm Lithuanian, trained in the old ways. Has anyone got a piece of amber? Even a bead?"

Heads shook, a few people making gestures to ward off his insanity.

"Give me a bead, and I can get us free." Bold words. Would that he could make them true. "Please." Jogaila swallowed. He slid his hand into the satchel, and Zaltys stirred, coiling up his arm, emerging to his warmth.

"Give me a bead," he repeated, "and I can get us free."

People pulled back around him, and he heard the word "witch" in three different languages.

The grieving mother pushed between the others as the truck picked up speed, as eager as he was to complete its mission. She opened her clenched fist to reveal a baby's teething ring, a loop of chipped, irregular amber beads held together by a string. Their eyes met, and she pushed it toward him.

"If you can. If you've done that—" she tipped her head toward the camp. "Do what you will to them."

Jogaila accepted the beads. The snake wrapped around his wrist, tongue flickering. He started toward the front of the truck, toward the engine, stumbling as people drew back from him, as the truck rocked over the damaged road.

At last he fell against the forward slats. One of the men inside the cab twitched and glared back through the little window. The man brandished a gun, gesturing for Jogaila to retreat. Three men, all of them armed.

Jogaila sank down, out of their view. He had no spark now, but the engine did. He brought his hand to his lips. "Look for the warmth, Zaltys. Carry this to the heart."

He snugged the bead string a little tighter as Zaltys wriggled through the loop, taking a bead into its mouth. Jogaila reached his hand through the slats down low. The little snake slithered away, beads clunking. If they even reached the engine, was there any way that Zaltys survived? Let the goddess be kind. He leaned against the slats, holding on as he sang the dainos.

The noise of the ruined camp fell away behind them, and the motorcycle escort resumed its proper rhythm, the soldiers shouting back and forth, curious and worried, more vigilant now than ever.

At the back of his skull, the vibrations of the truck's motor rose as the snake worked its way closer and closer. Hotter, too, and surrounded by the smells that other snakes avoided. The smells that, to Zaltys, might be home.

The truck shuddered and the sound of its engine changed, lower at first, then higher, churning and confused. Among the engine's familiar scent of oil and heat, Jogaila found the hint of burning pine as the beads smoldered. His mother's memory blazed to life, as if drawn by a new mother's grief.

Still singing, Jogaila brought his hand to the metal, listening and feeling. "These people are being taken to die, their souls to be scattered like yours." He addressed the amber glow that warmed his palm. "Help me, and they can live." To the truck, he said, "No need to serve a cruel master."

The engine growled, then the truck spurted forward, twisting from side to side.

In the cab, the driver cursed in German, wrestling with the steering wheel.

The truck jerked and spun. It bounced hard through a ditch and the passengers screamed, then the truck roared downward. Not so fast, not so fast! Jogaila felt the heat against his palm and the truck shivered.

"I'm sorry," Jogaila murmured. "We must break your sides to be free."

It turned again, more sharply, and the side scraped along a tree, snapping the slats. With a roar, the vehicle surged again, deeper into the trees.

The windshield shattered, and one of the Germans flew out as the truck reversed abruptly. One of the others slumped into the seat, gurgling, impaled on a branch. The third man fired his sidearm into the engine block. The truck lurched and crashed headlong, the rear end jolting up, then bouncing back again, tilting sideways.

Around him, people cried out, clinging to each other and to the bars.

The truck wobbled and ground steadily downhill, then the wheels splashed, and the truck stopped hard. The tires whined as they found no purchase.

On the road they'd left behind, soldiers shouted and flashlights bounced, hesitant to approach the crazed vehicle.

Jogaila pushed himself up, shivering. By the time he reached the broken side, others had already knocked loose more of the boards, scrambling free, helping each other down. The man who'd called him crazy put out his arm, giving Jogaila a steady grip to jump down to the muddy riverbank.

Stumbling out of the damaged vehicle, Jogaila pressed one hand to the hood. "Thank you."

The truck purred beneath his touch. From beneath the hood, Zaltys emerged, twitching slightly, and Jogaila gathered the snake close, then joined the others scattering into the woods all around.

Zaltys was singed but survived the mission. Jogaila cradled the snake as he slipped away down the bank. "I need a crossing—what do your friends say?"

"*Deep fast deep,*" buzzed the back of his skull over and over as he walked, then "*shallow shallow sandy.*"

Holding the satchel high above the water, he splashed into the river at an angle, finding his footing on the slippery muck, then across a sandbar. It would be slow going back to the Lithuanian camp on foot, and unshod at that, but he'd make it.

He emerged onto the Lithuanian side of the river not far from the stone bridge. The distant turmoil of the German outpost reached him over the river's grumbling. Jogaila set out on a parallel to the road, ready to duck away at any moment. Up ahead, something moved, and he hesitated.

"*Two wheels,*" the snakes told him at the same time he isolated the sound of the motorcycle, a low, dissatisfied rumble, moving away from the bridge at a painfully slow speed. It didn't sound damaged. It sounded…familiar.

"Gracija?" he whispered to the night.

The motorcycle's tone rose, then it swung about, turning an arc in the middle of the road.

"Ay! No—" somebody protested. The bike had a rider!

Jogaila jumped to the side of the road and dropped low, but the motorcycle stopped unerringly in front of him.

The rider panted, bent over and clutching his arm, not even touching the grips. "J—Jogaila?" A harsh whisper.

Jogaila inched a little closer. "Kelvas." He came up onto the road, catching the other man's shoulder to keep him on the bike.

Kelvas's teeth flashed in a sharp grin. "Not dead yet. It came for me. The motorcycle blocked their shots. Most of them." He nearly laughed, making room for Jogaila to take the steering. "You'd better…in case it…" He sighed. "Thank you."

The bike was, indeed, loyal and bold. Jogaila let the snake slide into the satchel as he climbed aboard his motorcycle, his mount, to carry them home.

Those Who Help Themselves

Donald McCarthy

I cannot be my everyday self, the one who works at a refueling station, the one who hears all the whispers about how the other post-Exodus worlds are so much nicer than this one. I cannot be the one who has to smile and tell the pilots that their spaceships are all good to go. I cannot be the one who pretends working brings me pleasure, that life is good, that a meager income satisfies me. That's why I smack myself across the face.

The stinging keeps me alert, and the pain makes it harder for the anxiety to slip in, so I can be a confident man when I step outside my apartment. I'll only have one shot at this. Back in parochial school, one of many that prided itself on funneling its students into the military, they used to tell us that we did God's work. I suppose that means God would hate me now. That's fine. I'm going to do for humanity what He should have done: incite revolution.

* * *

I keep my raincoat wrapped around me and wear a scarf so tight that it almost chokes. I prefer it when as little of the outside air touches me as possible. I'd wear a hat or a hood to fully insulate myself, but they banned face coverings a decade ago.

The streets remain silent. The gray and black buildings I pass contain no distinctive features. No windows, no decorations, no balconies, no signs of life. Inside them, hundreds of people work more jobs than could possibly be necessary; they're lucky in there, I suppose, as they don't have to do manual labor like me. Every day part of my body aches in protest.

This is life on Maldrove.

It's nothing like Earth, the place humanity left a little over two centuries ago. I think I knew that the moment I came out of the womb. The air smells ashy, the sky stays an angry red, and nothing can ever happen here that will make up for the fact that we don't belong. They terraformed this world just as the Earth fell apart. The terraforming only partially succeeded.

Specks of dust blow through my hair. They used to have a forcefield that would activate around the city to keep the dust storms' effects away from us. One day, as with so much of the technology on Maldrove, the field malfunctioned, activating without warning. It cut a transport straight in half. That put an end to the forcefield. It couldn't be repaired with full certainty an event like that wouldn't happen again. Such is the story of Maldrove. Nothing here is ever fixed.

Even though there are easily thousands of people within a square mile, I see only one or two others on the sidewalks. People tend not to go outside unless they must. My destination is only a few blocks from my apartment complex, but it will be impossible for me to not be seen by at least one of the Terrorizers, those awful humanoid guards that they insist we refer to as the Protectors.

A woman walks past me, avoiding eye contact. Does she not want to be noticed? Or do I alarm her? Usually, I try not to worry about how I come across, but today, I'm paranoid. To make matters worse, I'm also paranoid about my paranoia. Too much alarm can result in distraction, and I cannot fail. I have but one opportunity to make a difference.

I cross the street, where now there are individual stores instead of office complexes. Each storefront has a length of ten feet, a door, and an engraved title to let you know what you can buy inside. Nothing more. Not even windows where shop owners can advertise merchandise. A few years ago, certain storefronts featured advertisements that had what the police referred to as "dissident messaging" in them and that put an end to ads. Now, they just tell us to buy, buy, buy. It's our patriotic duty to be shoppers when we're not working or giving thanks for our supposed salvation.

There's one storefront that stands out since it's nothing but a black screen; such screens appear on every block. Emerald Eyes appears on them when she has an announcement. Whenever she tells us about a crackdown, those eyes become so bright you don't want to look. The crackdowns occur in various apartment buildings across Maldrove's three cities whenever the police decide the residents have been planning an illegal action. Or so they say.

You hang around the spaceport long enough, you hear uncomfortable truths, like the fact that every month, the police pick an apartment building at random and storm through it, brutalizing without thought of a person's age or fragility. It's the regular police who do that, not the Terrorizers. The Terrorizers wait outside, looking indifferent.

Emerald Eyes uses the police when she wants you beaten until your spirit breaks. She sends the Terrorizers in when she wants you annihilated from existence. That's how they can claim the police haven't killed anyone in decades. They make the Terrorizers do that part.

I turn into a tech store, the walls lined with miniscule ovals, referred to as Ovies, that fit over your pupil. They're only legal to wear at home for entertainment. Use at the workplace or while out on the street remains forbidden because twelve years ago, some people used them to organize a protest that almost breached the Administrator's building. The Terrorizers put a stop to the riot. One protestor had their head ripped off, and a Terrorizer held it up for the rest to see. After that, the crackdowns started to become a regular event. Dissidents were everywhere, the average citizen always in need of protection.

"Hello, sir," a salesman says. He's tall and thin, but nervy. His eyes seem to always move. He knows who I am, but we both have to pretend otherwise in case someone else walks in. We have to talk in code, which, frankly, I prefer to real conversations.

"I'm looking for a Chess Ovie."

"We have more exciting things than that," the salesman says. "Can I interest you in—"

"No, I like chess. I enjoy bringing down the king."

"Who am I to argue with the customer?" He spreads his hands. "But we need to match your skill with the appropriate Ovie. You don't want it to be so easy you become bored or so hard you want to jump out your apartment window."

"Too hard is fine," I say. "My windows don't open."

The salesman laughs. "Whose do? But right this way, sir, and we can get you fitted."

He opens the rear door and takes me in to see Ms. Jules.

* * *

The one good thing about the lack of windows in the stores? The red light cannot seep in like it does into my apartment. The lack of red doesn't mean I can trick myself into thinking it's Earth. People say you cannot sense that Maldrove's rotation is different from Earth's, that such a thing just isn't possible since I was born after the Exodus, but that's a lie. I can feel it. I can always feel it. The rotation, the gravity, it's all off. I saw holograms of Earth as a child thanks to my mother; when I looked at them, I became entranced, understanding our home world perfectly. Those holograms are banned now.

"I figured it was fifty-fifty whether you'd come," Ms. Jules says. It took me three doors and two corridors to reach her office. She sits behind a desk made of wood from Earth. I caress the relic. It's soft, sanded down, but I pretend it's still rough and in the soil, that it's part of a tree, that there's a scent of dewy grass around us, that birds chatter. I can pretend I'm on Earth. But only for a moment. I'm not where I want to be. I'm in a place where God rewards only those who help themselves, and they help themselves to us.

"Please stop disassociating in my office," Ms. Jules remarks. She's a decade older than me, early fifties, yet she speaks to me like I'm thirty years her junior.

I pull my hand back. "I'm not disassociating. Just rare to see something from Earth that's natural."

"It cost more than I'd care to admit. Not sure if it was worth it."

"It was worth it."

She gestures to the stool across from her, but I don't take it. She has a kind face, large eyes and always a hint of a smile. But in her profession, you can't be a kind person. She's wearing a mask she's perfected over years of practice.

A coworker at the spaceport told me about her shop and what she can do. Gossip lives at the spaceport because surveillance is lighter there. No Terrorizers. Even the police restrain themselves. The other worlds know what goes on here, but they like to pretend they don't. In the interest of lucrative trade, the government of Maldrove keeps the spaceports looking friendly. A person can find out a lot there, from where you can find contraband to whispers of how the Terrorizers are birthed.

I remove a chip from my raincoat and place it on that blessed table. "Here's all of it." I keep my tone steady, but I'm worried she'll back out at the last second. Not until I'm on the street again will I feel secure. And then there'll be other problems to worry about.

Ms. Jules stands and goes to her shelves on the rear wall. The shelves hold hundreds of water-filled cubes, all with an Ovie floating innocently in the middle. Some are small, just fitting over the pupil, but others are the size of an eye itself. The latter are very rare, used only by those with power, but it's one of those cubes that she picks up. She passes it to me before sitting down. "I told you this before, but I still want to be clear: this will replace your eye. It's not like the regular contact lens Ovies. You will have to use the machine in the back for the procedure. It'll numb the area, so it won't be painful, but I can't promise it's a pleasant experience, either. Once it's in, it should let you activate virtually any door in the Administrator's building."

I place my finger on the chip I set down. "I don't like that you said 'should.' I don't like that you said 'virtually.'"

She laughs and shrugs. "This is Maldrove, honey. Nothing works with certainty here."

I press down harder on the chip. "Here's a certainty: this is still my money."

"As soon as you walked in here, it was mine." She leans back, the front legs of her chair creaking as they rise off the ground.

I take my finger off the chip. I'm tired of feeling powerless, that feeling they instill in you day one in school and then reinforce for the rest of your life, but I have no choice. I need what she has. What's another moment of indignity? Especially when victory is at my fingertips. "Fine." I collect the Ovie. "The gun?"

"It's from Symoria. Made from a rare element found there. We'll call it a metal, but that's not quite accurate. It's funny. Symoria has such beautiful landscapes but look at what lingers under the surface. Look at what they're willing to mine." She taps the table. "I'd always rather get a punch in the face than a knife in the back. That's why, for all its awfulness, I prefer it here to anywhere else."

I pause. How much do I reveal? Perhaps more than usual. Perhaps more than ever. Nothing left to lose. "I'd prefer Earth."

She curls her lips, disgust evident. "Not anymore you wouldn't. And I doubt it was all that nice before the Exodus, either. Let's talk about your gun, though. What you need to know is that it has six bullets, and it cannot be reloaded. It's also undetectable in virtually all circumstances."

I'm positive she threw in the word virtually to irritate me. I don't take the bait. I do take the gun. It's light and painted dull brown. There's no obvious safety mechanism. But there's a trigger, and that's all I need. I don't want to shoot it. I think I can get this done without lethal violence, but I will not be defenseless. "Well, we're done."

"Almost." Ms. Jules smiles, and I don't like the smile. She's mocking me. She thinks little of me, I know. Just like my boss, just like my teachers, just like the priests, just like God. Has she looked into me? Does she know the reviews I received as a student? Does she know my teachers thought me weak and exhausting to deal with? Does she know they wouldn't let me into the military? Does she know how often the priests at my school told me I let God down?

No. No. No. I'm letting the bad part of my brain overrule the good part. I cannot do that. Not today. "What else is there?" I keep my tone even, which is an accomplishment.

"If you get caught and say you bought any of your materials from us, I will tell them you came in here and threatened me at gunpoint. I'll tell them you wanted to slaughter children. I'll tell them so many things that they'll make your death as painful as possible. They might skin you and display you in the streets. I don't want to do that. You seem like a broken soul. You do what you have to do. But leave my name and business out of it."

I pocket the gun and the Ovie cube. "I'm not going to get caught."

"Lot of people have said that over the years."

* * *

I put my eye against a cylindrical device that resembles a telescope. It presses against me in return. The area around my right eye goes numb. I can feel myself blinking, but the sensation is different, almost distant. Gentle brushes hit my cornea like a spider crawling over it. I keep my eye open despite my instinct to close it.

There is no pain, but I can tell my eye is being removed. I feel it moving inside the socket, slowly pulled outwards. It's fascinating to experience such an extreme moment without pain. If only life could always be that way.

The device inserts the Ovie into the now empty socket. The Ovie fits easily and will resemble an eye. I twitch a little, but there's still no pain, just the odd feeling that part of me is missing.

The machine turns off. I pull back, glancing around the small, dark room that's empty other than the transplant device. I blink a couple of times, reorienting. The right half of my vision is emerald.

* * *

Sometimes I have a nightmare. Always the same. I see a pile of bodies hundreds of feet high. The sky above is on fire, although I suppose that's impossible. Can you smell in dreams? I can. I smell the rot, the reminder that we are just as much meat as the animals we look down upon. On top of the corpse pile, one person, still alive, reaches out to a departing spaceship, trying and failing to get onboard. It's the last ship to leave Earth. The end of the Exodus, when the suspicion that we would leave people behind became ironclad truth.

That dream plays through my mind as I walk to the Administrator's building. Just a reminder that, much as I know I should live on Earth, the Earth I need is gone. Ms. Jules did have the right of that. That's why I have to follow through, have to wake people up to what this world is so that we can make a better one. It won't be Earth, but it can be better than this.

I pick up my pace. My heart races, and my throat tightens. I feel so parched I could be convinced I haven't drunk water in days. The redness of the sky seems more intense than usual, darker and more vibrant. The air thickened while I was with Ms. Jules; the dust content is somehow worse, like you can bite into it.

I turn right, the Administrator's building only one block away.

I've been too lucky. No drone flyovers this past hour. No announcements from Emerald Eyes. Empty streets. And Ms. Jules followed through. My plan was working, but now in front of me is a Terrorizer.

His arms and legs are double the length of mine, but his torso is that of a normal person, and he wears an ill-fitting suit. His eyes are black holes, and his mouth has been stitched into a permanent smile. I can recall, in school, teachers telling us the Protectors smile and never stop smiling because they're so happy with their God-given job to keep us safe. At the spaceport, though, there are whispers that their tongues were cut out, and they could no longer act for themselves, that they are victims like us and hate what they do.

The Terrorizer stares at me as he walks down the center of the street, his gaze following me, but he does not come closer. By some logic of his own, he must have decided I am not a threat. I almost say a prayer of thanks to God before I remember that I hate Him now.

* * *

The Administrator's building has a front hall with a glass ceiling. Once through the front, one reaches the skyscraper part, where the Administrator sits far above. The entry hall is where people come when they require help. If they cannot afford their rent, if their maintenance is not kept up, if they are struggling at their job, if they want to move to a new apartment, if their psyche suffers, or if they feel like, in some undefinable way, they just need assistance.

It's empty. It's always empty.

No alarms go off as I enter the hall, so I suppose Ms. Jules had it correct about the gun. The glass ceiling above makes certain the marble floor turns red. Connecting to the building's system, the Ovie activates. I halt and look up. I quietly ask Him, "Do you see me now?"

He does not reply.

I refocus. The Ovie gives me what I need: a map appears in front of my right eye, and I can see the route to my plan. Take the elevator at the other end of the hall up twenty floors into the skyscraper portion of the building. Enter the communications room. Locate the footage of the crackdowns. Connect the footage to the communications system. Air it throughout the city so the people learn the truth that the crackdowns are nothing more than sheer brutality. Let the people know there are no dissidents, no rebellions brewing. There are just people who enjoy being cruel and people who have to withstand said enjoyment.

Easy plan. Very easy. The difficult part is done. So, why do I breathe so hard and fast? This will work. The elevator doors will open for me. Everything will go right because it must go right. There's been too much injustice, and I know it must one day be balanced out with justice. I am not the chosen one to do this. I am the opposite. God has ignored me, so I am the only one who can reform the poisoned world He's allowed humanity to create.

"Can I help you?"

A surge of anxiety rises into my throat and twists. I almost choke. I see a young man dressed in a suit a size too large for him. An attendant who intakes those who arrive here? I'm probably the first person he's seen in ages. "I've been requested to speak with the security officers on floor three. I work at the spaceport." My voice sounds so weak, just like when I was— No. Now is not the time to think about those days. "I overheard subversive talk and was asked to come in for a conversation so I can detail it." That sounds good.

"Uh huh," the attendant says. He straightens his tie. He must think it gives him an air of authority, but I think he's as nervous as me. "I wasn't told about this."

"It's quiet."

"What's quiet?"

"The situation. The one I'm reporting. It's quiet." Damn it. Words do not match meaning. "I'm supposed to be keeping this quiet."

He's wondering if I'm dangerous, and then wondering if I am a threat, does he really want to risk his life by confronting me. It's what I'd be considering in his position.

His right eye briefly flickers blue. "You have an unauthorized Ovie in your eye. It's a— Oh, my God. How did you get that?" He reaches into his suit jacket, presumably for a gun.

I'm faster. It's sick, isn't it? I pull fast because that was the only part of all that military prep in school that I was good at. I couldn't think straight, couldn't hold back from crying, couldn't manage my terror and loathing of authority and God himself. But I could pull my gun fast. "Hands up."

He puts his up.

"Okay, you're gonna come with me." This could turn to my advantage. A hostage could work, especially since I only have six bullets. God forbid the police enter this building; I can't win a shoot-out with them. A few security guards, sure, I could take them—well, maybe. But not a police battalion. Or, worst of all, the Terrorizers. Would they be reluctant to shoot if it meant they could kill this kid? Maybe, maybe not. But there's no other option now. I've relied too much on belief. Christ, isn't that ironic? I say, "Walk slowly to the elevator. If you make any sudden movements, you're dead." Yes. That sounded good. Authoritative. I speak just as I used to be spoken to.

The youth walks slowly, and he won't meet my eye. He's saying something under his breath. Is it a prayer? Did he go to the same school I did? Did they break him down, too? Is he also one of God's castaways?

I almost ask him, but I hold back. I don't want to be made to think of those old days. It'll hurt my concentration. Besides, he might think me crazy, just as so many do, and decide to fight back.

We're almost at the elevator when the doors to the Administrator's building swing open. They bang as each door slams into the wall. The cruel outside air storms in on an aggressive wind. For a second, I think the youth's prayer actually worked and God is coming down to send me to Hell.

Instead, it's the Terrorizers. They do not walk in. They crawl on all fours, maybe thirty of them, maybe more. They crawl up the walls, onto the ceiling, blocking out the red, shadowing us. They just keep coming. I'm pissing myself, and they keep coming, and the attendant is shaking, and I'm grabbing him. I'm screaming, and the Terrorizers swarm. They're not screaming and not laughing and seem to take no joy in this. Their eyes are all black, yet somehow sad. I think they are marionettes, and I know they will kill me if ordered to do so.

The Terrorizers freeze. They're like insects on the walls and ceiling, waiting to pounce on prey. Their unmoving smiles remind me of piano keys. Even their breathing is shallow, barely causing movement.

The attendant resumes praying. I do not have the heart to tell him it's pointless. He knows his prayer well, though. He's still a deep believer. Perhaps he's not one of God's castaways. Perhaps he's valuable. Perhaps killing him could do something. One quick pull of the trigger, and he's gone.

But I drop my gun to the floor. I won't kill the boy. I don't care if he's important. They can and will take everything from me after this, but they can't take this decision away from me. Maybe it's the right decision, maybe it's the wrong decision, but it is mine.

Footsteps. They are steady, the sign of someone in total control of their body. I shouldn't know who it is, but I do. I know before I look to the doorway.

Emerald Eyes, our beloved Security Chief, walks into the hall, hands clasped behind her back, wearing a black leather jacket. The emerald Ovies in her eyes shine brighter than any Ovies I've seen. They detach, flying around the room before returning to her eye sockets. "There's no one else unauthorized in the building," she announces to the Terrorizers.

I don't have the energy to be petrified anymore. In fact, if she had not broken the silence, I could have convinced myself I am not here. There are benefits to disassociation.

"Tyler Morrison," she says. "Mediocre student. Failed out of military training almost immediately. Utility man at the spaceport. We can also add moron."

I don't let the words hurt me. I glance at the retreating boy, who appears confused about why I let him go. That saddens me. "How long did you know I was coming?" I ask Emerald Eyes.

"You were asking too many questions around the spaceport. It became clear from the intensity in your demeanor and conversations that you'd do something. We watched. We waited. We realized the opportunity. We told Ms. Jules to give you a gun and an Ovie. Insane man intent on killing everyone in the Administrator's building? So many crackdowns justified by that." She smiles. "You're the dissident we've been waiting for."

Anger flares in me. They've made me someone I'm not. They're good at that. Always have been. "I wasn't planning to kill anyone."

"Is that a fact?"

"I was going to expose the mutation that's grown on humanity. That's *become* humanity. I was going to air the crackdowns. I was going to show people what they've been ignoring. I wouldn't have to kill anyone myself, because the people would rise."

"Oh." Emerald Eyes looks to the side as if she must reorient herself. "That's funny, actually. That's really quite a funny plan. Not a moron, then. A martyr. But perhaps that's the same thing."

Two Terrorizers drop from the ceiling and fall to my side, obeying some silent order from Emerald Eyes. They grab me tight by the arms. They smell sanitized, like every inch of them has been scrubbed until it hurts, until there's nothing left to even admit an odor. I see in their slightly ajar mouths that the rumors are true: they have no tongues. Their mouths are voids. I let them drag me towards Emerald Eyes. She's concentrating, which means she must be manipulating a system with her Ovies.

"Let's go outside," she says.

The Terrorizers take me out, and it's red, so red, all red. For a minute back in the hall, I felt like I'd never have to see the red again.

I spot the sick joke, the one that Emerald Eyes must have come up with when I told her my plan. The screens on nearby buildings, which usually project Emerald Eyes' announcements, now show footage of the crackdowns. The real footage, the unfiltered truth about what we've become. Police storming through apartments, beating without mercy. It didn't matter who the victims were: they were beaten bloody.

Time passes, but I cannot tell how much. The footage keeps playing throughout the city, loud and constant. Eventually, it stops bothering me. Eventually, it's like nothing plays at all.

When the farce is done, Emerald Eyes whispers in my ear, "Should we wait together to see if the people come to the streets?"

* * *

As a child, they sent me to school outside the city proper, just as they do the children now. They beat me and worse. But that's to be expected. They taught me about discipline, about honor, about strength, about listening to others. They told me about the importance of income, the importance of rising high in the ranks of whatever it is you do. They told me the other colonies are weak, that their citizens are lazy. They told me that the three most powerful words in language are "law and order."

They told us that God helps those who help themselves, which means you should never ask for any help at all.

I realize now, after the incident with Emerald Eyes, that they wore us down so that we wouldn't complain when they wore us down more. I want to tell everyone this, that I finally figured it out, that I finally understand why none of us can ever think straight.

I try. I do. I see people every day on the street. They walk past me looking so frightened. I want to tell them the truth so badly that it hurts, but my body is not mine to control. My legs were broken and bent, my arms smashed and stretched, my real and fake eyes turned to pure black, but I still know the awful truth, and I still want to tell people that God won't help us, but we can help each other.

But I cannot as I have no tongue.

About the Authors

E.C. AMBROSE writes knowledge-inspired adventure fiction, including DRAKEMASTER about a clockwork doomsday device based on Su Song's astronomical clock of 1090 CE and the Dark Apostle series about medieval surgery. As E. Chris Ambrose, she writes the Bone Guard archaeological thrillers and the new Rogue Adventures. She is a graduate of, and instructor for, the Odyssey Speculative Fiction Workshop, and lives in the blustery Granite State where she thinks of plot twists from the bench of her floor loom. Find her on Facebook or visit her website to learn about all of her work.

CHADWICK GINTHER is the Prix Aurora Award winning author of The Thunder Road Trilogy, *Graveyard Mind*, and over thirty short stories, some of which have been collected in *Khyber: Sinister Tales of Sword and Sorcery* and *When the Sky Comes Looking for You: Short Trips Down the Thunder Road*. He lives in Winnipeg, Canada where he writes stories full of skeletons, giants, and dragons. Find him online at www.chadwickginther.com, ChadwickGintherAuthor on Facebook, and @chadwickginther.bsky.social on Bluesky.

JASON M. HOUGH is the New York TImes bestselling author of THE DARWIN ELEVATOR, ZERO WORLD, INSTINCT, and seven other novels. He lives near Seattle with his family, and enjoys a life free of social media (though he's always happy to chat via email). Get in touch at https://www.jasonhough.com

TANYA HUFF lives and works in the Canadian countryside with her partner Fiona Patton, five cats and six aquariums. She's the author of thirty-four novels and almost a hundred short stories ranging from military science fiction through contemporary fantasy to high fantasy with a little horror for seasoning. Her last book was INTO THE BROKEN LANDS (DAW '22) and her next will be DIRECT DESCENDANTS (DAW spring '25). She's on Facebook, Bluesky, and the platform previously known as Twitter as Tanya Huff, and, although she has an Instagram account, she never uses it.

BLAKE JESSOP is a Canadian author of sci-fi, fantasy and horror stories with a master's degree in creative writing from the University of Adelaide. His short fiction has been nominated for Aurora, Pushcart, Lambda, Locus, and Ignyte awards. You can read more about the upcoming drone war in ZNB's 2018 anthology "The Razor's Edge," check out his catalog at amazon.com/author/blakejessop, or follow him on Twitter @everydayjisei and Bluesky @ blakejessop.bsky.social.

GARY KLOSTER is a writer, a stay-at-home father, a martial artist, and a librarian. Sometimes all in the same day, seldom all at the same time. He lives among the corn in Midwestern America in a house haunted by cats and surrounded by crows. Previous work of his has appeared in Analog, Apex, Clarkesworld, and Escape Pod. You can find him cluttering the internet at garykloster.com, and infrequently posting on Bluesky as @garykloster

DONALD McCARTHY is an author from Long Island, New York. He's published short fiction with Mythaxis Magazine, James Gunn's Ad Astra, Pseudopod, The Creepy Podcast, The Grey Rooms, and more. His non-fiction has appeared at Salon, Undark Magazine, The Huffington Post, Nightmare Magazine, and more. A full list of his publications can be found at www.donaldmccarthy.com.

RUSSELL HUGH McCONNELL stumbled into the world somewhere in the vicinity of Toronto, Canada, and since then he has wandered around North America, never settling anywhere for very long. At the moment, for reasons he can no longer remember, he finds himself living just outside Dallas, Texas. By day he teaches university students, and by night he writes fiction. Every now and then, someone agrees to publish one of his stories, which is pretty swell.

D. THOMAS MINTON is the author of the Calypto Cycle, a series of espionage thrillers set in an alternative 1920s eastern Europe and the middle east. His short fiction has appeared in many publications, including Asimov's, Apex, and Lightspeed Magazines. He lives, works, and writes from his home in the mountains of British Columbia, Canada, but his idle musings can be found holding court at dthomasminton.com.

L. E. MODESITT, Jr., is the author of 85 science fiction and fantasy novels and nearly 50 short stories. His five fantasy series include the Recluce Saga and the Imager Portfolio. His most recent books are *Contrarian*, the third book of The Grand Illusion and *From the Forest*, the twenty-third Recluce novel. He has been a U.S. Navy pilot; a market research analyst; a real estate agent; director of political research; legislative and staff director for U.S. Congressmen; Director of Legislation/Congressional Relations for the U.S. EPA; and a consultant on environmental, regulatory, and communications issues. Website is: lemodesittjr. com

DERRYL MURPHY is the author of the math-as-magic novel Napier's Bones, two short story collections, and, with William Shunn, the novella Cast a Cold Eye. He lives with his wife and dog in a famously flat and cold place and is working on a non-fiction book about an even flatter and colder place.

STEVE PERRY has written scores of novels, short stories, animated TV shows, the odd unproduced movie script, and reams of non-fiction articles and reviews. His current projects include: *Kosmic Blues* a novel in collaboration with Daniel Keys Moran; the final book in his Matador series, *Churl*; as well as a can't-talk-about-it movie script with Mike Richardson, of Dark Horse Productions. Perry is a long-time student of the Javanese martial art *Pukulan Pentjak Silat Sera Plinck*, plays blues and geezer rock on the tenor ukulele, and resides in the Pacific Northwest with his wife of fifty-some years.

EMBER RANDALL is a software engineer who specializes in user-centered design and accessibility. They got into tech to make the world a better place, which is the same reason they write – if their stories or the products they work on make at least one person happy, they count it as a success. In their free time, they enjoy reading, running, hiking, and generally exploring the outdoors, as well as creating new tales via larping. Their stories have been published by *Cast of Wonders*, *Zombies Need Brains*, and other venues. Find them at www.emberrandall.com.

HAYDEN TRENHOLM is an award-winning editor, playwright, novelist, and short story writer. He was formerly publisher and managing editor of Bundoran Press. His first novel, A Circle of Birds, won the 3-Day Novel Writing competition. His trilogy, The Steele Chronicles, were each nominated for an Aurora Award; Stealing Home was a finalist for the Sunburst Award. Hayden has won five Aurora Awards, thrice for short fiction and twice for editing. In 2022 he was inducted into the Canadian Science Fiction and Fantasy Association Hall of Fame. He lives with wife and fellow writer, Liz Westbrook-Trenholm, in Ottawa. See more: www.haydentrenholm.com

EDWARD WILLETT the award-winning author of more than sixty books of science fiction, fantasy, and nonfiction for readers of all ages. His most recent novel, his twelfth for DAW Books, is *The Tangled Stars*, a humorous far-future space opera. Ed has won an Aurora Award (Canada's top science fiction award) twice, for his novel *Marseguro* (DAW Books) and for his podcast, *The Worldshapers* (theworldshapers.com), and been shortlisted multiple times. In 2018, Ed founded Shadowpaw Press (shadowpawpress.com), which publishes the *Shapers of Worlds* anthologies among other science fiction and fantasy titles, as well as books in many other genres. He lives in Regina, Saskatchewan. Find him at edwardwillett.com, on X @ewillett, or at edwardwillett.substack.com.

NEMMA WOLLENFANG is a prize-winning, speculative fiction writer who lives in Northern England. Generally, she adheres to Science Fiction – perhaps as a result of years in the laboratory cackling like a mad scientist – but she has been known to branch out. Her stories have appeared in several venues, including: Beyond the Stars, Abyss & Apex, Third Flatiron, Speculatively Queer, Cossmass Infinities, BFS Horizons, Broken Eye Books, and Flame Tree Publishing's Gothic Fantasy series. She is a recipient of a Speculative Literature Foundation grant and a participant of Writers on the Moon. She can be found on Facebook and Amazon.

About the Editors

GERALD BRANDT is an International Bestselling Author of Science Fiction and Fantasy. He is a member of the Science Fiction and Fantasy Writers of America. His current novel is *Threader God – Book Three of the Quantum Empirica*, published by DAW Books. His first novel, *The Courier,* in the San Angeles series, was listed by the Canadian Broadcasting Corporation as one of the ten Canadian science fiction books you need to read and was a finalist for the prestigious Aurora Award. Both *The Courier* and its sequel, *The Operative,* appeared on the Locus Bestsellers List. By day, Gerald is an IT professional. In his limited spare time, he enjoys off-roading, camping, and spending time with his family. He lives in Winnipeg with his wife Marnie, and their two sons Jared and Ryan. You can find Gerald online at http://www.geraldbrandt.com, on Facebook as Gerald Brandt – Author, and on Twitter @ geraldbrandt.

****

TROY CARROL BUCHER served thirty years in the U.S. Army, where assignments took him to three wars and places like Turkey, Albania, Iraq, Afghanistan, Kuwait and Korea. Troy holds a Bachelor of Arts in English and is a graduate of Seton Hill University's MFA in Writing Popular Fiction program. Before traveling the world for Uncle Sam, he spent his childhood traipsing around the Verde Valley in Arizona. Along with writing and editing, Troy currently works as a government contractor, training and preparing military units for deployment.

Acknowledgments

This anthology would not have been possible without the tremendous support of those who pledged during the Kickstarter. Everyone who contributed not only helped create this anthology, they also helped support the small press Zombies Need Brains LLC, which I hope will be bringing SF&F themed anthologies to the reading public for years to come. I want to thank each and every one of them for helping to bring this small dream into reality. Thank you, my zombie horde.

The Zombie Horde: Cory Williams, Axisor and Firestar, Lisa Kruse, Chris Matosky, Ian Chung, Kathryn Smith, Karen M, Sheryl, John Markley, Jaq Greenspon, Raymond Lowell, Beth Coll, Jamieson Cobleigh, Sarah Cornell, Kerri Regan, Henry W. Schubert, Anne Burner, Kris W, Robyn DeRocchis, Richard O'Shea, Jeremy Audet, Rowan Stone, Andrew Hatchell, Nicholas Stephenson, Ian Harvey, Becky Boyer, Stephen Ballentine, Phillip Spencer, Cindy Cripps-Prawak, Andrija Popovic, Millie Calistri-Yeh, Eva Jayet Alaminos, LetoTheTooth, Miranda Floyd, Wulf Moon Enterprises, Michael Axe, Lindsay Knight, Claire Sims, Taia Hartman, Cathy Green, Wolf SilverOak, Beth LaClair, Duncan and Andrea Rittschof, Patricia Bray, Megan Beauchemin, Stephanie Lucas, Mark A Kiraly, Rich 'Razmus' Weissler, Michael Kohne, Beth Lobdell, David Rowe, David Lahner, Michael Hanscom, Edward Ellis, Mary Jo Rabe, J.R. Murdock, Arej N Howlett, David Hankins, R.J.H., Niall Gordon, Michael D'Auben, Jakub Narębski, Ezra Lee, Juanita J Nesbitt, Piet Wenings,

R. Hunter, Dina S Willner, Jenny Barber, Todd V. Ehrenfels, E.M. Middel, Sasha, Tania, L.C., Rory King, Joe Hauser, Dino Hicks, Charles E Norton, Stephannie Tallent, Mustela, Jennifer Berk, Michele Hall, Owen Blacker, Jeff Eppenbach, Kit Rodgers, Jason Swensen, Leah Webber, Random Yarning, Jörg Tremmel, Carol J. Guess, Kerry aka Trouble, Jen1701D, Shayne Easson, Hoose Family, Richard Leis, Jenn Whitworth, Jackie Coleman, Curtis Frye, Helen Ellison, Jacen Leonard, Angie Hogencamp, Joanne B Burrows, Jessica A. Enfante, Colette Reap, Maggie Laigaie, Vulpecula, Colleen Feeney, T Lynn P, Kat Feete, Vana Smith, Sandy Bryant, Ruth Ann Orlansky, Samantha Sendele, Craig "Stevo" Stephenson, Margaret Killeen, Ron Currens, Alicia henness, A. Kristina Casasent, Kelly Snyder, Jo Beere, Cherie Livingston, Chad Bowden, Keith E. Hartman, Kate Stuppy, A.H. Gillett, Brenda Rezk, Ryan C, Rebecca Buchanan, Darren Lipman, Lorri-Lynne Brown, Andy F, Margot Harris, Rebecca M, Lace, Christopher Wheeling, Susan Simko, Bonnie Warford, Heidi Lambert, Tina M Noe Good, S Horvat, Brynn, Sheryl R. Hayes, Robert B Tharp, Annette Agostini, Charlie Russel, MykeTea, Debbie Matsuura, Trisha J. Wooldridge, Anthony R. Cardno, Svend Andersen, John 'Doc' Strange, Howard J. Bampton, Robin Hill, John H. Bookwalter Jr., rissatoo, Ilene Tsuruoka, Tris Lawrence, Jim Gotaas, Cyn Armistead, Margaret Bumby, Keith West, Future Potentate of the Solar System, Sonya R.Lawson, Katy Manck - BooksYALove, Brita Hill, Elaine McMillan, Ane-Marte Mortensen, Chris McLaren, Crysella, Randall Brent Martin II, G. M. Persbacker, Simon Dick, Ashley Clouser Leonard, Sidney Whitaker, Elyse M Grasso, Senhina, Mary Alice Wuerz, Chantelle Wilson, Jerrie the filkferengi, Elektra Hammond, Patrick Osbaldeston, Lou/justloux2, Niall Spain, Mark Carter, Bess Turner, Stephanie Cranford, Ryan Hunter and Cameron Alexander, R.G. Roberts, Bona Books, Adam Goldstein, Jesse N. Klein, Scott Raun, Brad L. Kicklighter, Penny Ramirez, Lynn R, Joshua McGinnis, Ian F Bell, Craig Hackl, Konstanze Tants, Eric B, Michael Fedrowitz, Terry Williams, Eric, Brendan Lonehawk, Anonymous Reader, Ronald H. Miller, Steve Arensberg, Steve & Beckey Sanchez, Patrick Dugan, K. Hodghead, Caroline Westra, Chris Huning, Sharan Volin, Kari Blackmoore, Robert Claney, Jonathan Brown, Krystal Bohannan, Cliff Winnig, John Senn, Kat Haines, Jim Landis, Jamie M. Boyd, Nathan Turner, Helen Cameron, Jeanne Talbourdet, KennyBoy, Robert Bull, RJ Hopkinson, Heidegger Dart, JMC, Janet Piele, Sue Phillips, GMarkC, Vicki Greer, Leane Verhulst, Dana Carson, Chris Munroe, Jenni P., L.C. Parfomak, Kate Malloy, Tanya K., Joshua Hair, Brooks Moses, Melissa Tabon, Lisa Dees, Mark Newman, Nightwing Whitehead, Tommy Acuff, Pamela Lunsford, Richard Hailey, Steve Blount, Gail Z. Martin, Craig Maylor, Kenyon Wensing, BOBBY ZAMARRON, Brent J, Olivia Montoya, PunkARTchick "Ruthenia", Brian, Kay, and Joshua Williams, Misha Dainiak, Yankton Robins, Bethany Jezerey, Tina Connell, Patti Montgomery, Jennifer Flora Black, Deborah

Nossaman, Kevin, Yosen Lin, Dagmar Baumann, Clarissa C. S. Ryan, Jessica Meade, Robert K. Barbour, Abi Scott, Mallory A. Haws, The Other Yvonne, Paul & Laura Trinies, Tara Paine, J.L. Gerrard, Shirley, Amanda Saville, Aysha Rehm, Daniel Hopersberger, Alice "Huskyteer" Dryden, Katie Mergener, Mike Rimar, Ryan Power, Bobbi Boyd, Taylor Munsell, Jackie Duckworth, Tasha Turner, Susanne Schörner, Joseph Jerome Connell, Shay Dinur, Steven Halter, Alice Bentley, Elaine Tindill-Rohr, Jonathan Olsson, Elise Power, Julia Hart, Risa Scranton, David Myers, Michelle P., Regis M. Donovan, Robert D. Stewart, Herbert Eder, John T. Sapienza, Jr., Thomas Booker, Rolf Laun, Max Kaehn, Lorraine J. Anderson, Donna Royston, Mervi Hamalainen, FOS Grace, Andrea Tatjana, Kristin EvensonHirst, In memory of Tammy Greco, Rob In AU, CL McCollum, BT McMenomy, Hayden Trenholm, Francesco Tehrani, Katherine, Barb Moermond, Tibs, Ian, Brenda Carre, Venessa Giunta, Andrew Foxx, Miriah Hetherington, jjmcgaffey, Emy Peters, Jacob H Joseph, Holly Elliott, Keith A. Kline, Joachim Verhagen, Paul Alex Gray, Sandy Komoroff, Michael M. Jones, Gail Morse, Fantastic Books, Edward K. Beale, V Hartman DiSanto, Yosef Kuperman, Meyari McFarland, Gary Ehrlich, M Glasser, Stephen Buchanan, Deborah A. Flores, J Millwood, Alison Scott, Sarah T, Cyn Wise, Karen Dubois, Pat Knuth, Dale Cozort, Blade McMicking, D.I., Jennifer Crow, Brad Roberts, K.tee Magrowski, kayliealien, Tim Jordan, Julie Pitzel, Lee Dalzell, Bob D. M, Adam Nemo, Anne Walker, Sheila Huijbregts, Abra Staffin-Wiebe, Matthew Egerton, Merav Hoffman, Mervi Mustonen, Arin Komins, Louisa Swann, Sylvia Greenwich, J.P. Goodwin, Michael Abbott, A. L. Kaplan, Arinn Dembo, Julie Halperson, Kathy Brady, RickyD, Tracy Popey, Darrell Z. Grizzle, Wingnut, R Kirkpatrick, Agnes Kormendi, Ellery Rhodes, Robin Schwarz, Alan Smale, Fred and Mimi Bailey, Mary Ann Shuman, James Enge, Caryn Cameron, Sarah L., Karen Fonville, Gavran, Tal S, Cat Ellison, Amelia Smith, Coleman bland, Winter Hart, Jason Palmatier, Will Gunderson, Geoffrey Willmoth, Cynthia Porter, Stuart Hall (aka Celt), Alexander Gent, Jeff G, David Keener, VikingSnail, Carol Mammano, Linnéa G, Lavinia Ceccarelli, David Futterrer, Bob Thibodeau, Alphonzs, Katelyn Cserjes, Carver Rapp, Mandy Stein, Connor Bliss, John Jason Lau, Tania Clucas, Holly J, AM Scott, Author, Robby Thrasher, CGJulian, Tracy 'Rayhne' Fretwell, Leah Smith, Stephen Kotowych, Gary Phillips, Lotta Fjelkegård, Katrina Knight, Kat D'Andrea, Powell Zucks, Michèle Laframboise, James Olsen, Jon Nepsha, Nick Mandujano III, Chris Vincent, Mike Smith, Jakiette, Acer R., Zalyn Schwartz, Fren & Edna, R. McKean

Printed in Great Britain
by Amazon